The Mischief-Maker

The Mischief-Maker,
or the Loathsome History
of a Malcontent

JULIA LACEY BROOKE

RICHMOND: TIGER OF THE STRIPE

Published in 2014 by
TIGER OF THE STRIPE
50 Albert Road
Richmond
Surrey TW10 6DP
United Kingdom

ISBN 978 1 904799 66 5

Typeset in the UK by
Tiger of the Stripe

For Jim, Helen, Kate and Tom,
in beloved memory of Nicholas.

Prologue

Well! Did he snort or was he spiked? Did he fall or was he pushed? Was he dragged or invited to that little party by the River? Oops, we can't ask questions like that, not even metaphorically, not ahead of the Crowner's Quest. It's sub-judice, and all very proper to keep schtum. But before Kinseyder involves this noble publication in yet another libel suit, just remember you probably read it here first. In the meantime, get a load of the picture on the right. The grieving widow of Britain's favourite Telly Tubby bravely does the shopping as usual... Black hat in that Harvey Nicks bag, Lady Louise?

It's a funny thing, death.

So final. That's it. No more. The end. In the famous words of Basil Fawlty, 'Whoosh! What was that? That was your life, mate...Well, do I get another go? Nope, that was it.'

Thing is, when most of us go, death really is the end: the last gasp, the tubes removed, the machines silenced; the respectful murmuring of the staff, the grim little family conference in the car-park, the awkward hugs and handshakes; then the inevitable phone calls and arrangements with the over-priced funeral home (Jesus Christ, funeral *home* – have you ever thought how grotesque that is?) followed by the pathetic little ceremony at the crematorium where you'll have some sort of clergy-person or you won't, but they'll play 'My Way' or a bit of Bach, depending on all the demographic, sociological crap, you know, the stuff which decides our preferences, or more likely decides the things that we'd like the outside world to think we prefer. But almost certainly the deciders will be the rellies and what have you, not the wishes of the dear departed. I mean, who'd instruct 'play Abba singing "Super-per Trouper-per" at my send-off'? (Though some cretins actually do put that sort of stuff in their wills and instructions, and that makes you wonder... I mean, suppose you've gone off Abba by the time you kick the bucket. Will you twist there in the hereafter, wishing instead that you'd put that famous thing from the St Matthew Passion from the start of *Casino* where Robert De Niro gets blown up in his Cadillac instead? Or 'Mull of Kintyre'? 'Smoke on the Water'?) But seriously, most of the time, the nearest and dearest will decide, and pretend it was 'his dearest wish, his favourite tune', and they'll all snivel a bit as the final curtain flops back over the departing casket, and then they can relax, and the whole shebang will be an excuse for a bit of a knees-up in the local boozer or sherry and cucumber sarnies at Aunt Caroline's, depending on all that sociological stuff. Or whatever.

Thing is, it's *quiet*. Private. One handful of specks bidding farewell to another speck snuffed out. We're just *that* small, bub. I mean, just *think* about planets and the sky – and that's just the bit you can see. Now imagine limitless numbers of galaxies... enough to make you puke with vertigo. Down here, you get a bit of noise in the street, maybe, while someone helps a legless Uncle Frank into a taxi; a trio of women weeping into their fourth bacardi 'n' cokes in the Royal George, or maybe a spillage or two on Aunt C's shagpile, a spot of projectile vomiting over the rhododendrons, while the old dames in the kitchen help themselves to more sherry with their pancake running saying, 'he was a lovely lad, he was, such a charmer, God rest him…' Nice and sentimental, but not very much in terms of a lasting memorial. And sooner rather than later, the dear departed disappears into his appointed oblivion, to re-appear only in photographs, in the family archive of video tape, maybe, and slides away into the past tense, to become a 'was' rather than an 'is'. And that's just for the departed who really were dear… most of us just disappear as if we never were at all. Look at Angel. Look at me.

But now look at Fairbrother: right now, Fairbrother is the biggy. Wars, revolutions, riots, Olympic Games, another dead adolescent warrior in Afghanistan… forget it. This one beats the band. At the funeral in Hatton, Cambridgeshire, they've even rigged up a PA video system outside so that the mourners who can't get ringside viewing can have a good gawp at those that can. And they're not mourners, as such; they're audience, this lot, having a sort of collective blub-in with the frisson of knowing that any moment now, they'll be just feet and inches away from – gasp! – celebrities. About old Jerry himself, most of them probably couldn't give a flying fuck. They didn't know him, he wasn't anything to them, not personally. This is just a crowd, gathered for the reasons that crowds do, feeding off each other, making each other cry, pretending they know the corpse in question like a personal friend. I mean, *remember* that stuff for Princess Diana? Now, everyone's waiting, all united in misery, it would seem, for the sudden loss of a figure who had come into their homes, made their days, been part of the fabric of their shallow lives, but they're also united in anticipation. There's been a rumour of Silvie Snape, Jilly Tantram, and Kylie, and Gwyneth and Liam and Robbie; *and* Boris, who met him on the charity circuit, apparently, and Sir Bob and even Sir Paul; and there's bound to be Denise, and Davina, and Simon, let alone those saddo-celebs-for-a-nano-second, the ones Fairbrother gave a leg-up to on that talent thing, as well as the ones he helped on *Sort It*.

Me? I've got the best seat in the house: my own, plus a bottle of scotch.

'…*And now, over to Hatton for live coverage of the funeral of Sir Jerry Fairbrother, who died ten days ago, and is being buried today in the village of Hatton, Cambridgeshire, where he grew up and where many people still remember him as a boy… a sad, sad day for everyone: for his family, of course, and for his many, many friends in the television and celebrity world, and of course for his millions of fans… many who have gathered patiently for several hours now outside the village church of St Mary, Hatton, to pay their tributes, say their goodbyes, pay their last respects…*' The pretty *Round Britain* anchor on the telly is professional – they train them well. But she's stumbling a bit, as well she might, poor love. '*Mike Bennett is there at the scene, among the waiting crowds… At the funeral in Hatton, Cambridgeshire where the cortege should be arriving at any moment. Mike? Are you there, Mike? In Hatton…?*' (Sounds almost desperate. Dear, dear! *Coraggio*, Suzy, my poppet.)

Here we go. Pan to a crowd scene, and zoom on Mike 'Gordon' Bennett. Here he is, stolid in his customary crumpled Barbour, centre camera. The Barbour hat hides the balding pate: a posh Wurzel Gummidge. Mike's mike at the ready, as ever, and a furry boom in evidence to catch the soundbites. Cold February day in middle England. Pinched, dazed-looking faces in the fenland chill, determined to wait it out. Subdued voices, some evidence of hankies, and not just for the flu – after all, this isn't a street-party. Some of them might even be sincere. It doesn't do to underestimate the brightness such as old Jerry brought into sad little lives.

'I'm here, Suzy...' Almost fatherly. How touching. Good old 'Gordon' – trouper if ever there was one. A reporter to his extremities and not a sincere bone in his body. The Media come to mourn, praise and bury their own, and every journo from the ambitious cub on the local provincial daily to the seasoned hacks on the *Torygraph* and the *Times*, the *Mirror*, the *Mail*, the *Sun*, the *Screws*, and the *Mercury* – they're all out in force, and of course there's the turnout of colleagues from the BBC, from ITV, from Channels Four and Five...

Me? Well, I too knew the man personally.

'Yes, well, Suzy, here we all are waiting. As you say, Suzy, it's a very sad day...a strange day for everyone...I've been talking to Local Councillor Clive Upton... Councillor?'

'Well, it's tragic, obviously. A tragedy,' agrees a tubby gingerish geezer dressed in an anorak and a muffler into Mike's mike. Personally, it irritates me that 'tragic' is the adjective used to describe any untimely misfortune. Tragedy properly concerns the downfall of a flawed hero. Hmm. 'We're proud and glad that this village of Hatton will be Sir Jerry's final resting place, but it's – well, he was sort of an institution, wasn't he? We're all very sad and shocked. It's, you know, all a bit strange...' And what else can he say? Apart from all the rioting speculations, it is strange: hard to get used to the idea that now there will be no more family quiz programmes, no more talent shows, chat shows, no more em-ceeing... and no more *Sort It* (Fairbrother is Looking Out For YOU!) Apart from the flower-heaped coffin that will doubtless arrive on the scene at any moment, and whatever nauseating corruption has already begun inside it, he truly is no longer with us. Nowhere on the planet, no matter how far or how wide one might search, my friend. Old Jerry's death – in human terms, it could have been anyone's. Yours. Or mine...

But right now it's not the metaphysical that bothers anyone. They're too busy in the here-and-now, having a circus, waiting for the star turn, only this time, he won't be doing the talking. All the up-beat introductions, letting his voice fall to a suitably solemn pitch when the hearse heaves into view. Now, everybody else can do that. And as circuses go, this one's got three rings at least: the wife – sorry, widow – with a Past, the details of which were just nicely edging their way into public prominence before Jerry's death eclipsed everything. It's got the pathos of three fatherless kiddies, and the memory of the untimely accident that killed the eldest one's mother – he's an orphan, now, and the sentimental press has had a field day with that in the hypocritical way it does, pretending not to wish to expose the child and his grief, yet making copy out of it all the same, complete with all the psychobabble.

Mostly, though, this is about a dead-famous dead telly celebrity. Cut off in his prime in 'mysterious circumstances'; the beloved hero of middle-England's middle-aged; the telegenic alternative comic turned cuddly household name with the racy humour that no longer offended anyone. All good family viewing; gently challenging, liberal, but no known alliances; bit of a time at uni, obviously (and who didn't?) and a bit of a bad lad image in the early days, but nothing *that* extreme by today's standards. True, there were a few notorious escapades with girls in the studios (and a few bank-rolled tabloid stories there, maybe, in the weeks to come?) but regular as the milkman if we still had one, a reminder, perhaps, that we *did* once have one, a recent relic of a Golden Age that never quite was, like (remember?) John Major's warm beer and village cricket. Jerry was part of the fabric, completely uncool, completely unquestioned, safe. In short, a national institution, and this is doubtless how the majority of this loyal public will always remember him, only the most sour and vindictive dwelling on his untimely end, or the manner of his passing...

'*A very cold day in Cambridgeshire, by the look of things, Mike...*' observes the pretty anchor again. When in doubt, comment on the weather. They have to fill the gaps, you see. Call me cynical, but I reckon that if you were to cut out this sort of inanity, many a half-hour news programme could be squeezed into ten minutes of the real thing. *Private Eye* has got a column dedicated to just this.

'Gordon' Bennett comes back on cue. '*Yes, well, Suzy. It is certainly chilly here in Hatton... but the rain seems to be holding off, which is good for all of us waiting*.'

'*Yes, Mike. We're all waiting for the cortège, now, aren't we? Outside the church? St Mary's in Hatton, Cambridgeshire?*' (Suzy, sounding desperate again, trying very hard not to lose the plot. Attagirlie!)

'*That's right Suzy... Still more people arriving... this crowd is far bigger than expected...*' Camera on the fresh droves arriving to join the throng. There must be a big-league match crowd's worth by now: a few uniformed police, being unobtrusive; the odd individual caught in the camera, suddenly self-conscious. Behind them all, the unprepossessing countryside of Cambridgeshire in all its bleak flatness... Jesus, if I believed in Purgatory, these flat fens would be it. That and saddo crowds like this one. Pale ugly faces, close up shot of bucolic jaws chewing like so many cows – gum, I suppose, and there's some bored kids handing out sweeties. For them, it must be a day out...

Necks craning suddenly. Something's happening at last. '*I think I see some arrivals now, Suzy...*' says 'Gordon' to camera. Now a convoy of sleek limos glides up, pausing to issue the first contingent, a flurry of photographers, dark-suited men, women partially hidden under big hats, designer shades useless in the grey of the day, part of the uniform. Faint organ music tinkling from the church, a shot of St Mary's rather pretty fourteenth-century spire. More flat fens. How can anyone can live in country like that? Living death. I mean, imagine. The old days, especially, what it must have been like. You got born, you got 'educated' in big inverted commas, at least enough to sign your name on your bond, your landlord's will, what have you, learned the ABC and a few hymns, got confirmed, all that stuff. Then you got married, had kids, worked picking peas and turnips, your kids had kids, and then you died of ague or dropsy or the 'old cough', and people shed tears for a day and then they forgot you, carried on, being born, learning to read the Bible and write their names, singing hymns, shagging their neighbour's girl if they hadn't already shagged their sister – no, really, these backwoods places are famous for it, I'm telling you – and people were sort of strapped into this harness, escape unimaginable, unless it was the Army, or to sea. Worse for the women, I guess. And worse in Ireland. I've got this poor old Uncle Ted who could tell you volumes of this social history malarkey. Then you died, and there was a funeral, a wake, and then it was all over. Again.

Not for good old Jerry Fairbrother. Sir Jerry. For him, or at least for that part of him that is public property, death is not the end, but the beginning. First the newsflash interrupting *Eastenders*, then the first item on the TV news channels, followed rapidly by the shock-horror headlines on the front-pages following the Coroner's summing up of the post-mortem analysis. Then the obits, the feature articles, the tearful interviews, the retrospectives and re-runs, and all those unrestrained speculations on the internet... Now those really did upset a few sensibilities before they got blocked. But nothing is ever really blocked. One can access anything if one knows how, and some embarrassing things have doubtless yet to emerge. More shock-horror! Prurience, that surreptitious crotch-itching fascination with the nasty, it's human nature, and not a modern phenomenon at all. If you've got a sense of history, you will recall that the Middle Ages had its versions of the middle pages. Think of the stocks, name and shame with a vengeance, and probably about as fair. Oh, this thing will run and run, believe me. Until the next thing, that is; let's not kid ourselves. Prurience requires new itches to scratch all the time. One day, probably sooner than you think, Fairbrother will be just an old scab, no longer suppurating, not worth picking.

I'd guess they'll probably bring in a verdict of misadventure. A nice, euphemistic blanket, 'misadventure'. Old Jerry, troubled by his much-publicised rocky marriage to the delicious but rapacious Louise, and further saddened by the recent death of his agent, not to mention a workload that must have been punishing, let's be fair. Old Jerry was stressed out, had taken too many prescription tranquillizers, and then taken himself to a party at the home of an old acquaintance where he had apparently consumed a modest amount of coke and a lot of wine. Then he seems to have needed the air, wanted to go home, perhaps, and left via the fire-escape to avoid any lurking news-hounds, lost his balance on the steep iron stairway, and plunged twenty-five feet to the ground, breaking his neck when he got there...

Of the dead has-been found in the snazzy riverside warehouse conversion party venue, 'misadventure' is likely in his case, too. Too much, too often, and, on this last occasion, too pure. Foul play and malice aforethought are still open questions, and the Met are still trying to track down others present, including the suppliers of the more interesting party-bags. In the meantime, pending the who and the why, they have the how and the what, and now they can bury Jerry.

On the screen, old Sir Brian, that stalwart of light entertainment, being handed out of a gleaming Roller, leaning on his stick, blinking at the assembled crowd, shaded by discreet minders, by stolid-looking fuzz in uniform. And now, a sort of loud hush and a swish on the gravel as the hearse-limo noses its solemn way towards the lych-gate... flashes of cameras, a child shrieks, a loud murmur as the coffin gets unloaded from the serviceable if unromantic trolley, and hefted onto the shoulders of six good men and true, well-matched six footers, doubtless picked from his production team from *Sort It* and the *Big Quiz*... I can't say I recognise any of them except Ben Young in his thick specs, grizzled, old-looking now, shouldering his burden, determined to do his bit, and let's hope he doesn't have a heart-crisis on the way in. Bet you there was a fight for places! How Lion Barley would have given his eyes to have been there if he could, except he was a midget. The coffin pauses, waiting for the mourners to form a sort of guard of honour.

Little murmur from the crowd, because now here's Louise, in quick close-up, in the regulation big black hat and shades, expensive black cashmere coat and boots, the chief mourner, out-glamorising Sir Jerry's sister Gwen by quite a lot. On the steps of the church, she is greeted by the Rev. R. C. H. Browne (who will doubtless be interviewed later, since he knew Fairbrother as a boy) and she goes to take his outstretched hand, spots a camera, ignores it like a stage-direction. Black gloved hands clasping the vicar's, retroussé profile elegantly half-hidden under the hat-brim... but now she looks around as if she might have forgotten something. She has, but here they troop with Aunt Gwen, the littlest one clinging to her auntie's sleeve. Lady Louise, as she insists on styling herself, puts out a consoling motherly arm. The camera catches the beautifully constructed wan little smile at the scowling Charlie, Charlie who is growing up to be a beefy specimen like his papa, and who gives his stepmother a look of pure murder. I've a certain sympathy for scowling Charlie – he's a bit stuck now, poor kid. Anyway, that's one for the paparazzi, splashed all over tomorrow's red-tops, bet you. Poor Lulu. Never mind. Her time will come. As it is, she's been saved the nastiest divorce since Paul and Heather, and now she gets the whole shout, not just the legal team's notion of a fair alimony pay off.

Now, as the coffin is borne slowly into the church, the organ wheezily audible, the crowd stands agog. Here is Kylie, if I'm not mistaken, and roll-called in old 'Gordon' Bennett's voice-over, here they all are, all pulling long, sad, lovely faces, dabbing with hankies under shades, walking purposefully forward past the waiting saddos gatherered outside. Close up. Yes, Kylie indeed, greeting elderly Sir Brian with a sweet sad kiss, and here's Silvie on the arm of some beau or other, and Gwilym Jones, Jonesy, looking very Welsh and suitably saturnine, accompanied by his latest leading lady, the lovely Laura MacFarlane, his Olivia, whose nude scene in *Twelfth Night* has caused quite a little sensation... And finally here's old Broadbent, OBE, pausing to have words with 'Gordon'. The old boy is visibly moved. *'A very sad day indeed, Mike...it's an appalling tragedy...'*

That word again. The hero with the fatal flaw. Or troubles, anyway...

Jerry's troubles? Well, I guess he began to be aware he had big ones early last year. Come to think of it, quite a lot of people began to have troubles early last year. Not in single spies but in battalions, eh?

Part I

1: Early Last Year...

It's a love thing. Year in, year out. You work so hard for it. You lag its pipes, prime its woodwork. You paint its walls, you mow its lawn. You take care of it with devotion and pride. Isn't it time for it to take care of you? Why wait? Your home is your greatest capital asset... contact...

Scavengers! Jerry Fairbrother muttered under his breath, and scribbled a note.

You don't take spam personally, even the ones that address you as 'Jerry'. Jerry's spam filter was efficient, but as he had a professional interest in the contents, he frequently found himself sidetracked into the extraordinary nether world of unsolicited and possibly downright illicit advertising, and wondered who sat and wrote them, and whether it could possibly be worth it. Somebody, quite a lot of somebodies, must fall for it, seriously consider all those impertinent questions: do you lie awake listening for bumps in the night? (house insurance); what happens to your loved ones when you can't take care of them? (life insurance); is she put off by the paunch? (slimming aids)... and the exhortations: give her what she deserves! (erectile aids); give yourself what you deserve! (a bigger penis, a retirement plan)... not to mention all the ones that told him he had won a unique opportunity to enter a Spanish lottery, or beg him to allow someone who addressed him as 'Dearest' to use his bank account.

Lately, *Sort It* had devoted a small slot to spam, and the slogan – 'if it seems too good to be true, it probably is!' – had been his own idea. The programme relied on a team of experts and ideas-persons, as well as constantly inviting stories, complaints and suggestions from the public, but Jerry prided himself on hands-on involvement, on being a real team-member, not just the public face.

The spam was actually Suzy's job, amongst many others. Very often, he found himself retracing her footsteps, as it were, producing a note, an idea, that Suzy had thought of already. Little Suzy, so staggeringly efficient, so bright, so scrupulous and keen. She took care of the official programme site. She probably spent hours doing unofficial overtime at home. He leaned back in his chair and stretched. Today, he could forget the programme, forget the studio. And forget about Suzy, in that vaguely itchy way he could always almost forget about Suzy... Sometimes, he felt a little guilty that she was so forgettable.

Saturday morning, home in Wimbledon. Showered and changed after his morning run on the Common, and back in his den in jeans and a jersey, fresh coffee in a flask on his desk, a steaming, fragrant mug. Shrieks from upstairs. Dorota dealing with it. Back to the keyboard, and the careful email to his sister, Gwen; Gwen, whose daughter, Elise, was in big trouble. In her first year at university, Elise had been doing the driving. On the way back from a party, accompanied by five friends crammed into her tiny car, she had managed to turn the car over into a ditch. Elise herself had escaped with cuts and bruises, but now she faced jail on a rap for reckless driving causing loss of life. Ecstasy had been mentioned. One of her friends had been killed outright. Another might not walk again. His niece, daughter of his only sister, the blonde curly child who had shrieked with delight in the sea in Sardinia, who had been infatuated with the handsome uncle on the television…and who had later dismissed his fame as one of those things, growing up in the sort of schools where nearly everyone had a wonderful uncle…

It had made big news. First, the breaking story on the national TV and radio networks ('student killed, others injured in accident in South Wales') and then, inevitably, 'Fairbrother's niece driver of Cardiff death-car…' They had asked him for comments, quotes. 'Celebrity TV host Jerry Fairbrother said, "I'm deeply shocked and saddened. My heart goes out to the family of Tristan Holmes, and I pray for Fiona James's full recovery…"' His private secretary had briefed him with the correct names, and he had managed to evade demands for his views on recreational drugs. In the papers, a grainy picture made him look ten years older, weirdly unfamiliar without the camera grin. He had had to dodge the *paparazzi* for several days. He shuddered, remembering. Appalled for Gwen and David, and for Elise, whose scared, tearful face at the inquest was ample testimony to how she must be feeling, he could not help but acknowledge that he was pretty appalled for himself.

He wrote: '…I'm thinking of you, dearest Gwennie, I really can't imagine anything worse, except to thank God that Elise herself was unhurt…only so dreadfully sorry that her connection to me has exposed her to so much glare. I'll be over as soon as I can. Please give Elise my love. I hope you can all find a way of coping…' Coping! Why did everything have to sound so trite? And how did one 'cope' with a thing like this? Memories, sickly surfacing, of his own youthful follies… Something about the nature of Elise's accident caused him a very deep disquiet. The telephone was at his elbow, and he picked up the receiver to call in person, then put it down, stared out of the window at the blackbirds fighting in the flowering currant which was sprouting with that almost impossibly green green of new leaf. Spring… 'Whatever, I'll try to come over, work permitting, next weekend. All my love, J.' He pressed 'send'.

Jerry drained his coffee and poured another, and reached for the weekend papers. The stack was smaller than usual. Dorota had taken the *Mail* and the *Mirror* up to Louise, and had left him with the broadsheets. Even so, with all the colour supplements they made quite a bulky pile. He made a brief scribbled note to himself to run the 'volume of newsprint' problem by the *Sort It* team. *Sort It* was running a 'doing your bit' slot, aimed at raising the public awareness of environmental concerns without antagonising the average householder. That had been his idea, too. But it had been Suzy's slogan 'think before you print' that had captured the public imagination, and was just possibly responsible for a nation of convert recyclers and rejecters of junk-mail. He dutifully read the latest on the Japanese earthquake and a depressing piece on the disappearing rain forests, and then glanced at a travel supplement's offering on Sicily, which looked appealing, but he wasn't in the mood. Now, he wanted nothing more than to immerse himself in an orgy of Louise's preferred tabloid reading, just for fun... and then comforted himself with the knowledge that newsprint media was his business, his homework, however much it seemed as if work was play, and play was work...

He was always catching himself out like this: little guilts, little hypocrisies that, if he cared to dwell on them, all too easily undermined his sense of himself. Take his latest alter-ego: the hero of *Sort It*. The friendly, approachable face, with its good-humoured grin, wry sense of fun, and incisive authority when the need arose in the name of fairness (and that pun on his name – Fair Brother!) This man was solid, unswerving, trustworthy. Such a man would not transgress. But the private Jerry had and did. He did not deserve the public's good opinion, or at least he didn't deserve what he began to perceive as the *adulation* – it made him nervous, made him feel afraid that he couldn't turn back, couldn't just say hey, I'm just this bloke, okay? I've just been – well, lucky. I got some breaks. I'm just like you.

He believed this. He had never been overtly ambitious. On the contrary, it often seemed to him as if his success – his succession of successes – had sort of slid into place without his having had to push very hard at all. He had had to tread on very few necks, he had made very few enemies and a great many friends... Lucky breaks, just lucky breaks. (Interview, last year when the new programme was launched, nice woman from *TV Choice* magazine: 'But you work so hard, Jerry! You have the *Big Quiz*, the *Step On Up* talent show midweek, and now *Sort It*. Are you telling me you're not a workaholic?' 'I certainly spend a lot of time in the television studios, Sandie, but – well, ho, ho, I'm a fraud, Sandie. It's true I put in a great deal of effort, as do my wonderful teams, but you can't call it work. I love it...') But so often, these days, he really did feel fraudulent: that the 'Jerry Fairbrother' in the public image was actually nothing like the impostor sitting here at his desk. He was not so much living a lie, as a lie was beginning to live him.

This morning, possibly because of the presence of his almost but not quite estranged wife in the house, he felt more than usually lonely... which was of course the oldest cliché in the book – fame's such a strain! cried a mocker in his head – and now, also mostly because of Louise, he was feeling sorry for himself, unattractive in anybody, but probably unforgivable in someone with his extraordinary good fortune. But it was surely true that fame did bring a kind of isolation and exerted its own tyranny: statistically speaking, there must be very few people in the world that couldn't have a family crisis without that world looking on and judging. And it *was* scary, how rapid had been this transition from 'popular TV presenter' to 'major celebrity'. Now, with three programmes on the go, he was almost ubiquitous, on three channels and in millions of living rooms at prime-time three nights of the week, and that wasn't counting the ads. This was the meaning of 'public property' – and now, whether he liked it or not, he had a duty to maintain their image of him. He was no longer entitled just to be himself, fallible, peccant – like everyone else. Now he was Everyman's Mister Super Nice Guy, fighting on the side of all the other average Mister Nice Guys who could fall out with their wives, their colleagues and their accountants without making so much as a ruffle in the public consciousness unless they invoked, say, the might of such as *Sort It*. Mostly, everyone else could swerve their way through their bumpy lives in private.

The letter from the Palace was tucked, hidden, in a drawer of his desk. He could hardly think about it without feeling slightly sick. If only he could avoid the worst of the inevitable publicity. With Louise, he knew all too well, that would be damn nigh impossible. She would be steely, utterly ruthless, and determined to take him for all she could, ripping apart his public image along with his home, his sense of stability. It had been a rocky stability for a long while, but, wrongly as it turned out, he had imagined it was contained, with no nasty surprises, no horrible confrontations... Now, it seemed, Louise wanted to bring things to a head, obtain 'closure', whatever that was. She wouldn't care about shrieking headlines, giving interviews – she seemed to thrive on that sort of stuff. In fact, she would almost certainly have to paint him in the worst possible colours, just so that she could justify the whole thing. He could see it all now: 'Why I can't live with Jerry, says Tearful Louise...' And 'So Mean! Jerry's Wife Cleans Houses to Buy Shoes!' Cleans houses! He knew only too well how things would get twisted. Since her return from the States, and her decision to be home more or less permanently these days was more cause for alarm than relief: she was plotting something, he was sure, strengthening her position, limbering up. Trust Louise to come home, just at the moment when she was actually planning to leave.

Very soon, she would go on the offensive, all guns blazing: he had known Louise far too long to imagine she would do anything other. And, because of his public self, Mr Nice Guy, and because, whatever else he was in private life, he was a loving and responsible parent, he couldn't ever fight back. She had him by the proverbial balls. He, who had made so few enemies professionally, had to acknowledge that he had recently made two rather significant ones in private: his wife, and soon, surely, Suzy. She could so easily turn into an enemy once she realised that he had no intention of making her the next Mrs Fairbrother...*Lady* Fairbrother! He knew he should tell her, end it. But when he imagined the scene – tearful, recriminatory, guilt-inducing – his mind winced and bolted.

Jerry looked at his watch: another hour before he had to face more of the music. Sometimes, he longed for the days when he was just a humble writer of alternative comedy sketches, a face on late-night TV, when he was nobody special, when nobody over the age of thirty-five had heard of him... He missed Jenny so often, too. His sweet, capable, sunny-natured Jenny, content to be the helpmeet at his side with no monster raving ego to placate. And sometimes, only seldom now, but when it happened it was with a terrible poignancy, his thoughts took him further back still, and he longed for the real old days, the Edinburgh fringe, for the camaraderie of *Plug & Socket*, for Jonesy and the rest... even for Marie. Even for Drex.

He could hear the children's thudding feet upstairs, and Dorota's voice, attempting to calm. Ignoring it for what he knew could only be a few more moments, he turned again to the papers. Dorota must have missed something, for here was the *Weekend Mercury*, with its familiar blazon, and on the strap, 'Kinseyder's Inside Job – High Court Judge's Disgrace', which he seized guiltily and gratefully, quickly becoming immersed in the centre-page human-interest story: a heart-wringing tale of a disabled girl and her mother and their wrangle with a heartless housing association landlord, and he drew a thick circle round the pertinent details in red biro, planning his next *Sort It* team meeting. Mostly, these tabloids made him angry. They moralised while making copy from such tales of misery, but never, as far as he could tell, did they ever do anything to help. That was where '*Sort It* – Fairbrother's Watching Out For You!' came in. Popular, populist entertainment it might be, but it always sought to help. As for Kinseyder and his kin, they were parasites, pure and simple, the sort of leeches who sucked out the last drain from stories like his own niece's tragedy, and who would doubtless make a ghastly meal of his collapsing marriage. The prurient accounts of the peccadilloes of his fellow celebrities gave him little satisfaction. There but for the grace of God… He made some more notes.

Pandemonium broke out suddenly outside the door.

Emily's voice, plaintive, shrill, with a new transatlantic intonation that had startled and rather annoyed him ever since her return. 'I want Daddy to come. It's not fay-er!' And Charlie's gruff tones, older than his eleven years: 'He can't. He's busy, stupid…' 'I'm not stupid, and you musn't say that, you pig!' There was an audible thump, and a little shriek, and now Dorota, ineffectual, 'Children, children!' trying to quell the racket. 'Where's Mommy?' wailed a little voice. 'Dorota! Tell those kids to can the noise will you? I'm on the phone!' Louise yelling from the upstairs landing. 'Oh, Jesus,' said Jerry under his breath. 'I'm here, darling,' he said, emerging from the den into the hallway, and scooping up the smallest in his arms, the five year old Jemima, and smiling conciliations at the nanny, called out, 'It's all right, Lou. Dorota's taking care of everything…' He heard his wife snort some inaudible obscenity, and helped the children into their coats and boots. 'We're going skating and you've got to come too, Daddy,' said Emily. 'Skating,' echoed Jemima. 'On a sink…' 'A rink, darling…' 'Sink!' Charlie said, raising his deceptively innocent blue eyes to heaven. 'Pooh! Ice-dancing. We did that last week. I want to go to Harry Potter…' 'It's not on until the next week, Charlie,' Dorota reminded him. 'You have to do skating today…' '*Again*,' said Charlie heavily. 'Girls' stuff…' 'Nonsense,' said Jerry. 'Some of the best skaters have been men. Let's see, there was Tim Curry…and Torville, or was it Dean…?' His children gazed at him, puzzled. 'Can't you come, Daddy? It's just not the *same* without you,' wailed Emily, gazing up at him winningly. 'Dorota says I'm getting very good…' She twirled in demonstration. Emily was eight and turning into a beauty. She was also, Jerry noted with some dismay, becoming remarkably like her mother, and not only in looks. 'Not this morning, sweetheart. Mummy and I have got to have a meeting with a man. But we'll go and fly kites this afternoon after lunch, I promise. Or if it rains, we can go to Henley or Richmond for tea. Would you like that?' 'With Mommy?' asked Jemima. 'Perhaps… We'll ask her, shall we? She might be too busy…' 'Louise won't come,' said Charlie sullenly. 'She never does…' 'Now, you lot, you all go with Dorota, and become skating stars, okay? Jemmie, you be a very good girl for Daddy and do what Dorota says, like a little angel?' 'Okay, Daddy…' 'Charlie? Take care of these women, okay?' He winked at his son, and pulled a face. Charlie worried him. The eldest of the three and very bright, he was old enough to know something was going on, and too young to be able to understand an adult explanation, if there was such a thing. He ruffled the boy's hair, and Charlie ducked from under his hand. 'Charlie?' 'Okay, Dad...' 'That's better...' He was tying on scarves and adjusting hats, and something in his chest felt as if it might burst suddenly. How he loved them! His children, these three precious beings, the only people in the world you'd probably literally die for, and who knew him only as Daddy, and loved him whoever he was...

'This has come for you. It arrived this morning,' said Dorota carefully, wrapped in a coat and furry boots herself, and sniffing – whether with cold or disapproval was left ambiguous. She handed him a small jiffy-bag. She was proud of her English, and seemed to expect praise for the smallest well-constructed sentence. For her part, she was deeply unhappy in a household where she expected to be treated with respect, but where the children were unruly and spoilt, and where the mistress of the house came and went as she chose, and was rudely dismissive, treating her as if she were reclaiming territory whenever she returned. She, Dorota Przwalska, a Polish girl of good family and who had been used to very different things, very different indeed, would have left the whole lot of them at a moment's notice were it not for her quite desperate need of a roof and some money, and for her English employer's sad, wry smile and cuddly countenance. Jerry Fairbrother had that effect on people. 'I found it, you understand, in the mat.'

'On the mat?'

'No, in the mat.'

'On the mat. Or do you mean under the mat?'

'Look, Dorota, 'on' is like this, 'under' is like that,' said Charlie, miming. He had taken it upon himself to supervise Dorota's English improvement.

'Yes. No. I mean under the mat. Put it under the mat,' she repeated, lesson-wise.

'Oh. Thank you. How strange. Oh, well, thank you, Dorota. Now be good, you lot. Charlie, I mean it, so put your tongue in. Emily, look after Jemima. Bye... bye, darlings...' He stood on the doorstep watching them, a brief, second-nature glance right and left for lurking reporters, relaxed slightly, watched them pile into the Fiat Multipla, watched Dorota's careful 'mirror, signal, manoeuvre' before she pulled out into the road through the electronic gates, watched their faces – Charlie's steadfastly looking ahead, and the girls', staring back and waving, watched the exhaust fumes billowing into the clear cold March morning as they drove away. 'Bye,' he said again, knowing he was inaudible, and trying not to look as sad as he suddenly felt. He went back into his den, wishing there was more coffee. He checked the time. Ten-thirty. Angus was coming at eleven. He hoped Louise would be ready in time. Suddenly, he felt furious with Louise. This split, the totality of the break-up of the home, the family, was at her insistence, not his. He would have continued – not happily, but somehow – just as they were (and that, he could almost hear her say, was just typical! Bury your head in the sand, Jerry, pretend everything's as perfect as one of your family entertainments, as one of your advertisements for instant Italian risotto or sofa-beds!) No, of course it couldn't go on like this…they hardly saw one another anyway. But wasn't divorce rather extreme? Couldn't they work something out? And the children… he worried so much for the children…

The jiffy bag was still in his hand. It was a small package, about five inches square, and addressed simply to 'jeremy fairbrother' in lower case letters, written carefully in black marker pen. No address, no stamps, no postmark. Perhaps Dorota had actually found the thing under the mat, which must mean that someone had come to the house to deliver it in person… Fairbrother frowned, suddenly unsure whether to open it. It was not the first time he had received unpleasant things delivered to the door. 'Oh to hell with it,' he thought. 'If the thing was going to explode, it would have by now…' He prised the staples, and eased the slim contents out: a single DVD in a blank cardboard slip. The disc itself was of the kind one could buy in tens and twenties at WH Smith, and it bore no identification at all. Most mysterious. He examined the packaging again. There was something tucked inside. A folded sheet of A4, typed and printed.

Hi, Jerry! I know you've got troubles of your own, but I'm afraid this is another one. You know, not single spies but battalions, as your man said. Artistically speaking, this is about as erotic as a trip to Kwik-Save, but I can't vouch for the good British public to be so discriminating, can you? Frankly, this will be the proverbial dynamite, really quite embarrassing at a time like this, isn't it? But Kinseyder's going to just love it, and the You-Tube kids are going to go wild! And think how proud your kids are going to be when they see their papa's – er – talents. Cheers! Call me, why don't you? There was a number…

Jerry Fairbrother felt slightly sick. He switched on the TV console and inserted the disc. Damn them, damn them, he was thinking. And damn me for being so bloody careless. That week, the Spanish trip to film condemned ex-pat villas and interview the poor ex-pats for the first series of *Sort It* last September. Yes, that blissful, idyllic week based just outside Barcelona was a serious mistake. Suzy had to be there as his PA, of course, but they should have been more discreet, even though they had had separate rooms on different floors. But they had felt irresponsibly free, and he had padded up to her room in the early hours, and been woken by the coffee and papers crew there in the mornings… Hell, there must have been dozens of waiters and flunkeys all too easily bribed to spy, take photos. He remembered with a sort of delighted shame a certain morning in the shower… Or perhaps it was more sinister still, someone recording them on their Friday assignations in the Barbican flat… Oh, *hell.* This was going to be awful. Poor Suzy! But this could be a *disaster* – just the sort of ammo Louise needed. Now she could really play the wronged wife, nobly blind and stoical while her husband fooled around with his junior staff. He was not even sure that Louise was not somehow at the back of this – so like her to play a double game, wrong-foot him. He'd better see the damage. He pressed 'play' with the greatest misgivings…and then jumped as Louise knocked on the door. 'Angus is here, Jerry,' she said. He snapped off the computer, opened the door, shook hands with Angus and said his good mornings, and followed his demurely-attired wife and their legal adviser into the sitting-room.

In the course of the day, he almost forgot the existence of the disc. Angus had advised a civilized separation; he had also advised (as Angus would) an outrageously high figure in settlement for Louise; Jerry had objected; Louise had accused him of being perennially mean. 'He *knows* I have nothing of my own, except what I earn,' she complained. 'He's so *cruel*, Angus, you can't believe! I can't even talk about it!' She had even begun, very tidily, not smudging her very understated make-up, to cry. The point of Angus, Jerry began to realise, was to provide Louise with a sort of sounding-board, someone to edit her remarks before she went public. He wanted to grab her by the shoulder, turn her to face him, make her talk to *him*, make her be honest, for once. Fat chance! He wondered, not for the first time, how he could ever have loved her, and yet, at one point, he knew he had, or at least been so mad for her that he had let her cloud everything else.

At one o'clock, the children had burst in with Dorota, pink faced and excited after the skating expedition, and they'd had hot bean soup and toast. Even Charlie had grinned and looked cheerful, showing off his bruises and joking, accompanied by his sisters' delighted giggles, that there was one he couldn't show them. After lunch, Louise had actually joined them on the Common with the kites, after rather pointedly giving Dorota the afternoon off... and he thought, she's doing this deliberately, playing the loving mummy, even being nice to Charlie, almost as if it's being recorded for the benefit of reporters hidden in the bushes. But there was a moment, as he watched them, the mother with her arm round the smallest girl, smiling at the child's joy as she watched her butterfly kite tug and rise, the older brother and sister nearby, teasing a great tiger-tailed kite into the air, when he thought: I wish I could snap this, keep this forever... but he had no camera with him, and anyway, people don't stay still. Louise caught his eye and her smile vanished; the butterfly fell, and Jemima wailed; Emily and Charlie began to fight. Again, he began to feel inexpressibly sad.

After Louise had gone out for the evening, and Dorota had put Emily and Jemima to bed, and Jerry had played a game of draughts with Charlie, who had won easily, and then demanded to go and watch TV in the rumpus room, Jerry, heavy hearted, remembered the mysterious DVD, poured himself a large glass of the Bergerac he freighted back from France, and sat at the computer and pressed it into action. More shit, he was sure, for the waiting fan. He winced in anticipation.

Whatever he had expected, it certainly was not this. Terrible picture, barely in focus, lurid colours; some blaring, out-of-tune fanfare, grainy opening titles in – yes, in Italian – and a gathering of people dressed in togas on a set which, even despite the poor quality of the picture, was so obviously cobbled together from boxes covered in sheets and velvet curtains as to be laughable. And somehow it was familiar, but he couldn't place it.

At a gestured command from one of the actors, the toga-clad people lay stretched on low benches round what passed for a table (a trestle with the legs cut down and a bed sheet spread over it?) and pretended to eat some sort of feast which looked like a modern *rosticceria* takeaway, to pour wine from coloured

[14]

jugs, and to drink from very implausible goblets. Every now and then, someone would throw a chicken bone to a waiting greyhound. Hang on a minute! Surely this wasn't? There was some accompanying lute music – very wobbly and out of tune – and no dialogue at all: the actors were miming as if in a silent movie. This is ridiculous, Jerry thought. He fast-forwarded a bit. The action had hotted up a little. Not so much a banquet now, but an orgy, with dinner neighbours feeding each other, stroking each others' exposed flesh, a mouth suggestively sucking on a drumstick... And now the Emperor (it was the Emperor because he wore a purple sash thing) stood up and summoned one of the young women. She came over on hands and knees, knelt at the Emperor's feet, blonde hair cascading over his sandals. The imperial toga parted.

'Oh shit! I knew it! Oh Christ! I don't *believe* this!' He pressed pause, and stared at the protagonists, barely suppressing a roar of laughter, remembering the children upstairs asleep, Dorota in front of her television. 'Oh God!' He stared at the out of focus image: yes, there he was, unrecognizable, surely, to any but himself or an intimate – one day, he might share this with his sister Gwen – thirty years younger, thirty years thinner, and with a mane of light brown wavy hair, the undergraduate Jerry Fairbrother, playing Emperor, in a highly unseemly pose with a young German woman whose name he had entirely forgotten. He remembered the studio, if one could call it that, and he remembered – hang on, fast forward – yes, here he was, dressed as some sort of slave: old Billy 'Whizz' Barnard, about to be that greyhound's object of attention, a complete impromptu but they'd kept the camera rolling. The animal had nearly bitten his balls off... Oh shit! How gorgeously embarrassing, how utterly inane, stupid and impossible. And all the time, he'd been thinking...shit! He slugged his wine down and poured another.

He and Billy the Whizz, and that girl, Chloe Whatshername, Cunningham – the one who ended up as a very grand theatre correspondent on the *FT* – yes, she was there too. That crazy long vacation trip, hitching through France, Switzerland and Italy, where they'd suddenly been so broke they'd spent a foetid, uncomfortable night on the platform on Rome Termini, been moved on by the Carabinieri, and told to report to some office or other with their papers...it was all coming back now. Chloe, who had had a smattering of Italian, had pleaded their bona-fides, but they would need papers of employment in order to stay – and they had had no money between them to eat, even in Italy in the seventies, let alone get home... And then, someone's bright idea: the film studios. *Cinè Cittá.* They were always looking out for extras. Filthy and hungry, they suddenly found themselves employed – even supplied with rudimentary documents – bathed and fed, not to mention dressed in togas (the film was some sort of life of Caligula) and pampered by make-up girls... and all for two thousand lira a day, and a dormitory that only had fleas if you noticed them. And then there'd been an 'approach' – someone making an art-film in some smaller film lot, someone looking for three good-looking young *inglese* like themselves.

The 'art-film' had attracted almost every down-and-out foreigner under the age of thirty-five in Rome: Germans, French, Armenians, Brits, even an American, bit of a Bible-basher, who had fled, scandalized, on the first day's shoot. For ten days they'd earned three times the ordinary 'extra' fee, and they'd put up at a local albergo, where Jerry seemed to remember putting in a spot of extra rehearsal with the German. Gisela? Lenneke? It had been, Jerry remembered, quite an experience...

So all this just an elaborate leg-pull, eh? Somehow, this *must* be from Billy. The relief was immense. He must get in touch. There was this number... Blimey, after all these years! Old Billy Whizz! He realised tears were running down his face.

'Dad...?'

'Yes, Charlie,' Jerry said, snapping off the image hastily. He had forgotten his young son, still watching TV downstairs.

'You were laughing...'

'Something very silly and funny on You-Tube, darling. Isn't it time you were in bed?'

'Yeah... suppose so.'

Charlie seemed disinclined to go. Never mind, Sunday tomorrow. 'What were you watching?' Jerry asked.

'You. The Big Quiz. I didn't get all the harder questions, but I answered one or two, and before the contestants did. I got the Eiffel Tower right – about them going to take it down like the O2 Dome. That woman didn't, did she? And I got the twenty-five thousand one, about Hadrian. We've been doing about him at school.'

'Have you, now? Well, you're a very bright lad, because I didn't know the answer when we recorded the programme...' It had taken him some time to impress upon the children that he did not know all the answers – they were on a card hidden in an envelope, top secret. 'Don't you think it's time to get in to your jarmies?'

'Yeah, soon...Dad?'

'Hmmm?'

'Dad...are we really not going to live here anymore? Are you going to make us go away? If it's true I think you should tell us...' Charlie was growing up: less like Jenny now, more like a miniature version of himself. It was disconcerting. He felt the boy's solemn eyes staring unwaveringly at him.

'Of course not, darling. Look, um...' It was time to be a bit frank with Charlie. 'Mummy and I might live in different houses quite soon, okay? But that's not a problem, is it? You'll have two houses to live in...and I'll be here.'

'But she wants to go to America. Emmy said.'

'Well, now...she might want to spend more time in America, with Grandma and Pops. But that will be fun, won't it? And to see New York? The girls loved it.'

He mumbled something Jerry didn't catch.

'Say again, old son?'

'S'pose so... Sometimes...' Charlie was mumbling again. Sure sign there was something very much on his mind.

'Tell me so I can hear, old thing...' Jerry put his arm out towards the boy, but Charlie remained stolidly facing him.

'I said it's not the same. For the girls. I don't mind *seeing* America, but I want to live with you. I want to live here. And go to school like normal…'

'Don't worry, Charlie. Mummy and I are working things out, and our first priority is you and the girls. Okay? Get on upstairs to bed, there's a good kid.'

'Okay. But it was still better when she wasn't here, when it was just you. And Dorota. Dorota's okay, I guess.'

'Oh, Charlie! You kept saying you missed them.'

'Huh. I missed Emmy a bit, I s'pose…but she's silly now she's back, talking *American*… And Louise has gone sort of weird. And it's not…not like…'

'Not like..? Tell me, Charlie. Come on, kid. You can say it.'

'It's not like she's really my *mum*… My real mum died, in a car-crash. Louise is Emmy and Jemmy's mum. And she doesn't like me, she hates me!' said Charlie in a rush, his eyes on the floor.

'Charlie! Charlie, look. She may not be your real mum, but she likes you…of course she does, especially when you're nice to her and don't argue. She likes you a lot better than she likes me at the moment.'

'I still want to stay with you…' There was a small sob in the young throat.

'Come here…' Jerry pulled the boy close to him. 'So you will, darling. Nothing terrible's going to happen…' He felt a lump in his own throat, and prayed it was true. 'Fun today with the kites, wasn't it? And you even quite liked the skating.'

'S'pose so. I fell over a few times, but I didn't hurt myself. Dorota can skate. She's not bad. She's got a boyfriend.'

'Has she now? Well, lucky old Dorota, eh? Was he at the skating rink?'

'Yeah… he's a gangster.'

'How do you know he's a gangster?'

'He wears shades…and he's all in black.'

'I see. Mystery man, eh? Does he skate?'

'Can't…he's got this bad limp. I reckon he must've got shot up some time.'

'I see… How do you know he's her boyfriend?'

'He kisses her – well, you know. Soppy stuff. He got us ice-creams and coke. He's called Derek, or something, and he speaks funny.'

'Sounds as if Dorota's met a Pole… Well, good for her, I say. Off to bed, now, old son, okay?'

'Okay, Dad.'

'Sleep well, kiddo. Give us a kiss goodnight.'

If only, thought Jerry, as his son closed the door behind him, if only I can keep their childhoods decent, keep them safe, free from all the shit… Charlie was still only eleven years old, time enough for him to have to face all the ugliness, the disillusion… Pray God he might keep the hopes and dreams of all his children alive for a little longer! Like it or not, and Louise aside, there were wreckers, destroyers out there. All too easy to get paranoid. That guy in the park this morning, strangely familiar, and he would have sworn the guy had spotted him and was following. And now this latest prank. Price of fame. But it was almost certainly Billy Barnard behind the Roman thing. Old Billy. Just fancy! Jerry shook himself, and poured another glass of wine. Perhaps tonight, he might sleep.

[17]

2

Sleep beckoned. Eyes gritty and his leg beginning to ache – these days, it wasn't his foot and ankle but his hip, the side that took the strain – the man who called himself Drex Bello emerged into the light from Liverpool Street Tube and made his way back to Brick Lane. Colours, soft as they were in the deepening after-noon gloom, glared unnaturally, and the flickering shop neons, harsh and sickly flaring, made him feel unsteady as he walked. An old-fashioned come-down, no less. In the past, there would have been another line, another chemical catapult back into buzzing energy. Now, all he wanted was a large scotch and his bed. I'm getting too old for this, he was thinking. Time to retire from this senseless game.

He had been having a bad day. It was about to get worse. His sense of forebod-ing only increased as he turned the corner into Stinson Street where, glancing up by habit at the second floor of his building – the only ugly, purpose-built thirties utility dwelling in a street of mostly rundown but picturesque late eighteenth century London terraces with atelier fourth storeys the Huguenots had built to weave silk. He could see the blinds were pulled and the apartment had a private, keep-out look. Reassuring, a little. No raid, then. Not so far. And I'm not being followed, he thought. He would know; and despite his sense of exhaustion, he had kept checking.

In the street, newspapers and polystyrene cartons blew about on little gusts of stale wind, bringing on it the faint but persistent reek of the Halal butchers. The kids just let out of school with their backpacks flapping, shrieking and joshing each other, barged into him as if he wasn't there.

And now, when all he wanted to do was let himself into his own private fug, pour himself a whiskey, put his head in his hands and try to think, or at least get drunk and allow himself the luxury of worrying, like a dog with a sore, he would have to face out Angel, Angel of the angel-face and the filthy habits, the liability he could no longer afford. Or not. Wouldn't Angel, in a fit of pique, re-sentful, self-righteous, be even more of a liability? It was a showdown he had been half promising himself, half putting off, for the last week. Week and a half. Several weeks. What difference would a day make? Except that today had prob-ably changed everything anyway... and Angel would leave soon enough once the truth was out in any case. Perhaps that was the best way. Tell Angel what had happened, and Angel's sense of self-preservation would have the bags packed in no time at all. And that was the good case scenario... The worst – well, the worst didn't bear thinking about. In that case, they had best both scarper. Probably within the next thirty minutes...

That drawn blind was ominous, suddenly. Suppose Angel were not alone? Be-ing interrogated? Or maybe it was just that the flat was strewn, as it had been last Friday, with squalid discarded female apparel, the glass coffee table a Drug Squad paradise of debris? This was by far the most likely, the stupid little toe-rag! Angel had to go. But then there was the thought of the tears, the apologies, those soft yielding apologies... Fuck Angel. Nowadays, *that* thought left him entirely cold. He felt his resolve rise up again like clean new energy as he climbed the dark staircase, found his latchkey in his pocket and opened number four, his bile increasing as he now heard unmistakable low moans coming from behind the closed sitting room door, which he flung open with a violence that made the wall shudder.

'Oh, hullo, Beautiful. Wasn't expecting you back yet!'

'Evidently,' said Drex sourly. In the sitting room, Angel was in a sort of lotus-position on a floor-cushion, and naked apart from the white silk Armani scarf that had been Drex's birthday present, which he wore, python-fashion, wreathed around his thin pale-freckled frame. The gas fire was going full blast and the tiny over-furnished room was unbearably hot and rancid – the sickly stink of cooked opium and raw, fresh semen hit Drex like a sock on the jaw. A leather miniskirt and a pair of shiny boots, haphazardly discarded, littered the floor. Naked bodies writhed and groaned on the outsize television screen. 'Turn that fucking thing off,' said Drex, his voice ominously quiet.

'Before you ask, this is homework,' Angel squeaked. 'You know how it gets me.'

'Who's been here?' Drex said. But already he knew. He felt his wrought up anxiety subside very slightly.

'Only Mitzi. And she's off for the evening, lovey. But she had a good time – we had this new consignment from Ahmed. There's one that's going to interest you. Tell you all about it...' Angel adroitly used the remote, and there was a thick hush as the surreally-silent bodies continued to writhe. 'If I'd known you'd be back so soon,' Angel said, his perky little face full of winning, puckish smiles, 'I'd've put t'kettle on...' He always exaggerated his York accent if he thought Drex needed placating. 'Don't be cross,' he added sweetly, and rose lithely from his cushions. 'I'll do it now...' He sashayed from the room very fast, and Drex, despite himself, wondered at that extraordinary combination of elegance and speed in his friend's movements, and felt an unbidden stab of desire as Angel's tight, white buttocks atop small, ballerino's legs flashed from view.

Homely clattering sounds from the kitchen. Drex's fury had diminished to a dull smoulder, and he perfunctorily turned down the gas fire, spun up the black blind to let in the last of the weak early evening light, opened the window to let out the fug, before he sank into the only proper armchair, from where his eyes took in, almost idly, the spoon and the bloody needle on the coffee table, and the litter of paper tissues, the empty bottle of Coke and the plastic cases of video films strewn over the grubby fawn carpet.

'Da-dah!' Angel placed a laden tray, complete with brown teapot with a knitted cosy ('me gran's') and some chocolate biscuits on the table. He had also dressed, which perhaps was unwise as it hardened Drex's resolve rather than the one part of him which might, conceivably, have undone it. All in black – drainpipe jeans and a skintight longsleeve spandex teeshirt and dancer's plimsolls – Angel had the look of a junior stage-devil, and Drex suddenly found the staginess intensely annoying.

'What is it about this pusillanimous stuff?' Drex said. The film was still playing soundlessly on the enormous television screen, the squirming bodies ridiculous.

[19]

'You don't even like pussy. And it's hardly erotic, even if you did. All that heaving and squealing and doughy flesh. It's crap.'

'Your orders, pet. And some of them sailors and slaves…ooh-er. Wasted on pussy, but I mean to say.'

'You are disgusting, Angel. You make me puke. You're supposed to be looking at the faces.'

Angel poured a steaming mug for Drex and curled himself round the back of the armchair and stroked Drex's hair. 'Poor old love, have we had a bad day? Woops, shouldn't ask. Have some tea…' His hand slid down.

'Look, never mind about tea! Or *that*!' Drex exploded suddenly and, straightening up in the chair and pushing Angel from him, spilled a great deal of hot tea into his lap. 'Shit! I suppose you've left me some whiskey in your squalid solo debauches…' He got up and found the bottle in the ugly fifties cabinet that took up most of one side of the room. Poured himself a large tumblerful.

'Never touch the stuff myself, but proper little hypocrite, aren't we,' said Angel. 'I mean, we all have our own poisons, at least you always said so.'

Drex ignored him, waved an angry hand at the glass table. 'And what's all this, I want to know? God knows what you're doing this muck for. Shit, I haven't seen this stuff for about twenty years. Where the fuck do you get it?'

'You're not the only one with friends,' said Angel, pouting. 'Besides, it's supposed to be more natural.'

'Natural?'

'Natural. More organic. You know, you and your quorn and tofu and stuff when you went veggie.'

'You mean needles are natural and pure, I suppose? *And* it's still illegal, my pet. And it doesn't cost *nothing*. Where are you getting all this crap?'

'I thought we'd agreed we wouldn't ask each other – questions,' said Angel primly.

'You're such a silly little bitch.'

'O 'ark at Miss Proper. And who's talking if you please? Uncle Charlie comes round and it's mirrors out and roll up the tenner and straight up the nose and no messing! I prefer something more macrobiotic, and you come over all mardy. It's cheaper, too.'

'Macrobiotic! It stinks. Let me see your arm…' Drex lunged for Angel's long tight black sleeve, but Angel dodged neatly, holding his thin bony wrist in his long, rather raw fingers as if he'd been struck. 'None of your cowin' business…' His back was turned to the grimy window, and his sharp, childish cheekbone jutted in profile. His huge blue eyes were filling now. Drex could see the quiff of whitened hair shaking in the paling light. Angel snorted back tears unattractively. Real tears, not just theatre then, which he would have made sure were pretty. That was the problem with Angel: just when you were convinced his naïvety began and ended with a kind of worn theatrical performance, all a prostitute's pretence, what with his faux-Northern poor bad-lad act, the Orphan Annie bit, there'd be a real appeal to his feelings, and he surprised himself, often, by not being as immune as he'd like… How he hated him! How he hated them both, Angel and Drex, these roles they played. Drex and Angel…and Mitzi. Not a real name between them. 'Pour me another whiskey.'

'It stinks,' mimicked Angel. But he was coming out of his sulk.

'Shut up, Angel. Listen. I don't actually give a flying fuck if you wank yourself silly to the accompaniment of exceptionally squalid movies all afternoon. I don't care that you're risking vile infections by sticking needles into your lily white arm. I don't even care how many tricks you turn at the baths, or whether they even bother to pay a pathetic undereducated little tart like you. But I do care about this flat because – I do hope you're listening to me, Angel – because it's actually all I have. After today – yes, you're quite right, it's not been very pleasant – it'll doubtless interest you to know that I shan't even have this soon. I'm broke, Angel. I'm flat broke. Skint. Cleaned out. The details will keep…'

'C'mon, lovey. It can't be that bad. How come?'

Drex sighed. His exhaustion washed over him in sickly waves. 'Chris the Whisper's scarpered. Disappeared. With all the stuff and the entire investment. Including one Lockhart's.'

'Lockhart? Shit! He'll kill us.'

'Kill me, you mean.'

'But where is the Whisper? Where's he gone?'

'If I knew that, you sad little moron, he wouldn't have disappeared, would he? Think about it. We'd better hope that he's done a bunk, that he's hitched a ride back to Bolivia or Argentina or wherever, in which case he's only got me to worry about if I ever find him. Do you know what the alternative is? Well, do you? Can you work it out?'

'You mean the Whisper's *dead*? Bloody 'eck!'

Drex laughed out loud, mirthlessly. 'Now that, my little cretin, would be too much to hope for. Just *think*, for once, will you? That stuff – it's made your brain go soft…' He drank whiskey morosely.

'Oh…*oh!* You mean he's been? Oh, bloody Norah!'

'Yeah, bloody fucking Norah. Right this minute, he's probably singing his scabby heart out on the advice of some Old Bailey lawyer, trying to get his sentence reduced. He's got form, remember? He'd do anything.'

'Oo-er,' said Angel. 'But not necessarily… he might have just, well, *gone*.'

'Well, we had better hope so, hadn't we? Actually, I think we'd have heard. He's been gone twenty-four hours, and the Met are normally quicker off the mark than that. No, the swine's done a runner. Which doesn't mean he won't get picked up at any time. They strip search at airports, and there's probably an international watch. He's a hostage to fortune. And if he doesn't get his deal, Lockhart will be after my sodding neck. So I want you to get this shit – this *mess* – off my table and my carpet, and stick Ahmed's crap into a bin-liner and tell him to stick it, using my house as a porn scrap-yard, while I think.'

'You were pleased enough with that Italian thing,' said Angel, pouting. 'I'm your research assistant, you said.'

'That was different. I've got far more immediate problems now. And I'll begin with you. You can pack your bags, precious, and hitch a ride, because I can't afford your fare. I can't afford you. Even if I could, I think I'd rather be without a schizoid little northern junkie catamite with the brains of an intellectually challenged insect. See? And for fuck's sakes, get bleeding Mitzi out of here. She's getting on my tits. You both fuck my head, you hear? ...' He was yelling.

'Shh! She'll hear you. Anyway, you'll change your mind when you see what I've found you. And about Mitzi.'

'Oh yeah?' Whiskey always made him angry before it made him depressed. Now, in a dull way, he was both, and suddenly too exhausted to have anything more to do with the re-arrangement of his household. His last forty-eight hours awake and sweating with apprehension had left him craving nothing more than to sleep, to forget everything, before he had to think again. 'Gotter call in some debts... that's it. Debts.'

He must have dozed and heavily, because when he resurfaced the sitting room, apart from the indelible stains on the carpet, was spotless. At first, he thought that Angel had obeyed him and gone, and the thought suddenly gave him a thrill of pure panic. He had visions of Angel, tearful and pathetic, spilling all into the sympathetic ear of some Yard social worker...

'Coo-ee,' Angel said, and the relief must have shown briefly in his face. 'Welcome back to the land of the living. You don't half snore! Look at these. I blew them up big...' Angel shoved some A4 sheets into Drex's inert hands. 'Wait,' Angel said. 'I'll adjust the light.'

'Christ, not too bright, bloody hell...'

'In your own time, Beautiful...' He skipped from foot to foot behind the armchair.

'Jesus Christ,' Drex said, after an interval.

'Told you they were good. Mitzi took them – the ones of the Snake. Fancy dress party. She sort of blended into the background. Good, innit?'

'Probably dynamite,' admitted Drex. His brain was whirling. He wondered if he hadn't found a solution to an immediate problem. 'Get me another whiskey.'

'Not until you say sorry for the hissy-fit.'

'Sorry...'

'Okay. Coming up.'

'And find the mobile. I've got to call Lion.'

'Oh? Why him?'

'Because he's going to be useful for once in his miserable little existence. And stop pouting like a jealous six-year-old.'

Angel passed him his mobile and a refreshed glass with his eyes averted and his mouth crimped. 'I just don't know why you bother with that tosser, that's all. He's –'

'Useful. Thanks, sweetie-pie. And I decide who's the tosser round here, okay? Now shut the fuck up, will you? I've got to think.'

3

Bad Girl Silvie Snape Grows Up! And here she is, folks, with agent Jake Durphry, sipping skinny-lattes at her newest exclusive hang-out, the Graven Image in Mayfair, where a breakfast table for a latte and an organic croissant-ultra-lite will set you back a cool thirty quid. Best save up for the octopus salad lunch, the Supermodel's nutrish-dish of the day. Our Sylvie is the new 'face' for City Girl, the cosmetics giant Cosmix's newest spin-off that appeals to the young and trendy on a budget. Says a spokesperson, 'City Girl is delighted by the recent signing. She's got the look. And our clients love her!' Nasty rock-star boyfriends? A reputation for powdering her nose in the rest-rooms of Paris hotels? Trashing holiday cottages? Forget it! According to the long-suffering Durphry, La Snape is 'all grown up...' Time will tell, eh? Kinseyder is not taking bets...

Silvie Snape was in bed in her Notting Hill flat, still trying to sleep off the night (or rather, early morning) before, when the letter came. Dayna Nboku, the latest assistant (and Silvie got through assistants like other people got through kleenex) had tip-toed in with a tray nearly an hour before and, seeing that her employer was still sound asleep, had left it, with its simple order of black coffee, a multi-vitamin pill, a glass of water and a sachet of alka-seltzer together with the morning's post, on the table by the bed. Dayna had fielded three telephone calls already (I'm so sorry, sir/madam/Mr Durphry, but Miss Snape is not available to take your call...) 'Well get her out of bed, there's a lovey, and tell her it's urgent, okay?' And Mr Durphry, who was always quite polite and didn't use language, had sounded a bit agitated. Dayna was wondering whether to risk her boss's wrath (which could get violent, and was always accompanied by very extreme language indeed) and was putting off the moment with another cup of coffee herself, when she was startled by a piercing scream. She hurried to her employer's bedroom.

Dayna took in the scene with alarm. The tray had been knocked to the floor, the coffee-flask was on its side, a viscous black stain seeping onto the pale pink Chinese rug; the water glass had smashed on the polished pine floor, and Silvie Snape herself was reared up in the bed yelling blue murder and waving a brown envelope. 'Look! Look at this! Christ albleedinmighty!'

'Oh God, Silvie, have you scalded yourself?' cried Dayna, rushing over. 'Here, let me see.'

'It's not me, you stupid cow! This! Look at this!'

'But this *mess*! And your lovely carpet! I'll run and get a cloth!'

But Silvie grabbed the girl by the wrist. 'Fuck the mess! Just look at this, will you?' She thrust a typed letter into Dayna's rather trembly hand. When the opportunity had come up to work for a famous fashion model, Dayna had jumped at it, thrilled to bits. Now, she wasn't at all sure. All these dramas (and there were at least two, every single day) made her very nervous. Dayna had been increasingly nervous for the past three weeks. She read, but it didn't make sense.

'Hello Petal. This amused me a bit, especially as you'd promised that nice beauty company you were a reformed character. Woosh, good gear, eh? I don't like the Fuzz anymore than you do, but I think it might amuse Kinseyder, don't you? Not to mention C.G.'s Board of Directors. Call me, do ...' There was a number.

'What does it mean, Silvie? I don't understand. Who is this Kin - Kinseyder? And why does he call you Petal?'

'Kinseyder's that gossip-columnist cunt in The Mercury. He's got a blog, too. And nobody's called me 'Petal' since Lion... I've gotter think. Shit! Shit, shit, shit!'

'I still don't understand, Silvie.'

'I thtill don't underthtand, Thilvie...well try this. Perhaps this will explain things even to someone with as tiny a brain as yours.'

It was a photograph, rather grainy and out of focus, but it was clear enough. In the foreground was some sort of low table with a mirror laid flat on it, and something – it looked like some sort of white powder – was laid in neat parallel lines on the mirror. Perched on one of the lines was what looked like a little silver tube, about as wide and half the length of a biro pen. The other end of the tube was inserted into a famous nose. A famous nose on a famous face, which grinned and winked, not at the camera, but at someone off the picture...

'Oh,' was all Dayna said.

'Yeah! Oh! This just about bollockses me with City Girl, doesn't it?'

Dayna frowned. 'So this, this Kinseyder, what does he want? Is he trying to – to blackmail you, is that it? He wants money?' Dayna's mind was reeling. Things that up to just a few weeks ago she had only read about were now happening for real, right in front of her.

'Oh very quick. But not Kinseyder, you little prat. Someone's threatening to give this photo to the papers, YouTube, Facebook, you name it – and City Girl. Shit! Let's just hope it's the Lion being just really fucking stupid. Fuck him! Christ, I'll have his bollocks cut off for this!'

'But if you don't pay...Oh God, it's like a film! Is that, that white stuff – is it cocaine?'

'Oh Christ albleedinmighty! Look get me the phone, will you? I've gotter call Jake.'

'Mr Durphry rang already, Silvie. I was going to tell you. He wanted you to call him back.'

'So now I'm calling him back, okay? Jesus Christ!'

'Your cell-phone or the portable?'

'I don't care which sodding phone, you fuckwit. Just get it!'

'You mustn't speak to me like that, Silvie,' said Dayna, retreating, and followed by a heavy silver cigarette lighter, which missed her head by half an inch and clattered to the floor. Dayna fled.

She grabbed the portable from the hallway. Panic confused her, made her unable to think straight. On the short journey from the bedroom suite and back, however, she had the glimmer of an idea.

'Silvie,' she began.

'What? Have you got the phone? Gimme it.'

'That photo.'

'What's his frigging number? Come on, you should know.'

'Just do last number received. Look, can't you say like that photo's an old one? I mean, well – sorry but you, you did, like, used to take drugs, didn't you? But you don't any more, and so like no one can get you for it.'

Silvie Snape screamed again, and her shoulders began to shake. It took Dayna a moment to realise that her employer was convulsed in helpless laughter.

'You – God, you'll kill me, you will! Look at the hair, you cripple! Look at the *hair*!' She waved the print in the girl's face.

'Oh...' The famous face, the less famous new elfin haircut, all ready for City Girl's new campaign... 'Oh,' said Dayna again with widening eyes. The new image had been the talk of the fashion pages. Just a fortnight ago. Which must mean... 'So you *were*?'

'Yeah! *I* was, but Lion wasn't, was he? I've not seen that balding little prick for six months. This is bleedin' *serious*. Where's fucking Jake? Come *on*, Jake... Jake? At last! Silv. Look, something really shit's come up. Urgent. I mean like an emergency... how soon can you get over here? What do you mean, you know? Oh Jesus...Jesus...Yeah. Like soon. Like now. And while you're at it, you can look out for another domestic assistant. Little miss prissy-arse can't take the pace...'

'God, you took your time. Dayna!'

'She's not here, Silvie. You sacked her, remember? And if we're very lucky, she won't sue. Get real, Silvie...' Jake Durphry looked miserable. It was, after all, partly his reputation too.

Silvie Snape wore shades over an un-made-up face, and the coffee was foul, mostly because she had made it. 'All right, Jake. What do I do?'

'Find me a decent drink? No, not bloody Perrier! Got any gin? I think you have to go along with him, Silvie. Do whatever he asks within reason, keep it discreet, and let's hope that's an end to it. I can't do any more, Silv. Sorry. I've had enough trouble getting you this deal with City Girl as it is.'

'You mean just cave in? To that shagging bastard?'

'Silvie, you asked. That's my best advice. Let's give him what he wants, and keep it as dark as possible. Sorry.'

'But he can't do this to me! He wants fifty sodding grams! That's criminal!'

'Silv... please. He's doing it to me too. Let's just be glad it's not more, for God's sakes. And who's in any position to argue?'

'Not you, by the look of it. Can we get it? Like now?'

'I can, Silv, but this is the last time. I can't go on like this, babe...' Jake Durphry shook his head. Since taking on his first and only truly big-account modelling client, life had been one long series of lurches from crisis to crisis. He should have stuck to the music business. 'Are you sure you haven't any gin in the place, Silvie? Or vodka?'

'God, you're pathetic. I'll have a look in the fridge.'

Durphry stared beakly at the disordered room. Silvie must own about a thousand pairs of shoes...

'There's only this bit of grappa,' she called from the kitchen. 'You know, but it's weird,' she said, bringing him the drink neat in a smeary glass. 'At first I was convinced it wasn't him. And I'll swear he wasn't at Figgis's party. I wasn't *that* out of it.'

'So? He's got friends. Everybody stoned to fuck, waving mobiles about. Piece of piss… Anyway, it was a costume do, wasn't it?'

'Oh come on, Jake. Nobody goes to costume parties in *disguise*. *He* wasn't there, and if he had of been, I'd of recognized the little scumbag. This just doesn't seem like him, that's all. He's too much of a worm.'

'Worms turn, Silv…and it was him on the phone, no mistaking him. The way I see it, we don't have a choice. You don't have a choice. Call his bluff, antagonize him, and City Girl goes down the tubes. You might even be arrested.'

'Puh! They can't prove it wasn't talcum. Not just from this picture. He knows that. How dare he, the sad little wanker?'

'So you want to risk it? Christ, what is this, motor-oil? You don't want a great set-to in the papers do you? That's what'd happen. You've run out of lives, Sylvie. Christ, this stuff's disgusting.'

'It's all there is, so tough. I think you're being the bleeding worm, Jake. I'd like to cripple the little bastard.'

'You mean, get me to cripple him. No can do, Silvie. We're both in this up to our necks. Give Barley what he asks and then clean your act up, for Christ's sakes, Silvie. I put myself on the line for you.'

'You punning or what?'

'What?' Durphry looked more miserable than ever.

'Never mind. Christ, you get enough out of it, out of me, my fucking hard work! Look, Jake, suppose I agree? But I can't do this by myself. I'm too known. You've got to meet him. Give him the stuff. Christ! What a waste! Let's get shot of the miserable little moron. Fuckin'hell, Jake – he's *such* a moron, I'd have thought something like this was beyond him, honestly. You don't know him like I do.'

'I know him pretty well. He's probably desperate.'

'Well, I still bet you he's not working alone.'

'I don't think that matters. And whoever it is, we're in no position to tell them to stuff it, Silv. Way I see it, we just don't have a choice.'

4

Are Jerry and Louise headed for the divorce-courts? They, or 'sources close to the couple' deny strenuously that there is any bad blood between them. 'It's a fit-up by the press, and you couldn't find a more devoted pair,' the loyal sources say firmly. But this 'devoted pair' has been apart since Christmas. Louise has been in the US 'visiting with family' and Jerry has been 'throwing himself into his work' – apparently with the indispensable help of his latest assistant on Sort It. And if she wasn't actually dragged back to accompany hubby to last week's BAFTA bash, Louise must have just stubbed her toe as she got out of the limo if that grimace is anything to go by... Keep smiling, Louise, honey! And buy a tiara! A little bird told me that someone's about to be Regally Honoured!

Suzy Merritt's hand hovered over the receiver of her internal phone. Should she, or shouldn't she? The more she hesitated, the more ridiculous she felt: after all, what more normal thing in the world than she should call her immediate employer and ask if there was anything he wanted? God, who was she kidding?

'Jerry?'

'Aah – Suzy!' Slight hesitation. Embarrassment? 'You must be psychic!' The light-toned laugh: lazy, easy manner all in place. 'Just about to call you, as a matter of fact...' No you weren't, you liar, Suzy thought unhappily. Misery, shame and anger, most of it directed at herself. 'Thing is, I have to leave early this evening, darling. Bit of a hurry on at my end.'

She felt her voice go tight in her throat. 'I see. I – um – take it you don't have time to see the Green Document after all, then?' The 'Green Document' was their code.

'Really haven't time this week, my love. Got to get my skates on, I'm afraid. I'm so sorry, darling. We'll go through it in detail next week, don't worry. You'll be okay?'

'Of course. I understand, Jerry. Have a good weekend. See you Monday...' Louise, of course, was back. It couldn't be coincidence. Something must have changed.

Bastard! An explanation she could have swallowed, and been tolerantly sympathetic. But he was going to just slide out of the premises, let her find out from a colleague that he'd already left. Bastard! Anger sustained her while she grimly tidied her desk, threw things into drawers, snapped off electronic equipment; while she walked the short distance to the station through the hurrying, heedless, homing crowds; while she fought her way onto the tube in the rush-hour crush, and clung onto a strap for most of the jerking, swaying journey. Sheer misery was ready to overtake her when she got off at Angel into the pungent evening, however, and, unable to face her flat-mate Becky, and revolted by the thought of a lone miserable drink among the happy-hour crowd in one of the rowdy local bars, she paid for a single stalls seat at The Screen on the Green. The film had already begun, and she didn't even notice what it was. She sat alone at the back of the cinema, silently crying her eyes out.

5

So much of the time, you scrabble, scrape and eat shit, like the business with Lockhart and the vanished Whisper. Sometimes, though, things just fall into place and into your lap.

I have a lot of strings to my bow. I also have a useful number of clients.

Angus Tremain and I have just concluded our bit of business in the Park. He trusts the goods these days, and doesn't feel inclined to sample immediately. He also trusts me in the matter of weights and measures, and we're not talking big deals here. Just a small party supply of the best, for personal use only. Hyde Park makes as good a rendezvous as any, therefore: no embarrassing visitors to his office, or to mine, for that matter.

The old-fashioned methods are the best, I find. We sit and chat for a bit, and he's carrying a copy of *The Times*, which he lays on the bench between us. I slip in the package between the folded pages. He picks up the paper, pockets the goods, slips in an envelope with the agreed number of notes inside it, passes the paper to me, points out an article... Deal concluded, with goodwill on both sides.

'Have a pleasant weekend, Angus,' I say sociably.

'You, too. I say, Todd. I am right, aren't I? In thinking you still operate the sideline? The – um – tracking business? Are you still up for it?'

I got to know Angus through a former client of his. Forget the small ads, the pop-ups and Yellow Pages. It's all recommendation in this game. A delicate little operation, as I recall. I did a decent job, more than decent, and Angus was grateful, mostly because he made a stack out of it. Didn't do too badly myself, come to think of it.

'Sometimes,' I say carefully. 'If it's sufficiently – interesting...' These days, I've had cause to be nervous, and this had better be good.

Angus gives one of his small smiles. 'I think you might find this suitably – intriguing.'

He tells me the gist. A client of his, a woman, wants her husband followed. The usual. Except, apparently, this isn't just any woman, and as for the husband...

'I see. Well, all right. I can think about it...' I am seriously expert at a straight face.

'I'd thought of others, naturally. Someone more – mainstream, let's say. But then I thought that maybe you would be – suitable...' Angus examines his well-manicured hands. He's one of those geezers, thin, sleek, colourless, quietly dressed, forgettable in a crowd, who is always on the verge of sliding away from whatever he's doing or saying. Or not saying. It flits through my mind that he knows I might have a personal angle on this one, but naturally I don't say anything and neither does he. He coughs. 'I would need an early answer. It's rather essential – for my client – that the thing gets wrapped up. Soon. It will doubtless require a bit of – delicacy.'

We talk figures.

'When do I get to meet the lady?' I ask.

'As soon as I've spoken to her and she names a venue. Cheers, Todd. I'll ring. I have to run.'

6

What-ho! Aristo bean-spiller short-listed for literature prize! Ex-junkie turned memoirist, the Honourable Veronica Dearborn is in the running for the small but serious Victor Punter Memorial personal writing award for eloquent dirt-dishing near the top! 'Too Big to Cry' is a crying sensation, it would seem. Kinseyder can only hope Mummy (ex Lady Fitzrivers, ex Lady Callington, but now just plain Mrs Gilbert Wardley-Hill – it must have been lerve) and the rest of this frightful crew choke on their suing breakfasts. Whitbread next? More power to your elbow, Veronica, and all your other well-covered pointy bits...

'Vee! Honey! Hi!'

'Louise!' Veronica Dearborn stepped into the familiar dark interior of Bistro Brunero in Walton Street. 'So nice to see you. I'm not late, am I?'

'Don't worry, honey. I'm early,' said Louise, air-kissing in the vague direction of Veronica's face. 'Let's sit down. I just ordered some white wine for you. A Chardonnay. They told me it was half-good. I take it you still drink wine?'

'In shoals. I mean, thanks. How nice. Oh dear, I'm not dressed up or anything. This place didn't use to be at all *smart.*'

'Still isn't. I mean, just look at me!'

Veronica looked, and reflected that there was a time, once, when she would have almost killed to look like Louise – had indeed felt her life blighted by the fact that she did not. Now, she was perfectly sure that to look like Louise would be to inherit an awesome burden. The upkeep alone must cost the earth. And the *time*... How many hours did Louise take to put herself together? I've just got better things to do, Veronica thought. Louise could have been anywhere between thirty-five and fifty-five, and would have admitted to no age at all, but nevertheless, Veronica and Louise had been contemporaries, and she wondered seriously if surgery had helped; one mustn't peer too closely – too rude – for possible telltale scars under the perfectly-finished face. She wondered what would happen, when would come the moment when *anno domini* would win over intervention; a moment when Louise would gasp, horrified, at her reflection, like Plath's 'terrible fish' in the poem. Not yet, anyway. Now, Louise simply seemed to be suspended, as if she had arrested time: she was slender, sleek and well-groomed in that understated way that always manages to look *careless* (when Veronica was careless, she just looked a mess) and today it was tight denim jeans, kitten-heeled purple ankle boots, and a Missoni jacket (in those typical Missoni horizontal chevrons, in dark violet, fuchsia and cranberry which, Veronica had to admit, was lovely, and she said so) over a lavender scoop-neck top. Understated jewellery, understated make-up, a look that was at once young, elegant, casual, and very, very expensive. Veronica *knew* about clothes – with a mother like hers, who couldn't? She just couldn't wear them. Now, it had almost ceased to matter. 'How was your trip?'

'Fine...feels like an aeon ago. And I do want to hear *all* your news, honey. But hell, don't even *ask* how I am! I'm just so - so *exasperated* I could scream. Sorry.

Here's the wine. And do have something to eat...' A waiter came with bread in a basket and a bottle, opened it, poured it, and hovered. 'No thanks. I'm fine with mineral water. Another moment, please...' The waiter melted.

'Jerry?'

'Of *course*. Ever since I came back. It's obvious. All I need is some goddamn proof! I mean I know for a *fact* that he's playing away. I just can't seem to get anything on him, apart from the crap in the papers. It's as if he's second-guessed me, the bastard!'

'How very inconsiderate of him,' murmured Veronica. Louise was toying with the lemon in her glass of Perrier, twirling it round and round on its stick with extravagant care not to spill any. 'To behave badly, I mean. Cheers.'

'Cheers. I'm just so goddam furious, I can't tell you! I'm not hungry at all but do please have whatever you want.'

Veronica studied the chalk-board menu and felt her empty stomach growl. Louise was making an impression. Two businessmen at an adjacent table stole regular, covert little glances at her, each trying, Veronica saw with amusement, to keep his glance secret from his companion. Automatically, and without the slightest sign that she had noticed them, Louise sat a little straighter in her seat, wriggled her slim shoulders fractionally under the subtle weave, flicked a lock of her thick dark-blonde hair away from her face, thrust her angular retroussé profile in an attitude, all in one graceful, fluid movement, as if she were being photographed. Watching the effect on the men was really frightfully funny. On the other hand, at this moment, Louise's anger was palpable – she positively radiated fury – and the men went back to the topic of toppling hedge funds just a little more vigorously than before.

Another waiter came and smiled expectantly. 'What? Oh, okay. I'll be sociable, I guess. The octopus salad thing for me. And the pasta carbonara for you? You sure, Vee?'

'Yup, great. Bacon and egg! Breakfast! God, I could eat a horse! I feel I haven't eaten in about four days. All this writing. I forget about food...' Sooner or later, Veronica thought, she would be told why she had been summoned, at the last minute, to have a lunch that Louise obviously did not want to eat.

'*Still* writing? But you finished the book ages ago, surely. But what's all this about a *prize*? Have you won a lot?'

Louise could be fantastically irritating. Would she say to an artist 'You finished the painting *ages* ago, surely'? Perhaps, being Louise, she would. And whatever might she say to a brain-surgeon, or a mortician, an astrophysicist? *Still* preparing corpses? *Still* looking at the stars? In a world in which she felt increasingly at odds, it was with such private absurdities as these that Veronica often comforted herself. 'Oh, that's nothing, honestly. Just a sort of university honour, and I haven't even got it yet. The papers blew it up, as usual. This is something else. Far more exciting, actually. A commission – the publisher wants my next one...' It was so new that there was still a small thrill in saying it aloud, even to such as Louise.

'Oh, that's *wonderful* – er, isn't it? I mean, how thrilling! Well done you, writing *another* novel!'

[31]

'Not a novel, Louise. I don't write fiction, at least not yet. No, this is going to be a biography…' Veronica buttoned a sigh.

'Wow! "Dearborns Two," eh? Your family must be getting fairly worried, honey. Is brother Jamie still going to try to sue you?' Louise had read Veronica's savage oeuvre about her ghastly-sounding family. Or at least she'd begun it, read several chapters in fact, and she knew lots of people who'd finished it. For a while, everyone was reading it. So nasty! Odd, for someone like Vee. What a dark horse! Made you think.

'Don't know. Don't care, really. And it's not *auto*biography. I'm sick of ripping chunks off myself… No, this is biography, about someone else. The life of Henry Cuffe – he was the Earl of Essex's batman. And a spy. In the late sixteenth century, Elizabeth the First's government. Don't worry if you haven't heard of him. Almost nobody has…'

'Oh, *history*! My, how clever! I just *adore* historical novels – good ones, that is. I absolutely adored Georgette Heyer when I was a kid. And Jean Brodie…she was wonderful. I absolutely fell in *love* with Charles the Second, and I wanted to grow up to be Lady Barbara Castlemaine. Just imagine!'

'Jean Plaidy. And it's not a – oh, never mind. But it really is rather fun. Henry Cuffe was rather interesting. So were his times. He was probably Essex's brains, you see…but he probably couldn't have cared less about Essex's rebellious tendencies, the outcome, or at least not from an idealistic point of view. It was the fun of it, not politics as such, not overthrowing Elizabeth. Maybe. That's my idea…'

'Fascinating!' Veronica saw Louise smother a yawn, and she glanced at her watch, hoping the food would come. Already, she wanted very much to be at home, to get back to it, stop having moronic and meaningless conversations. Only serious hunger prevented her from making an excuse and leaving. 'You wanted to talk to me, Louise,' she said, deciding that subtlety was useless.

'Well now – yeah, I did. I was just wondering, you know, honey, about the apartment? How the sale's going, all that?'

'I haven't sold it yet if that's what you're asking. Bad timing at the moment. Besides, I'm not so pushed for dosh as I was, so I thought I'd hang on for a while…'

'Now, I'd call that wise, I really would. If you can afford to, hang on until all this mess recovers. That's what I'd do, sweetie… So it's empty? No one there at the present?'

'Do you want to extend the arrangement now you're back?' asked Veronica bluntly.

'Well, you know, Vee, that would be just wonderful. I mean, just for a little while. It means so much to me just to be able to get out of Wimbledon once in a while on my own, and be a bit creative, you know, just to come and go. It's so *sweet* of you! I'm having such a *time*, you know? I'll pay you the going rate, of course…'

'Oh, don't be silly,' Veronica said, almost without thinking, and almost as instantly regretted it. That is how, Veronica thought, Louise gets her own way every damned time. It would take a far stronger character than her own to stipulate a charge, or to refuse altogether. 'Use it when you want. You still have a key. I'll warn you if I've got people coming to look at it,' was all she added, despising herself. If it hadn't been for a chance meeting, shortly after her release from Holloway, Veronica probably would never have seen Louise again after the fifth-form at Duddingdale, but then one thing had led to another, and Louise had offered to do up the little Fulham house that Veronica had inherited from poor old cousin Leo. That had worked fairly well – half Louise's fee in exchange for Louise's unlimited use of the middle flat until it was sold or let. A bolt-hole, Louise had called it, ha, ha… That poor twerp Jerry! She hardly knew the man, but living with Louise couldn't be any picnic… (and why, she thought tangentially, do we associate picnics with an easy time? Picnics, in Veronica's experience, were fraught with irritable nannies, squawling siblings, sand in one's food, wasps, and a dreary mess to cart home…)

'Of *course*, honey,' cooed Louise. 'And you know I always get Nesta in to keep it pristine. After all, it's partly my showcase! It's *really* kind of you! And of course I'll pay you. That's not the issue. The thing is…'

The food arrived. Louise pushed rocket and pieces of baby octopus round her plate, trying not to observe Veronica tucking in greedily. Veronica: tall and large-boned, a woman who despite being overweight might have been handsome but for an overall impression of sloppiness. A disastrous perm in the reddish hair was growing out in unbecoming frizzy straggles; her fingernails were ragged and not very clean; she wore a baggy grey cardigan-coat over a shapeless navy jersey frock with dirty suede boots of indeterminate colour. She looked, frankly, as if she had just nipped down the road unwashed after a meagre breakfast (which was more or less the case: alone in her flat, realised she didn't even have so much as an egg in the place: Louise's call had been timely.) Somehow, Louise was thinking, one ought to be able to expect something a bit more – well, *classy* from an Honorable. But Veronica was Veronica, and there'd been that prison business. Obviously that must have affected her. And they'd known each other since school. But strange how odd she'd become, all this writing, how she'd turned into this edgy, unpredictable person who used words one didn't understand, and who seemed to be laughing behind one's back, making clever-clever comments, as if she was trying to catch one out all the time. And it was perfectly *gross*, watching her scarf food down like that! What did it cost to make a bit of an *effort*? Louise looked away as a strand of eggy pasta snaked into Veronica's mouth.

'The thing is?' prompted Veronica indistinctly, munching.

'The thing is, I don't want Jerry to find out about Maxwell Road. It's absolutely essential this is completely – well – discreet. Things couldn't be more, well, delicate, if you know what I mean. I have to catch him, and I have to be not a *little* bit sneaky. You know? You'll keep this to yourself?'

Veronica shrugged. 'Why not? It's none of my business. But it sounds horribly complicated. Can't you come to some sort of civilized agreement?'

'You sound like our legal mediator. God, he's pretty damn useless! He's all for making it as easy as possible for Jerry, and he's supposed to be on *my* side. But you have to promise you won't say a *word* to the papers?'

'You know I never talk to the papers if I can help it. I leave that to my mother...' This was true. 'Call me dense. I thought you just both agree you've irreversibly broken down or something, and work out the sums. If you really do want a divorce. Do eat. That looks delicious.'

'I'm too upset to eat. Nauseous. I arrive back to find the papers full of hints about that little tramp assistant, and it's just so *humiliating*. After all I've done for him! He goes and does this to me! Again!'

'Oh God, the gutter press. Ignore them.'

'All very *well* to say ignore them! But I know it's true, and what's more, I'm about to prove it!' Louise's voice was rising again. 'He can't fool me, any more than he fooled me about the one before. And the one before that. He goes for those, the underlings, so they'll be grateful, and keep schtum. After all, that was what his first wife was. The famous Jenny. The great *official* rumour is he's messing around with that Natasha, Natalie, or whatever her name is, all that verbal fooling around for the camera, but that's just shamming. He's only interested in kindergarten, the sad prick. I *know* my husband!' She glared at Veronica as if daring her to contradict. 'Shee-it!'

'You mean he wants to marry her? This studio hand, or whoever she is?'

'Christ no! He's just getting laid – and by someone half his age, as usual, fooling himself that he's still desirable, when it's just these dumb kids getting celebrity-struck. They throw themselves at him...' She speared a piece of baby octopus on her fork and it hovered between the plate and her mouth. 'He's done it once too often. This time he's going to *pay...*'

'Call me dense,' Veronica said again, 'but I don't really understand what the problem is. I mean, you don't actually care do you? I mean about him. You said you hardly shag him yourself... Are you *sure* it's worth it, all the public row?'

'Screw that! He's going to squirm, this time. The more public the better as far as I'm concerned...' She pushed her plate away.

'Are you really not going to eat that? Seems a pity...' Veronica had finished her carbonara. The octopus was beginning to congeal.

'No! Have some, why don't you! God, I wish someone would just *understand* instead of casting me in the role of Cruella DeVille...'

'Well, perhaps a smidge if you really don't want it...' Veronica helped herself, and poured a liberal slug of wine from the bottle while Louise glared. (No wonder Veronica never lost any weight when she ate and drank like *this*...) 'It's not that I don't understand, Lou, but can't you work something out? In private? I mean, think of the publicity. The circus would be just horrible, I'd imagine. Heather Mills, all that. It'd be a Pyrrhic victory, bound to be.'

'A what? Oh, yeah. But he can afford it. Christ, can Jerry *afford* it! He's humiliated me long enough. Now it's my turn!'

'I meant that the papers would mangle you, Louise. They always do. They can be unbelievably savage. I should know.'

'Not if I get him first, they won't. He's got more to lose than me, remember.'

'The children, of course.'

'Are you *kidding*? The kids will come to New York with me. No question. No, I meant his great birthday honour.'

'Oh…his K. But suppose he puts up a fight? I mean, for the kids?'

'So? Any court in the land would decide I'm absolutely the obvious person, and Jerry is quite unstable as a father because of his work. It's a shoo. Completely obvious. And the kids – the girls just *loved* New York! My parents, the upstate country, and Manhattan. And he's got to provide for them, properly. Schools, everything. America's expensive, New York especially. It's only reasonable. The kids'll love it. We've got to go free of him…'

'Including Charlie?'

'Of course including Charlie! I don't expect you to understand this, Vee, but just because I didn't physically give birth to Charlie doesn't mean I'm not his *mother*…' Louise reminded Veronica so much of her own mother sometimes, it was uncanny. The whole conversation was beginning to depress her. 'Of course, if Jerry plays fair, then perhaps Charlie might stay with him most of the time. It's all up to him.'

'Up to Charlie?'

'No! For chrissakes, Vee. *Jerry!*' The two hedge-fund brokers got up to leave, casting a last stare at the stunner in a towering temper. She lowered her voice. 'If he plays his cards right, I might concede over Charlie. But there's such a thing as justice. He can't go on with this Mr Whiter-than-white bit for much longer. I need to catch him out, that's the thing. I need evidence.'

'Whew! Well, rather you than me. You'd better have him tailed. You know, private detectives. Investigation Agency. Must be easy enough. I'd imagine there are plenty in the book…'

'Hmmm…Actually, strange you should say that. In fact, I've already hired someone…a firm. Small. Very low key.'

'God! I wasn't even being serious! What are they like?'

'Like?'

'This Private Dick outfit. Whiskey in the drawer stuff, talking out of the sides of their mouths, seedy office – like Philip Marlowe?'

'Who? Oh, yeah. Bogart. No, not a bit. Professional, businesslike. Nice premises on the river, like a broker or a consultant or something. Well, sort of. And it isn't 'they', really. It's 'he'…' Louise's mouth curved in a little smile.

'I see. Real Philip Marlowe stuff. Well, good luck to you! You know he's probably a fraud. Or he'll start blackmailing you.'

'Oh, thanks a million. Actually, if you must know, he's really rather cute.'

Veronica wanted to laugh. 'All the more reason! The worst ones are. Sorry. Good hunting. Have some of this wine before I polish off the lot?' Now that she had eaten her fill, she was longing to smoke, which was of course not allowed. Lunch over, all she really wanted to do was get back to her laptop in her untidy flat, smoke her head off and think about her new project.

'No thank *you*. I make it a rule not to have alcohol at lunch, but you go ahead. Everybody *drinks* so much here! My God, I mean, no offence, but …' Louise sighed. 'God, how I just want to get back to the States! I hated coming away, and so did the girls. It's really all I dream of now. I'm an American! I should never have married an Englishman. Once this crazy divorce thing's through, that's where I'm headed. New York, new start. I'm so sick to *death* of this creepy little country!'

'O my America! My new-found land,' Veronica could not resist saying, thinking that if ever she were to write a novel, a character very like Louise would be in it.

'Newfoundland? But that's not in the United States, sweetie. Honestly.'

7

'I don't like this – this under the cover thing you ask me to do. It feels – dangerous...' But Dorota laughs a little.

'You're so very pretty, you know that? Especially when you smile...'

'Noooo! You laugh – you tease – too much.'

'I mean it. You are...' I pick up her large square hand, put it to my lips.

She isn't, of course, but women always want to feel desirable, desired; and it's actually not hard to desire Dorota a bit. She's comely, to use an old-fashioned term: rosy and compact as an old-fashioned apple, a Pippin or a Russet, thick fairish hair that she wears in an old fashioned way, plaited into a knot at the back of her head; roundish face with those very middle-European high cheek-bones, small bright ice-blue eyes, fair lashes, no make-up, skin as fresh and supple as a teenager's – and she can't be much more than twenty-eight anyway. Her clothes are frankly hideous – unflattering wide skirts bunched at the waist, and embroidered blouses and cardigans in off-puttingly garish reds and greens, and if she ever gains weight, she'll begin to look like an extra in an old Russian movie. But all in all, I'm not at all ashamed to be seen with her. The only reason we're tucked into this dark corner of the Hand in Hand is that we have some private business which we don't want prying eyes to see. Otherwise, we're just a nice if slightly odd couple having a bit of a discreet snog in the snug over a couple of glasses: sweet apricot wine for her (a house speciality – they make their own. It's something that appeals to her sentimental Polish heart) and honest Irish stout from the tap for me. Homesick, is Dorota. I'm cheering her up.

It's her night off. It's also nearly time she was back on duty. She looks at her watch with heavy resignation. 'I have to be back in a half hour.'

'Relax, plenty of time. So, there's no problem about this?' I give her bag a tap. 'You understand what you have to do?'

'Of course,' she says, slightly scornful, as if I've underestimated her. It's my guess that her employers treat her a bit disdainfully. 'Derek, I am thinking that sometimes that is only why you meet me. To deliver envelopes. To help you make this intrigue?' The small blue eyes are very intelligent, challenging.

'Oh please, don't think it's just that, my dear, truly. I can't tell you how much difference seeing you makes to me. You're so – *understanding*, so sweet...' She allows a small smile to break over her face. I kiss her hand again. 'But I have to be very honest with you, Dorota. It was an amazing coincidence to meet you and find out you actually work for Mr Fairbrother. I'm trying to help him, you see, with this very private, important business. But it's difficult with Mrs Fairbrother there all the time now. I don't think I could do it without you. You see, I need to get some very important information to him, but it's my fear – you understand? – that she might intercept his post, look at his emails, all that kind of thing. Which is why it is extraordinarily kind of you to help me. I don't want to ask you to do anything you don't want to.'

'She is a bitch,' Dorota says succinctly. 'I don't like...'

'She must be a difficult person to work for,' I say, supping my pint. She gives me an eloquent look.

'She is very rude. Unpolite. Not...' she fishes for the word. 'Not civilized. Not at all...' That's Lulu. 'And the children, they are not respectful too. You meet them, and it is true, yes? The little Emily especially. She is like her mother I think. I am glad when this work is over. So much I want to go home, back to Wegorzevo, the lake. I miss. Like you miss your Ireland...' Her eyes brighten. A little apricot wine goes quite a long way with Dorota.

'We two, we are both exiles, Dorota, my dear girl. What about him? Mr Fairbrother?'

'Mr Jerry...ahh. He is very different...' Her eyes soften again. 'He is a good man I think. He considers me with good respect. And kind, generous. I say him I leave before, I can't stand any more the conditions, but he want me to stay. Pay me more. She – Mrs Louise – she is away much. He need me there for the children without a mother. He is very famous, well-known man in television,' she explains, not for the first time. 'Caring for those people unjustly treated by the state. And the quiz programme.'

'I know. A very important man.'

'You are in politics with him, I think,' says Dorota wisely. 'I understand. My own father, also him a famous man in his town, he too was in politics, fighting for justice, how is it said, on the side, in secret. Very brutal, the politics in Poland once in the past. Different, now we are in Union of Europe... Once, when I was just small, it was all very – too – private, secret, of necessity. And even after, people were killed. Murder... Not many people know this, but it happened. My uncle, the brother of my mother, he was a famous professor in politics history, and he was put in – how is it said? – house-arrest. And he was prevented to teach in his university many years. It is all the Communists who did this to us. And now the Jews again, whatever they say. Poland, she is not free. We still have terrible history.'

'That must have been hell,' I say sincerely.

'So I am happy to do, Derek...' She mispronounces my name rather charmingly: I have never bothered to correct her. 'You and Mr Jerry, you are in good politics together, and I will help you.'

'Come on, my dear,' I say, drinking up. 'I'll walk you back to the top of the road...' We set off across the dark Common, her arm tucked in mine.

8

Coffee in big flasks, croissants, crumbs littering the table, making greasy splodges on the paperwork, but this was Jerry's idea. Extended working breakfasts, he called them. Took pressure off the cafeteria, he said, but he was joking. Lynne disapproved, one could see that, on the grounds that it was less than businesslike, and Lynne wiped her businesslike mouth on a napkin. But Lynne effectively worked for Jerry... and there was no doubt that the informality, the relaxing of protocols on these Monday mornings tended to produce ideas, even flashes of genius. Jerry knew what he was doing. With apparent nonchalance, he was calling the meeting to a close.

'So! For the small potatoes, we've got wood-shavings in the organic porridge, and a spam ad for dog training that seems to sell electric-shock collars, and another scam to persuade people into parting with their housing capital, as well as the market greengrocers in Hampshire who're being threatened with prosecution for advertising their weights in imperial. That one's a runner, and Suzy is following up with other regional greengrocers, right Suzy? The newbie is this Robinson eviction case. And we're following up the piggery story. And we get interviews with our pet squatters and their legal eagle for the next broadcast. Great. Okay. AOB?' he asked genially.

'Mostly fine, Jerry,' said Lynne Berry. 'Look – I don't want to be a wet blanket...' Lynne flicked stray crumbs from some typescript. 'But I'm not at all sure about this piggery thing. Frankly, this Mr Pacey sounds a bit of an old crook...'

'Oh, come on, Lynne. This is fun...after mothers and disabled kids ejected from community shelters, and squatters faced with litigation, we need some fun. Pigs are always fun, aren't they? Yes, Suzy?'

'Jerry, I think I agree with Lynne on this one. The man's built an illegal extension and put central heating in it and called it a pigsty. According to my sources at the *Eastern News,* he's pulling a fast one on the local council. Can we afford to be seen to back him?'

'Quite...' said Lynne Berry, looking at Suzy strangely.

'I still think we should get to the bottom of it,' Jerry said. 'Strict impartiality, of course. This Mr Pacey seems to think he's got right on his side – but as usual, we check scrupulously before we place *ourselves* on his side. That okay, Lynne?'

'I suppose so, but I think we mustn't give it too much time and attention. Gavin – you're our new property expert. Here's a small bone for you to get your teeth into...'

'Not so small, now,' said Gavin Macavity happily. 'It's all over the redtops... broke in the *Mercury* this morning. Mr Pacey's been busy...' He was on his third croissant, licking buttery fingers.

'All the more reason to check. See what they're all saying, can you? Broadsheets and Sky as well as redtops. We don't want to get caught with egg on our faces, do we?'

'Or pig-poo...oops, sorry. Sure thing, Mizz Berry – Lynne...' He caught Jerry's grin. 'I'll get them all up this morning. There's bound to be a latest in the East Anglian locals by now.'

'Great,' Jerry said. 'Get Suzy to give you all her contacts there. We might talk to the local hacks, but the main thing is this Councillor Whatshisname, and Mr Pacey himself. Even if Pacey's in the wrong, it still makes a good story. Illustrates the might of the planning-permission gestapo and all that. Okay, everybody? Lynne?' Jerry beamed round the table. He was irrestistable when he was like this, and Suzy wrenched her eyes from his face, scribbled notes.

'I don't deny it might make a good story,' Lynne Berry sipped the remains of her coffee. 'But I'm not having this programme involved until we've found out more. I really must stress no involvement for the time being...' Lynne seemed sour this morning, and she was mostly avoiding Suzy's eyes. 'Well, everybody, if that's everything, Emma and I have got work to do on this Robinson case. We're going to interview the mother, Jerry, and speak to the landlords' representative. Natalie, we need to discuss this. I'll see you at four, Gavin...' She gathered her papers, tsk-tsk-ing at the crumbs, and sailed out of the conference room, with Emma and Natalie North in tow. Emma gave Suzy a sly wink as she went. Gavin Macavity got up to follow.

'Gavin!' Jerry called him back.

'Sorry, sir. Mr Fairbrother. Jerry. I took it you didn't want me...'

'Don't take anything of the kind, Gavin,' said Jerry. 'Go up with Suzy, and get any line you can on this piggery thing. I'm relying on you to suss the credentials, okay? If we decide to run it, this Mr – um – Pacey has got to have some sort of legal angle. I'm hoping you'll be able to sort it...okay?'

'Sort it! You bet!'

'You'll need to sweat over a hot computer for most of the day, I guess. Suzy will show you.'

With the new recruit Gavin stowed and set up with a terminal in a small ante-office, Suzy Merritt went back to her own desk and googled the green-grocer story, waited for it to come up. She had a great deal of work to do. *Sort It* was a magazine-show – new material being processed all the time, so that even during a season of planned broadcasts, the research team was all hands on deck gathering and checking material, interviewing people, visiting locations. The team, with Jerry at the hub.

Now, after the deceptively relaxed breakfast meeting, a flat-out 'office' morning, with the latest stories to sort, as ever, into 'queries', 'possibles' and 'must-sees' for Jerry's personal consideration, and the week's broadcast schedule to organize and agree with Ben Young, Suzy had no time to brood about 'Green Documents'. Her routine was divided, sometimes fairly erratically, into 'office', 'studio', 'producer conference' and 'meetings', and at any time these meetings could be called, disrupting any normal schedule. Suzy enjoyed this unpredictability: it was part of the fun, the challenge of the job, *her* job, most of which was to keep a semblance of order, of routine, everything ticking smoothly; her job to liaise between Jerry and the rest of the team, keep the stories coming in, not miss a single thing, provide Jerry with his diet of carefully sifted material, weed out the obvious non-runners; keep Lynne or Emma minutely informed (but take care never simply to inundate Lynne's office with what Lynne would call 'squit'. Squit was Suzy's job. The squit stops here!) Suzy's was a job which required tact, balance, shrewdness and an abilitiy to cope with the unpredictable, all qualities she valued in herself.

She still had vivid memories of her interview – a gruelling two days – and she had been terrified, but she had been confident too. 'Basically...' Lynne Berry had said, 'This post *is* the programme. The front line. We would be absolutely and totally relying on you, the whole team...' But her CV had glowed, been checked scrupulously, glowed still. She had shone at the interview. She had got on in a friendly way with everyone she had met from the team. And, since she was to be his assistant, it was Jerry Fairbrother who had had the final say. He had made a special point, over a pleasant and relaxed lunch with Lynne and Ben Young, the show's studio director, of telling her that the job was unpredictable. 'If you can cope with that, Suzy, keep me on the straight and narrow, that's all I ask...' 'I can try,' she had said, meeting his professional twinkle with one of her own, for she was no slouch in her own estimation. And so they had hired her, Suzy Merritt, the bright ambitious girl from local radio in the sticks, into the job of a lifetime. 'You know that John Gibson at Radio Anglia said you were the best at coping with the unpredictable he had ever worked with?' said Lynne Berry, smiling warmly. 'Welcome to *Sort It!*' And she had borne with the jibes – half envious, half joking – from her colleagues on Radio Anglia, even when Steve Catchpole, the presenter who had always had a bit of a 'thing' for her, played 'Wild World' three times on his breakfast show on her last day...

Her brave new world was a little strange at first; but 'wild', in the Cat Stevens sense, not at all: no 'bad things out there' so far as she could see. She had settled in happily into her quarters in the small rented flat in Clerkenwell which she shared with Becky Marsh, an old friend from college; the new job was all-absorbing, and seemed to involve a pace that demanded her whole attention. When it was not rushed off its feet, the programme team was friendly and welcoming. Emma, Lynne Berry's assistant said, over cafeteria sandwiches during her second week, 'Lynne's okay. She can be a bit overpowering sometimes, you know, wants to be everybody's auntie, wants to *know*. She'll take you for the usual pep-talk soon, I'll bet...'

'The pep-talk?'

'About He whose Name must not be Uttered,' said Emma, giggling. 'Don't worry – we've all had one. Some of us have had two or three!' And Emma had run off, pleading a meeting, leaving Suzy feeling a little like Alice in Wonderland: everyone, it seemed, lived life on the run and spoke in riddles. Not many days later, however, Lynne Berry had sought her out, taken her to a pleasant lunch in a nearby bistro.

'Suzy...I've really enjoyed this, my dear,' she said as they stirred their coffees. 'I always try to have a sort of private girl-chat with our new female recruits, just make sure everything's okay. I feel I know you a little better now, and it's always satisfying to know that one has made the right choice. I know you're going to enjoy working on the programme very, very much.'

'I'm frankly having the time of my life,' Suzy had said, mellowed by a glass of good wine and her hostess's skill at putting people at their ease. 'I love the job, I love working with the team. And you've all been so kind, helping me to find my feet. I know I made the right choice too.'

Lynne Berry's eyes crinkled in an intimate smile. She leaned a little closer across the table. 'And what about our Jerry? How are you getting on with him?'

'He's – well, he couldn't be nicer. He's so, well, you know, so *easy*. I mean, he's so easy-going, patient. And – well, approachable.'

'You were expecting him not to be?'

'No-o. Not exactly. Maybe I was expecting more of a prima donna, someone with more of an ego. I mean, sorry, I'm putting it badly, but when someone's so famous and you've only seen them on TV...' *He whose Name should not be Uttered...*

'Prima donna?' Lynne Berry chuckled, her eyes twinkling some more. 'No, Jerry's no prima donna. Easiest of them all, I'd say, and I've worked with some right charmers. Let's see, Jerry, Jerry... Our Jerry is a dear man, a great colleague, and he'll always say his pleases and thank yous. He'll even say sorry, which is more than some people. He can be exasperating sometimes, gets distracted, loses the plot from time to time – who doesn't? But he relies on us all, and we all take care to see he gets it right... He'll be relying on you a great deal, Suzy...' She took Suzy's hand, apparently impulsively. 'Suzy...I'm going to be frank with you. You know, woman to woman? You're a very attractive girl, Suzy. I'm sure you've met all sorts of men in your time, I mean, in the workplace. Always the odd predator, yes? Jerry – well Jerry's not predatory. I'm not suggesting anything of the kind. But he is a bit – well, he's like a little boy sometimes. A little boy in a sweet shop. One has to be aware of Jerry's – well, of Jerry's *susceptibilities*, if I can put it that way. He never means it seriously, and I *mean* never, but some young women – well, they've had stars in their eyes, if you know what I mean.'

'You mean, you think that? Oh, no...' Suzy had shaken her head, smiled into her cup. 'That's absurd. Honestly, Lynne, the only stars in my eyes are Johnny Depp and Brad Pitt...' Suzy now fully understood the reason for pep-talk and hoped her response put paid to any of Lynne's doubts. 'I am serious about this job, you know. Very...'

'Of *course* you are! Now, please don't be cross, my dear. Sometimes it's just best to get these things straight right from the beginning...'

But I wasn't remotely cross, Suzy had thought on the way back up to her office, more annoyed than she had cared to admit. She had been warned off, and it had even crossed her mind that Lynne herself might have – no. That was just silly. Surely.

'Emma? Did JF have, well, office flings?' Another hurried lunch-time sandwich a few days later.

'Uh-oh. I detect a Lynne Berry lecture. Right?'

'Right. But is it true? She said he was like a little boy in a sweet-shop.'

'Lynne's like a boarding-school matron. Just nod and smile and take no notice.'

'I did sort of. But is it true?'

'Well, mmm, I believe he's had his moments,' Emma said, draining coffee. 'Before my time though. Bloody hell! Half past already! I've got to run. See ya!'

A little boy in a sweet-shop... It had been a Friday about three months later, after a working lunch in the Blue Fleece to discuss details of the trip to Barcelona, when the sweets had been sought, offered, and in Spain, a week later, greedily devoured. Under the eyes of the whole team more or less, they became not only lovers but conspirators, thoroughly enjoying the game they were playing: professional to the point of curtness in public; engaged in an ecstatic mutual discovery in the privacy of the small hours...

'Have you said the 'L' word?' Becky Marsh, an avid romantic if only by proxy, had wanted all the details. Her friend's new job was far more thrilling at second-hand than anything that happened first-hand to her in a chain of West End estate-agents.

'No!'

'But you do, though, don't you?'

'Yes – no. I don't *know*. I just can't resist him. I've only got to smell him...you know?'

'Jee-sus, Suzy! He must be old enough to be your dad. And he's fat, let's face it.'

'Portly. That's what I'd call him. And only a bit. He goes running. He's big... tall. And he's just, well, gorgeous. And he's only forty-nine.'

'Pull the other one!'

'It's true. I looked him up on Wiki.'

'They write their own. Common knowledge, Suze. Besides, that still makes him twenty years older than you even if it's true.'

But Jerry's age didn't matter. Suzy had got him like a disease, and in private she was almost ashamed of herself. This was so much what was not supposed to happen. She was certain, for instance, that Lynne Berry knew. She had been expecting it, as she had made perfectly clear. Suzy didn't imagine those looks that Lynne sometimes cast in her direction. 'Old fashioned', her grandmother would have called them. And Ben Young knew, too, and somehow, this was worse. He was the knowing kind, and sometimes he looked at her, just looked, with an unfathomable expression that could – just – have been interpreted as sympathy. *He never means it seriously...* She always found herself looking away, or down, when Ben looked at her like that.

Her desk telephone rang, snapping her out of her reverie. 'Jerry?'

'Nope. Just Gavin Macavity at your humble service. Can I have a word, Suze?' Gavin, who was so absurdly, slavishly formal with his superiors had decided to treat Suzy with the utmost familiarity and it irked her for any number of reasons.

'You're having it. Say on.'

'Could you spare a minute in person?'

'I'm fantastically busy, Gavin. The computer's not playing up, is it? I've had tec. sup. out to it twice this month.'

'Computer's fine. No, it's partly pigs, and partly something else… I think you'd better see it.'

She sighed, and went through to where Gavin was sitting in front of the monitor, his hair disordered and his tie askew. 'Pull up a pew, Suze. See the screen? Great…o-*kay*.'

Suzy peered. 'I haven't got time to sit down. It's just a row of codes and figures. I don't understand. Is it re-booting, or something?'

Gavin gave her a look that Suzy interpreted as indulgent scorn. 'You really don't know what this is, do you?'

'No, I don't, since you ask. I thought you were supposed to be in deepest Norfolk doing pig-farm research. Look, if it's all the same to you –'

'Hold your horses. The pig-farm's a piece of cake, for a start, and definitely a story, I'd say. The Will-Co chain – know it? A local string of supermarkets in East Anglia. Well, now – seems they were trying to buy Pacey's field. He refused their offer, and later applied to build a bungalow. Permission refused. He built a pigsty. No one could object to that – animal accommodation comes under a different legislation, and he's a farmer. Then he puts in electricity, plumbing, et cetera. Can't object to that either. Pigs need water and enough light to read the piglets bed-time stories…all right, *joke*. It was the windows, double-glazed, mark you, that did it. That and the shower and flushing toilet.'

'So? He was pulling a fast one, like Lynne said. Pretending a house is a farm-building, sneaking it in past the planning officials. He's in the wrong, and we haven't got a story. Pity. You'd better prepare a short report for Lynne and Jerry, Gavin, and we'll file it under "D" for dismissed.'

'Hang on, hang on, Miss Hasty! First, there's no legal reason why Pacey can't build a bungalow, or six bungalows if he wants on this particular bit of land. It's not protected green-belt, and that's why Will-Co was so interested – new outlet in Sowerby Stanton. That's for starters. Second, guess who the chairman of Will-Co is? No? Okay, it's none other than Councillor John Charmers… who just also happens to be chairman of the local planning board. This is quite a biggy, I reckon, Suze…' Gavin Macavity tried to look modest and failed, smirking up at her.

Suzy decided to sit down after all. 'Can we prove all this?'

'Yep.'

'Wow! Well that's – that's brilliant, Gavin. No, I mean it.'

'Thanks. What do I do now? For the programme?'

'Okay. You need to prepare a detailed report, setting out everything you've just told me, and all the corroborating evidence and so on, and get it to Lynne as fast as possible, and a copy to Jerry. Wow! This is when things begin to get exciting. It's what I love about working here. Well done, Gavin! I really mean it.'

'Thanks, Miss Merritt. Suzy. It's very decent of you to say so. Now, about this other thing.'

'Hang on, Gavin. That's my phone. I'll be back.'

But it was Jerry Fairbrother, wanting to discuss Green Documents in private conference, and that day, Suzy Merritt did not learn Gavin Macavity's other mysterious piece of intelligence.

9

It's difficult to imagine Louise has actually whelped twice. I'm pretending to be asleep, but I can see her through half closed eyes as she soaps herself in the shower. What's more, I know she knows I'm watching. There's something in the way she does it, and besides, she hasn't been too careful about drawing the curtain. She's worth watching, too, vain little bitch. I think it's called the well-toned body. Tanned, lean enough to be almost athletic, just about curvy enough to be feminine; stomach taut, buttocks ditto, little breasts still pert, not a sag or a wrinkle or a stretch-mark anywhere…and she must be what, forty-five, forty-six? Nearer fifty, probably. She must have had a good-ish frame to begin with – fairly tall, slim legs, all that; but even so, it's quite an achievement. A lot of time, effort and money goes into that body, I'd say. Difficult to imagine it heaving and sweating, as I say, in the travail of childbirth, the pains making her forget all about what she must look like: nice, regular features waxy, paintless, jaw jutting, all twisted up in agony (although I must say, she heaves and sweats quite prettily on top of me, and doubtless she heaves and sweats quite vigorously at the gym, or wherever she goes) but even so… Less easy still to imagine her a *mother*, cuddling a sucking infant, changing nappies, reading stories, kissing goodnight – the things mothers are supposed to do. Impossible, actually, to imagine Louise looking at anything with love, unless it's got Louis Vuitton or Dior or something stamped on it.

In temperament, Louise must be a little like I imagine my own mother must have been…

The shower squirts and splashes, and I can hear her tuneless humming. Happy girl, eh? I should hope so, too. On my day, I'm pure gold, or so they tell me. I think I must have passed the audition. I stare at the white wedding-cake ceiling, wondering who lives upstairs… and downstairs, in the basement, although I expect they call it the garden flat now, although there's no garden. Such is modern London real-estate. I doze a little.

'What are you looking so pleased with yourself about?' Scent, expensive, and a soapy steaminess that pervades the room. She flips the corner of her towel-turban in my face. She's grinning down at me with white, even little teeth; all clean and pink and wrapped in a fluffy white towelling dressing-gown. 'Wakey, wakey. We need to talk business.'

'Oops. Sorry, doll,' I say, stretching.

'I wish you wouldn't call me that all the time,' she says, and a little frown clouds her pretty face. It's a pretty little frown, like she's rehearsed it.

'Sorry, doll,' I say again, being deliberately annoying, and knowing now that I can get away with it. Prop myself up on my elbow, give her a look. She apparently finds me very hard to resist. 'How about *bambola*?' I run the word round my tongue, and she gives a delicious little shiver. '*Bambolina? Bambina mia?*' I reach over and part the fluffy dressing-gown, finding the slightly damp fluff of her perfectly coiffed pubic hair. She's almost back in the bed. 'I like the Italian language,' she purrs. 'It's got a certain – something…'

'*In somma,*' I agree, reaching to pull her towards me.'*Si rifà? Ti va' un bis, bambola mia?*'

'What?' I whisper the translation in her damp little shell-like. 'You devil! No!' She backs away from the bed, laughing. 'I've got a date.'

'Really? Now that's what I call dedication.'

'Not that sort of date! It's a Child Labour Project meeting, since you're so interested. Not that it's any of your business. Whatever, the last thing I can afford to do is reek of you…' She bends and kisses me, teasing with her tongue, tasting of toothpaste, dodging my hands. 'Italian stallion…you'll have to wait…' She sits down at the dressing-table, hunts for creams and potions in a compendious bag.

'Italian stallion, eh?' She pronounces it 'Ital-yun stall-yun', the up-state New York twang still faintly present. 'Is that how you'll describe me to your girl-friends?' I'm watching her toilette with some fascination.

Her hands stop for a second in mid-air. 'Why should I talk about you to my girlfriends?' She resumes the hair-styling. 'I don't talk. Not in the way you mean…' Women always do, even one who plays her cards as close to her chest as Louise.

'What, never? What about the friend who lends you this place? Not even about when not to suddenly turn up and interrupt the – er – the interludes?'

Again the little start and pause. 'No. Never. Why should I?' Whirr of a porta-ble hair dryer. She says over the noise: 'She doesn't need explanations. She doesn't use it. And she's not exactly – well, you know, a confidante.'

'Fair enough, but you must tell her something. What's your excuse?'

She turns from the mirror, frowning slightly. 'Why do you want to know?'

'Curious. 'Satiable curiosity. Like the Elephant's Child.'

'Who?'

'Skip it. So who is she? This generous friend who lets you use – now let's see, obviously not her home, not nearly lived-in enough. No nick-nacks, no fol-de-rols and no books, unless you count *Interiors*, *Harpers* and a Penny Vincenzi, and I rather imagine that tripe's yours, dollink. So, a spare apartment. An investment, but with no tenant unless we count you, so no immediate return. *Ergo*, richish woman, doesn't need the income, with spare house in fashionable Fulham which she lends on an expenses-only basis to a not particularly close friend who claims not to confide. Interesting. I'm beginning to think this friend – …' I make curly quotes with my fingers – 'is a bit of a chimera.'

'A *what* ? God almighty! She's an old schoolfriend. And a client. I did this place up for her. What is all this, the gestapo?' The hair, longish, blondish, art-fully coloured, is now moussed and piled, held by styling clips, on top of her nicely-shaped head.

'Just detecting, dollink. I'm a detective. You have this free shag-box – sorry, sweetie, *pied à terre* for when you feel like a bit of – privacy, shall we say. I'm just intrigued.'

'Well get unintrigued, will you? It's none of your goddamn business what my private arrangements are…' Louise applies some sort of lotion to her face with controlled little upward movements. Fascinating to watch. No, really.

'But it is my business,' I say.

'Like hell it is…'

'I disagree. Listen, dollink. Basically, if I'm going to do what you're paying me to do, I need to know. I need to know who can be trusted, who can't. To know that one's movements aren't open to scrutiny, so to speak…'

'*What?* Oh, go to hell. You're just trying to needle me…' Back to the face. That's the trouble with people like Louise. They think they're immune to the things that might occur to normal people as possible banana-skins. It's called hubris, and it isn't very clever.

'Not in the least. I just think we need to be certain that there aren't too many – um, hostages to fortune, shall we say…' Actually, of course I'm trying to rattle her. I always like to see unwarranted composure decompose.

'What? You don't have to worry about this, honey. For one thing, I can and do use it as an office, a studio. Any visitors could be here on business.'

'Well that's all right then. Isn't it? Mmm, must be rich, this mate of yours. Natty interior design by a socialite demi-celeb.'

'It *is* kinda natty, isn't it?' Louise pretends to be an interior designer, and people actually pay her for all the Feng Shue crap, and telling them what colours to have and where to put the lamps in relation to the sofas, what have you. Pay through the nose, if I know Lulu. But this pad is good, I have to say that, if you happen to like the ultra-modern outré from several periods all at once. I mean, this is nouveau meets deco meets Bauhaus, more or less in descending order from the ceilings down. But it sort of works. Maybe Lulu has some talent after all.

'It would have been a whole house once, this. Integrated,' I say, musing. 'Upstairs, downstairs, and a nether-downstairs, in the basement, where there was a big old-fashioned kitchen with a range…damp, perennial damp, and a sour-smelling scullery with beetles and mice and an old fashioned jakes off of that, opening out onto a pokey little yard with a high wall…and attics for the lodgers…the maids, once, I dare say…all very chilly, with lino on the floors… Your girlfriend, the owner – owns the whole place, does she?'

'Oh, for Chrissakes! She divided it and rents the top flat and lives in the basement, okay?'

'Ah.'

'She wants to sell this middle apartment. She'll get a decent price for it if she hangs on in there, like if this slump ever improves. Why all this interest in interiors? Doesn't sound like your thing…' She's applying subtle colour to her face now, in tiny, precise little dabs, concentrating.

'It's not,' I say. 'But I used to live in a place a bit like this. As a kid.'

'Oh. How quaint…' She has entirely lost interest.

'Do you believe in Fate, dollink?' I ask.

'No, not especially. Well, I don't know. Maybe I do. I'm a Leo… Why? Do you?'

'Not much. But I quite like the Chinese proverb that goes that if you sit by the river for long enough the corpses of your enemies all float by sooner or later… So. This old school chum, she won't go ratting to the headmistress, eh?'

'What? Oh I see! No. Why should she?' Lulu moves on to the eyebrows, neat golden half-moons.

[47]

'Not even for a serious cash inducement? Money has a weird effect on people, doll. It bends the best of us, and as for the worst...'

'Oh, she's not like that. She's a writer.'

'A writer, no less, eh? And you think her noble intellectual mind above such venal squalor, presumably. Who is she? Has one heard of this lady-writer?'

'God, what *is* all this? She's called Veronica Dearborn, if you must know, and I don't suppose you *have* ever heard of her. She's hardly Ruth Rendell.'

I digest this information. 'Veronica Dearborn. Book about her crazy family. And she's actually the *Honorable* Veronica, yeah? Lot of trouble with naughty substances, late daddy an earl? Am I right, or am I right?'

'Only an hereditary baron. But, yeah, that's the one. How strange *you* should know.'

'Oh, I read the papers, even the intellectual ones,' I say airily. Louise's rudeness is almost entirely unconscious. 'It got the odd good review, too, her book. Well-written, all that. Makes a change. Most dirt-dishers can't string a sentence together, and debs are usually the worst. Well, well. Rather an unusual friend for you to have, the Hon. Veron., I'd have thought...' I can be rude, too.

Actually, it's not at all unusual, if you think about it. The Honorable Veronica Dearborn represents the arty-inty set to which Louise loves to think she belongs these days. It gives her a kick to have these vaguely aristocratic English chums as mates. What's much odder is that the Hon.Veron. can bear to spend more than about fifteen minutes in the company of Louise. Lulu has the intellectual scope of Barbie and just one topic of conversation: herself.

'Oh, why? What a silly thing to say. And she'd hate to be called a lady-writer, by the way. Old fashioned feminist principles.'

'Those don't bother you, I notice. I mean, here you are, shagging the hired help...'

'So? What about you? Do you lay all your clients?'

'*Touché*. Only when they're as easy as you are, doll...I mean, on the eye...' I wink.

She frowns. It wasn't the answer she was expecting. She doesn't know which way to play this one, not quite. 'This,' she says evenly into the mirror, 'was something of an unforeseen complication...' Busy with an eye-shadow wand. 'I hope you realise – rats! Smudged it! – I hope you realise that nothing's changed. That you are still working for me...' She turns to face me, one eye on, one eye off, as it were. The effect is a trifle bizarre. It is probably dawning on her that I have got her over a bit of a barrel, except that she thinks she has me over one too. 'I mean, we're still on *strictly* professional terms.'

I grin. 'Regrets, *bambolina*?'

'Not exactly, no. But I need to be able to trust you. Professionally, I mean.'

'And do you?'

She takes a big breath. 'I've got to haven't I?' Practical girl. 'But it's got to be clear. You won't get your very handsome fee unless you deliver, and that means not screwing this up...' Fair enough. Like all entirely selfish people, Louise is capable of ruthless realism. I have to admire this – cuts out so much of the bollocks. She goes to work on the naked eye. 'I've simply got to catch him out, and that's your job. Speaking of which, I don't seem to have had much from you in the way of results.'

'Unless you count multiple orgasms during a working afternoon. Perhaps you shouldn't be distracting me from my work,' I say, catching both her eyes in the glass, now mascara'd, shadowed and perfect. I'm enjoying winding Lulu up. She winds so very easily when you know which which levers to pull, as if she treated her temper to Kegel exercises too. She turns and throws an expensive gilt lip-stick-case with a rather nice aim and quite a bit of main force. It clouts me on the shoulder.

'Bastard!'

It hurts. I blink, but watch her steadily. 'Of course. By nature. Had the maid-enliest star in the firmament twinkled at my begetting.'

'What? Oh, you're quoting. I wish you wouldn't. Just tell me you understand the deal...'

'Misquoting, actually. Okay. I catch Jerry-boy with the flopsy, evidence, pho-tos, emails, whatever, everything nice and clear. You drag him through the di-vorce courts, big alimony package, divvy up all the jolly property. The des. res. in Greater London, farmhouse in the Dordogne, apartment in New York... and I get my percentage. There's his flat at the Barbican, too, isn't there, although you probably won't be able to get your mitts on that.'

'Probably not. But the villa in Grand Bahamas is mine outright. And Jerry's place in the Barbican's where you should be right now, with a telescopic lens. Hey...hang on...' It's sunk in. 'What percentage? We agreed a flat fee, plus your expenses. I don't even know you're earning those.'

I lean back and yawn. 'Just a manner of speaking. But I think the terms could change, doll.'

'Like hell they could. That's *outrageous*! You can't do that. You absolute *bas-tard*! I'll pay what we agreed...' She's dressing rapidly now, wriggling into smart tight black pants, zipping them over her narrow hips. 'You're in no position to pressure me, you know,' she says, brushing invisible lint from an elegant little jacket.

Al contrario, Lady Fairbrother, I'm thinking. 'It very much depends on what you actually want...' I light a cigarette, which I know will annoy her quite in-tensely. I watch her pretty nose wrinkle, but she doesn't say anything, just glares at me flicking ash into a sweet little Casa Pupo saucer thing by the bed. 'Just think,' I say dreamily, leaning back on the pillows, smoking, with an arm behind my head. 'All that lovely property chopped in half...pity. Still, even then it's far too much for just one girl, even one with tastes as expensive as yours, doll.'

'I'm thinking of the children!' she spits. You bet she is. Her image depends on them these days. 'I want to get him, catch him in the act, and preferably in time for them – the Palace – to withdraw his knighthood. Got it? And it's time you got your lazy ass out of that bed. I have to leave very soon. We can talk business again if you ever come up with anything that remotely earns your expenses...' Game to her, or so she'd like to think. 'Speaking of which, there's an envelope on the night-table. I suppose you'd better check it.'

[49]

'I trust you not to diddle me,' I say. I do: she wouldn't dare. But this is one of her games. She wants me to feel like a bit of a whore. Takes one to know one. 'So. Old Jerry-boy. Sir Jerry, soon, Lady F. I imagine he'd do quite a bit himself where the children were concerned. Wouldn't he? I mean, it's something he feels strongly about.'

'So? And stop calling me Lady F. It sucks. He only cares when it suits him. They're good for his cuddly image.'

'Of course. But he might play the kiddy-card for all it's worth, mightn't he?'

'What are you saying? *I'm* their mother, and this is about *their* future. And mine. Have you any *idea* of what I've been through? No! You haven't...' As far as I can tell, all Louise has 'been through' is having some of her very generous allowance curtailed and her wings clipped a bit in the interests of favourable publicity. As for her motherly devotion, call it window dressing. Not that you can necessarily take the gossip columns seriously.

'I'm saying you're not thinking straight, dollink...'

'*What*? All I need to do is prove that he's been the rat, the hypocrite. And Jerry doesn't care who I'm *seeing*, for God's sake. It's gone way beyond that. He'd only care if –'

'If it helped his case. His custody rights for instance. Has it occurred to you, dollink, that in certain circumstances he might care very much indeed?'

'Of *course*,' she says, exasperated. 'That's why I've got to get in *first*. The press is bound to be on his side. Sure, they take the rise out of him. I mean, who wouldn't? All that cuddly Uncle Jerry stuff and downhome grandmas knitting him sweaters. But they adore him, truly. No one's any idea what a complete lying bastard he is! And they hate me, because I dress well and go to fashion-shows and parties and I'm *American*. It's so *unfair*... ...'

'Hmmm,' I say, nodding, giving the problem real consideration. 'The press isn't the judge, necessarily, dollink. Not here...' (Like hell it isn't.) 'But he could fight dirty. Do anything it took, even if it did mean smearing his precious children's *mammina* all over the gutter press, making her look like a greedy little gold-digger, maybe? All sorts of unwelcome hostages to fortune emerging – if you get me.'

'I don't know what you mean! I've always behaved with absolute – well, I've always been...'

'An exemplary wife and mother. Of course, of *course*. And occasionally careless. I'm speaking as your professional adviser, dollink, it could happen to anyone. If this drags, and it probably will, well, that's our problem, *bambina*. Stuff coming out that isn't welcome. You know how things can get distorted, sweetie. Perhaps you should tell me. Give me the dirt first.'

'There's nothing! Nothing at all!' She's looking a bit worried now.

'Like Ginelli? Name mean anything to you? Apart from posh handbags, I mean?'

'Just how in *hell*?'

'Oh, come on, babe! It's stale news, and it's hardly private. Any more than Rickie Castello...and that little *movie*...' It was disappointingly tame, but even so...

She turns and does something furious but careful in the mirror, then takes a deep breath, fixes on little gold earrings, fluffs the hair out: beauty as active meditation. Her face has relaxed again, into its lovely expressionless blank. 'It seems as if you know all about it. It's past, done. Over...'

'Of course it is, dollink. I use it simply as an example. Your main problem, as I see it, is your image.'

'Look!' she hisses. 'I'm not paying you to be pessimistic. Just get my husband, okay?'

'Oh, I will. I'm just wondering. Perhaps you've been thinking of all sorts of alternative solutions to a protracted and expensive divorce. Especially with so much that could damage a none-too-pristine reputation. His advisers will be urging him to leave no stones unturned, you know. This could get, well, uncomfortable. Bound to. I'm amazed you think it's worth it...' I let the suggestion hang.

Her chin makes angles this way and that, and she smiles that little private smile that women do when they're pleased with their reflection. It's a reflection to be pleased with. She really does scrub up superbly well, does Lulu. Then she says evenly into the glass: 'I suppose you mean I might have him killed. Rubbed out. Of course I've thought about it, believe me...' Lipstick. 'You're not shocked?' She's really something, this Lulu. I've met very few quite like her. Perhaps it's just as well. I tell her I'm not shocked. 'Of course I've *thought* about it. But I thought it was a bit drastic. Anyway, I don't know any of the right people. You can't just look hit men up in the Yellow Pages. Can you?' It's a serious inquiry.

'Noo-oo,' I say slowly, stubbing my cig out in the porcelain thingumajig. 'I guess. Not as such. But then I'm not exactly an expert. It's done by word of mouth. So I've been told. People who know people. In low places... So I understand.'

'Do *you*?' She's serious. 'Know people, I mean?' Her voice is light, casual, very steady and even; in her eyes, though, is a certain powerful emotion which I interpret as high excitement. Whether it's at the prospect of having someone take a telescopic pop with a rifle at old Jerry from out of a parked van, or whether it's because she thinks she might have just been rogered silly by a member of the hired-assassin fraternity is hard to say. I suspect it's a bit of both.

'I have had the misfortune to have met with a few undesirables in my time,' I say diplomatically. 'In a day's work, so to speak...' I'm watching her very closely. 'Bound to.'

'How much?' she asks, straight to the point. 'Theoretically?'

'Expensive. More for a rush job. Er, so I'd imagine. The best are real professionals. They do their homework and they don't miss...' I watch her pupils dilate. 'I can make discreet inquiries. If you like.'

'Perhaps it's too much of a risk, though. I mean I – one – would be in their power for one thing. And it is a bit well, extreme. Silly, maybe. No. It's absurd, isn't it?' She laughs and bites her lipsticked lower lip with small, white front teeth, like a naughty child. A naughty little girl quite seriously contemplating murder. 'No. Yes. Okay. Do it, then. Inquire. Whatever it is I do, I've got to do it *first*.'

'And you're sure that you have, *bimba mia*?' Naughty of *me*, but I can't resist it. After all, she doesn't seem to be acknowledging just how much she'd be involving me.

'Have what?'

'Got in there. First...' I leave this one hanging in the air for a nanosecond. Watch her face undergo some extraordinary changes.

'You mean? Oh, holy shit! You don't think?' She's really quite put out now, first staring at me in a sort of wild incredulity, and then leaps to the window, goes to twitch the art-deco printed silk curtains, then thinks better of it, sits down on the dressing-table stool, staring at me again. 'Christ! You mean he? What do you *know*? Have you found out something? Has he got someone *onto* me?' Her agitation is a joy to behold: wildly looking into corners, at the framed print above the bed – it's that Escher thing with the interlocking cockroaches. Strange choice, but she's the interiors wallah. 'Ohmigod,' she whispers. 'Are there? Have we got *bugs*?'

'*Piano, piano, stai calma, bimba...* Relax! I'm only guessing. But honestly, Louise, isn't that what you would do, if you were he? Get in first?' She bites her lip again. One can almost see her nightmare vision. Paranoia with knobs on. I'm not laughing, but it's an effort.

'Oh God! It's not *fair*! It's not fair that he can *do* this to me!' She's almost hysterical. 'Get out of bed! Now, for Chrissakes! You've got to get the *fuck* out of here! No! Wait! Let me think. If we leave together, you can cover me... Oh God! Hurry. Oh *God*...' This babe sees too many movies. 'No! Wait! We'll go separately. You could have been visiting one of the other apartments...' Now she's beginning to use her noddle.

'Whatever your ladyship pleases,' I say amiably, throwing back the sheet, see her eyes light on my goat-foot, and light away again. 'I take it a quick shower is allowed?'

My turn to go tum-te-tum under the hot water. 'I shot the sherriff...' I can sing quite well. 'But I did not shoot the deput-eee.'

'For *Chrissakes!*' she shrieks. Tum-te-tum.

I peer from the shower curtain with soap dripping down my face. 'Tell you what, I'll stay and do a reccy. Make sure there aren't any you-know-whats...'

'*What*? But suppose? Ohmigod! You really do think? What the fuck were we *saying*?'

'Shhh. Can't be too careful, dollink!' I dodge back into the shower. I hear urgent murmuring. She's doubtless phoning for her cab.

She puts her head into the bathroom. 'I'll go. I'll call you. Just shut the door behind you. That's all you need to do.'

'And the other thing?'

'I said I'd call...' Sounds of Louise gathering her things, closing the door. Tum-te-tum...

Me? I'm in no hurry. I'm drying off as the door slams. In a leisurely fashion, I rub my hair on a fluffy towel, pick up the envelope from the bedside cupboard, count the notes: small currency, no traceables. Our Lulu has all the makings of a smooth operator if only she could keep a consistent thought process in her head. A tactician, Lulu, but no strategist.

Once I'm dressed, I take a peek round the house...that is, of course, as much of the house as I am able to see. This middle apartment has a main door, a stout, glossy racing-green affair with a double Chubb lock onto a wide landing – part of the communal access, which is smartly done out in what I think of as 'posh utility'. How times change. I prop open 42B with my lighter. Off the landing and along a small passage, another secure door bars the entrance to the attic apartment: also racing green, and marked '42C', in smart brass figures. No name or obvious sign of occupancy, but that doesn't mean anything. At the end of a narrow corridor that runs beside the staircase, another Chubb-locked door, the proverbial baize door, once, bars admittance to the basement flat. 42A boasts an electric switch-bell and a name, handwritten rather carelessly in biro on a card in the little perspex window: 'V. Dearborn'. V. Dearborn, the Honorable lady-writer, who rather intrigues me…

Back in the middle apartment, no bugs, unless you care to count Escher or the tiny device in my cig packet on the bedside-table that I now stow carefully in an inner pocket. From the long casement window, I can see no obvious signs of lurkers in doorways or behind plane trees, but if they know their job, there won't be. I stand there watching the street, watch Louise getting into her mini-cab without a backward glance. All normal: modicum of traffic negotiating the calming-humps; parked cars; a loose dog peeing against a lamp-post; a ginger cat on a wall; someone in an anorak putting leaflets under windscreen wipers… everything as it should be on this quiet weekday late afternoon in this narrow gentrified backstreet in fashonable Fulham. In the house – Number Forty-Two (now subdivided A, B and C) Maxwell Road – all is nice and quiet. Apart, that is, from the ghosts. The light turns melancholy. I fish out another cigarette.

10: Winter 1966–7

Captain Leo Rollitt, DSO, smoking his third forbidden cigarette, watching from the casement window as he has been most of the afternoon sees, at last, the taxi draw up. 'Is it her? Is she here?' Nurse Streatham, excited, tactfully ignoring the cigarette, and more than pleased with her charge in his heavy maroon wool dressing-gown, smelling as he does of old-fashioned clean gentleman, all shaved and smooth, that lovely aroma of bay rum in her nostrils (and how she relishes this change from the Jeyes Fluid she left behind at the Royal Free!) peers out agog from behind him; they watch the street below together. The woman standing beside the cab: long feet in brown brogue shoes, thin, thin ankles visible beneath the thick hem of her tawny-coloured coat as she turns to count out change in a gloved hand, a fluff of pale chestnut hair tucked into a high tweed collar. The taxi man's breath billowing into the frosty air, heaving bags out from the cab…

'Oh,' exclaimed Nurse Streatham. 'So she's not in black. Just fancy! *And* she's got on one of those new swing-style coats, all folds from the shoulder. *Very* nice. And there was me! I'd expected her to be in black – but everything's changed now, hasn't it? *And* she's been in the South of France!'

'She probably doesn't own another coat, you silly female,' murmured Leo inaudibly, too happy to be annoyed. Lottie wouldn't be in obvious mourning anyway even if she did have a black coat, he thought.

'Poor young lady, losing her husband like that! So *very* sad…' Nurse Streatham was still staring down at the street. 'And you'll be *very* happy, I dare say, sir, now she's come to look after you,' she added. In Nurse Streatham's book, family was family. Only right that a sister should come and care for a sick brother. But she wondered whether *this* sister, who looked a lot like how she imagined a French film star might look, would be quite what was required. Her mind went to practicalities: what about *baths* never mind about all the rest of it?

'Yes,' agreed Leo simply.

'Not but what you haven't turned the corner,' said the Nurse. 'I hope she's prepared for everything. I'd better have a little word with her, I suppose…'

Try stopping you, Leo thought. 'Yes, of course,' he said, limping without help to the day-bed slowly with the aid of his crutch, and hitching himself and his bad leg into his customary semi-prone position. The bad leg was almost an extra appendage, something that still wouldn't quite obey the automatic commands of his brain. Movement tired him abominably still, but he had got to that stage of convalescence when the fatigue made him impatient. His hip had begun to pain him more than the bad leg. Unaccustomed stress on unused muscles, Nurse Streatham said.

'Now then,' said Nurse Streatham, as she straightened the pillows behind his head, 'I've spoken to Mrs O'Ryan. She's promised a light supper for two which she'll put out, and she's done the spare room just as you wanted, and I've insisted she light the gas-fire for Mrs Walters in her bedroom. I mean, she'll be expecting a bit of warmth in our old London after the Riviera…' He did not bother to correct her: that his sister had actually returned directly from their aunt in the Midlands. Nurse Streatham beamed, evidently expecting praise.

'That's super,' Leo said, 'but look, I say, Nurse, we mustn't go upsetting Mrs O'Ryan, putting her out too much. She's had quite a lot to put up with already with me, you know...'

'Huh,' sniffed the Nurse. 'She'll manage. She's got that Mrs Pell in the mornings now. *She's* a bit of a one, if you ask me. Nosy parker. Always asking questions. And I think I must tell you, Captain, that I found That Child on the stairs *again* as I came up. Lurking as usual. I hope he doesn't go upsetting poor Mrs Walters. He's not quite right if you ask me! All big dark eyes and innocence, but he doesn't fool me, all those spy-games and blood and thunder. I blame the American picture papers. Comics, they call them, but blest if I can see anything funny. And the films. The television's full of them now. *Says* he's only playing. Eye-tie, that's what he looks like. Or Spanish...' Another meaningful sniff.

'Well that's always possible, Nurse. There were a lot of Spaniards in Ireland after the Armada, you know. He's a good-looking kid...'

'Hmph. Not that I don't feel sorry for the lad. But he's a sly one...' Nurse Streatham, at the window again, watched the billowing diesel fumes as the taxi drove away into the grey November afternoon. Turning back, she became efficient. 'Now then, Captain Rollitt. You've got everything you need, and your dose for tonight. I'll be back tomorrow morning for the massage and there'll be your bath and the bandages...' She hovered with her hand on the door, 'There'll be some things that young Mrs Walters won't want to be bothered with, I'm sure...' Leo was listening to the heavy slam of the front door and the murmur of voices below and did not answer, and the Nurse coughed significantly.

'What? Oh certainly not, Nurse. Let's keep to the present arrangement, shall we? And anyway, Nurse, as you say, I'm round the corner. On my feet properly in no time. Be able to take a bath like any civilized person. And – um - thank you again for everything, Nurse. I'm really terribly grateful for all you've done. Are doing,' he corrected himself.

'Oh, now that's all part of the service, as they say,' said Nurse Streatham briskly, but he could see she was pleased. 'And I must say it's always pleasant to work for such a – a cooperative and gentlemanly patient. It's not everybody who appreciates ...' Her plump cheeks had gone a little pink, and she smoothed her uniform over her ample stomach and added quickly, 'Now then, I'll just have a quick word with Mrs Walters and take myself off. Not too much whiskey, now. Remember what Doctor Baines said...'

'Promise, Nurse...' He heard her firm footsteps thudding down the staircase, and listened to the voices in the hall: Nurse Streatham's, voluble and insistent, Mrs O'Ryan's, interjecting in shrill Dublin, and now his sister's, quiet, husky and somehow pervasive. He opened his book at a random page – it was Rex Stout's *The Doorbell Rang*, lent to him by his friend Bollinger, to cheer him up – but Leo could not read for the life of him, and allowed the book to fall onto his lap. 'The Captain's doing really *very* well, Mrs Walters,' he heard Nurse Streatham say. 'Round the corner, definitely, I'd say...' And Lottie: 'Yes, I'm sure he is, Nurse, and

I'm certain it's all to do with your excellent care. Can I go in to him?' (Darling Lottie. Always diplomatic, always knowing the right things to say to people.) 'Of course, Mrs Walters, of course. He's expecting you. I'll just have a quick word with Mrs O'Ryan and then I'll take myself off...' And now light steps running up the stairs and the door opened and then there she was, and in black, as it turned out, beneath the coat that she had left in the hall, but on Lottie, a little black jacket and knee-length skirt looked chic rather than widow's weedish. 'I think the FF is leaving,' she said in a stage-whisper. 'FF' stood for Frightful Female, and it took him straight back to the nursery. 'I know,' Leo mouthed. They listened, arrested, to more exchange in the hall, and then to the clang of the front door. 'If you've met the O'Ryan,' he whispered. 'FF isn't in it...' 'The tiny Irish witch who let me in? She's just called me "me dear"...Oh *Leo!*' And she flung herself onto her knees at his side, and he held her very tightly for what felt like a very long time.

'You musn't feel that you have to.'

'Mmm? Have to what?' Lottie Walters was curled up on the floor with her shoulders on a pouffe at her brother's reclining feet. She jiggled the ice in her glass, meditatively staring ino the gas fire which was intended, with simulated licking flames, to look realistic and failed rather dismally. Nothing, however, could detract from the gaiety of their mood.

'Look after me, of course. I'm not quite as helpless as I look, whatever the FF has been saying.'

'Nonsense-constance. This is just perfect, and it's so bloody wonderful to see you.'

'You'll regret it, you know. When you've seen Ma O'Ryan's housekeeping, and you've been kept awake by friend Welham the lodger stumping about and counting his encyclopaedias at all hours of the night, let alone been sprung at on the stairs by that engaging but alarmingly sudden O'Ryan youngster, you'll be booking a ticket on the first plane back to Nice...'

'You are idiotic, Leo darling. I've done ghastly Menton to *death* with Aunt Jessica. I don't know why she asked me. I hate bridge, and her cronies are like waxworks with blue hair. Hugh was there for a bit, which was nice, but he wasn't exactly chatty, poor man. You've heard Anabel's left him, haven't you? Run off with one of the Callington brothers, apparently, just bolted. And since then I've been shivering with cold from Aunt Rosalind's Rutland, so I'm sort of on holiday, you realise, in this blessed, fabulous *cuddly* London with your wonderful central heating and fake fires. If the price is plumping your pillows and making you the odd lightly boiled egg, I'm more than happy, you know. Truly...' She turned and smiled at him radiantly, and the faux-firelight caught her reddish hair and made flames in it.

'Are you?' Leo said seriously. 'I mean, I was rather expecting...' There was a brittleness about her that worried him. Her face, dear as it was, seemed to him far too thin, the bones jutting, and the 'London' make-up too harsh for her delicate colouring. Girls were going in for a sort of bloodless lipstick these days, and making their eyes look black and hollow, like pits. Fashion rather annoyed Leo.

'Gloom? I know. But I'm over all that. The worst, anyway. Really, I am. Do you know, Aunt Rosalind made me sit through the entire recording of Verdi's 'Requiem' the other night because she was feeling guilty she hadn't come to the funeral. And I'll swear she was really put out that I didn't *cry!* But I nearly did, with sheer boredom. You know what, it takes almost three hours and it's on about forty records – imagine! And she'd given me just one glass of gin and I was expected to make it last. She sends you lots of messages, by the way. Her love, of course, and not to brood, but she says that to me too, and she also said, all very mysteriously, to have patience for your time will come. You're her favourite nephew, you know. She kept saying so. I rather think she means to leave you the Hall now that poor old Phil's dead. There aren't any other Bullivants in the offing...'

'You're joking!'

'I'm not. She kept hinting things. She hasn't got any heirs, now, except us and Hugh, and Hugh's got the Dearborn estate, of course.'

'Oh my God! It's falling to bits. Or it was. Is it still falling to bits?'

'In spades. Tiles tumble off the roof with every passing breeze, and the stables are officially unsafe. Condemned. All propped up with scaffolding. She's had to move the horses to Mrs. Jenkinson's in the village. There's still the wonderful garden, but the topiary's all out of shape, and the roses are all reverted, as far as you can tell this time of year. They need an awful lot of attention, Leo. The whole place does. Do you know, sometimes I think I'd love to really learn about gardens and actually have one of my own. Roses especially. Poor old Henry can't cope with it any more, and Aunt Ros is too mean to hire on anyone else. She put me in the Hogarth room.'

'Good Lord! A sigh for lost innocence.'

'Quite. Do you remember how we weren't allowed in there as kids? Said she thought it would cheer me up, but really I think it was just the only spare room that wasn't completely uninhabitable. But anyway the Hall's still the same – sacred downstairs, if you don't count Uncle George's grizzly trophies, and quite unbelievably profane up, if you can possibly regard Hogarth as anything but sweetly antique, and of course those ghastly French nudes. They're probably worth a bomb, Leo! She doesn't think of them that way, of course. I offered to find her a valuer, someone from Sotheby's, maybe, but she's not having any of it. She's got more stubborn then ever.'

'I always loved Aunt Rosalind's dual personality, didn't you?' Leo said. 'All that huntin', shootin' stuff side by side with the music and the outdoor Shakespeare. Poor old girl. I really ought to go and see her. Soon, if this leg behaves itself.'

'She'd love that, I think,' Lottie said. 'But she really is a bit of a poor old thing now, Leo. It's all fairly squalid, really. She's confined to about three rooms. The poor Henrys do their best, but they're almost more doddery than she is. Everybody's got so old, Leo, it's sad. Mrs Henry confided to me that she really didn't know how they'd cope this winter without more help, poor old love. And honestly, darling, the place stinks. Really, I mean *stinks*. Paraffin, cats, mice – and drains, I'm afraid. And the damp you wouldn't believe! Real black mould on the walls and in my bedroom the ceiling was peeling.'

'The ceiling was peeling, and we don't care anything more,' chorused Leo. 'Oh, Lottie, darling! You can't believe how good it is to see you. And to see you so well...' He was about to add 'in spite', but stopped himself.

'Which is more than we can say of you, sausage…' She knitted her carefully sculpted eyebrows. 'Are you still in lots of pain, darling?' She hated the way his hands shook. Trauma and the drugs, Nurse Streatham had said, more than pain, preparing her. She put out a hand to his pyjama'd leg, but let her hand hover just above the shin.

'Ow! No, just joking. It just aches a bit, I suppose. The septicaemia's cleared up, which is the main thing. *That* was painful, and pretty revolting. But mostly, I'm just fed up now, apart from turning gradually into an opium addict. Those pain-killing jabs pack quite an amusing punch, let me tell you. The atrophy's a bore, but the FF is quite good on the massage, strangely enough. No, don't laugh. But I've not been able to do anything much except read. And no visitors to speak of, unless you count Bolly, and he only visits because he can't afford to do anything else now that Sophia's cleaned him out over that divorce. He just drinks my scotch and complains about the stock market. He thinks everything's going to go robotic, or something. He's scared of the new electronics, whatever that means, thinks computers are going to alter the 'Change beyond anyone's comprehension, everything done in a split second across the world to hedge your bets, or whatever they do. Imagine that! But then it's all beyond me anyway. I don't pretend to understand Bolly when he gets technical. Bright sort of bloke in his own field.'

'Oh, Leo, poor darling. You must have been so lonely.'

'A bit. Thing is…that is, I think until recently, I'd begun to remind everybody else of Death…' Leo's hand picked at a pill on his dressing-gown.

'Even Phyllida, I gather,' Lottie said, more sharply than she meant to.

'Her too…' He paused. 'I think the sight of me all crocked up in hospital put her off. You know. I suppose you've heard that she's – um…'

'Well, yes! Sort of couldn't miss it. Aunt Rosalind shoved *The Times* in front of my face at breakfast last week. I gather it was all pretty sudden. I'm truly very sorry, darling.'

'I learned it from the announcement too.'

'Leo!'

'Well, nothing was ever official. No diamond solitaire. Of course we'd intended to wait until all that bloody Middle East business was resolved. Only made sense. She was away when I got back, visiting relatives, so she said. And then, well, she just faded out…'

'But that's horrid. Cowardly. She might have at least, well…'

'Come to see me and said darling Leo, I'm so sorry you were blown up, and you're a bloody hero but you're also the most frightful crock, and by the bye I've fallen for someone else far more glamorous and rich, but while he's away madly winning everything at Aintree and Cheltenham, let me bathe your poor hot forehead? Come on, Lottie.'

'Well I still think it's absolutely despicable. No, I really do. And what a *shock!*'

'It was on the cards. She got nerves, I expect. Most people are cowards, when it comes to it, including me.'

'And you never heard from her? You mean not a word?'

'Not a sausage. Actually, that's not true. Her mother wrote a rather rambling screed about regretting her daughter's peremptory behaviour. She more than hinted I could have been more forthcoming, if I'd really wanted to marry into the family, if you please, but how much she regretted I wouldn't be her son-in-law after all, because she had always been fond of me. I burnt it. The letter. I was rather angry at the time.'

'Oh Leo, that's *outrageous*! I mean, really! *And* typical, I suppose. God, she's a ghastly woman. I thought she looked just like Toad as the washerwoman. God knows how she had such a pretty daughter. And the worst kind of ambitions. I met her just that once, at the Dysons's party, remember? She told me she thought I was courageous, in 'my position', whatever that was supposed to mean, being an academic wife in Cambridge, I suppose. I think she thought I was dirt poor and never saw anybody except desiccated professors! A toad, darling. Your children would have looked reptilian, or is it amphibian? You got off lightly in that department anyway. Oh, Leo, I'm not making fun, honestly. I really am terribly sorry. You couldn't have burned it in this,' she added, staring at the fake flames.

'The stove in the kitchen's real. Coke. But paper takes appalling ages to burn in it, and Mrs O'Ryan hovers. I tore it up and had a conflagration in an ashtray, if you must know. And no, you're not sorry, you liar. You hated her, remember.'

'I protest! I never hated her. I just never particularly, well –'

'Liked her! Be honest!' They giggled like children.

'No, really. I suppose I was a bit unfair,' said Lottie, suddenly serious. 'I didn't exactly like her. But I didn't exactly hate her either. I mean, we seemed to have precious little in common, and I didn't think she was really nice enough for you, but I'd have behaved myself perfectly well if you and she had, you know...'

She stood up, looking round the room. Between the long windows was Grandmama's ottoman, with its shabby green and rose pink brocade, one corner torn to shreds from Pookie's claws. And she recognised the faded rust velvet curtains from Anstey, the ones that had moved with them to London when Anstey had had to be sold. So *much*, so much that was the past, their past... And here on the top of Leo's pretty Edwardian baby grand piano, his twenty-first present from Aunt Rosalind, the photographs of Ma and Pa, one young, 'BC' – before children – they both looked so *young*; and the other one much later, which she remembered being taken in the Anstey garden by that strange godson of Ma's, the one from Kenya who became a professional photographer, with Ma, obviously so ill and gaunt by now, poor darling, holding the silver Egyptian fruit dish that had been Grandpa's 'trophy' from Cairo, from his days on the Judiciary, and Pa looking on with such a sad but sweetly indulgent look; and here was one of Darkie the labrador, fancy keeping that, sentimental old silly...and this other in a silver frame, which she picked up and hastily put down, of herself and Giles, just married, on the steps of the Shire Hall in Cambridge. She thought, I'm absolutely not going to dissolve, not going to let this evening turn to me, my emotions, my troubles. She twinkled the piano keys, and said brightly, 'Are you still practising?'

'Yes, a bit. Not enough. Pedals are a bit difficult like this, and I can't sit straight for long. I always turn to it, I suppose, when I'm in the mood. I'm always slightly afraid of upsetting the O'Ryans, though the old girl says it does her a 'power o' good to hear all the old choons'. And I still have the odd… pupil.'

'You toyed with the idea of being a proper musician, when you were at school,' Lottie said, sounding suddenly like the older sister.

'Oh *that*! Toyed is the word. I was only ever just a dabbler, Lottie. Never did have the, you know, the staying power. Or the talent. I'd have ended up doing third rate provincial orchestra stuff, teaching in a boys' prep and reffing the rugger in my spare time. I do rather miss the concert-party, though. Only good thing about the Army. I'm very light and frivolous, these days, my dear. Old fashioned stuff. Cole Porter, all that. And I always preferred Fats Waller even as a kid. Fun stuff. I offend myself trying to play Schubert properly…' He wanted to tell her all about his second thoughts about the Army, about his second thoughts about just about everything, but it would keep. He lay back on his pillows with the blessed sense that things, now, could keep. 'Hey! While you're up, pour me one, will you?'

She poured him a large whiskey, and an even larger one for herself. 'The FF would disapprove. She warned me especially not to let you. I remember your Schubert and stuff. And Chopin. I loved Chopin. I just used to sit there on the stairs, listening to you practice, did you know? I wanted to be jealous, because you were always the one, you know, Mamma's favourite. But one couldn't help loving you. Your hands on the keys. Mamma always thought you were concert pianist material.'

'Mamma was ambitious for both of us, wasn't she, bless her? You with a 'suitable' marriage and me, well God knows… Well, then, cheeri-bloody-o, as Aunt Rosalind would say…'

'Cheeri-bloody-o. Poor old Aunt Ros. She's no coward, though, I'll say that for her. Still goes out with the Cottesmore in all weathers and rides side-saddle on an elderly sixteen-hand grey called Nimrod, the whole works. Rouged up to the eyebrows and a bowler with a veil, terrifying the bejesus out of the kids in the local Pony Club. Can you imagine? Tell you what, she'll have a frightful fall and break her neck, and then old Lovell will ring to tell you you've inherited the entire ruin… I suppose we both disappointed her,' Lottie said after a pause. 'Mamma. Me and my crazy lefty poet and not getting married in church, and you – well no, you couldn't have disappointed her. Army hero, if nothing else…' She picked up a portrait photo of Phyllida. 'She really is frightfully pretty, I suppose. For a complete pill, that is, as she's treated you so badly. Perhaps you had a lucky escape.'

'Or perhaps she did…' Leo's face cracked into one of his wry smiles. 'Tell you what, you can put that photo away…second drawer in the bureau…' He paused, frowning into his glass.

'There.'

'There! A piece of the pointless past consigned to where we can't see it.'

'Really as easy as that? You really don't regret anything?'

Leo watched her restless movements round the room. Her thinness rather appalled him. She had lost whatever she had had of a bosom, and her legs and arms seemed like sticks. He was aware that the look was supposed to be elegant, but he simply worried for her. When she sat down again, plaiting her thin legs under her chin on the pouffe, he said, 'Do you mean, do I resent the cowardice, do I want to biff the horse trainer or do I miss her?'

'The lot, if you like. But we can talk about something else. I'm supposed to be cheering you up. Don't let's talk about her if you don't want. I just wondered, that's all.'

In fact Leo was far more content to talk about the absconding Phyllida than about his lingering injuries. Absently, he ran his hand through Lottie's springy chestnut hair. 'I suppose I miss the – well, you can imagine. But no. No I don't really regret anything. I think, you know, I'd have probably suggested doing the deed before I went out to Aden if I'd really been that serious. Lying here like this makes you think.'

'Poor Leo,' Lottie said, this time actually stroking his injured leg, very gently.

'Actually,' Leo said, considering, 'I don't think she was frightfully keen on me in the first place, deep down. I mean she didn't ever really seem, well – I mean, perhaps things might have got a bit more hearty once it was all official, but...'

'Oh *I see!* Scheming little minx, all that pretended virtue! Makes me sick, that sort of thing...' She frowned and stared into her glass, and slugged the contents back. Whiskey was making her garrulous. 'You know, if I'd been her, I shouldn't have hesitated, ring or not. I mean, you're rather a gorgeous old thing really. Silly, silly Phyllida.'

'Silly Phylly. Silly us all. Actually, since you ask, she didn't hesitate, as such. She was very sweet – and, well, perfectly willing. Just didn't like it much when she got there... But that was probably me. I daresay I'm not a very good lover. I gather men often aren't.'

'Giles was...'

'Ah. Good old Giles,' Leo said loyally. He had never been close to his brother-in-law, had felt indeed rather at a loss with him. Cambridge, mountain climbing, motorbikes and Eng. Lit. Strange mixture. Leo said, 'A lot more of a tough than you'd have expected of a poet. But a good bloke. I mean, obviously...'

'You never liked him much either.'

'I mostly felt he didn't like me. You know. Sandhurst idiot with no learning. He must have thought your brother was a bit of an ape...' He looked at Lottie and felt glad that Giles had satisfied her, that she had had that in her life. 'But he was basically decent, wasn't he? I wasn't up to him, of course, and I can't pretend to understand a word of his verses, but I really thought he was, well, a good bloke.'

'Yes,' said Lottie. 'Good bloke as you say...' She smiled the briefest of smiles. 'You're a good bloke, Leo. The best. What are you going to do next, darling? I only ask because I haven't the smallest clue myself. I've been doing a few hours at the Fitzwilliam, but it's hardly a job. And I can't go on living in College, you know. They're being very nice about it, but basically they want Giles's rooms back for someone else.'

'The shits,' said Leo, frowning.

'No, Leo, honestly. They have to. And they're not on my back or anything, and I still have Giles's University pension. I think they might even give me what the Italians call a 'buonuscita' to get out. Caius is quite a rich college, you know, and sort of paternalistic. Giles was always very scathing about that, but I've been rather pathetically grateful for it. The Master and his wife have been dreadfully kind. But I am expected to go, to make room for the new man. I honestly don't want to stay even if I could. I'm rather a spare part there these days, obviously. I know I ought to start applying for things, and it just always feels like putting pins in a map. It's not even money, really. I get Giles's royalties, and his publisher says sales are on the up since…' Her eyes were too bright. 'But I was asking about you. What next, after the leg's mended?'

'I don't know, dearie! Let's see…draw my pension and practise becoming an young old buffer? Take up golf and bridge and all that sort of thing…or play gentle jazz in a refined night-club? Join an amateur dramatics outfit? Sing Gilbert and Sullivan with the Basingstoke Players?'

'Silly.'

'Sorry. Not being entirely serious, but I'm too much of a cripple to go back to the active Army. And there's something so very depressing about a desk job at the War Office. It's the Ministry of Defence now. I wish I – well – still believed in all that.'

'Don't you?'

'Not really, no. I can't help feeling there must be more to life – you know, a spot of optimism, something less – defensive, less military. The world's changed quite a bit since I last looked at it, Lottie. I feel I ought to…well, I'm not sure, exactly, but I'm not a natural soldier, you know. Even less a natural civil servant.'

'I know…and I'm not a natural widow. Nor a natural art-historian either, probably. Aren't we a pair, eh?'

'You – um – you must miss him so very much,' he said gently, and felt thoroughly inadequate. Pride notwithstanding, he really did feel he had had a lucky escape from Phyllida, whereas Lottie's loss was surely immeasurable.

'Yes. Rather horribly, in fact. But that's not really all…' She bit her bottom lip and her brow furrowed. She was losing her fight. Bravery was possible – essential – at Aunt Jessica's horrid bridge parties in the south of France, and for fending off Aunt Rosalind's bullying attempts at 'cheering' in the chill Midlands. But now the London warmth and Leo's whiskey had got to her, and Leo, without realising it, 'got' to her like a second self. With him, her customary pluckiness was a game, a shop-window she knew they could both see through. She slugged at her empty glass and then stood up to pour herself another. 'You know,' she said, rocking slightly on her feet, 'I've never told any one this, but I can tell you. I mean, while we were frightfully happy together, and everything in the physical department was absolutely hunky-dory, and he was a thoroughly "good bloke," as you put it, he worried me like crazy, actually. He'd never, ever talk about it. Or anything very much, about what he was *really* feeling. He had the blackest of moods, Leo, and it wasn't just going all distant and broody while he was working. I even thought that his accident – well – wasn't…'

'Lottie?' Leo sat up too fast and winced. 'Whatever do you mean?'

'Oh, yes. I think he did it deliberately, darling. There he was, after falling most of the way down a mountain and concussed to the point of brain damage, about forty stitches in his head and bandaged like a mummy, the doctors not liking him even being out of hospital. Well, he insisted on coming home, back to College – he'd got this group he was schooling through the tripos, and he was getting seriously agitated, but they warned him even about walking and sudden movements. But after about a fortnight, after the vivas, he went and took the bike on a train to Lancaster and insisted on making it up that dreadful hill to Wanswater. The ride was a bet, for God's sake. He really was a bit bonkers, darling. He must have known he was bound to black out and have the most frightful smash. I think, oh God, I think it was something sort of inside him, something he couldn't help... And he just *hated* being the Modernists' darling. He felt as if he'd sold out... Sorry. I'm not making sense, am I?' The nightmare vision of his smashed body on the mortuary table came back with terrible presence. 'The awful thing –' her mouth twitched – 'the truly awful thing is that I should have tried to stop him and I can't stop blaming myself...' And then suddenly her face crumpled and she began to cry.

'Oh, Lottie, darling! Oh, Christ! Dearest, don't, don't.'

Andrew O'Ryan was squeezed on his haunches inside the heavy wardrobe in the attic bedroom. The interior was pitch-dark, and it stank rather horribly of dirty socks and of Mr Welham's spare pair of shoes, and Andrew's thighs and knees had begun to ache, and it was cold, too – the house had no radiators in the top rooms – but he bore with his discomfort, what with the pong and all, as stoically as he knew how, and he kept his right eye firmly against the hole in the wardrobe door. The hole, now the size of a sixpence, was Andrew's own handiwork: a tiny woodworm bore in a natural knot in the oak which Andrew had patiently worked at with his penknife while Mr Welham was out, selling stockings and encyclopaedias and whatever it was he sold. Mr Welham sold anything going, apparently, and the goods in his cases changed from week to week. Andrew was proud of his hole. You couldn't tell there was a hole unless you really looked, because of the knot in the wood, and Mr Welham couldn't really look, because his glasses were thick like the bottom of a beer-mug. Now he heard Mr Welham's awkward tread on the carpetless stairs, and his thick, glutinous cough, and the thump of the cases outside the room, and he quickly allowed himself a small shift of movement before he froze like a Commando as the door clicked and swung open on its noisy hinges. A click. Light. Now, Andrew could see the door – just – and the narrow single bed, and part of the window where the faded pink curtains had never been drawn back since the morning, for Mr Welham tended to leave very early and his grandmother had the rooms 'done' mid-week when she changed the laundry. Grunts, as Mr Welham heaved the cases inside. Encyclopaedias this week, probably; the cases made a heavy sound, like big books would make. Andrew was very proud of his sleuthing abilities.

The door closed. He saw Mr Welham, a thinnish, bespectacled middle-aged man with a straggle of hair smoothed over his rather high, yellowish crown, and a little gingerish toothbrush moustache, to Andrew's fancy like a little hairy animal between his nose and his lip. He was carrying a small newspaper parcel under his arm, and he deposited it, out of Andrew's immediate view, onto a rickety table in the corner. Now a sound like 'ouf!'as Mr Welham crouched down, and a hiss and splutter as Mr Welham lit the gas fire with a match. A jingle of keys – Mr Welham had taken his jacket off and put it over the chair. A treading on the floorboards, and now, the clatter of cutlery onto a plate. Grammy didn't like the PGs eating in their rooms, although she provided a little gas-ring for kettles for coffee and tea. A soft 'pshh' as a bottle opened, and the blub-blub of liquid pouring into a glass. A rustling of paper. A new smell reached Andrew's nostrils: the reek of lard and fried fish and chips. His eye saw Mr Welham carry his plate and glass to the bed and climb onto it, in his shirt and braces but without removing his shoes. Grammy would be very displeased: Grammy was very particular, Grammy was, about what PGs got up to. Mr Welham pressed the switch of his transistor radio on the bedside table, and some tinny band-music made it possible for Andrew to draw a proper breath behind the sound. Mr Welham ate his meal with a sort of joyless deliberation, licking his fingers not so much with relish but as if he were determined not to waste an atom of his supper. He slurped at his beer, and then burped loudly without bothering to put his hand in front or to say 'Pardon'. That's what you did when you were by yourself without somebody to remind you of your manners. Mr Welham put the empty plate onto the floor. Then he fished in the pocket of his trousers for a very grimy handkerchief and his Park Drives. He wiped his lips and then lit a cigarette with a match, and now another smell, which Andrew liked. Mr Welham would smoke his cigarette and stub it out in the bakelite ashtray that said Guinness beside the bed. Soon, he would get up and go to the lav down the corridor, and then Andrew would be able to slip out of the wardrobe and out of the room. He tested himself, every time, on his accurate timing, and on his noiselessness. He was especially proud of his ability to creep silently, on account of his boot. It had taken a great deal of practice.

He would like to stay, to see Mr Welham take off his shabby grey trousers and his grubby white shirt, and his grey-white vest and underpants, to see his stringy grey-white body with the small red squirrel hanging between his legs and put on his faded striped pyjamas, and he was very curious to see if Mr Welham would come and fetch his magazines – the ones with the pictures of young ladies in the nuddy, tucked away in the wardrobe drawer beneath Andrew's hiding-place. If he did, Andrew would have to hold his breath for at least thirty seconds and then let it out silently as Mr Welham took the mags into bed to read them through his thick lenses, and then take his glasses off and put them by the radio and turn out the light and begin to make the shaking and grunting under the thin covers and then make the strange tiny squeak, like a rat being killed, and then, suddenly, as if felled by a blow, fall snoring loudly asleep…

That was what had happened last week, and Andrew had had to make sure that Mr Welham was really asleep and not shamming (the way Andrew some-times did when he wanted to fool Grammy and have some night-time to himself with the battery torch and his comics) before he plucked up the courage to open the wardrobe door and uncramp himself in utter silence and steal noiselessly over the lino to the door, open it without making the hinges groan (really tricky, this one), slip out of the door, and close it, silently, like the Commandos. But to-night Grammy would be missing him surely, and already she was probably look-ing for him, to make him brush his teeth and order him to go to bed. Tomorrow was a school morning.

Welham, still reclined on his bed, his supper-plate on the floor beside him, and the reek of fish and chips and a recently-extinguished cigarette fugging the air in the foetid room, yawned so wide that his head seemed almost to split in two, and his spectacles nearly fell off his head. Andrew had to stop himself from laughing. Mr Welham was very tired. Andrew realised that he was tired too. He nearly 'caught' Mr Welham's yawn, and stopped himself just in time. He waited. Perhaps Mr Welham wouldn't get up to the lavatory. Perhaps he would just go to sleep as he was. Andrew waited some more, and the tinny band-music continued to play. Then – unstoppably and fatally, and without any warning at all – An-drew suddenly sneezed. He couldn't help himself, it just happened. Mr Welham gasped and sat up with a look on his face that was really very funny indeed, but now Andrew's eye was no longer at the hole. He tried to make himself very small in the wardrobe, burrow into the darkness. Then a rapid thud of feet on lino, and the wardrobe door flung open, and a violent flood of yellow blinding light. 'Bleedin' Jesus Christ almighty!' said Mr Welham.

'Ow!' said Andrew, blinking. He was not afraid especially, although his heart was thumping vigorously enough in his chest. Mr Welham's fingers seemed to flutter at him rather than to grab. He extricated himself from the wardrobe and stood uncramping his legs in front of Mr Welham, who seemed to be trembling all over.

'Shit!' said Mr Welham. 'You nearly gave me a 'eart-attack. What the flamin' hell are you doin' in 'ere, you little bleeder?'

'I fell asleep,' lied Andrew.

'A likely story, *and* beside the point. What was you doin' in here in the first place, I'd like to know. Eh?'

'I was hiding from me Grammy,' Andrew said. That was partly true.

'In trouble are you? Well, you won't hide from your Grammy no longer, sonny jim, not 'ere you won't. You're a nasty little sneak, that's what you are. A little spy, a little Irish Commie, coming into people's private rooms and 'idin' in people's private cupboards and scarin' 'em witless after a 'ard day's work. I'll tell your gran'ma what you are, all right, and if she beats the livin' daylights outer you, it's what you deserve. Bleedin' 'ell fire. Bleedin' '*ell!*' Mr Welham's outrage was sufficiently comical to eradicate Andrew's last scrap of fear.

'So? Like I'll tell her about fish and chips in your room and your shoes on the bed?' inquired Andrew, his big ink-blue eyes round with innocence.

'Never mind that, you little toe-rag. A man's gotter eat. Your gran's almost 'uman, the old witch, and you shouldn't be 'ere. You're the one in trouble, make no mistake. Gettit?' Mr Welham gave Andrew a shake at the shoulder which was supposed to hurt but didn't. Its ineffectuality made the boy bolder still.

'What about all them saucy magazines, then? Girls without a stitch? My Grammy'll have plenty to say about *that!*'

'Why, you little b – !' began Mr Welham. 'Christ!' He had had a shock, but he was collecting his nerve at last. He stared at Andrew for a moment, swallowed, and then he seemed to slow down and make his voice go quieter. He said, tapping the side of his nose with a yellow finger, 'You're a fly one, ain't yer? Nah, then. Nah, *then*. Let's not be too 'asty. You're 'aving a game, ain't yer? Ow old are you?'

'Ten,' said Andrew. 'And a half.'

'Ten, eh? *And* a half. Bit of a shrimp ain't yer? And a gammy foot...' Welham was staring at Andrew's built-up boot, and Andrew conceived a sudden hatred for him that almost took his breath way. 'And what do you want to be when you grow up, sonny?' Mr Welham was chuckling nastily now. 'Spy for MI Five? Sexton Blake? Sexton O'Blake? Cripes, that's a laugh that is. Bloody Irish, siding with the Ruskies and comin' here and free-loading off all them boats from Liverpool.'

'I'm going to America,' the boy burst out. 'Rochdale, Texas, America!' When he repeated it often enough, it was true.

'*America*, eh? The FBI, Elliot Ness n' all that? Well now, I expect we'd all like to go to *America*! You're a right one, you are, sonny. Rochwell, Texas, America! You're out with the fairies, ain't yer?'

'It ain't a story,' said Andrew. 'And it's Roch*dale*, Texas, America, and I'm goin' there just as soon as me mammy can 'ave me, ask me Grammy if it ain't true! But I'll talk to me grammy first, about what youse doin' in her room!'

'Nah then, nah then. Keep your hair on, sonny-jim...' The man Welham was softening, apparently. 'Tell you what – ...' He forced a sickly smile under the ginger moustache which showed long front teeth yellow with nicotine, and fished about in his trouser pocket. 'S'pose 'alf a crown might settle it? I 'spect you like pocket money. I did when I was your age. The fair an' that. Picture house. Half a crown's a lot of pocket money. A lot of rides at the fair. Y'can spend it before you go into Yanky-land and the Almighty Dollar. How's that? Nah then. You don't say nothink to your gran'ma, the good Mrs O'Ryan, about my bit of supper, and I don't say nothink about you 'idin' in this 'ere wardrobe in my room, and we've got a deal. What about that then? Deal? Man to man, like?' The salesman's stained fingers held out a coin.

Andrew's eyes were on the half-crown, but he kept his hands resolutely behind his back.

'C'mon, son. I'm bein' lenient. Generous. A man's room is his private territory...' He flashed the coin again, temptingly.

'It's Grammy's room,' Andrew reminded the lodger. He was almost enjoying himself now. It was always interesting to know what people – especially grown up people – would do next. He enjoyed watching Mr Welham's yellowish face flush an ugly red.

'It's mine while I pay the rent, you little bleeder, which I do, every fourth Sunday, regular as clockwork. Bleedin' 'ell, I'm 'avin' a argument with a sodding kid!'

'There's plenty of people would pay good money for a nice room like this,' countered Andrew in a precise echo of his grandmother. 'And what about that sauce-stuff? The girls in them mags? Grammy runs a respectable house. That's what she says.'

'You little – ...' Mr Welham grabbed ineffectually for Andrew's throat. Angry grown ups were sometimes very scary, but for some reason Mr Welham wasn't. Andrew dodged, and positioned himself between Mr Welham and the door. 'Five bob,' he said firmly. 'Or I tell...' Andrew held out his hand. Mr Welham swore. Then he counted out some more silver change. 'Shit!' he said, and roughly shoved the half-crown, and a florin and a sixpence into the boy's grubby hand. Andrew clutched the money tightly in his fist, and dodged neatly out onto the landing, leaving Mr Welham to slam the door closed and swear quietly and insistently to himself behind it. 'Watch yerself, Smelly-Welham,' said Andrew loudly, knowing the man could hear. 'I'll be back!'

It was Andrew O'Ryan's first proper extortion operation, if he didn't count some of his dodges at school or his grandmother and her purse, and it had been roundly successful; but it was Mr Welham's face, the contorted, impotent anger on it, and the surge of power he had felt that gave him his true satisfaction.

He limped happily down the two lots of stairs, no longer concerned with silence, whistling softly under his breath, jingling his spoils in the pocket of his grey school shorts, past the landing and the wounded Captain's rooms where he thought he could hear the sound of a lady crying. Perhaps it was that lady who had come this afternoon, the Captain's sister, so Grammy said. He longed to linger and try to hear through the door, but, genuinely afraid of his grandmother's wrath, he forced himself to go on by, down to the basement apartment he shared with her, and where his bed awaited him. Dodging the old lady dozing in the kitchen in front of the television, he sneaked into his tiny room under the back staircase. He too had a wooden wardrobe, a smaller version of the one in Mr Welham's room and, like his recent hiding place, it also had a built-in drawer at the bottom. He emptied the pocket of his shorts and counted out his treasure, and then hid it in a red Oxo tin, where it joined his various other treasures. He was sure that Grammy wouldn't look. She never looked in the right places for things.

12: Spring Last Year

Detection is all about knowing where to look. And what to look *with*, get me? I mean, technology is fine when it works. There's this nifty little device – the amateur spy's agenda, they're beginning to call it – that allows you to subscribe to a service that lets you track anyone you like. Literally. No kidding. 'Always know where your loved ones are...' goes the slogan. This thing – it's operated from a central database like Sat Nav – it can track any active mobile phone to within two hundred yards. No. Actually, given its precision, it could probably tell you if your loved one is in the kitchen or at the bottom of the garden, and all at a reasonable monthly rate of about thirty quid. To a professional private investigator, this is potentially revolutionary: no more hiding, lurking behind doors, skulking behind newspapers, all the foot-padding is done for you. All you've got to do, once the blip stops, is freeze your nuts off as usual in a parked car with your flask and your telescopic digital, waiting for the flopsy to arrive...

But this is neat, eh? Except, of course, that being operated from a central database, presumably the tracker can be tracked... this stuff is paranoia with salad-dressing on it, I promise. And here's snag number two: before yours truly the PI starts to make significant savings on shoe leather, and before you break into a cold sweat lest her indoors knows you're not working late at the office this evening, or that your boss is now fully aware that you spent your twenty-four hour stomach bug supporting Chelsea in person, be comforted to know that there is one little obstacle: you have to give your consent. (Imagine: George, I need to know where you are at ALL TIMES! Okay, petal, just tell me what I have to do...) But it's true, you do. So, George, my friend, you're safe from this appalling intrusion unless you agree. But – (so you can panic some more) – amazingly, it involves no forms, and no ID. I mean, all you have to do to be electronically stalked is answer 'yes' to a texted message that will appear on your mobile screen when the subscriber supplies the details. Or not, as the case may be. So, you decide to say no, to ignore it, for as long as she lets you, that is: (WHY can't I know where you are, George? You're up to something, aren't you??) But, George bub, if you object, or if she's too wise to you to ask you in the first place, all she's got to do is pinch your mobile when you leave it lying about, out of your jacket in the hall, off the kitchen table while you go to answer the house phone – she'll have a million opportunities unless you actually sleep with it under your pillow, and you possess the reflexes of an SAS man – and answer the message for you. If this happens, bub, you'll be a little green blip on a minutely precise map if she's got the most sophisticated technology. And even if she hasn't, she'll be able to locate you to within a distance that would place you fairly precisely in the Bricklayers' Arms, or at that red-headed trollop's at number twenty-six... Then, I'm afraid, the only safeguard is to keep the thing switched off. Or even not own one at all. I hope I've got you good and rattled, George mate. Cancel the subscription, I would.

For reasons of a more old-fashioned paranoia, the rich and famous often don't carry mobiles – too risky. If they have them, they give their numbers to a very selected few. The canny ones don't even own one, or they register them in the names of their minders. Jerry Fairbrother still has several, though. One's a top of the range job, I'm told, the kind that can do everything but butter the toast, but he leaves it in his desk, according to Dorota the nanny. Never takes it out, only uses it from the house. So much for all this personal tech. All so potentially public. Bit of a waste, really, since Jerry can afford some really snazzy gear.

Tracking Fairbrother on behalf of my client, therefore, I have had to resort to entirely old fashioned methods. Which means, at the moment, God help me, one Lion Barley... More about him soon, I dare say. He's a squirming pathetic little amateur, but he suits my purpose for the moment. It has its tedious moments, believe me, and I keep my temper with difficulty.

'Look, like I said, get his route and his routine, right? Just *follow* him,' I say testily into my mobile. (Yeh, yeh, I know.) 'Bloody hell!'

Lion's voice, out of breath, being unused to outdoor exercise. 'I have been, for godsakes, man. Studio, Wimbledon. Wimbledon, studio... Studio car both ways...Lunch in a dark little dive called the Blue Fleece on Aherne Street with colleagues most days of the week...surrounded...and the girl's often with him.'

'We know all that, you stupid prat. Christ. Anything further there? The girl's flat? The Barbican?'

'No...you might say thank you...'

I grunt. The photos were hardly arresting. 'What do you mean, no?'

'I mean *no*. Totally doesn't see the girl now, not except for work. Of course they could be having it off across his desk, Bill Clinton job, hey.'

'Shut up Barley. Nothing, really nothing?'

'Not for two Fridays, not together...that's definite...' Barley actually sounds pleased with himself.

'Sounds like he's getting gagey. Shit...Okay. So now it's the jogging. You must have something by now, you cretin. Where he goes.'

'Goes? He runs on the sodding Common! Goes home after. For fucksakes, man, I've been on this night and day. What the fuck am I supposed to do? And don't tell me to get up at this hour again! I'm not built for this, man. I'll totally have a fucking heart-attack.'

'Big loss. Wife there much? In Wimbledon?'

'Sometimes...not always. I could get more joy out of her...meets lots of friends in the West End, goes shopping, taxis, comes home with parcels...and she heads off to Fulham sometimes, takes the tube in a scarf and dark glasses, like she's totally fooling anyone.'

'Forget that! It's him I want. Just get his run-routine, will you?'

'You keep *saying* that. What the fuck do you mean, run-routine? He runs on the Common, like I said. Near Windmill Road. Saturday mornings regular. Some evenings.'

'Not enough. I want his route, you cretin! The pathways. And his routine. They all have routines. Run, pause on a bench, smoke a cig, make a call – fucking hell, Lion, take notes! Use your gumption! Have you got *any* gumption, Lion?'

'Look, man, I've been in shorts and trainers every Saturday morning since you put me onto this, and all I've had out of it is bad ankles. If you don't come up with something down, I'm totally out, okay?'

'Whooa, Lion. Whoa! Anyone would think you're in a position to dictate terms. Listen, pillock, just give me a run-routine. Then you can have a down. Sunday. Usual place.'

'That's better...shit man, this is a bummer! He nearly caught me, you know that?'

Big pause. 'Where?'

'Well, I was in that pub, the Fleece, just off Aherne Street. I had a couple, blending into the background, you know...and one of his minders got suspicious, told me to lay off. All very polite, but look, I can't go on with this! All I could say is I'm a crazed fan...it worked...he gets lots...but well, I mean, it's *humiliating*. Shit, man. Me, a fan, of *his*.'

'Barley, you're a pathetic little arsehole. Just don't let him catch you being obvious. On the Common you're just another keep-fit idiot. Let him catch you, think he's being followed, change his routine, that means you're out of a job, okay? Okay? Get it? I don't have to spell out what will happen if there's a major fuck-up, do I?' Silence. 'Do I?'

There's an ambiguous grunt on the line.

'I will kill you. That's a promise. Okay? Don't go back to the Fleece, don't lurk round his house. You're just another jogger on the jolly old Common, get me? So, I want to know what route, which bench, and what time. I want details, and good ones, or no little party on Sunday... I've got a rather nicer job for you, too, if you're a good boy.'

Lion is exhausting. Soon, I shall be rid of him, the dur-brained little twerp.

13

'Come on, Beautiful!' Angel tucked his arm through Drex's, and tried to dance him through the tiny flat to his armchair.

Drex sighed and allowed himself to be led. He was happier. His damage-limitation tactics with Lockhart – sort of a double whammy with the Snake writhing in what must have been agony, or at least a humiliating slither – had worked, and, while the Whisper's disappearance remained a mystery, it had now been more than two weeks. The more time that elapsed, the less threatened he felt.

'Here we are. What you said you wanted…' said Angel, pirouetting. He slotted a tiny blue chip into Drex's lap-top, and placed the lap-top onto Drex's knees. 'Watch.'

Drex looked up at Angel's face. 'My, my. We *are* trying to earn our keep.'

'Look at the screen, you soft pillock. Look!'

Drex looked. 'Christ…' The face of the man in the foreground was as visible (as was as a great deal of the rest of his person) as it was also entirely recognizable. Drex shivered involuntarily. He had dreamed of something like this for many years. 'Angel! Christ's teeth! That's Paluticowski's club! You didn't go there yourself?'

'Brr. You must be joking! Friend,' said Angel modestly. 'Friend of a friend. For a consideration-like.'

'Not too big or too persistent, I hope. No, I don't want to know, as long as there aren't too many hostages.'

'To fortune… No. Promise. Owed me one. The friend.'

'Good. I want a glass of whiskey. And all right, Angel-mine, you and Mitzi can consider yourselves re-instated.'

'But who is he? Apart from a punter?'

'Little Miss Inquisitive. He's just a man…' Drex closed his eyes for a moment. 'A man with a great deal to lose…'

14

There's always a hostage to fortune. And fame. No hiding place. If there were, face it, bub, you'd be a has-been. So now you're always under the scrutiny of the public eye – you know, the Public, the ones whose interest you have to have or you wouldn't be a celeb, would you? The Public may behave as shamefully and as nastily as you do, but the Public isn't news, and you are. It's envy, partly. Human nature. Fickle. You're rich and beautiful and that's why they *lerve* you...and they aren't, and that's why they hate you too. So they'll just eat it when you fuck up, when you fuck someone you shouldn't, or look as if you're about to. When you get tired and emotional as a newt on a long-haul from the USA, when you fall over and show your knickers in a night club, or reel out of it and puke in the taxi, when you punch a photographer in his avid, ugly little mush – well, this is a red-letter day. So is the morning when, supported on the arm of your agent (who'll naturally say 'no comment' on your behalf to the flashing press) as you check into the Priory because only last week the same little camera-toting tosser snapped you snorting all that naughty white powder in the bogs in a private club and now you have to be seen to be doing something about it... It's their job, the *paparazzi* – all in a day's work to them. They're just waiting for you to screw up and snap you doing it and a fist in the kisser is a small price to pay – and there's the possibility of a double-whammy with a lawsuit for assault into the bargain. There's big money for these shots – and I mean big, bub. Tell you what, that agent of yours probably set them up in return for a bit of the action, know what I mean? You can't have a private nervous breakdown, a private line of coke, a private any-thing, bub, including a private conversation these days. It's the price you pay. It's what you wanted. Now you've got it. Good luck to you...What? You're sea-green incorruptible, squeaky-clean? I don't believe you – but even if you are, there'll be those prepared to make it up, set you up... It's very lonely at the top, as somebody once remarked.

But suppose you're not a celeb, as such? Suppose you're just a bloke we'd pass in the street without a second glance? You're not a famous face, you're just a voice, *ex officio*, an aide, a press-officer, say, someone in a position of trust. In the service, maybe, of Someone Very Important. You – you're news in the front-pag-es sense of the word *only* when you screw up...

What beats me (oh dear, pardon the pun) is why you take such amazing risks. I mean, I can understand the saddo-celeb-for-five-minutes mentality. Up to a point. Fame, notoriety, what's the difference? No press is bad press, in both sens-es. You lose one lot of fans, the moralistic, hypocritical lot, but you gain a whole lot of others, the ones that wish they were snorting lines in the Groucho rather than just getting hammered on their hard-earned in the boozer on a Saturday night. But if you've actually got a vested interest in being at least seen to be clean – well, why throw it all away? Why kid yourself that you're immune? Is it hubris? An extravagant belief in your guardian angel? Or do you simply imagine that you're sort of invisible?

'Is there anything wrong, Dom?' Gillian Mann looked at her husband with concern. *The Times* had fallen to the floor, and he was staring rigidly at a printed sheet of A4 clutched in his hand. His face had blanched nearly as white as the paper. 'Darling? Dominic, whatever is it?'

'Nothing. Nothing, dear...' His chair screeked on the terracotta tiles as he rose abruptly from the breakfast table, gathering up whatever it was and shoving it back into a brown envelope. 'I have to call the office. Something rather, er – annoying has come up. I'll be in the study. Don't let anyone disturb me for a bit, will you? Thanks...' His mouth contorted into a bleak little smile.

'All right, dear. I hope it's nothing serious. But you haven't forgotten that Toby is coming home today, have you? Or that we've got the Johnsons for lunch? Speaking of which, I'd better do something with that lamb...' But she was talking to herself.

In his study, Dominic Mann re-read the single page of typescript over and over again. Gazed in horrified disbelief at the accompanying photograph and hastily put it back in the envelope in disgust. Scrutinized the envelope for any kind of distinguishing mark – Mount Pleasant. Of course. Told one nothing except the sender had posted it in London...or not even that, necessarily. He put his head in his hands, rubbed his greying temples, re-opened the envelope and pulled out the contents, as if studying it further could somehow make it less threatening than it obviously was.

'Oh dear, Mr Mann. Or perhaps I can anticipate and call you Sir Dominic, or may I call you 'Neanderthal'? Those girls are so naughty, and doubtless worth the sore botty, you bad boy you. Bliss, ain't it? But what would Sir say to all this? Embarrassing! I don't expect He is one of Kinseyder's regular readers, but I bet his wife is! Call me.'

Kinseyder...that society-scandal merchant on the *Mercury*. That didn't mean anything. The writer could have put anyone: that Dempster person (except he was dead) or that other one, whatshisname, Ephraim Hardcastle, and he was a pseudonym... But the meaning was clear. This was going to go to the papers unless he took steps. But what? *Who*? There was nothing, no clue that he could see... 'Neanderthal', 'Neanderthal Mann', his stupid school nickname, and later the soubriquet that *Private Eye* had given him a few years before when, from out of the Environment Office, he had come out firmly behind the farmers in the matter of pesticides – a reference to a paranoid American book by some hysterical woman about DDT, apparently – trust the *Eye* to indulge in over-educated obscurantist stuff like that, and the reference had been lost on most people, doubtless, even though the nickname had stuck... Only mildly embarrassing, and all in a day's work for a senior politician. And he was very 'green' these days. Had to be. Now he felt green to his gills...

Mustn't panic. Call someone. His lawyer? John Johnson – and hadn't Gill said John and Jean were coming to lunch? Thank God! But could he bear to be candid about this, even with John? *Especially* with John? Oh God, oh *God*... His head whirled, visions of his royal employer's dismay, visions of his children, of Toby, about to spend his Easter vac with them. And Gillian! How could he ever explain to a living soul? Suddenly, he felt horribly, frighteningly alone. He mustn't lose his head. He must try to think *straight*...

Someone wanted to damage him very badly, that was obvious. Naturally he had made enemies over the years. That Fletcher woman, or Cartwright – yes, Cartwright must still be feeling pretty hostile. But even so, it was hard to imagine that even he... Or perhaps they only wanted *money*. That was right, nothing personal necessarily. It was blackmail, pure and simple. And blackmail is a crime, punishable by a heavy term of imprisonment. Whoever it was shouldn't get a penny, and deserved to be punished very hard indeed! But not everyone had the courage to say 'publish and be damned'... and, dear God, certainly not he, when he thought of *what* would be published, and who would see it...sickening images again... *think!* Blackmailers want to be paid, and he must find out what they wanted, pay them... Visions of anonymous brief-cases, left-luggage offices in stations...fiction? Where the hell did one go? And it was doubtless collusion under the law (perhaps he could pose the problem to John as a kind of hypothesis?) But, yes, that might be the answer! Damage-limitation. This number...

His hand went out to the telephone, hovered, hesitated. Blackmailers want to be paid over and over and over, didn't they? And he was comfortable, but he wasn't a rich man, nothing to spare since that Equitable Life policy had gone down the pan. Just this family house, and the cottage in the Lakes, Gillian's jewellery...and his job, his job. Oh God!

If only he could find out *who*, he might at least know the type of thing he was dealing with. He forced himself to take out the revolting photograph again. *Someone* had taken the wretched thing. He had always been so careful! The girls were like old friends...one of them must have been bribed... He must force himself to remember, to *think*. Someone in that room, that day (little club, South Ken, last week, first time since Christmas). He must force himself to *look*. Himself, naked from the waist down with his shirt-tails ludicrously hitched up over his thin, flabby buttocks, and in an obvious and grotesque state of arousal, bent over a gilt empire-style chair, and with his face turned towards the camera, all too recognizable despite the grimace of pain and ecstasy... He felt sick. A sort of blur, like a comet-tail, in the background behind him, which, he realised, must be the whip, caught in action, swishing through the air, and Mollie (or was it Maisie? They all had names like that, Maisie, Milly, Mandy – all doubtless aliases) her arm raised and her breast bare above the red, mock eighteenth-century stays, Lady Hamilton as dominatrix...

He *had* to try to remember who else had been there! Perhaps it was just a camera hidden in the room, automatic, and someone had – had... His head whirled again, and he grabbed the waste-paper basket only just in time to catch his recent breakfast.

15

Well done, Jerry! Or should we anticipate and say Sir? It's not often that Kinseyder gives his unalloyed approval, but join him now in three hearty cheers for Sort It!. *Sowerby Stanton, in the crux of three counties in East Anglia, is a rotten borough if there ever was one. Its vile little council has been forced to back down over farmer Leslie Pacey's planning permission after a splendid and splenetic exposure on TV's best representative of the rights of the little guy. All poor Mr Pacey did was apply to build a bigger piggery on his own land, and when he ran out of patience he was threatened with court action for building without permission, remember? But his persecutor in chief, Cllr. John Charmers, is none other Chairman of the Will-Co chain – which had put in a bid for Mr Pacey's land to build an out-of-town shopping mall. Now, thanks to* Sort It!, *this outrageous example of local corruption has been named and shamed...*

'And that's all we have time for this week, indeed until after Easter, so wishing you goodnight are tonight's team, Natalie North...' (Close up Natalie: 'Goodnight.' Little dip of helmet-like brunette bob, bright lipstick smile.) And Gavin Macavity... (Close up Gavin: 'Goodnight!' Cheery little grin.) And of course the rest of the *Sort It!* crew, all the ones you don't get to see, beavering away out of sight. So from me, and from all of us, have great holidays, take care, and remember – if it doesn't do what it says on the tin, get in touch with *Sort It!* Watch the credits for details of our address and website. If *you* have a problem you'd like *us* to look into, Fairbrother is watching out for You! Goodnight!'

Brief, silent pause for cut to credits and signature tune, which of course the team could not see or hear. 'Still seems weird saying goodnight in the middle of the morning,' Gavin Macavity, the new recruit, hissed to Natalie North, the stalwart. 'Sshhh...You'll get used to it,' she replied, *sotto voce*. 'Big' Ben Young glared at both of them, as he silently counted down with his hand.

'And cut!' Ben Young took off his headphones with a sigh. 'Great, everyone. Thank you. Run away and play until Monday. Team meeting, 9am, Lynne's office. See you there. And you – yes, Gavin! *Mister* Macavity!'

'Yes, sir!'

'Gawdelpus! Drop the 'sir', for gawdsakes. Stick to the agreed script and shut up until I call 'cut', got it?'

'Sorry, sir. Mr Young...Ben...I am trying to get it right...' Gavin Macavity seemed to Ben Young so young he could hardly have left school, let alone finished a law degree. Lynne Berry's choice, not his. Ours not to reason why or who, although for how long and how far and wide she had searched before lighting on this particular specimen – all Essex vowels and spunky manner on camera, all puppy-anxious-to-please off it – was anybody's guess. There must have been other young, dynamic, telegenic experts in property law. If he weren't so young, Ben Young thought, you'd suspect this Gavin of being the worst kind of ambitious little toady. As it was, Young, who was today feeling particularly old, read simply 'little twerp'. 'Yeah,' he said to Gavin with a sigh. 'Sure you are. Buy Natalie lunch and get her to tell you the recording ropes...' He saw Natalie North, a trendily turned-out woman in her late forties, roll her eyes to heaven behind Gavin's back. She gave him a pleading look, which he ignored. They were all the same, these roped-in research professionals. Bloody experts! Boffins, they'd have been called once. Hard not to think of them as outsiders, however clever they were, and (you must admit) however much there wouldn't be a programme without them. The North female, for instance, been with them through three series, almost part of the family, yet you could almost see her thinking, 'gawdelpus these TV folk' with that half-hidden scorn of hers, as if having a life, a profession on the 'outside' somehow gave her an automatic superiority, although he doubted if La North, the Citizen's Advice expert, any longer did her voluntary stint in Basingstoke or wherever it was now that she was a 'face' on prime-time. He shook himself. He had other things on his mind.

'Jerry? Have you got a mo?' Jerry Fairbrother was scooping up papers, and placing them in the waiting arms of Suzy Merritt, his PA, who was hovering at his elbow and appeared to be trying to have an urgent conversation. Whatever it was must wait. If it was what Ben thought it was, the longer it waited the better. 'Jerry?'

'Sure, Ben. Five minutes at the Fleece? Just bung this stuff back in my office, Suzy, thank you. Yes, love, soon. Of course I'll call you...' Fairbrother was aware that Ben was witnessing Suzy's hurt, angry eyes, and his own embarrassed ones. He turned to Ben resolutely as Suzy stalked out of the studio. 'Come on, old boy,' he said, patting his jacket pockets. 'Pub. Now.'

'Don't you want to go to make-up? Get the goo off your face?'

'Nah. What's the point? They've seen just about everything at the Fleece.'

'So that's about the sum of it, Jerry. I wanted you to be the first to know...'

'I'm stunned, Ben. Nothing will be the *same*... Christ...' They were tucked into one of the Blue Fleece's many convenient dark alcoves. It was a favourite haunt of the Studios because one could hide. And if there was a fear that the hyenas were waiting outside, the men's room had a convenient fire-escape route into one of the alleys off Aherne Street. The Fleece did unpretentious lunches and real beer and didn't charge the earth: a miracle of comfort, in short. The only problem was that one was always running into one's colleagues. On the other hand, one's colleagues also did not necessarily wish to be seen, and the alcoves were frequently, between the hours of noon and two, little islands of carefully preserved privacy.

The two men were running out of beer, and Jerry automatically rose to get the next round.

'Sit down. My turn,' Ben said, getting to his feet.

'Are you sure that – um?'

'I told *you*,' Ben said, his huge frame looming over the table with the old-fashioned mugs in his hands, his grizzled beard and thick spectacles suddenly out of proportion, 'because I thought you'd be the one person who wouldn't treat me like a ninety-year-old meringue. I still think so. So I'm ignoring you, and when you're ignored by me, you're being ignored by a real ignoramus, got it? Same again? Bacon sarnie?'

Jerry watched Ben's broad back as he ordered the beers at the hatch. Dear old Big Ben. The programme wouldn't be the same. The Studio wouldn't be the same. He brushed away all traces of emotion before Ben returned.

'I'm not finished yet, Jerry, so you can send that jacket to the cleaners...' There was a smear of make-up on Jerry's fawn linen sleeve.

'Thought you were supposed to be sight impaired, you old bugger!' They drank. 'Does Lynne know?'

'We're thrashing the details out this afternoon. No unpalatable shocks. She'll deal with the Old Greys. It's her job.'

'What about Horst?'

'Be holding my hand through the whole thing, he says, bless him. Loyal boy, Horst. I've been a lucky old queen, Jerry. Job I love but not so I'm married to it, and a nice boy to cuddle up to. D'you know it's been fourteen years now? Settled sort of life, which is all I ever asked. Good friends, nice colleagues, holidays in a Tuscan cottage. I'll be spending a lot of time at Il Molino in future. Reading. Growing tomatoes and olives, like a retired Mafia don. Watching episodes of 'Taxi' on Sky... Actually I'm almost looking forward to it, and only scared slightly shitless. Mostly of having to give up this stuff...' Ben gave one of his outsize guffaws, drained more beer through the laugh, and gave way to a fit of coughing. Jerry looked on, anxiously. 'Look,' said Ben recovering, 'they do these triple by-pass things everyday. I'll be in good hands, and I'll survive – if the rest of the arteries don't give out. Now, don't stare at me like that, gawdelpus! But, look, Jerry, there is something you can do to help.'

'Anything, Ben. Hell, of course.'

'I'll have to tell Lynne the works, obviously, but as far as everyone else is concerned, I'm taking a break on health grounds but no details, right, and nothing about retirement. I really can't do with a party right now. Keep it down, Jerry, that's all I ask, at least until I come out of the ether...'

The dark interior was suddenly lit by a gash of light as the door opened. 'Looks as if your advice was taken...' Natalie North entered with a sheepish-looking Gavin Macavity close on her heels.

'So what do you think of Lynne's latest experiment?' Natalie was steering Gavin into a distant booth, and they were lost from sight.

'Young *Mister* Macavity? Mmm. Bit of a token, typical Lynne. Camera-friendly. Looks and sounds like an Essex snooker star...lots of popular appeal, therefore. And I rather like him. Clever kid, engaging. Genuine. Seems to really know his stuff, and I liked his approach on that Sowerby Stanton story. Hasn't quite got the hang of the studio protocol yet, but what the hell? You?'

'Hmmm. Bit of a gawdelpus with all his sirs, and forelock tugging. But yeah, I was impressed by how he handled Sowerby Stanton. Natalie thinks he's an infant, which is just as well, maybe, when you think of how superior that prat Jonathan Danes was with her, just because she's CAB, as if it was too low to count. I think the balance works better with this younger guy. Now she can do the credit card debts and wills stuff now without thinking she's being scrutinized by the High Court. Important to keep Natalie sweet. Let her think she's queen bee. That about sum up your judgement, colleague?'

'In one, colleague...' Jerry, was beginning to feel sentimental again. He said, 'Say, how do you think they're getting on? Perhaps she should seduce him, you know, rite of passage. Okay, joke.'

'Gawdelpus, Jerry!' They both laughed, but this had given Ben the cue he had wanted. 'You know, Jerry, we've been friends since the earliest days of the *Big Quiz*, let alone this shenanegans...it's been a long time. What, ten years? More? Anyway, I've always been impressed by how basically sussed you are on this job. You're a pro to your toes, Jerry. At least you are on the set. Look, as I'm very shortly going to be packing my spotty hanky and taking to the highway, I just wanted to say something to you, personally. I mightn't get this opportunity again, so trust an old man and hear me out, okay?'

'Oh, shit. Pi-jaw time, I knew it. Go on, Ben. Bet I know what you're going to say. Say on.'

'You know what I'm going to say?'

'Yep. In a word, Suzy. Right?'

'So what are you going to do, Jerry? This could get ugly.'

'Suzy Merritt, delight of my stolen nights. Well, afternoons. All right, Ben, I know, I know. I've been a bit of a fool.'

'Bit of?'

'Big fool. And a cad. I know it, Ben. She's in love with me. And she's gorgeous. Oh, God. I'm not exactly proud of myself, you know. I've been an idiot.'

'Gawdelpus. You've been a stunned mullet. I thought you'd learnt your lesson after Lindi...and that Martha dame. Look, Jerry. It's far too late now, but you were crazy to start this. That girl could get pissed off. You know my dictum: never fool around with colleagues, especially junior ones. That was always your weakness, Jerry. And this one's not mistress material, colleague. She's ambitious. In my opinion, for what it's worth, she could turn dangerous, start making demands. Don't you see? And it's not really fair on the poor kid, either, is it? She's got a job to do, and she can hardly do it well if she's nursing a resentful broken heart in the next-door office. Well, can she?'

'I know, I *know*... God, you're making me feel despicable as sin, Ben. I have been trying to bring things to - well, I've tried to cool things off a bit. It's difficult. We've - we've fallen into a bit of a routine, and I have to keep inventing things... Oh, hell, Ben, I'm up shit creek, if you must know. Louise is rolling up her sleeves for the big fight. This is serious. She'll take me for everything if she can. Mostly I'm just scared as hell about the kids. And if she finds out about Suzy, gets evidence, it will be just more ammo for the hearing. On the other hand, I can't have Suzy throwing wobblies at the moment. And I can't bear to hurt her, either. But she's not vindictive, Ben - in fact, she's an absolute sweetie. And I've got to make sure this doesn't damage her career. Everything's all a bit - well -'

Ben Young sighed. 'Oh Jerry. Are you *never* going to learn to keep your dick behind a zipper? Bloody hell, mate. Gawdelpus! Don't you ever consider *your* career? Nobody's immune, you know, and you've taken some fantastic risks. And what about this K?'

'Oh sod the K! That's just embarrassing.'

[79]

'See you turning it down, telling Lilibet where to put it.'

'Well, no, all right. But there's worse, Ben. Don't laugh. I think I'm being black-mailed.'

'What? You *think* you're being blackmailed? Don't you *know*? Gawdelpus!' Ben spluttered.

'Well, it's weird, okay? A little while ago, I got this mysterious package. A DVD, complete with anonymous note, threatening YouTube, the scandal columns, all that. I thought it must be something to do with Suzy. I was shitting bricks.'

'I bet. And?'

'It wasn't. It was a – well, a soft porn movie I and a couple of uni mates made in Rome. I'd forgotten all about it.'

'What? Gawdelpus, Jerry, but you're priceless...' More gales of laughter, more spluttering.

Jerry slurped beer. 'It was the late seventies, a bunch of us hitching round Europe. We were completely skint, starving, and there was that film studios in Rome, remember? *Cinè Città*. Bad costume dramas, cod Taylor and Burton stuff. Dubbed into Dutch, German... and they were always wanting extras, and we jumped at it. We could eat at least, but the pay was as lousy as the beds, never mind all that hanging around four hours in togas and make-up. And then some dodgy tout made us this offer. We knew it was decidedly unsavoury, I suppose, but we thought, what the hell.'

'Like you do.'

'Like you do. Anyway, suddenly here it was, on my doorstep, literally, with this cryptic note. The thing is, the movie as such isn't worth anything to any blackmailer. I'm hardly recognizable – thirty-odd years younger and thinner, for a start, and the picture-quality's crap. If it hadn't been for the fact that I'm pretty jumpy these days about Louise, I'd have just laughed it off. I mean, it was a joke. Had to be. It wouldn't have mattered if it had been screened prime-time. I mean, who cares? I suspected one of the uni mates having a go. Just a leg-pull, you know? So I rang this number.'

'And?'

'And nothing. It was a mobile, with just an answering service. I didn't record a message, naturally. But then, just out of curiosity, I tried to track down this mate I suspected. God!'

'Yes, and? Go on, for gawdsakes! Honest to God, Jerry, your private life's better than a soap. Sorry, shouldn't laugh.'

'Well, it's not so funny really. I found him, the uni mate. He was the biggest dealer of class Bs on the campus in those days. We called him Billy Whizz for ob-vious reasons. Anyway, after a lot of boring white-pages stuff, I got hold of him. His wife answered. Turns out he's the headmaster of a top-of-the-league-tables girls' comprehensive in North London. He couldn't believe it was me. We met for a drink. It was quite embarrassing. He's got some sort of selective amnesia about his earlier activities, including that Rome escapade. In fact, anyone would have thought I was trying to blackmail *him*.'

'So it wasn't him, then?'

'No *way*.'

'So? It could still be a prank. It really doesn't sound too serious, Jerry.'

'No…not so far, but wait. So, I don't know who sent this disc, right? And what with one thing and another, I just put it to the back of my mind. Then, the other morning out of the blue I got another.'

'Another disc?'

'No – photos, prints. And another note, but phrased exactly the same way, threatening the internet and the press, that Kinseyder column in the *Mercury* specifically – and left on the mat like before, not in the mail. Only this time, like I said, there's this handful of photos. Of me leaving Suzy's flat. We'd been using the Barbican place and then I thought we'd better be more anonymous, and she suggested her place while her flatmate's out…' Jerry gulped more beer. 'Yeah. I know it's sordid, but better than a hotel for obvious reasons. But in the photos I'm completely recognizable, and so's Suzy's front door, her street… And there's the same number. I rang it, and again just the answering service. It's – well, it's a bit – I'm getting a bit unnerved, Ben.'

'I should think so, too. Have you told her? Suzy?'

'Christ, no! I don't know what to do now. There's no demand, no anything. In a way, that's the most disturbing thing. What should I do, Ben? What would you do? I can't even pay them unless I know what they want, who they are.'

'You don't want to start paying, that's for sure. Shit, I don't know, Jerry. I agree it sounds a bit serious.'

'If I only knew what they wanted. This could be dynamite to Louise's legal team. She wants to ruin me. But mostly, she just wants to take the kids to the States, to her parents on Long Island. Oh, Christ, Ben! This is all getting completely out of hand. The thought of losing the kids! Sorry Ben. You've enough on your own plate. Honestly it's, well, a bit of a relief to get this off my chest.'

'You've really no idea, apart from this squeaky-clean headmaster?'

'Well, obviously I wondered about Louise. But it's a bit fantastic. The blackmail bit. I'm yours truly mystified.'

'You have, well, thrown caution to the wind a bit, Jerry, to put it mildly. You're not going to like this, old son, but I advise the good old CID. It's what *Sort It!* would advise. Blackmail is illegal, you know.'

'I know – but is it technically blackmail if they're not asking for anything? And if I report it, they'll publish at once if I do that, won't they? Whoever it is. And the police probably won't take it all that seriously, not without some proof of where it's come from. The first thing the police'll ask is, have you any enemies, Mr Fairbrother?'

'Well – have you?'

'Apart from Louise's lawyers? No. I mean, well, *no*. I've mostly been decent, Ben. Professionally, anyway. You know that.'

'Sure. You have. But people get jealous, resentful. Particularly of apparently effortless success. I'd have a bit of a think if I were you. And I still think going to the police is the answer, Jerry. If these crapsters are serious, I should think they'll be back in touch to define terms quite soon – I mean, there's got to be something in it for them, hasn't there? When they do, go straight to the Met. They can trace that number for a start. Honestly, it's the best way. Trust Uncle Ben. And in the meantime, I'd have a good think about who might want to do you down, bear you a grudge. I don't want to sound over-dramatic, Jerry, but if it's not Louise, it might be someone you've forgotten you ever offended.'

Jerry stared into the remains of his beer. 'The only person I ever really offended is dead,' he said.

'Handy. Well, old girlfriends, then. Ever think about them? Perhaps whoever it is just wants to get you rattled.'

'They've succeeded. It's the not knowing. Jesus Christ!'

'And break it off with the Merritt girl. Like at *once*.'

'I have to. But how? I work with her.'

'I might be able to pull a string or two. I'll promise nothing, but I'll do what I can, colleague. Gawdelpus, Jerry.'

'I don't deserve it, Ben. Thanks a million. I really mean that.'

'Forget it. I'm actually thinking of the programme. And her, poor little idiot. In the meantime, I suggest you take a trip down memory lane.'

Part II: Memory Lane

16: Last Year

'Where the fuck did you find *that*?' Drex Bello was in a sour humour. His visits to Fulham sometimes depressed him.

Angel gazed up innocently. 'Just been having a bit of a clear out. That's you, innit? Get the doublet and hose. And the cod-piece! Suits you.'

'I didn't even know that thing still existed. Bloody hell! Christ, Angel, no more surprises today, okay? I'm off to bed. I'm shagged out.'

'But what is it?'

'Just a silly vid of a uni production we did. A play. *Tanti anni fà*...like before you were born. Let it rest, will you? Or at least let me.'

'Shakespeare? You were acting in Shakespeare? *Hamlet* and stuff?'

'Close. Guy who wrote this was a sort of colleague of his. There are academic arguments about the authorship. It's called *The Revenger's Tragedy.*'

'Coo – right up your street, then. 'Cept the tragedy bit, pr'aps.'

'You never know, Angel. What's the sound production like?' He turned it up. *'Great men were gods if beggars could not kill 'em...'* 'Not bad. He's got a point there. Watch it properly. You might get some education. It's a good play.'

'Whatever you say, Beautiful, but it's all over my head. I don't even know if it's sad or happy. Can't understand a friggin' word they're saying. Coo, fancy you having to learn all them lines! It's like speaking foreign. Worth it for the costumes, though.'

'Huh.'

'Why didn't you get to be an actor?'

'Allergic to limelight. Angel. I'm half asleep. Keep the vol down, okay?'

'Course. Ay-oop! That's him, innit? That's Fairbrother! Him in the golden robes?'

'The very same, Angel. He plays the evil Duke's son.'

'Bloody Norah! He was really quite a dish before he put on weight, weren't he? Is that when you two fell out? At uni?'

'We didn't...oh, for fuck's sakes, Angel, give it a rest! I'll have a whiskey...' He was staring at the grainy picture despite himself.

'Here you go. So what happened?'

'Happened?'

'Yeah! Bet you were shaggin' him, right, and he threw you over, and...'

'Why, Angel, does everything have to come down to shagging with you? No, for what it's worth, I was not shagging him. Perish the thought. Fairbrother is probably the most dedicated heterosexual I ever met.'

'But you knew him really well, didn't you, and you hate him. So what did he do?'

'Let it rest, Angel. Look! Vindice, that's me – he's about to dupe the Duke with a poisoned skull. He's going to make him kiss it, and the Duke will fall down dead.'

[83]

'I still don't understand a bleedin' word. And I like horror films as a rule. Don't just nod off, watch it! Ay-oop!' He prodded Drex's knee. 'Look, here she is again! There's this really strange chick in it – here, this little blonde babe. S'funny. She looks really familiar.'

'Yeah?'

'So who's she? Did she get famous, too?'

'I'll tell you all about her someday, Angel...' Drex yawned. 'I've got to sleep.'

'Did you shag her?'

'You disgust me, Angel, as I've said many times.'

'Well, did you? I like your pussy stories.'

'They'll keep. And yes, I did. Not that it's any of your business.'

'Oh, I get it! You were shaggin' her, and then Fairbrother stole her off you, right?'

'No. And yes.'

'So *that's* why you want his guts. Don't blame you, neither. If I was into girls, she'd be, well, I mean, daggers out!'

'*Angel...*'

'S'funny,' Angel's eyes were rapt to the screen. 'I keep thinking I know her from somewhere. She must have been in summat else. What's her name?'

'Marie. Her name was Mary, but she called herself Marie.'

17: Christmas 1977

Allergic to limelight. Yet still they bang on my door, try to expose me…

'C'mon, Bello, you lazy git,' someone cried, accompanied by more banging and a great deal of laughter. 'Yeah, c'mon, Drex. We're going to be late!' 'Is he in there?' I heard a female voice inquire. 'Perhaps he's gone out. Perhaps he's down at the Snakepit already…' 'No, he's in,' said another voice, authoritatively. 'You can smell the brimstone…' More bangs and thumps. I nearly ignored them all – they'd get fed up and go eventually. 'Please, Drex,' said another female voice. Marie's. 'You promised…' That was when I decided to open the door.

'What?' I said, glowering into the harsh neon-lit corridor.

They were all there, a gang of about seven of them, but they shut up in mid-giggle, their childish rosy faces falling. I sometimes have that effect on people. It's nearly always comic, and I nearly laughed out loud, but I was actually rather angry. Some of them had those daft reindeer head-bands on, joke antlers with winking lights. 'Oh Jesus Christ,' I said, sighing. 'C'mon, man,' Jerry said, determined. 'Snakepit time…' 'Look! He's yawning! He's been asleep!' yelped someone else. 'Lazy *arse!*'

'What?' I said again, still glowering. 'I'm in no mood to come to some stupid party…' But it was all beginning to come back to me.

'Come *on!* It's the Revels! You've written most of it, you prat, you've *got* to be there,' said Jerry.

With drama students, it's never *just* a party. I wasn't a drama queen, merely a sort of hangbye collaborator, a humble literature student and co-editor of *Howl,* a fairly bad satirical paper that Jerry and I had launched in our second year, but this is what you got, apparently, for lending some creative input to things like Christmas 'revels'. 'Shit, man, are you ill, or something?' Everyone, including Jerry, said 'Shit, man' in those days. I told him I was fine, that I just wanted to be left alone.

'But you wrote it,' pleaded the tiny blonde girl in a strong Yorkshire accent. '*Please…*' She wore gauze fairy wings.

I said heavily, 'I didn't write it. I just tidied Jerry up. He knows that…' I glared at Jerry. 'Look, just follow the script and do it without me…' I had, genuinely, forgotten all about it until now. *The Fractured Shakespeare Panto:* a 'light-hearted glimpse of the Bard on speed' or somesuch idiocy. I'd got myself roped into this piece of lunacy at the prompting of Jerry about a month ago, and probably at Marie's as well. I had no interest in the performance: my task was over. I said so.

'We've learned the script,' Jerry said, offended. 'Besides, you're *on.* You're doing Richard Four, remember?'

'Well, put the Whizz in a wheel chair, or stuff a cushion up the back of his shirt or something. He can do it. Can't you, Billy?'

'Well, er…'

'No he can't. Billy's being Lear's Fool,' Jerry said. 'Aren't you, Billy?'

'Sure...' The Whizz grinned idiotically. He had on a red nose, and a Harpo Marx wig, which on a second glance looked so much like his own hair it probably was. 'C'mon Drex,' said the Whizz, coaxingly.

'Yeah, c'mon, Drex,' chorused the others. 'Work can wait, man. It's Christ-maaa-ss! Fuck the essay!' said an idiot called Dave, who never wrote any, but who could do seriously competent Fats Waller impressions on the piano. (Later, after scraping a third in Biological Sciences, he joined a band called Feet First, which even had a minor hit in 1979 before it disappeared from view.) 'It'll be a real blast, Drex,' drawled a tall girl called Chloe, who wanted to be a BBC announcer. 'Speaking of which,' put in Billy the Whizz, whose future should have been pre-dictable, 'have a toke on this. Get you in the mood. It's best Red Leb – and only a fiver a half ounce to you, this week's special offer, no kidding, no strings, no –'

'No *thank* you. And I wasn't working, since you ask. I was asleep. I had turned my brain off. You cretins have just woken me. Thank you. Thank you all very much.'

'Told you he was a sort of android,' said Dave. 'Oh, do come on, Drex. Be a sport,' Jerry said. ''Tis the season of goodwill!' A dismayed chorus of protests.

'Then merry Christmas, goodnight, and kindly fuck off...' I went to close the door, but someone's foot was in the way. 'Please,' I said testily.

'Whoa! Humbug!' said someone, and the inevitable chorus joined in. 'Scrooge! Ebenezer! Want and Ignorance!' and, irrationally, 'Let them eat cake!' which was probably Dave, who in addition to never writing anything, never read anything serious either, only Phillip K. Dick. 'Will we have to pull the Richard Four thing?' asked someone anxiously. 'Oh, that's not fair,' wailed Chloe. 'And the *Faculty's* going to be there. Everybody, both Petes and even old Prof Mac's said he's com-ing!' 'All the more reason,' I said, deliberately unreasonable. 'He's your head of sector, not mine. Wish him a merry humbug...' I gave the door a particularly vicious shove, and the foot in it moved hastily. Then the girl in fairy wings said, to me, and not for the benefit of the others, 'Let *me* in, Drex. Please...' Marie was tiny, a little scrap of a girl, dressed for the party like a child, gauze skirt sticking out from shapely little thighs in white tights. She was suddenly inside my poky room like Tinkerbell, like a magic vapour. Despite myself, I thought she was the loveliest thing I had ever seen. Again. Marie had this effect on people. At least she did on me, and I told myself then, as I had been telling myself for the past several weeks since Marie and I had been having what we called then 'a bit of a scene', that this was a bad thing. For one thing, Marie was supposed to be Jerry's girl, or at least one of his many girls. Far worse, she could make me feel almost human. Marie could make me *feel*. I found it disturbing. Disturbing and irresistible, es-pecially when she was this near, this close...

'You lot go on,' Marie said to the others firmly. 'I want to talk to Drex. I'll join you down there...' 'Whoooa!' yelled the cretinous Dave. 'Here we go a wassailing among the leaves so green,' someone sang in a pleasant tenor, probably Jerry, and someone else cried out 'That's a new word for it! Woossalling, eh?' And with raucous oaths and ribald insults, they careened off on their merry way, clattering and shrieking down the neon lit corridor, leaving Marie in my still darkened room, and me aware that it smelled of smoke and my socks and my lone take-out burger, the remains of which I'd just shoved in the waste-paper bin, and not taken the crockery to the communal kitchen as one was supposed to do.

She didn't say anything, she just wrapped her arms round me and kissed me. Her long silvery fair hair had glitter in it, which sparkled in the orange light coming in through the thin window blind. I realised you could buy glitter sprays, knew the secrets of the dressing rooms…but the magic was there just the same. 'We don't have to go, if you don't feel like it,' she said after a rather delicious inter-val. I didn't feel like it – I never did feel like parties. Now, I just felt randy. I also felt guilty. There she was, all dressed up, and I remembered she had some sort of turn or other, hence the get-up. Damn it, I'd written the piece for her. 'Don't crush me wings,' she said softly, her Yorkshire vowels doing as much to my groin as the feel of the ribs under my hands beneath the silver dress, the tiny breasts jutting softly into my shirt. 'C'mon,' I said, making my mind up suddenly, and thrusting her from me. 'Let's go. Party time…' 'Oh, Drex,' was all she said, but her eyes – very blue, and tonight huge with stagey mascara, luminous in the semi-dark – said it all. I remember thinking, 'Jesus.'

That was the trouble with Marie. She made me – let's be precise about this – think of someone other than myself. Have you ever done this? I mean actually put aside your own immediate desires, compunctions, passions, paranoia and all that, for the sake of the pleasure of seeing someone's face light up? No, my friend, I do not mean one of those ghastly, dutiful sacrifices, which leave one feeling at best, well, dutiful. Neither do I mean mere lust, or the slavish service to whoredom. I really do mean *pleasure* – the sense that someone's happiness actually means more than one's own gratification; more, that this person's happi-ness *is* one's gratification. It's a question of connection. And if the person is sweet and lovely and feels the same way about you, wants *your* happiness more than her own – my friend, I guess this is Love. Something precious, almost holy. All that stuff that the better Elizabethans wrote, when they weren't merely postur-ing and posing and getting the lines to scan – *they* knew about this. They knew that to love was to serve… I almost had it, that once, that night. And I learned something about myself, as well as about the so-called Silver Poets I had been wrestling with all that last term.

These were the last fragments of my adolescence, my third year in a British university, a place where it was most unlikely I should have fetched up at all, let alone put to good purpose given everything, yet it was there that I found the free-dom to study and work and read, which is what universities are for, or were. It was there that, so improbably, I learned about Love, and Delight. I even learned why God might come into it.

At that moment, skipping (yes, bub, skipping: it's amazing what you can do when the right hand is holding yours, even if you aren't shaped for sportive tricks, as the man said) down the corridor with Marie in her fairy get-up, it was as if I'd been shown a glimpse of heaven. Even the dreaded Snakepit cabaret bash was fun that night, what with the Whizz and Dave on piano doing a sort of Flan-ders and Swann turn as Lear and the Fool, which was witty, even though I say it

[87]

myself… And then my little Marie, in her fairy-costume almost androgynous, singing that Aerial thing, in her sublime Yorkshire ('we're the bee sooks, there sook aye..') and I didn't even have to get changed for Richard Four because I wore black anyhow, and I remember (will I ever forget?) hugging Jerry afterwards, after his Orsino piece with tall Chloe in doublet and hose as Viola, who clutched his hand possessively and passionately kissed him; and Marie, looking on with that extraordinary triangular smile; and she came up and hugged us all, but she had a special hug just for me, and we lifted our glasses to the assembled faculty dons who were just as smashed as we were on mulled wine with cinnamon in it at the very least, and we all said Happy Christmas and I squeezed Marie's hand and knew she would be leaving with me, sleeping with me…

Halcyon days, as they say. There we all were, on the brink, had we known it, of a fantastic success. Jerry and I would get involved with a gang of talented luvvies, invent an amusing fringe series called *Scrape the Barrel* out of which would emerge the famous and cultish *Plug & Socket*. Marie would realise, very briefly, and after a false start or two, her dream of stardom. Chloe would become one of the more well-known high-brow theatre critics, and Dave would play in a professional rock-band, and the Whizz would go straighter than anyone could have imagined… But, my friend, because this is life, because this world is truly a vale of tears, and lived for no apparent purpose except to shout for a bit and then just go phut, phizz – make no mistake, I was about to learn something else, as if I didn't already know it. You probably do: Life is shit. And if you don't know this yet, think of me watching that moment when it hits you.

18: That Fateful Summer 1982

Loud hilarity. Celebrations. A wake, a baptism and a confirmation, as old Jonesy put it, all in one: the death of *Scrape the Barrel*, that wacky, off-beat alternative comedy sketch show he had helped to create; the birth of its various spawns which had taken the Fringe by surprise if not entirely by storm, and the continued life – a second TV series in rehearsal – of its most famous spin-off. It was also his birthday, and he should have been jubilant. His friends and colleagues were all gathered together, drinking champagne cocktails and feasting on canapés and garlic bread and snails in 'Il Bistrot' in Charlotte Street – the venue for many a similar innocent debauch and, incidentally, the birthplace of *Plug & Socket*. He had chosen it again for sentiment's sake. But there was an end-of-term feel, an atmosphere of finality, something vaguely melancholy; and now sentiment threatened to wash over him. A great many toasts had been drunk, and Jerry gazed almost tearfully round the table at the assembled faces, wondered when they would ever be together in this way again. This was the watershed, the moment of leaving childish things behind. He had lost the battle not to feel maudlin. Someone was snapping non-stop with a Polaroid camera.

'Speech!' somebody cried. 'Speech from the birthday boy!'

Jerry stood up, swaying a bit. 'Well, then, now.'

'Oy! Those are my lines!'

'Shut up, Jonesy, you Welsh git. Since when have you been a Scottish thane? As I was saying. Oh, fuck, you say it, Jonesy. I'm hammered…' He sat down promptly, and his brow was mopped by the two young women sitting either side of him.

Gwilym Jones, stocky, dark, impressive – intimations of the serious actor he would become – stood, glass raised. 'Ladles, gentlespoons, pray silence – there ought to be two minutes' worth, but I am an ingrained Welsh pessimist, and anything approaching hush from you lot would be like asking the cat to cook the dinner. I give you first of all, the combined corps and pullulating corpse of *Scrape the Barrel!* It's officially, unequivocally, irrevocably dead, ladies and gentlemen, but it's died a lovely death…'(Cheering, and a chorus of moans.) 'Thank you! Here's to the Sod the Buggers team and bless all who've sailed in them, now we've shown those Scots morons the meaning of *satire*…' (Loud cheers. Much clattering of spoons on glasses.) 'Pray silence! *Silence!* And three hearty cheers – wait! I haven't finished speaking yet, you miserable dogs! – for the launch of *Petticoat Tales*, precocious brainchild of Wickens and Osborn, and showing on a TV near you sometime in October. Sally! Cathy! Stand up and represent your sex, if you'll forgive my prodigal use of the term…' (Cheering and stamping, accompanied by good-humoured obscenties in the feminine vocal register.) 'And now – wait, can't you! Here's to the continued success of *Plug & Socket*, a satire of renowned refinement, grace, mordant wit and the most synonyms for intestinal flatulence in recorded history, of which I have the honour to be part. It's only a small part… shut your rattle, Fairbrother, or I'll never let you hold the soap for me again! A small part, as I say, because I am only a humble actor. The biggest parts – ladies, please! – belong to the combined creative ego – sorry, genius – of the two writers of Puke and Soddit. I give you Drex Bello – he's the quiet sinister one sitting appropriately on my left – and the mouthy git in front of me, our own Jerry Fairbrother who is a venerable twenty-seven years old today, and doesn't look a day over a sort of used thirty-five... Jerry, everybody! Cue spotlight, bucket, sponge...' (Roars, barracking and general pandemonium.)

'Oh Christ! What can I say? Actually, I'm completely plonked... Thank you, Jonesy. Thank you everyone. Since I'm obviously rocketing to stardom, I promise all my next birthdays will be a badly-kept secret. All I can do is say none of this could have happened without the wonderful, tolerant, sunny, generous and utterly indispensable help of all the tireless stage and studio personnel over the last couple of years. As for the monster shrieking egos in front of the spotlights and the cameras, all I can say is the sooner I go solo the better... Seriously, though. I must just say something serious.'

'You really *must* must you, Jerry? Seriously?' (Girl at the table.)

'Yes, I must. Seriously. Everybody thinks that because Jonesy and I are moderately famous faces these days, that *Plug & Socket* is ours alone. Jonesy of course does bugger all except ponce about front of the camera...oh, and he learns a few lines and studio marks as well... Damn it, I *am* going to be serious for a moment... It's axi – axish – axiom – oh shit. They tell me that the viewing public imagines that actors make it up as they go along... that the ad libs are truly lib, not to mention ad.'

(Shouts) 'Get *on* with it!'

'Okay, okay... give a man a chance. As you all know, on Puke and Soddit, I am the credited co-writer, but this is actually a barefaced lie. I'm not 'co' or anything like. I only occasionally supply the odd idea. The real creative brain behind *Plug & Socket* – indeed behind so much of what we've been calling our jobs for the last couple of years or so – is Drex. Without him, there would have been very little Barrel to Scrape, let alone any Plug to put in the Socket. He's modest, he's allergic to limelight, he's a total neurotic, workaholic bastard pain in the arse, and if Plug famously never does the washing up, his inspiration was his creator, whose house is not called Typhoid Mansions for nothing... But, if this man could dance, he'd have turned Miss Piggy into Ginger Rogers. If he could sing, he'd have taught Cathy Berberian that one elusive roulade. Maybe. Um, anyway, he works with me, which is my profound good fortune as well as the bane of my life. Ladies and gentlemen – my colleague, my friend, my black dog. And I owe him almost everything, including a tenner for the essay he let me copy in my third year at uni on Jacobean villains. Mr Drex Bello, everybody! Drex, stand up if you can, there's a sport...Oh, shit!'

Drex, prodded by Marie next to him, stood, and the assembled company actually did fall silent, more or less. Drex sometimes had this effect on people. 'What a load of crap,' he said. 'A load of extravagant, hyperbolic *bullshit* delivered by a total *arsehole*...' If anything, Drex was drunker than Jerry. Marie prodded his leg again. 'Sorry. Very rude. My little friend doesn't like me being very rude, especially to Jerry. Jerry, there's no point in being nice to me, since I'm never going to be famous. Spare the arselicking for the producers. And I'm still waiting for that tenner, you bastard. What? Oh. Okay, Jer. Marie says to say something about your birthday. Birthdays…what are birthdays? In the famous words of Eeyore, here today, gone tomorrow. Jer, tomorrow you'll wake up with a head on you that feels like a rhinoceros has stamped on it, and you'll think, oh, shit, let me die, and I for one will wish you would, you nauseatingly successful git. Ladies, gentlemen, anyone else who has aspirations – I give you Jerry Fairbrother, may his star never go nova.'

'Drex, can I come home with you?' Marie said later.

'Sure. What do you want? One last gaudy night?'

'*Drex…*'

Her little white body, as she sat in his grimy bathtub soaping herself, was still almost like a pubescent child's, the breasts still tiny, the pubic hair a little wisp of blonde fluff. The bones jutted, as if Marie didn't eat. The pink punk hair, darkened with water and sticking up in tufts, looked less comic than pathetic. If he had had it in him to feel protective, she would have moved him so. As it was, he was waiting for the explanation, waiting because he wanted to hear her say it, not because he didn't know perfectly well why she had insisted on coming back to his lair. He perched dangerously on the edge of the tub. He was still fully dressed. It was about five o'clock in the morning, and neither of them was exactly drunk any longer. It had got beyond that. As the light was beginning to filter through the Indian bedspread that served for a curtain in the untidy, damp-smelling, roach-strewn sitting-room, they had shared a generous line of cocaine, and their mood had brightened, hardened, become chattery, and driven away any real closeness between them.

'You know I should have been a dancer,' Marie said, examining the soapy white calf and ankle of a small slender leg. 'Instead of trying to be a comic, I mean. I'm – well, I'm thinking of doing some training. Ballet…' She flexed the pointed, painted toes of a tiny foot.

'Too late, babe. Real dancers have to start when they're about twelve. You're twenty-six. Forget it.'

'I don't mean the *Bolshoi*! Perhaps it doesn't need to be proper ballet…something more modern-like. And singing. I've got a lot of talent. I'm going to spend all I've got on some lessons. But I want to do serious stuff. I've decided to diversify.'

'Diversify? Christ, Marie! Face it, babe. Your real forté is being a pet Yorkshire walk-on in yoof comedy. And they love you, provided you actually turn up.'

'Christ, you're vile! I can do it. I've got talent!'

'Yes, babe, but no discipline. That's why you keep losing opportunites. Opportunity knocks, and you're either out cold or heaving up your last meal over the porcelain pelican.'

'I was fine in Edinburgh! I didn't miss a single show. You're such a total bastard!'

'And you're priceless, Marie, sweetie. You had some nice sketch walk-ons with about three lines, and now we're supposed to applaud because you remembered the time!'

[91]

'Fuck off. I'm going to do it, Drex. I'm going to find a proper role. I'm going to do it. I'm going to be – to be…oh, shit…' She suddenly burst into a fountain of tears. 'I just – just – refuse – to go down the pan,' she sobbed. 'You've been such bastards, you *and* bloody Jerry!' She wiped her streaming eyes on a grubby flannel, smearing thick mascara down her cheeks. 'Bastards! You just ditched me. You wouldn't have me on *Plug & Socket* once you'd got the second series. Jobs for the boys. You *total* bastards! It wasn't fair. You two got slammed all the time on *Scrape the Barrel* and you still managed to work. I couldn't keep up with you and now *Scrape the Barrel's* gone!' She blew her nose into the flannel, and then wagged a silver-painted finger at him. 'You're the one who scares me. I mean it. You're so – so *savage*. And you make out you hate him, hate Jerry, but when it comes to closing ranks…Well, I'll show *you!* Oh, fuckin' hell…' She wrapped her arms round herself, hiccupping. Drex watched her dispassionately.

'Do you blame us? Jerry may think he's Jesus Christ on wheels, but he knows how to show up for work on time. He's too ambitious not to. And never be fooled by that nonchalance, babe. Or the friendly concern. It looks like kindliness, but Jerry has one interest in the world. Jerry. If you get in the way, he'll dump you. Don't shiver like that. Come on out. I'll dry you.'

She stood up obediently, still sobbing quietly, and he wrapped her in a towelling robe that had once, in the days when it was still white, been the property of the Holiday Inn chain. Her teeth chattered as she nestled into his black tee-shirt, the earthy smell of his sweat and tobacco pungent above the chemical odour of shower-gel. 'At least Jerry wants me,' she said indistinctly. 'He's promised to help.'

'Oh yeah?'

'Yeah! On c-condition I clean up. First, well f-first, he's taking me to F-france with him…and Ital-italy. A couple of weeks. I'm cleaning me act up…we're going to w-work out a plan.'

'Ah. A *plan*. I wondered when one of you would tell me. Don't bother sending a postcard.'

'I don't belong to you, Drex. I d-don't b-belong to anyone. But he – he w-wants me. More than you do…' He was rubbing the robe vigorously. 'Ow! Ease up. I'm not a wet dog!'

'Sorry. I don't dare want you, babe. I just don't dare…' Suddenly, he desired her terribly, and held her away from his swelling groin.

'Wh- why?'

'Because you'd always be a liability.'

'That – that's so bleedin' unfair!'

'You're also absolutely delicious. You always were, sweetie. You always were. Come to bed.'

'Jerry's going to find me an agent. Maybe Shelley. He's truly going to help. He said he wants to make it up to me. He said he felt badly.'

'Jerry never likes feeling bad,' Drex said, wearily. 'Come on to bed, babe. Sleep…'

19

'Wow! Fantastic!'

'Pleased?'

Jerry Fairbrother was sitting in Shelley Tasker's small, untidy, smoky Bloomsbury office. The message had been emphatic, irresistible; well worth cancelling a week or so of his holiday with Marie in Europe, worth dashing back to hot, grey, stifling London at the end of dusty, silly-season August. And now here he was, gazing from the fax in his hand through a thick haze of cigarette smoke to Shelley's pantomime face and back again. Her shrewd brown eyes behind the trade-mark outsize spectacles watched him intently as he read. The ashtray on the untidy desk between them was already piled high with long, lipsticked stubs.

'It's amazing, Shelley. Webster! I'm – I'm a bit gobsmacked.'

'Good, yeah? Hoped you'd think so. You can begin at once.'

'It's fantastic. God, thanks! Thanks a million.'

'You don't have to thank me, kiddo. For one thing, it's my job. For another, I didn't have to do a damn thing to get this. They came to me. At least Webster's agent did. We set up a meet with the light-entertainment guy at Beeb Two, and that was it. It's in the bag. Now – over to you…' Shelley Tasker lit another cigarette, and sat back, blew the smoke upwards. The front of her silver Mary Quant bob was stained permanent yellow.

'What next? What do I need to do?'

'Okay. Provided all goes well with the Webster, and it will, we do a preliminary pilot contract with Beeb Two, with a provisional agreement for a series. The draft's right here…' She pushed some typed sheets of A4 towards him, which he forced himself to read. That had been Shelley Tasker's own insistence: always check the contract, kiddo, even when it's me. And he did, forcing himself even when, as now, the print fuzzed before his eyes like excited bees.

'Shelley,' he said after a pause. 'Have I got this right? This seems to be suggesting… I mean what about *Plug & Socket*? Don't tell me I have to.'

The diamante specs nodded up and down. 'Yup. If you go ahead with this, you have to let *Plug & Socket* go.'

'Let it *go*? But we're still under contract, Shelley.'

'Only until the end of the autumn and a Christmas special. Then you'll be free. You can begin at once, like I said.'

'Yes, but we're working on the new one! We're writing the third. Oh, hell!'

'So? Nothing's been signed, has it?'

'No, not yet, but –'

'So what's bothering you, kiddo?'

'You mean, really stop doing *Plug & Socket*? Altogether?'

'Yup. Drop it. Kill it. Move on.'

'But, Shelley – God, what a ghastly choice!'

'Choice, huh? Kiddo. Jerry. You need to grab this. If you don't…Look, this is the best offer of your career to date. These things don't come along very often,

Jerry. Pass on this one, and you'll regret it forever. I mean it, kiddo. Don't hesitate...'

'I'm not hesitating. Of course not. Not as such. It just seems a bit, well, *unfair*.'

'Harsh, maybe, but entirely fair, Jerry. Those are their terms. If you sign up for the Webster deal, you resign all other commitments to all intents and purposes for a two-series deal. It's only reasonable, if you think about it. It'll all be okay, kiddo. Trust me on this one.'

'But to just drop a third *Plug & Socket*! They – they're going to be pretty unhappy.'

'Sorry, kiddo, but they'll be used to this. People move on all the time. Nothing's been signed. Easy-peasy...' Another billow of smoke. 'I can ring them at once. It's David Connors' office, isn't it? I can get you off the hook like that...' She snapped her fingers. 'It's what I'm *for*, Jerry, love. Don't worry. Leave it to me. All I need's your say-so.'

'Yeah, I know... But oh, shit, I didn't really mean the Channel. I meant, what about the others? I mean, what will Jonesy say? Does he know? And what about Drex? Christ, he's going to go apeshit...' A whole life was disappearing from under him, or that's how it seemed.

'Jerry. Thing is – bottom line – Webster wants *you*. He doesn't want *Plug & Socket*. He doesn't want Gwil. Or Drex. Only you...' She crushed out her stub like a punctuation. 'Anyway,' she went on, 'you don't need to worry about Jonesy. A little bird – well, his agent, actually – has told me he's in line for a Shakespeare. Petruchio in the *Shrew* at the Young Vic under Hall. Or *Comedy of Errors*...You didn't get this from me, okay?'

'No, of course not. God! Well, good. I wish Jonesy all the luck in the world. But what about Drex? Hell, I don't know how I'm going to tell him! We're a team. He writes most of my lines.'

'So?' Shelley Tasker spread thin beringed fingers tipped by scarlet talons that matched her mouth. 'Now you get to work with J. J. *Webster*, Jerry! Stop fretting. Look, leave Drex to me too. Who's his agent?'

'No one. Not as far as I know. He's sort of free-loaded with you, I suppose, because of the show.'

'On your ticket, Jerry. Okay. Well, I'll represent him personally from now on, if he wants that. I'll ring him, and I'll find him something, never you fear...' She paused to light up again.

'Something he'll like?' If only Drex could have something good, good enough to – 'I mean, *Plug & Socket* was always more his than mine.'

'Listen, kiddo. We've known each other long enough for me to be entirely frank, haven't we, yeah? Okay, well, it's time to drop Drex, Jerry. He's holding you back. That sort of show's holding you back., as I'm sure Gwil Jones knows perfectly well...'

'But you loved it! You got us the contract in the first place, for God's sake!'

'Of course! Of course I love *Plug & Socket*. Never miss it. It's great, hilarious... all good wacky adolescent fun, aimed at a narrow target audience, and it's screened at ten-thirty pm on what's still a minority channel. I don't have to tell you what its viewing figures are. Hell, Jerry, look, there's only a limited shelf-life for that alternative stuff, you know that. It's fringe-theatre on air. Now we're talking mainstream, kiddo, primetime. Webster's been in the game a long time, wants to explore new directions. In his hands, alternative comedy breaks into the popular consciousness. I don't have to tell you this. It's the zeitgeist. Jump on the train now, for heaven's sakes, kid.'

'And leave Drex on the platform,' murmured Jerry Fairbrother. But nothing could kill his excitement. It bubbled up, unstoppable.

Shelley Tasker leaned close over her desk, eyeing him hugely behind the giant glinting specs. 'Lose this,' she intoned, 'and it'll be fringe stuff for ever and ever amen, except it won't, because it's the way of the world that this stuff just drops out of sight after about six months and there's a new face every year. You've had a great run with it, Jerry. It made a series out of that *Scrape the Barrel* scrapbook, and you made a name for yourself. You all did. But it's over. If you want my advice as a friend, let alone as an agent, I'm telling you to grab this and not look back. This is your future, Jerry.'

'Shelley, look, can I think about it?'

'No. Webster wants to see you this afternoon at four. He's expecting you.'

'Okay. I meant, before I agree, sign.'

'How long do you want?'

'I don't *know*. A couple of days?'

'Make it twenty-four hours, Jerry. This won't wait. And someone has to talk to Connors at the Channel. I think I might as well ring him now.'

'Oh, shit. This all feels so sudden, Shelley...'

'Welcome to the world, kiddo! It *will* be okay, I promise.'

Jerry Fairbrother hesitated in the doorway. 'Look, Shelley, I accept. But at least let me talk to Drex, okay?'

'Whatever you say, Jerry. Good luck!'

'I mean, please let me tell him first. I owe him, you know.'

'Sure thing, kiddo. Promise...' When she heard the outer door bang shut, Shelley Tasker lit another cigarette, lifted the receiver and started dialling.

J. J. Webster in the flesh had been a surprise – older, tubbier, and somehow al-together *cuddlier* than he had expected: a round face sported an untidily fuzzy beard, a little slit of a mouth in the gingery whiskers seemed to contain oddly tiny, juvenile teeth. Webster had spelled out exactly what he wanted.

'I chose you on purpose,' Webster had said when Jerry remarked, diffidently, that he thought a collaborator might be redundant. 'I want to go in a slightly new direction, Jerry. Webster words fuelling the engine, maybe, but Fairbrother will be doing the navigating. You're my guide to the youth market, you see. What will go *down*, as I believe you say...' And his small, myopic blue eyes had twinkled above the folds of pink flesh, enjoying the irony. 'Every now and then, one needs a Virgil.'

J. J. Webster's comedy dramas, including his latest and most successful series, *Read All About It!*, set in the offices of a provincial newspaper, were characterized by a certain spikiness, a quirky realism that gave otherwise two-dimensional, formulaic comedy characters an edge of human individuality. People actually *cared* what happened to harassed editor Frank, ladies' man Clive, bossy Stella, raw recruit Gubby and all the rest; moreover, the nature of the setting gave plenty of scope for local colour and other featured characters, cameos for well-known actors. Several storylines, funny, tragic and merely banal, could be covered in a single episode; others, to echo the Clive character, could 'run and run' with a satisfying sense of continuity. The series had some of the ingredients of a successful soap, and it was hugely popular. Jerry himself never missed an episode if he could help it. But now, J. J. Webster was avid for something different, something to move on to after the third and possibly final series of *Read All About It!* finished. The new idea was to have some set pieces, continuing characters in a variety of situations in a vaguely futuristic London: a merchant banker and his shop-a-holic wife with kids at private school; a chronically unemployed family on the dole; an Indian newsagent who wants to send his daughter to university; a pair of male students (not a million miles away from Plug and Socket) scraping through life in a squat; some elderly residents in a rest-home; a couple of bemused Japanese tourists being cynically ripped off in the West End (to mention just a few of the ideas they contrived between them) and all brought together under the purview, scrutiny and commentary of a pair of endearingly amoral extra-terrestrials. Jerry was to play one of the ETs and co-write the series, and it was Jerry who came up with the title: *Earthwatch*. You were probably a fan.

20

'Jerry man? Heard you were back! *Ciao!*'

'Drex! You must be psychic, man! I was about to ring you...' This was the part he was dreading; the cloud in the blue sky of an otherwise perfect week, the prod in his sleep, the spike of a pricking conscience through the meetings, the handshakes, the glow of a fairly lavish BBC hospitality lunch; the queasiness in his giddying excitement. Jerry Fairbrother was still young enough, and inexperienced enough, to feel a child's thrill at a dream coming true. Young enough, too, to feel squeamish. He had yet to acquire the killer-instinct that accompanies true success. He felt as he had at school and university, charmed from stalwart but dull companions towards metal infinitely more attractive, obeying the secret instinct that he belonged elsewhere, in other circles. The memory of the sullen faces he had chosen to ignore and tried to palliate with true but phoney-sounding explanations (I'm rehearsing, I've got a session...) still had the power to haunt him. And now, here was Drex. Now that Drex had pre-empted him, he felt worse than ever. He braced himself.

'You first then, *buon amico*.'

'Well, um, I was wondering if I could see you...a bit complicated on the blower...'

'Look, Jer, if it's the script, it's almost done. The two last episodes by Friday latest, promise. I just wanted to run something by you, yeah? There's this moment with Plug on the bus, when he says to Socket –'

'Drex, old thing, we can talk if you come over. Save it.'

'Yeah, okay. Bar of the Grapes? Could do with a jar. Been at it for twenty-four hours solid...' An audible yawn, and Jerry could picture an unattractive scene at the other end of the line, in Drex's squalid quarters in Whitechapel, where the makeshift blinds were always drawn, blotting out all distinction between night and day. He went there as little as possible.

'No, not the Grapes. Come here to Goodge Place?'

'You're *da solo*, I take it? No complications?'

'Marie's not here if that's what you mean. Gone to stay with a mate in Shepherd's Bush...'

'Ah. Okay. *Va bene. Tra poco. Ciao.*'

'No chance of pinning you down to a time is there?' Jerry inquired, but the line had blanked.

Almost everything that had begun to irritate Jerry about Drex in recent months could be summed up in that call: the completely casual attitude to the time of day, let alone deadlines for one; for another, those phoney Italianisms, which had seemed funny, idiosyncratic once, but now seemed to be part of an adolescence that Jerry had begun to need to leave behind. Drex Bello might have affected an Italian surname, but he was basically London Irish, as far as anyone could possibly tell. Brilliant, though, and he knew it – another irritation. But they had worked together for practically ever, and the *Plug & Socket* thing had acquired a familiar rhythm. They were like a pair of dance-partners, a Torville and Dean of comic sketch writing. The plots came up as they talked, Drex would sketch in a script, Jerry would modify, object, suggest adjustments which, to be fair, Drex almost always accommodated, working his intimate knowledge of Jerry the actor in with his dramatic persona. It *worked*...a true collaboration. It was also – this was the crunch – a friendship which, if you had asked him, Jerry would have said he valued. Their working partnership remained solidly unbroken, in spite of everything: their sometimes uneasy collisions; their tendency in recent years to keep very different social shedules, and the crazy young woman who dodged between them like a shared toy. Jerry was firmly convinced that no one else could break this news. He could have left it to Shelley, but he had refused...

Honourable intentions are one thing, natural impulses another. Jerry Fairbrother's natural impulse was to avoid sooner than confront, and this particular looming confrontation made him feel horribly nervous. He paced about, unable to think straight until the thing was done. He was heartily glad that Marie had decided to go away. He would put off worrying about Marie for as long as possible. He made one beer last, and then opened another and drank it rather fast, wiped his lips at the sound of the doorbell.

'Drex! Hi, man. Hi! Almost thought you weren't coming. Come on in! Cold beer?'

'Great! Yeah. Could kill a cold beer, man. No air anywhere. The tube was like a gas chamber. Shit, this must be the hottest summer in London since seventy-six... remember seventy-six? Bush fires on Clapham Common? Cheers! I've brought the notes, and there's some perfectly gleamingly brilliant ideas for the new series I want to run by you. Shall we go up on the roof, get a hit of fresher carbon-monoxide?' Drex was chattering. Bad sign.

'Yeah. Good idea...' Jerry sighed. Morose, difficult Drex, the quirky genius with no sense of time or responsibility was bad enough. Drex out of his orbit on coke or amphetamine was infinitely worse. Still, it was as good as done now, and he had made up his mind how he was going to put it. They sat on the roof on deck-chairs as the evening darkened without freshening, a chilled six-pack of Becks between them, smoking a small spliff and watching from four storeys up the atelier windows opposite, and beyond, interrupted by the rooftops, the teaming, swishing traffic in the Tottenham Court Road. Blink red, blink green...

Drex slurped thirstily from the can and produced from a canvas bag a wedge of typescript, much annotated in Drex's tiny illegible scrawl. 'Now then, where is it?' He licked a thumb, flicked through the corners of dirty pages.

'Drex.'

'Right! Got it! Here we are. This new series, now...right? Okay. Listen. Plug and Socket are still sharing digs in somewhere very like this, but you know, scruffier obviously, and they're dreaming, fantasizing, Plug on about girls, as ever, Socket on about money, making his fortune. As ever. But this next one's going to be more inward-looking, less slap-stick, okay? This time, we're going to see the dreams. As ever, they're too broke to go out, and yes – why not a scene on the roof at night like this, watching the road, philosophising? And the Plug character, he begins to, you know how he does, to *romance* about the pubs and clubs down *there*…And he has this bit of a dream-vision, comes in on top of his dialogue, fuzzy edges, that stuff, girls, him pulling some go-go dancer, whatever. And of course they can't afford it, and most of the whole episode is Plug – Jonesy – conjuring this vision, about meeting the woman of his dreams, and trying to persuade the Socket character to go down with him, hit the West End where the gates of heaven will open and they'll both get laid… The usual impulses, and Plug's virginity hang-ups, all that. And you – Socket – he makes the usual objections, and of course in the end, Plug does persuade him, but they end up in the local, trying to find the dosh to share a pint, and some stage-business with the landlord who won't take tick and a woman who completely freezes them. No! Maybe two women, one each, but they might pretend to be lesbians or some-thing, mirror dialogue.'

'*Drex.*'

'Thing is, the way I see it, the next series will be more fantastical, feature this impossible dream-sequence each time, yeah? It's going to be good, Jer. But right now, I want to tweak 'On The Bus' a bit. Thing is, if the conductor throws them off too soon, we lose half the the stuff with the posh old lady and the Pekinese. Pity. Anyway, it's here. Have a look. Socket says, you say – oh Jesus, I do like this bit – he's tanked up to buggery, and he says to the conductor, right, he says, 'Make mine a double scotch' and the conductor –'

'Drex! Drex, man, stop!'

Drex glugged the last of his can, made a beery burp. 'God that was welcome! Any chance of another?'

'Sure, man, help yourself. Drex, I'm trying to tell you something. Oh, *shit*…'

'Now, my ideas for the next run, this new idea,' he pulled the ring tab, slugged at the new can, 'it puts a new slant on situation comedy, see? The situation is not really two broke morons sharing a house, but the situations they imagine precisely because they *are* two broke morons sharing a house, their dream life, you know, Plug's sad-herbert wank-fantasies, Socket's dreams of untold wealth… another kind of wanker's fantasy, if you like… The point is that it makes a log-ical third series, and plus, we get to put in some really raunchy stuff, and I've thought of the perfect upgrade – it's obvious! This is how we creep from under the fringe into the spotlight. We have some *guest cameos*, my friend. We get Lulu, Kate Bush, Olivia Newton-John – and hey, wait! Not just pop stars, we might get Anna Ford, Angela Rippon, even Valerie Singleton or Sue Lawley for a spot of bathos, all the posh totty fantasy-ass going – whoever. But they're all in Plug's head, right? How about Joanna Lumley? Whew! Older women, all that experi-ence! Man, Jer, just imagine!'

'*Drex!* Drex man, stop, okay? Look, it's brilliant, it would be brilliant, but the thing is – oh, shit, man, just shut up and listen to what I'm saying. They – they're going to pull the series. Thinking about it, anyway. Don't want to run it. Told me yesterday… I've been trying to get hold of you.'

'What?'

[99]

'I'm afraid it's true, Drex.'

'You don't *mean* it!'

'Fraid so...' Jerry's hands shook a little over his can. 'This, well, it couldn't be *worse,* man!'

'You spoke to Connors yesterday?'

'Yes. No. Well, sort of. Shelley spoke to him, then I spoke to her.'

'Christ, you're not joking. Are you?'

'No. I'm not joking. I didn't know how to tell you. I have been trying to ring. The contract stands – um – stands firm for this run, obviously. It's just they won't commit to any more...' Jerry heard himself stammering.

'Shee-it! In other words, they're wiping us. Christ!'

'We do still have this run. And the Christmas thing.'

'So why didn't that cunt Connors have the fucking bottle to tell us? They're pulling our *series,* man! First thing tomorrow, I'll be on that arsehole's office doorstep. Fucking hell! And what about your Shelley? Can't she do something?'

'It wasn't exactly like that. I mean, Shelley told me. She's pretty appalled. Obviously...' Jerry drank miserably from his can. 'We just have to accept this, I guess. According to Shelley, we're rapidly becoming old hat...or too new...or something...' Jerry glugged more beer. 'I guess it's just one of those things,' he said. 'Blame Connors' lack of vision...' He was even beginning to believe this himself.

'Well, I'm not going to take this lying down, man. Shit! All the ratings have been good, it's had raves in the reviews, it's got a fan-base, they've made tee-shirts, for fuck's sake, *Plug & Socket!* What have we done? That fucking blind *idiot* Connors! *Figlio di putana! Testa di cazzo!* What a stupid, visionless, quotidian, pedestrian, costive, pusilanimous *bastardo!* This is our fucking career down the tubes. Tomorrow, you're going to come with me. Jonesy too, if we can get hold of him. He'll go apeshit. We're going to take my roughs for the new series and go over Connors' head if we have to. Talk to that bastard Broadstairs...'

'Broadbent. Look, Drex, honestly I don't think a set-to with Connors or Broadbent is going to help. Truly. I'm appalled. Oh God!'

'Not have a *set-to,* you call it? I call that pretty fucking feeble, Jer. Like we're supposed to just sit here while someone flushes us down the pan with all the other turds! Eh?' Jerry looked at his feet and there was a very long pause. They sat in silence, listening to the traffic honking, the mingled sounds of the teeming London night. On the roof, moths batted into the glass-covered lamp. Below them, engines revved, tyres swished, heels clattered on pavements, voices brayed, shrieked, joshed, bellowed, televisions and radios chattered and blared, machines hummed and whirred – the collective agitated murmur of the night, coalesced into that continuous subliminal vibrating background buzz that never ceases in any large city at any time of the night. Across the street, a man argued violently with a woman, someone shouted for a dog or a child, someone in the next apartment put the volume up on Pink Floyd's 'Money', someone else yelled out to shut the fuck up... The woman cried out suddenly, as if in pain, and as if in answer, far away, a siren sounded. '...*that geezer was cruisin' for a bruisin'*... The hot, dusty, airless night was making Jerry's blood pound. 'Makes you think of *Rear Window,*' murmured Drex.

'Yeah. Scotch?' said Jerry eventually, getting up.

'Why not?' Drex continued to stare morosely out over the parapet while Jerry fetched a bottle and glasses.

'Here you go...'

'Thank you, my friend...' Drex took the glass and gazed up very intently at Jerry, his eyes almost invisible behind his dark glasses. Then he removed them, revealing the naked eyes slowly, his expression not wavering by a muscle; opaque ink-black eyes staring unblinking into Jerry's face. Then he winked with no mirth at all. Then he replaced the shades. Jerry turned abruptly, made rather a business of pouring his own drink. 'The way I see it, yeah,' Drex said in a more normal voice, sipping scotch. 'First, obviously, we've got to get hold of Shelley.'

'I, well, like I said, I already have. She's –'

'She's what?'

'Well, she's appalled, like I told you. She can't believe it. Naturally. She's going to do what she can.'

'Funny. Funny you should say that. Because that wasn't how she put it to me...' Drex let the words hang in the air. Jerry jolted in his deckchair, spilling scotch into his lap. And Drex watched him. He said, 'Shelley said to me, more like, 'this is show-biz, kid. Tough.' Like I said, we get hold of that bitch Shelley Tasker and we break her fucking neck.'

'Eh? You've spoken to her?' Jerry felt suddenly sick. 'Already. Obviously.'

'Obviously, my *friend*. She rang me. Just after she'd rung Connors to pull the plug on Socket, if I might put it that way. She didn't actually put it that way. She said, and I quote, 'We mustn't stand in Jerry's way.' That's what she said. After she told me all about your phenomenal success with J. J. Webster and your new deal...' He took another slug of scotch, his eyes behind the dark glasses never leaving Jerry's face. 'Just how long,' he said, his voice very measured and not much above a whisper, 'did you imagine you could keep this from me, Fairbrother, you contemptible cunt? Hmm?'

'I wasn't – I didn't –'

'Oh stop blustering, you lame fuck. You were going to let me bullshit you all night, weren't you, about the new series? Huh? Let me tell you, I came full of it deliberately, just to see how far you'd be prepared to go. Jesus, man, you make Judas Iscariot look like a loyal pal. A week near enough you've known, a *week*, and then I have to ring you, and even then you lie, you twist, you lisp, pretend it's the Channel that doesn't want us...a *week*, man! *Che stronzo!* You get a better offer, get that conniving Dame Edna cow who's fixed it all up anyway to do your dirty work and dump the series, and she at least has the decency to ring me, put me out of my misery as well as my job, while *you*! What were you going to do? Eh? Wait until I walk into Connors' office with a fat script for the new series and let him go all surprised, say 'Why, what are you doing here? Don't you know? Has nobody told you?' You know the reason that Shelley called me? Shelley called me because she didn't think you'd have the bottle to do it yourself. She was right. I'll give the bitch that. She even offered to help me. I told her in very graphic terms where she could stuff it. Here! Have this!' He sprang up from his chair, flung the sheaves of paper onto the ground, and his glass of scotch into Jerry's eyes.

[101]

'Ow! Drex, *shit!*' Jerry tried to blink the burning, smarting stuff away, clawing at his eyes, blundering in the sudden red blackness. '*Shit*, man, oh bloody hell!'

'*Ow, Drex!* You pathetic *schoolboy*, Fairbrother! I hope you're blinded! And I hope, and this is a curse, man, I hope you never have another quiet moment, ever again, not in your whole life. You're a treacherous, spineless piece of excrement. And before you ask, I'll never hurt Marie, but after you've dumped her, and you will, because she'll hold you back too, when you're least expecting it, my friend, I'll be round the corner, and I'll come to get you. I'll be there. I'll let this go cold, and then I'll *be* there!'

And then he was gone, his footsteps, slightly uneven, sounded on the atelier steps, grew fainter through the kitchen, barely sounded down the hallway. The door slammed.

'I'll be there, you cunt!' yelled Drex from the street below.

Jerry put his head in his hands, and sat motionless for some time. It was a long time before he could open his eyes. A tiny gust of wind ruffled the sheets of A4, and he was suddenly on his knees in his near-blindness, scrabbling to pick them up. He stumbled downstairs to the kitchen, spent several minutes with his head under the running tap, his eyes still smarting. And for the rest of the night his eyes watered painfully, and not just with single malt.

21: Last Year

'I wish you wouldn't keep watching this pusillanimous stuff, Angel. It stinks.'

'I like it.'

'I agree it's more wholesome than your usual fare. But it's dated and crude. I wish you'd be a bit more discriminating. Its only use now is some sort of cultural archeology.'

'Cultural what?'

'Skip it...' DVD has a lot to answer for. *Puke & Soddit* is enjoying its own mini-renaissance for an audience scarcely born when it was made. Royalties are handy, which is about the only thing you can say for it. To be fair, if I could watch it without feeling slightly ill, I would agree with my culturally challenged little friend that it wasn't half bad, once.

'Well, Mrs Sourpuss, I think it's funny even if half the jokes are about people I never heard of. But I love them rats and carrots having conversations. And that neat little blonde babe who plays the girl upstairs. Coo, and to think that you actually wrote it! Bloody Norah! I know, I know, *co*-wrote it.'

'I did most of the work.'

'You should've wrote more of it.'

'Possibly.'

'Why didn't you, then?'

How to kill a budding career – that is, if someone hasn't already done it for you? Go to jail. Go straight to jail, do not pass 'go', do not collect two hundred pounds... and learn who your friends are.

22: That Fateful Late Summer...

A ringing telephone clanging into his sick dream. A thumping headache. He stumbled from his bed.

'Hi, Jerry? Sorry if I got you up. It's Gwil. I'm afraid I've got a bit of bad news.'

'Who? Oh...Gwil...Jonesy...oh, shit, man. Look, I know, I know you've had bad news. It took me by surprise too – I can explain everything. What about a pint or a sandwich or something? A bit later, maybe. What's the time, anyway?' He sat down suddenly on the stairs, his brain hammering sickly in his skull.

'Half past nine. I'm sorry, Jerry. You sound terrible. Long night celebrating, eh?'

'No – yes – no. Not exactly. Look, Jonesy – I can explain if you'll let me. I feel like shit, if it's any consolation.'

'What are you talking about, consolation? Have we got crossed wires or something?'

'The series folding. *Plug & Socket*. I'm really sorry, Jonesy...' Jerry rubbed his head. His eyes – so swollen and sore. Memory began to resurface. 'Oh, Christ,' he said, groaning.

'Jerry – look, you've obviously got a five-star hangover. If it makes you feel any better, Drex is in a worse state than you. That's why I'm ringing. He's been nicked. Arrested. I've just come from the police station in Charing Cross Road. He was positively identified trying to set up a coke deal with an undercover cop in a gay dive in Soho, the bloody fool. They found enough on him to make it stick, but I gather there's about half a ton of various stuff in his flat and they've got a warrant. It's pretty incriminating. They'll do him for dealing. I did all I could, and I think they believed me when I said I was a proper colleague – one of the cops recognized me from *Plug & Socket* actually – but it looks bad, Jerry. They're sending for a duty solicitor, but my bet is he'll get sent down whatever happens, poor bugger. Thing is, if...'

'Wait! Look, how – how did you – ? I'm confused, Jonesy. How come you get mixed up in all this?'

'He asked for me. They rang me at about six am, and I went over. I'm probably one of his few acquaintances who's actually clean – er, present company excepted of course. Thing is, look, that's what I'm trying to *tell* you. They're trying to clean up. The police. They want to interview his friends, his known contacts – seems they think they're onto something bigger than just old Drex on his own, you know? I've been trying to do a bit of damage-limitation, but it's not been easy.'

'*Christ* – what's he been saying?' Jerry's head was reeling.

'Well, he's not being very helpful, to say the least. Just insists he was only trying to pick up the cop at the Cavalier. But anyone who's seen him recently is bound to be in the frame. He – well he told me he'd seen you last night.'

'Shit! We shared a spliff – that's all, I swear to God! We drank beer, scotch. Oh, shit. In his present mood, he'll probably say I planted stuff on him! Oh, fucking *hell!*'

'Jerry, calm down. It's none of my business if you two have fallen out, but I'd just get the story straight and hoover up a bit maybe, okay?'

'Jonesy! You mean they'll come here? Look, I can't get involved...oh *shit...*' Jerry felt his guts turn to water.

'I'd just be prepared if I were you. Anyway, I gather congratulations are in order. J. J. Webster, eh? Well, it works both ways. I've got the *Errors* and about sixteen thousand words to learn. Onwards and upwards, eh? Why don't we have that pint after the studio on Tuesday? Down the Tubes episode, isn't it?'

'What are you doing?'

'Jesus Christ! You startled me! I wasn't expecting you back so soon. Marie, we've got to get out of here. I'll explain everything later. Don't unpack. I've got to get out of here now!'

'Why? And what on earth are you doing with the hoover?'

'This is really serious, babe. Shelley's expecting me – she'll put you up too, I'm sure, if you want. This is an emergency. Take your bag back down and grab a cab, will you? Drex has gone mad, and the rozzers'll be here any time now...' He was shoving clothes, books, shaving kit, haphazard into a hold-all.

'The bag's empty, Jerry. Why are you so frantic? What's happened to your eyes?' Her voice was flat, a monotone.

'Nothing – accident with some bleach in the sink. I've cleaned up as best I can, flushed the roaches down the lav. What about you? You didn't leave anything – er – incriminating behind, did you?'

'Nothing. I'm clean, Jerry. Jerry, is this Italy come to get us? I knew it would... it's karma.'

'Stuff karma! Let's get out of here, okay? This is Drex, I'm *telling* you! He's been busted, and they know he was here last night.'

'I don't believe you...' She was swaying a bit, and her eyes were pin-points. 'You're not telling me the truth.'

He grasped her arm and turned her to face him. He spoke very slowly and deliberately, jerking her thin body slightly with each emphasis. 'Marie. Forget. Italy! We witnessed an *accident*. It wasn't us. *Wasn't us*, do you hear me? We'll go back to Italy and we'll be good witnesses and tell what we know. I promise you we will. Soon. In the meantime, Drex is in trouble, and we have to get out of here. *Now*. Understand me?'

'Is that where you're going? To help Drex?'

'NO! Yes. Later. Christ, sweetie, *please!* Come on! Come with me to Shelley's. We can help Drex from there...'

'Is he in prison?'

'As good as...Marie! Please!'

'So you're just going to leave him in trouble, like you do. Jerry, I came back to say I'm leaving. I'm staying with Chloe. I'm leaving you, Jerry. You scare me sick. I just came back for some stuff like, clothes, shoes...' The monotone scared him far worse than hysterics would have done.

'Not now, babe – really not now. Get it later. Tomorrow. Next week. I'm serious…' He grasped her elbow. 'Come *on*, for God's sake!' He more or less shoved her down the stairs. At the front door, he hesitated, his heart racing, hearing a siren. It passed. He jammed on a pair of dark glasses. 'Come on. If we get stopped, we're on holiday, okay?'

'On holiday,' Marie repeated. 'You're not thinking straight, Jerry. You never do.'

'We're on holiday,' he told the cabbie unnecessarily as he loaded his bags into the boot.

'I'm not on holiday,' said Marie. 'I'm in hell. I'm not coming with you any further, Jerry. I'll post the key. Goodbye…' She began to walk away, a tiny figure in huge lace-up boots and lace, all in black with pink spiky hair and a white peaky face that looked positively ill in the morning light.

'Marie! Don't – Oh God! Look, go straight to Chloe's, okay? I'll ring you.'

'Crouch End, did you say, mate?'

'*Marie!*' She fluttered black-painted finger nails without turning round. 'We had a bit of an argument,' Jerry told the driver lamely.

'Women, eh?' said the cabbie. 'Ere, ang on! Ain't you that actor from *Plug & Socket*? Like that thing, I do. Wife don't like the language but what I say it's realism, I do. Thought I reckernized you under the shades, like. You're good.'

'No, I'm not – I mean everybody says I look like him, but I'm not him. Unfortunately… Let's get on, can we?'

'Well, stone me! You could be his twin…*and* I was about to ask for your autograph. Get that, eh?'

23: Later That Fateful Year

Jerry Fairbrother, star and co-author of foul-mouthed alternative comedy series Plug & Socket, *denies knowledge of former writing-partner's drug-fuelled lifestyle. 'It's a great shame and a total shock,' Fairbrother claims, despite having known Drex Bello since their days at East Anglia University where, as students of the Drama Department, they began writing sketches that enjoyed brief popularity on Channel Four's youthful current-affairs satire,* Scrape the Barrel. Plug & Socket *which also stars young Shakespearean actor Gwilym Jones, is due to finish after the present series ends next week, and it is understood that Fairbrother is writing a new comedy with J. J. Webster of* Read All About It! *fame. Drex Bello was sentenced to three years for dealing and possession of cocaine earlier this week under his real name...*

She came to see me after I was sent down. There are those booths, you know? You sit in a long line of other lags waiting to see their nearest and dearest behind the wires. If you haven't got a visitor, you don't get called, but I did get called this one day and I sat, wondering if it was Jerry and knowing he wouldn't have the guts, or maybe Jonesy, but in she came, and they ushered her up. People stared at her pink hair, her navvy boots, her extraordinary prettiness under the gothic make-up. Mostly, she looked like a little junkie, and I steeled myself.

'Is it very horrible? You look so pale-like.'

'There aren't rats gnawing my toes, if that's what you mean. The food's better than they say, and if anyone spits in it, it's the screws, not the kitchen detail. I get off most of the square-bashing being registered disabled, and I've got a cell to myself most of the time. I write... And they let me use the library, and if I'm good, they'll let me be a librarian. Let's see...the communal lavatory flushes when you tip the night's leavings down it. And if I behave, they'll get me a transfer to some so-called open place, probably in the far north. Other than that I hold an 'at home' every Thursday, with tea, cakes and sherry and the butler calls me 'sir'. Why did you come, Marie?'

'Drex. I wanted to see you. And if there's anything I can do, bring-like...'

'A saw? A chisel? A fine double-bladed knife hidden in a birthday cake?'

'I meant books, something like that.'

'Library is more than adequately stocked, thanks. Look, it was sweet of Jerry to send you, but he's too late. I don't think this is a very good idea, Marie. I'd invite you into the best parlour but Her Majesty's staff are a little recalcitrant. I'm sure you understand, my dear. Now, if you don't mind...' Seeing her was doing something mangling to my guts.

'Oh, *Drex*! Drex – don't just send me away. Jerry didn't send me. He doesn't know. I thought he behaved like a complete wanker to just let you stew like this, not vouch for you or something. He should have stood up for you. I mean, you're *friends!*'

'You're a nice kid in some ways, Marie. It's as well he didn't. He's got that precious skin to save. I take it he saved it,' I said lightly, but she shivered.

'Oh, yeah, he saved it. Drex, we've parted. Jerry and me. For good. I wanted you to know. I really am here on my own.'

'I see. Threw you over too? Standing in the way of naked ambition, were you? Well, I'm sorry, but I'm not remotely surprised. And I'm not really sorry, actually. He was rather your choice, sweetie, wasn't he? Metal more attractive, all that. You decided he'd give you a better leg up for a bit of a leg over. Sorry to sound cynical.'

'That's not fair. I want to – to come back to you, Drex.'

'Silly career move, Marie. Yes it is. Go back to Jerry. *Il personaggio famoso,* the one with the face on the telly. He's the one ascending the wheel – jump on it with him. He must owe you that, at least...' She looked down, her heavily mascara'd eyelashes wet. 'Seriously, babe. I'm not kidding. He really is on the up. Stick with him, have a ball. Get him to introduce you to all his successful pals. Eat a square meal a day, don't puke it up again and lay off the speed and the hard gear. Do it. You can...' I doubted it, truly. Her pupils were enormous, her black-nailed fingers tremulous.

'Drex...don't, please. I know I deserve it if you hate me. I – I really have left him. It's not quite like you think. I mean, I know I said I was scared of you. Now I think I'm even more scared of *him.*'

'Well, really! What's he done? Tied you to the kitchen sink? Whipped you soundly into submission? I take it that holiday *al continento* didn't work out.'

Marie just shook her head and shivered again, as though trying to shake off some bad dream. Marie was always apt to 'register', play the little drama-queen. That was her problem, exaggerating, so that when she was really in trouble, no-body believed her. 'I'd wait, Drex, if – if you wanted.'

'So. What will you do next? While you're waiting?'

'Oh, you know. Chill out a bit-like, try and suss out some auditions.'

'Sounds a reasonable idea...' Except it didn't. Real ambition requires the kill-er-instinct. The only person Marie would kill was herself. 'Well, babe, *in bocca al lupo,* as the Italians say...' I tried to smile. I had loved her, once.

'Ta. What about you? What will you do next?'

'You mean apart from writing a hateful memoir and plotting to slay all my enemies?'

'I just hate to think of you in here, Drex.'

'They'll let me out,' I assured her. 'In time...'

In no time at all, they rang the bell. Five minutes for the last blown kisses, the last meaningless platitudes, the last cryptic messages to the ones on the Bricks, the other side of the big divide. Chairs scraped and uniformed guards began to move.

'Actually, there is something you could do, babe. Got a pen and paper?' She fished in her bag. It was something I'd been planning to entrust to Gwil Jones, but he was deep in rehearsals. And perhaps Marie was a better bet, except her spelling was always terrible. 'Okay, buy a cheap copy of Ford's *'Tis Pity* – yes, sweetie, of course the *play* – and just a single edition, not a Ford anthology. Post it to Mrs C. A. Walters, care of Captain Leo Rollitt. Got it? That's R – O double-L, I – double-T...yeah, that's it. Forty-two, Maxwell Road, sw10. No, no message. Just send it, okay? I owe them a book. I'll make it up to you later.'

[108]

'That doesn't matter. No message. Are you sure?'

'They'll know who it's from.'

'Okay, Drex.'

'Thanks. Be good, okay?'

'Yeah… and you.'

'Can't do much else in here, babe…' Her enormous eyes welled up a bit before she turned.

'Abyssinya…' The Sally Bowles wave with the back of her hand, painted nails fluttering.

I never got to know if she sent the book. In fact, I saw her only once more in person after that, much, much later. And after about nine months of real 'jug' I was indeed transferred. My next cell-mate – except they weren't called cells any longer, and he was next door rather than in an upper bunk – was a piece of interesting and unusual low-life known as Chris the Whisper.

24: 1983 La Casa dal Ruscello, Tuscany

When Lottie could not sleep – and sleep was often an elusive, fractious, fleeting commodity – she calmed herself with plans for her garden. Nowadays, as she confessed to her friend Alison Porter, she would far sooner shop for plants than for frocks and shoes. Every aspect of this small but delightful oasis of calm and richness delighted and soothed her. The main reason for buying the tumbledown house had been its once-lovely grounds, and Lottie with the help of the knowledgable and practical Umberto had mended the maze, made a secret amphitheatre of the old, defunct vineyard and planted roses, many, many roses, in the old *orto*, and on discreet trellises around the lawns. This was a Tuscan country garden in the old style, with wooded walks, little vistas over the valley; friendly rather than over-formal, it had been designed for pleasure, function and shade rather than any overt display of grandeur. It pleased her immensely that she had rescued rather than coverted it, and the roses round the walls of the orchard muddled in with the ancient spreading apricot, the cherry trees and greengage plums. Swallows returned each year to the mud nests in the courtyard, and they brought luck, so Umberto said. She had made a little clearing of the walnut trees down to the tiny river, where bracken and acacia and willow grew, and frogs mated in April, and toads, like animated lumps of clay, made their ungainly way over the little track. Wild birds – blackbirds, robins, chaffinches and jays – nested in springtime, and hoopoes boomed in the hills; at night, owls hooted, and she could hear nightingales, although Umberto, who told her they were becoming rare, had his doubts... No doubts about the wild boar, though, which grunted – shouted, to Lottie's fancy – in the night, taunting the labrador, Mr Bozo, who had finally learned after a badly bitten ear, that sows with piglets must not be confronted. Soon, the hunters would track and shoot them – supply the local restaurants with the local *cinghiale* dishes that made the region famous – and part of her wanted to shoot the shooters. She was always terrified that poor Mr Bozo would get caught in the crossfire, like the peppered spaniel she had seen at the vet's.

But Autumn suited her mood. The leaves were turning to gold and russet, and there was mist in the woods each morning. There was rain, and no need to threaten the fragile reserves of the well with over-watering. And the concert season was over, thank God! Her main worry in these last few years was the concert season. This was Leo's brief – he who had become involved with the local music-circuit, and had alighted on the idea of the amphitheatre as *the* perfect spot – and he who had turned the house, during the months of June and July, into a magnet for the local, mostly ex-pat, musical community, determined, as she had teased him, to have his Folwell come hell and high water. In fact, the smaller concerts took place in the shelter of the courtyard, where there would be a small supper laid on also. Lottie undertook these chatelaine duties stoically and unresentfully, and was even able to admit they were sometimes rather fun. Whatever else, it gave her an opportunity for people to admire the garden. But now it was over for another year! If Leo thought she 'hid' – and she did hide, just a little – he could never, surely, accuse her of a lack of courage.

Now, after a happy morning ambling round the roses with secateurs, snipping, planning autumn planting with Mr Bozo at her heels, she made her way back to the house. She had plans for the courtyard: hydrangea petiolaris, for that north wall, perhaps. And she must talk to Umberto about replanting the bits of the maze that had suffered in the latest drought She felt almost serene. If the house was still a bit of a building-site, so what?

In the dining room, she idly sifted through the bundle of post Leo had brought with him from his recent trip to London. Gardening catalogues from England – her favourite rose-grower in Norfolk, another from Somerset. A letter, in Barbara's writing, from Cambridge. And this: a small jiffy-bag addressed to 'Walters, care of Rollitt', the 'care of' spelt out and written in an unfamiliar hand. She knew perfectly well what it was. She didn't even need to open it. After so long, after she had almost allowed herself to forget, but this was Nemesis, waiting to get her. She felt her innards sink, and might have wailed out loud.

She was on her third gin by the time Leo returned from his errands in town.

25: 1983 and for Quite a Long Time After: HMP Stonethwaite

When you're in real jug, you know it. In some ways, it's easier to accept. You get banged up every night, if you can call it night at ten pip-emma. Your 'recreation' is supervised. Your 'association' is watched, your 'privileges' – and I mean things like being allowed to have pens and paper and use the library – are meted out like sweeties. You wake when they tell you, sleep when they tell you. Bars, barbed wire, keys, guards; altogether an atmos of a pretty tough institution, get me? Much of the architecture is so quaintly Victorian you might as well be in some history documentary about crime and punishment in nineteenth-century London, but there are the entirely modern CCTV cameras everywhere. You queue in line for grey, tasteless food, and the mess hall reverberates to the earsplitting din of men's voices and crashing cutlery and tin trays. You see the doc once a week, less often if you don't have a 'habit' or some other troublesome complaint. And of course there are the screws. Strange guys, these, doing this key-rattling stuff for a living. Unlock a door, immediately lock it again behind them – one wonders who the real prisoners are sometimes. They're as confined as we are. Some of them smirk, despising you from the moral highground. Some of them seem to have a sort of calling – fancy themselves doing good work among the fallen and disadvantaged, and these are far and away the worst, pretending they're doing something hot for their miserable souls, all that nauseating 'I'm here to help' attitude, all of a piece with 'accepting one's crime', which can only really amount to a hubristic pretence that they're really any different, that you got caught and they didn't. For yet others, I guess it's probably just a job, better than being on the dole.

Others are simply sadistic shits. I don't mean they beat you up, or at least not often. It's more subtle than that. Doubtless they all have to be a lot more careful now, but I bet it's still the same, however many internal inquiries and steering committees and official reports have happened since. Back in the 80s, it was blatant. You knew the screws you could trust and those you couldn't, the ones who'd look away at the appropriate moment and the ones who'd grass you into solitary with real enjoyment. You had to treat them like God, that's what they wanted; but swallow your pride, and you could work the system. You kept your nose clean, didn't annoy the heavies, you stood your ground if you did, but not too much. There was quite a lot of, 'Oy, you clocking me or what' by guys who just wanted some aggro to let themselves know they were still alive. If the screws didn't like you, they let them get on with it. But you never made it obvious you were pally with screws… and if you had any sense, you wore your learning very lightly indeed. I'm not the first to say this, but attending an English public school partly prepares you. Funny, isn't it, that the best training the educational cream of England can offer is how to be a model prisoner…

In the open joint, it's actually worse in a way. You can wear your own clothes, have a few personal possessions in your room (they aren't called 'cells' here.) You can use the bathroom when nature calls and flush it like a civilized human being. You can associate freely, up to a point. You don't get banged up at night, or at least there's no universal lights-out. They keep an all-seeing eye on you, inside as well as in the well-kept grounds, of course – not that there's anywhere to go in the remote high grounds of northern England – but there's this illusion of freedom, almost of a spartan hotel, a Butlins without the pretty animators, with activities that are supposed to be educational or physically enhancing. We had outside visitors, teachers, therapists. One sweet oldish dame, with wild greying hippy hair frilling out from a tortoise-shell pin like Spanish moss and a voice like she'd swallowed a fruit-bowl full of plums showed us videos of meerkats and used to give us smarties, truly, I'm not kidding, when we got our sums right. Grown men, given sweeties, and saying thank you. We were as good as gold. The place was a bromide. All those permitted freedoms, but we weren't at liberty. All those restrictions, but 'prison' was all but a dirty word. As existential metaphors go, it's a lot like real life. I'm not the first to remark that either.

In HMP Stonethwaite, there was a serious interest in sport. Football pitch, proper tennis courts, swimming pool, the lot, and serious coaches, many ex-army, guys with a natural affinity with boot-camps, some of them closet psychopaths. The sport thing wasn't compulsory if you had a bad foot. Very little was strictly compulsory, except behaving, submitting to spot-searches, getting the rehab boxes ticked. And not straying out of bounds, of course. 'Development' was the buzz-word. For those of us without the sporting bug, there was an old-fashioned recreation room with table-tennis, table football, pool, a vast TV, and a large collection of board-games. Soft drinks machine with almost decent coffee. Videos. Soft porn mags. Newspapers. Ashtrays. You might think you were in a social club of a very scruffy sort, a provincial boys' club, maybe. I played pool with Chris the Whisper and I got quite good. The Whisper was brilliant: on his day and when he hadn't got the shakes he could have been a professional. I won just often enough to keep him interested. He was this strange geezer, Argentine, maybe, by origin, or Greek. Or something. He never talked about himself. His accent was London but not quite, but as he never spoke above a characteristic hush, hence his name, it was hard to tell. We palled up for a number of reasons – he had a bad chest, and couldn't leap about on a sports pitch either – but the main one was that he was in for the same thing as me, and he was due for a parole any time soon. That we were being watched was a given, for obvious reasons, so we took to having most of our conversations in a rather clever code while we were playing pool. Like I said, we were quite good. It passed the time.

Sometimes, a new inmate was introduced. Some of us, a handpicked few, got to be mentors. That is, being the one on the inside who can explain the ropes to the new recruit. I'd kept my head down – you bet. You just get on with it, mark the time, don't make things difficult for yourself. When this kid Lionel was introduced into the fold, they appointed me as shepherd. Christ knows why – except that he was miserable, depressed, unmotivated, and seeing the shrinks who thought he needed Librium and cheering up. He really was a kid – only just eighteen, so old enough for adult prison, but actually as green as they come. He was also, with his mane of wavy gold hair and cherubic features and tight little buns in his tight little denims, an obvious target for all the wrong kinds of attention. For some reason 'they' thought that I could be trusted in that department...

Little Lionel. A kid from the sticks, Wiltshire, with a sweet little burr in his voice and a grudge against the world for plucking him, immature bud that he was, from (so he told us) a promising career in rock music for just a few quid-deals. Ha, ha, and pull the other one. But little Lionel could sing all right, as he proved on a 'concert night'. This was a handful of idiots playing an electric piano, drums and battered acoustic guitars wired for sound and doing Elvis impressions on a Saturday night (this was before karaoke took off, remember, and it was complete crap.) But this kid, he could actually hold a note, he knew the old standards and he really slayed them. I really had to keep my wits about me to keep him safe after that. Chris the Whisper let him play pool with us, and as long as Chris could win, which he mostly did anyway, little Lionel Barlow was accepted, a sort of rookie. Besides, it was no skin off the Whisper's nose – he was going out, any time soon. As he kept assuring us. The Whisper and I had a plan on the boil – the details don't matter now – but it had to do with putting him in touch with a certain contact of mine on the Outside, in return for some nice consideration when I re-emerged myself. In the meantime, the Whisper, Barlow and I knocked balls about a green baize table and Barlow was either too thick or too cushioned on benzodiazepines to worry much about coded conversations, and we started to ignore him. Like I said, it passed the time.

These things happen in the blink of an eye. I can get pretty feisty when I'm roused, but my natural instinct is to wait, keep my powder dry. I scowl, I'm known for sarcasm, and I don't blink, and sometimes this winds people up, but I very rarely lose it. The Whisper was much more obviously cool, this little strange guy with the bulgy head, slightly too big for his body, on which he always wore a battered fedora hat. He had a weedy little chest, on which hung an outsize gold crucifix. And there was the oddly sinister rustling voice. He had very few moments of anything you could call an emotion, not even a smile, not even when he slammed the last ball in. Then Big Doran wanted the pool table. Our pool table. There were three, and occupied, but Doran wanted ours. Doran was one of those specimens with a hard-man reputation, far more at home in Parkhurst or the Scrubs one would have thought, but for some reason he was here, with the petty dealers, the fraudsters, embezzlers and the non-violent thieves. He commanded quite a bit of respect. On the Outside, Doran was a legitimate used car dealer in Hayes or somewhere who received and made-over stolen vehicles as a sideline, and he'd clocked himself quite a long stretch for an expert job on some get-away cars in a heist that made national headlines. A set up, so he said. It's a protocol that nobody asks, but sometimes people tell, can't help it. And Doran told anyone who'd listen. Sometimes, he could sound like a man after six pints even on Coke and Fanta. His continual protestations of his complete innocence meant that he hadn't 'accepted' his crime, hence his parole was a long time coming. His wife had upped and left, and he was fighting a losing battle for the custody of his three kids. Basically, Doran was stir-crazy. He was also six foot four and broad.

'Reckon it's my turn now, Whisper, mate...' Doran tapped Whisper on the shoulder. Lightly. The Whisper was lining up a shot, and remained cocked over the table, squinting under his hat, concentrating all his puny power. Ignored Doran. Doran was not in the mood to be ignored. He touched the Whisper's shoulder again, harder, just at the moment that the Whisper's cue was about to go in. 'My turn, ain't it?' Jerked out of true, the Whisper's shot went all over the place, balls flying off the table. And then, suddenly, without so much as a change of expression, the Whisper sent the back end of the cue smartly into Doran's guts, sent him sprawling backwards with a winded yowl that brought all of our keepers running, but not before Big Doran had picked himself up and grabbed at the Whisper's neck with hands like paddles. It was the Whisper's reaction that I recall best. He would have had Doran's eyes out if he'd been tall enough, a demon of sheer fury, his little chest heaving, a weedy little David to Doran's huge, maddened, growling Goliath. No one was going to tackle Doran. He was going to kill the Whisper as easily as swatting a fly. My memory is of a whole load of us, just standing round, agape, waiting for Authority, and little Lionel whimpering, literally hiding behind me. Later, massaging a great red welt where he had nearly been garrotted by his own gold chain and what was almost certainly a broken jaw in the hospital wing, the Whisper morosely told me he had lost his chance with the parole board...

And that was when we started schooling little Lionel, visiting the sick in the hospital wing. Little Lionel, we realised, was anybody's, provided he could keep his dreams in tact. He was also due out, on probation, in a month or so. Just as well – prison's no place for a kid. He can pick up all sorts of unsavory friends inside, and learn all sorts of unpleasant things. As it was, in return for being more or less guaranteed an audition with an associate of mine, and guaranteed some serious consideration from an associate of the Whisper's, little Lionel went as free as he was ever going to be. He wasn't a bad little envoy on the Bricks. And he really did have what it takes. You next heard of him in a new incarnation, doubtless. He became Lion Barley, lead singer with that close-harmony Boys'R' Us band that won that TV talent contest in nineteen-eighty-six with a Beach-boys' cover, and then took a number one with that cover of 'Lady Be Good' a year later. A year after that, he went solo. Teeny-bopper jail-bait wrote him explicit letters enclosing tufts of juvenile pubic hair. Grannies wrote him letters offering their spare rooms and their accommodating bosoms. He did that famous ad for a chocolate bar. His star ascended. For a – let's say – consideration of loyalty, his secret was safe. Relatively.

It was when Lionel had left the fold for pastures new, and the Whisper was still laid up in the hospital with wires in his jaw that had caught an infection, where they could keep a better eye on his bad chest, or so they said, that I began to write again in earnest. I also watched a lot of TV. What else was there? Sometimes, I did both. I mean, rather than sitting in my room or in the library which anyway closed at five, I'd sit in the recreation room with the big TV, notebook out, scrib-bling the odd thing as it occurred to me, with the noises off filtered out by some magic trick in the human brain that can simply not hear things it doesn't want to. Behind me, pool games got won and lost, the card-players, betting vending machine tokens and fags, uttering the odd cry of triumph or dismay, the jukebox playing ghastly country and western – it's true, lags really do love Johnny Cash – and in front of me, the familiar strains of a Bond movie just finishing, or starting… and I just sat there, scribbling, not letting anything really bother me. Like in *The Producers*, I'd had this idea for some silly stuff set in an open prison.

Some things set off an alarm. You're listening and not listening. Vaguely, I was waiting for the news. Somebody switched channels. There was a shout – suddenly, the TV room began to fill up. 'C'mon, it's *Earthwatch*,' somebody said. 'Get that sound up,' said somebody else. 'Yeah, right…' I surfaced suddenly. 'What's *Earthwatch?*' I thought everyone had suddenly become hooked on the environment, and got up to leave, go back to my room before some doom-monger started showing aerial pictures of melting ice-caps and dying penguins…

'Don't go, Drex my friend. This is great, seriously,' said a small brown man called Tarik, sitting down next to me. Tarik was older than most of us, a modest guy reputed to be a master forger of passports and driving licenses. He never spoke of his skills or his sentence, only spoke indeed of his family, whom he missed. He had a photograph of his new grandchild that he showed us proudly. He was the main man in the Library, and if I had a real friend in the place, it was him. He grinned engagingly with white teeth, chewing on some red gum. 'You've seen it before?'

'No…' I watched the screen. It was one of those comedy sketch revue shows. A modern version of *Scrape The Barrel*. A very familiar face played some sort of alien, martian, whatever. It was Fairbrother, no less, and this must be the new J. J. Webster collaboration. I watched, in spite of myself, while Tarik laughed himself into paroxysms at a pair of Indians arguing about steak and chips in a restaurant. 'They've gone out for an English – good, eh? This is social satire, my friend,' he said chuckling. The alien character was providing a running commentary. Now a Japanese couple enter and get shown the tourist menu, and we can see that the prices are outlandish…it was fairly amusing, but I decided I could live without it, and the roars of laughter behind me. I stood up. Then the scene changed. Here were a couple of scruffy student-types arguing about whose turn it was to wash up in a filthy kitchen. 'You can't use bleach on the plates, Paul,' says one. 'I used the Fairy on my bike-chain, Alan,' replies the other, examining the bleach bottle. 'Kills all known germs…that ought to do it…' 'Ho, ho, ho,' said Tarik. 'This is the best bit. I love this pair! One's a medical student, and the other's a trainee dentist, and they share this – …' 'Filthy flat,' I said, sitting down again. 'And one of them's about to put a capful of bleach into the goldfish bowl…' 'So you have seen it!' Tarik said. 'No. I wrote it,' I muttered, and watched, repeating familiar lines almost word for word. It was distilled from an aborted episode of *Plug & Socket* called 'Hygiene'…

Favours, slights…some you should simply never forget. I have never forgotten Tarik. It has been an honour to repay a considerable material debt, and if Tarik cannot receive it in person – and I don't expect him to – there's the knowledge that he can collect the odd envelope at an accommodation address in Paddington and put it in his granddaughter's dowry-box. I smile, sometimes, thinking of Tarik on the Bricks, his smiling white teeth, his gentle ways, and his extraordinary skills, still doubtless employed… and every time some lunatic in a Ford Fiesta gets into reverse by mistake and nearly runs over my foot, I curse him, liberally. I also bless him abundantly every time my passport passes muster at the check-in. May your Gods smile down on you, Tarik. If you read this, know that I am forever grateful to you, not least for being someone whose sweet nature and erudite polysyllables prevented my going round the twist. On the other hand, I decided right there in HMP Stonethwaite that I would never forget Fairbrother's theft as long as I lived…

26: April Last Year

'You've got to co-operate, Barley. That's the deal. Nice, isn't it, the river at this time of the evening...' I gaze out of the enormous window at all the little tug-boats, the barges still full of Japanese tourists, and the Thames Police launches jaunting merrily along in the black water making little oily runnels in the pale descending twilight. 'Seems a shame to lose this view.'

'I'm not going to lose this view,' says Lion Barley petulantly. I notice he never stares at it much, despite having one of the more enviable addresses in our hallowed capital. I pull up the wheatstraw blinds pointedly every time I'm here.

'You are if you don't go to work and earn it like a good boy,' I say, drinking scotch and flicking ash very deliberately onto the stained creamy shagpile. This shagpile has seen better days, and deserved the pun once, before he stopped having the parties. The apartment, the third floor of what used to be a Victorian warehouse and could still be used in a Dickens film-set, was done out expensively by a young and eager newly-rich Barley in the mid 90s with the help of Harrods's and a ridiculously expensive designer from Milan. Illiterate male rock-star chic, plain and masculine, all black and cream and chrome, with angular Italian-style light-fittings and squishy leather cube-shaped furniture, very smart, and alas destined to look decidedly dilapidated within a very short time. There's a TV screen to rival a small commercial cinema, a giant sound system with speakers you could get yourself buried in, and his collection of framed advertising prints on the walls. An awful lot of them depict himself, younger, thinner, and with the trade-mark mane of hair, some with the chocolate bar that so nearly but not quite bore his stage name. Boring. I prefer the framed Pears Soap ones of the Edwardian barber in the bathroom where Barley keeps his anti-balding treatments.

Barley is complaining. 'I got you Fairbrother's run-routine. I got you those snaps of him leaving that assistant bird's place in EC1. You get this place to use as an office whenever you want, with me as office boy when you feel like chucking your weight about. What more do you want? I'm totally like your gofer when I should be concentrating on my *career*... And stop fucking up my carpet! It cost *thousands*, man.'

This carpet has been pock-marked by a thousand feet in a thousand Jimmy Choos, all Barley's barbarian celebrity friends spilling ash, vinaigrette, *vomito rosso* and spunk all over it.

'Stop whining, Barley. It's taken a lot of punishment, *man*. Time to get another, maybe.'

'I totally can't *afford* another! I'm owned! I'm totally owned by Todd Enterprises Limited!' Barley looks as if he's about to cry. I let him.

'Only for the time being, Barley...' Then I offer him another line, which he takes, mopping the snub nose that had pre-teen girls wetting their knickers more than a decade ago before they grew up and forgot he or his nose ever existed. The Met and the tax-man didn't quite forget, though, and that's why he owes me if not his life, then a life in more or less total obscurity in revue at the end of the pier in Dullsville-on-Sea. Which, incidentally, is more or less where I found him, as I frequently remind him. I remind him of a lot of other stuff, too, when I want to put on a bit of pressure.

Barley cheers up. It's not bad gear. 'So! You want me to get to the chick, yeah? This Suzy babe? She's quite a peach…' He smirks. Extra weight, a thinning of the hair and one of those fair, delicate complexions that doesn't stand up too well to the test of time, sunbeds and excess have given Barley the look of a supercilious baby. Or a shrivelling balloon. This hasn't done anything to curb his wholly un-realistic ambitions in the girl department, however. Lion still thinks he can not only pull, but command the pride like he did in the ad. Those 'Lioness' teeshirts have been shredded for dusters long ago and their owners are probably grand-mothers.

'If you like,' I say, considering. 'But she's probably too professional to come across with much, even despite all your fading charms, Lion. So's that frozen North dame. No…' I've had a bit of inspiration myself. 'Chat up that legal lad, Macavity, find his weaknesses. No – revise. *I'll* find his weaknesses. Then you go in with the equipment, okay? Then, if this means what I think it means, you get the new carpet.'

'It's not just the *carpet*, for Chrissakes. Do I get this place back in my own name? And some real work, like you keep promising?'

'Real work' is a sad joke, honestly. I say soothingly, 'Of course you do, Lion, of course you do! Once you've paid for your salvation.'

'And suppose he hasn't got anything, this Mac whatshisname, eh, man? I don't see what your down is on that Fairbrother guy anyway…'

'Yours not to reason why,' I say. 'You're my undercover research assistant, okay? For now, anyway. And if we get enough on Fairbrother, he'll do anything to prevent the publicity, including hiring you onto his talent-judging panel. No promises, at this stage, but…' This is the real inducement. Lion's pet idea is that with a bit of leverage, so to speak, he can re-launched himself into the rarefied world of showbiz that he misses so badly. The fact that he is basically an aging, almost talentless twerp who, with a mixture of chutzpah and a fair wind, once managed to leap onto an overcrowded bandwagon and hold centre stage for about five minutes is no deterrent to this singular delusion. Naturally, although I tease him mercilessly, I do nothing to discourage this. Actually, Lion's talent, for what it's worth, is in the sphere of photography, and I have my work cut out keeping him happy enough to prevent his selling the Leica XI I recently bought him in exchange for essential supplies, and desperate enough to keep working for me at the same time. It's a lonely life.

'Okay, Drex,' says Barley, almost humble. 'When do you want the office again? Just let me know.'

'Oh, I will,' I say. 'Here. Put money in your purse, bub…' I hand him some notes and a small self-seal plastic bag and his sulky-toddler face lights up pathet-ically. 'And make it last. I'm going on my travels.'

Whether I am or not, it's often necessary to put myself beyond the reach of Barley's prodigious appetite for cash and class As. Acting as Barley's regulator is franky wearing me ragged.

[119]

'*WHAT?*' Louise shrieks so loudly I have to hold the phone a good twelve inches from my head. 'What the hell do you mean, going away on somebody else's case? You work for me, remember?'

'Not exclusively, dollink. I have to eat, pay the rent. Be reasonable, sweetie.'

'Reasonable! *Reasonable*?' I put the phone down on my desk where it continues to make Disney noises for several moments.

'Lulu,' I say into it when the quacking has subsided. 'It's a week, okay? I can't meet you as agreed because I have to go away. My colleague is on the case, and we have some definite leads. Okay?'

'You'd better have, because all my lawyers need is some real evidence. They've been suggesting something called Specialists. They're a proper team of experts, in case you don't know what those are. And it can only be a hundred times better than your crap one-horse cowby outfit.'

'A hundred times more expensive, too,' I point out. 'And, well, not always to be trusted in the confidentiality department.'

She digests this. 'Well, there won't be a single penny more for you unless I get something solid!'

'Lulu, really. Keep it clean…' There's been another meeting or two at that snazzy Fulham apartment with the expensive cockroaches above the bed. My client is more than satisfied in some ways.

'Where are you going, anyway?'

'Washington,' I say. She won't believe me. 'I cannot tell a lie.'

Breathy angry silence. Then: 'All right, fine! *Be* mysterious!'

'My prerogative, *bimba mia*.'

'Okay. Okay! Look, I'm feeling a bit hysterical right now. Sorry. But you're sure he's being followed?'

'As the day the night,' I assure her, and ring off.

Now I have to get packing. I have to get to Heathrow. The US of A beckons. Like it always did.

Part III: The Summer of Love and Beyond
28: New Year 1967

'Grammy,' Andrew said, casual-innocent. He could still look – and sound – like a very sweet little boy when he chose. The trouble was, in his grandmother's presence he all too frequently felt like one: little, anyway, and much less bold than when she wasn't there. He was sitting at the kitchen table finishing his tea: a boiled egg with toast, and the last piece of the Christmas cake, dry and crumby by now, difficult to swallow, and amusing himself by causing very precise little crashes between his Matchbox London Bus and his Matchbox London Taxi, both presents sent in a parcel from his Uncle Ted O'Ryan who had the grocer's shop in Dublin. These toys were dead babyish, he thought, but good for crashing. But his mind was only half on the business, and the London Taxi clattered onto the tiles. He scrabbled to pick it up. 'Grammy?' His cheeks bulging with cake, he concentrated on the little vehicles, and kept his gaze from the armchair where she sat.

'Didn't I tell ye not to interrupt me programme,' said Mrs O'Ryan. 'It's Steptoe. Now shush, will youse, or youse'll get a smack in d' mout'...' He took the old lady's occasional threats of physical violence for the affectionate hyperbole they mostly were. He, after all, had power of a sort over her: he could make her laugh.

An old man on the television said in a whining, London voice, like the other kids at school, but funnier, *meant* to be funny (and he had learnt the difference the hard way): 'Ow, Arold! Just wot I orlways wanted,' and someone else said, 'I fort you'd like it, Farver,' and there was laughter on the television and Mrs O'Ryan joined in. 'I fort you'd like it, Farver,' Andrew mimicked in a loud whisper, so that Mrs O'Ryan could hear. She chuckled, despite herself.

Prudently, he waited. Andrew didn't find the programme funny as such, but he knew Grammy did. She was wiping her eyes on her tea-towel. There was more laughter and clapping, and now here was the familiar tune played at the end, like a horse clip-clopping, because the programme was about two men who sold scrap stuff from a horse and cart. Andrew decided to seize his moment, before the old lady got stuck into another programme. 'Grammy. I want to ask youse something. Serious-like.'

The television voice said, 'And now, here is the Nine O'Clock News,' and there was the bonging of Big Ben. If Andrew listened hard, he could often hear the real Big Ben bong too, but now he had other matters pressing.

Mrs O'Ryan sighed. 'Yes boy. And 'tis time youse was in bed. School in the mornin', remember...' The word 'school' sent a slight sick feeling to his stomach, for last term, just before the Christmas holidays, he had been called into the Headmaster's study, and had had to say that yes, of course he had given the letter to his grandmother, and that she must have forgotten all about it. It had stuck in his craw, a bit, to tell a lie about Grammy who would never have forgotten any such important thing. Soon, probably tomorrow, there would be another letter, by post this time, surely, and his grandmother, an impossibly early riser, would

[121]

give him no opportunity to intercept it. He crashed the vehicles, by accident this time, and they clattered noisily to the floor. He made rather a business of picking them up again.

'Sshhh! All your noise'll disturb the Captain!' She always said that.

'No it won't then. He's still in Italy or somewheres, ain't he?'

'So he is, so he is to be sure. But you can still hush your noise and leave me in peace.' For some reason, Mrs O'Ryan found the idea of the Captain absent from his upstairs rooms unsettling. Andrew, for his part, was very glad. He had every good reason to believe he was in the Captain's bad books by now. America had got to happen *soon*.

'You know the Captain, him upstairs? What got wounded in the Middle East and all that.'

'What about him?'

'And he's in Italy?'

'To be sure he is. Ain't ye just after sayin' so yeself? Now let me see the News.'

'Is it a war? Him being a Captain in the Army?'

'Course not, y'daftie. He's on his holidays. Now shut yer mout' won't ye, while I watches me programme.'

Andrew waited a few seconds. Then: 'P'raps he's Eye-talian...' He knew that would get her. It did.

'Course he's not Eye-talian, you great eejit. He's an English 'ero, that's what he is. Eye-talian indeed! The very t'ought!'

'Uncle Ted says my dadda's Eye-talian...' He had picked up trifles of information, dropped casually when people thought he wasn't listening, or not around to hear. Nobody would give him straight answers.

'Ted ought ter watch his big mout'. Come on, now, Andy. Eat up. School to-morrow.'

'I *know*...' He caught the bus neatly before it slid over the edge of the table. 'I spect the Captain's gone to Italy with that lady...' That lady. When he wasn't dreaming of America, he was dreaming of her...

'What lady?'

'The lady what came here before Christmas. From France. Very grand, she was. Is the Captain going to marry her?'

'You and your nonsense, ye daft child. That'll be the Captain's sister. Mrs. Walters. A real lady, she is. Always polite, which is more than you can say of some. Now shhh!' The grandmother kept her eyes firmly on the screen.

He fell into a troubled, puzzled silence. Because he knew he had not been wrong, mistaken in what he had seen from the lavender-scented fug of the airing-cupboard on the Sunday before Christmas. And the vision vividly remained: four o'clock in the afternoon after Sunday dinner, Grammy snoozing in her chair with the television turned low, and he with a sudden whim to inspect what might be going on upstairs... The Captain's bedroom door slightly open, and the Captain gently snoring in the big bed, and *her*, emerging from beside him, throwing on a thick tweed dressing-gown and padding in bare feet across the corridor to the bathroom, giving him just seconds to dart into the linen cupboard with a thudding heart, keeping the door a little ajar; her passing so close by him he could hear her breathe, smell her musky smell… From his lair in the cupboard, squeezed into a tiny space that would very soon be too small to accommodate him, with the almost overpowering fragrance of clean linen and lavender making him feel faint, he watched her bend to twist the taps, the hot water sputtering and then gushing, steaming into the bath, the hiss of fragrant bath salts in the vapour, the dressing gown loosened and barely covering her nakedness, a small breast with its pink nipple protruding, her mussed hair… He had almost gasped out loud. When he thought of her like that, he felt frightened and excited all at the same time, a bit like when he had seen Mr Welham's pictures in the magazines, but far, far worse. He almost gasped again, at the thought, and suddenly he felt very embarrassed to have conjured up such a vision in the presence of his grandmother. Better to remember her as she had been the last time, two days later, when he'd made her swallow the butterfly story…when she'd promised not to tell on him… He concentrated very hard on the taxi and the bus.

'*The Queen Mother, elegant in a snug plaid coat and matching hat, set off by a seasonally cheerful red scarf, was evidently touched by this very splendid bouquet of winter greenery and holly presented to her by this deputation of young Brownies invited on to the Balmoral estate… Here she is on the arm of the Prince of Wales…*'

'Now that's another real lady, whatever Ted says,' murmured Mrs O'Ryan with a snort of satisfaction. 'Him and his politics.'

'Grammy?'

'Shhh, can't you! How many more times? 'Tis t' Queen Mother.'

'Grammy! 'Tis t'New Year, isn't it? …'

Pause, while the old lady concentrated on the smiling Dowager. '*And now Southern Rhodesia. On Tuesday, the Prime Minister, Harold Wilson, will meet for talks with delegates…*' A snorted dismissal for Mr Wilson: 'What of it, boy?'

'Well – …' Suddenly, he couldn't say the words *Rochdale, Texas, America…* 'You said, remember, New Years! I'm goin' to America, ain't I?'

The old lady sighed. 'America! S'that *all*? Jesus, Mary and Joseph!'

'Only wondered…' He concentrated on his toy vehicles.

But the old lady pulled her eyes away from the broadcast. 'What's your hurry, anyways? Youse happy here, ain't ye?'

'Sure…' In fact, he wasn't *un*happy exactly, if 'unhappy' meant actually miserable and sad. His life here in London with his grandmother had a certain solidity that he scarcely needed to examine. But he was bored, often, for all his invented amusements. And he hated school, except perhaps for Mr Bartram, who was just a weed. Sometimes he hated school with a hard, dry, private passion that occasionally erupted into actual violence, but mostly he simply managed to escape the school grounds unnoticed. That was about to be his undoing: if he wasn't very careful, this particular crime ('Truancy is a crime, my lad!' the Headmaster had said, flanked by Mr Bartram who had not disagreed) was about to be exposed. Yet Andrew hugged a certain, special knowledge to himself and whenever things became unbearable, he could remind himself that his was a misplaced life, that he actually belonged elsewhere, and that his troubles in number forty-two,

Maxwell Road, Fulham, London, or at the Gladstone Lane Junior Boys didn't matter, for soon, soon, his new life would begin in Rochdale, Texas, America. 'I just wants to go an' see me Mammy, like...' He tried to make the appeal sound casual.

As if divinely intuiting his train of thought (Grammy could do this; it was disconcerting) his grandmother said, her voice shrewd and hard, 'Youse not in any trouble, are ye?'

'No,' said Andrew at once. 'Course not.'

'No monkey business at school?'

'No, Grammy,' he said, but he felt himself going red.

'And you ain't been upsettin' me PG?'

'No, Grammy...'

Mrs O Ryan got up from the sagging armchair and began to clear the tea things. 'I don't believe you, Lord help me,' she said and, bending over him very close, her blue glare defied him to lie. Whereas the likes of Mr Welham, Mr Bartram and the Headmaster had no power to scare him, and the Captain only a little bit, maybe, this tiny, spare, elderly woman, with the unnaturally black, curly hair, and wearing her blue nylon overall and clutching a tea-towel as if always prepared to cope with some domestic mishap, inspired a powerful respect. 'It's Mass for you on Sunday, and confession, ye hear me? The good Lord will know when youse not tellin t' trut'! He will, surely to goodness...'

His grandmother's vigilance over his religious observances was erratic. Mass, at the Roman Catholic Church of St Saviour was not a weekly ritual for either of them, the old lady herself tending to 'pop in' whenever she had a spare moment during the week. His own attendance, however, was something invoked as a punishment, or at least as a sort of precautionary measure for his many misdemeanours. He was still at an age where he could almost believe that the Lord could see his sins. 'Yes, Grammy.'

'Hmmph. I want to watch the rest of the News. Off to bed with ye! Go on, will ye! Pygwammies. And your teet'!' She stomped on her stick-thin lisle-stockinged legs back to her chair. *'And can we turn to you for one last comment, Sir Jonathan? The stability of the Smith regime in Rhodesia now surely depends on...'*

'Grammy?' He was standing in the doorway.

'What *now*? You have to go to school in the morning. And let me hear another word from that Mr Barton about you, and you won't know what trouble means. Now goodnight, boy.'

'Bartram... Grammy?'

'Ow, what now, for the Lord's sakes?'

'Me Mammy. She is going to send for me, isn't she? To go to Rochdale, Texas, America? Soon?'

The pleading in the young voice caught at a heart which was used to hardening, and she said grimly, 'Soon, boy. Soon, let's hope. Now, will ye off to bed, or do I have to pick up a broom to ye? Jesus, Mary and Joseph, the sooner youse's off to America the better, so far as I'm concerned!' And this almost cheered him, and so he went obediently, and re-read his latest Superman comic by torchlight in his chilly little bed under the staircase and eventually fell asleep, dreaming of America. Waking and sleeping, he dreamed constantly of America, that promised land. The more discontented he became with his life *here*, at home in London, and at school where he stood out as odd, and where the other boys pulled his curly hair and made fun of his accent, mimicked his limp, and called him bog-boy, the bogger, and 'Spud', and 'Murphy' (which really was offensive, since it wasn't his surname) the more obsessively he planned his new life *there*, where things were surely better and bigger, and just like the films, but he must stop pronouncing it 'fil-ums', because of the boys at school... There'd be big limousines, and men in wide hats, and great tall buildings such as Superman could push over... The buildings loomed at him, giddy-making, and he felt lost, felt his head whirling as he gazed upward. It was *this* America, this half-awake America, that lurked under the surface of his passionate hopes and dreams of escape, a New World full of strangers, where there would not be a simple reunion with a Mammy to whom he had in his heart's dream always belonged and in whose arms he would know a true home and a blessed peace, but a confrontation, awkward and stiff, with a stranger called Rose, Rosie, Rosaleen... He repeated her name, her names, very often... Rosaleen. And there would be the Others... There'd been the whisperings and the conferences, about the other children, a brother and a sister, and now a new baby boy, and this man called Hank, his new dadda as he would be... A new family who might find him as strange as he found them, a family who would all talk in American, as if he'd stepped by accident, like a Martian, into a film where nothing and nobody was real. In his dreams, his uncertainties crowded in his busy young mind, and sometimes he shouted out loud in his troubled sleep.

Alone with her television, his grandmother sighed. He wasn't a bad little feller, Andy, but he was turning into a terrible handful. Drat that Rosaleen! She would have to get hold of Ted. And she would speak to the Captain when he returned. He would know what to do.

29

Leo and Lottie had settled down into a pattern in his London rooms: she would wake him with the French coffee she had brought back from her sojourn with Aunt Jessica, and then the Nurse would come and help him bathe and dress and give him his injection and massage. Gradually, as his leg strengthened, Leo and Lottie would walk in the Square, and began taking longer excursions to the Chelsea Physic Gardens, to the Brompton Oratory, in a taxi to Kew, to the odd concert. With great tact (oh, please, Mrs O'Ryan, don't *ever* stop making your wonderful bread for us) Lottie had taken over most of Mrs O'Ryan's duties as Leo's personal cook, and made him appetising little meals on the upstairs gas-stove and helped eat them herself, and she grew steadily a little less thin. She thinks she's looking after me, thought Leo, but the truth is, I'm looking after her.

One night, shortly before Christmas, about three weeks after she had arrived and her blessed presence had given him the courage to heal, he lay reading in bed. He had heard her come in after a dinner party; heard her tread rather unsteady on the staircase, but soft, shoeless (she always took them off, tactfully, on the landing) up to the bathroom and the lavatory; heard the flush and the plumbing screech, and then her footsteps again, stumbling a little, on the corridor to her room next door to his; then the quiet, definitive click of her bedroom door. And then, a little later as he was settling to sleep – he would never have admitted to himself that he had been waiting for her – he heard her sobbing her heart out. No sound could hurt him more. He hitched himself out of bed with an agility which surprised and also inspired him, and he padded out into the corridor hardly feeling his lame leg. He opened the door and saw, lit dimly orange by the streetlamp through the drawn curtains, her huddled body convulsed with grief. He eased himself into her bed and curled himself round her, stroking her hair, her shoulder, and her great choking sobs subsided eventually, and her thin body relaxed against his. When she turned her hot, wet face to him it was with a quite unstoppable desire.

One has shared a nursery; one has shared, for God's sake, a womb. They barely needed to speak, except that they both delighted in the funniness of conversation. 'If only Giles had enjoyed, well, just *talking*,' Lottie admitted, unable quite to dismiss the thought that her late poet, one who had taken *words* very seriously indeed, had found certain aspects of herself, her unconscious *family* self, a little silly, frivolous. 'He doubtless had weightier matters to consider,' Leo said, staring up at the wedding-cake ceiling. She glanced and saw the trace of a wry smile. 'What would he have made of this, I wonder?'

'Giles? Giles was a champion of personal freedoms, of self-government. He – I mean I'm sure –...' But privately Lottie pondered. For all his *avant-garde* opinions, for all his famous inveighing against the Establishment, moral, civil and political, for all his theoretical championing of rebellions, revolts and riotous assemblies from the solid established comforts of his Cambridge rooms, Giles Walters might well have been a little shocked by this more homely reality. And it unnerved her, a little, to imagine Giles with feet of suburban clay…

'You know we're committing a crime, I suppose?' They had spent every night for a week in Leo's bed.

'Mmmm. Does it matter?'

'No…no, it doesn't. At least it doesn't to me. Does it to you?'

'No. Not one bit, actually. Frankly, I just feel glad I'm still alive.'

But if crime, as such, didn't matter, Lottie found herself taking careful precautions: simple, practical steps to protect them from prying eyes, from speculation. She mussed up the bed-sheets in her room for the benefit of Mrs O'Ryan's charwoman; she tried to ensure that the doors that connected Leo's private apartments to the rest of the house were kept firmly closed. Total privacy was impossible, however: the main staircase from kitchen quarters to the attics ran past Leo's rooms, and Leo's wide landing contained the household linen-cupboard. The thought of exposure made her feel always a little nervous, jumpy. To this household, she was still the object of curiosity, still the interloper. And, sometimes, with reason, she felt as if she were being *watched*…

'What the *hell*? Good *God* you gave me a shock!'

She looked formidable this time, in a smart little grey jacket over a dress that showed her knees. Her shoes had high, square heels. There was paint on her face, and her face was furious. The last time he had seen her, she had looked so entirely different, and despite his own heart-stopping shock at being discovered – just his luck that she should want a towel – his secret knowledge nevertheless inspired a sense of power. Now he tried to superimpose his previous vision of her, to make her less fearsome. A good trick, that: you imagine your enemy in the altogether, or doing something embarrassing or silly, like being on the toilet or farting, and they lose their power. It worked. Imagining her as he had last seen her, he even found himself unaccountably excited under his grey school shorts. She grabbed his arm and yanked. The rest of him tumbled out of the linen-cupboard. 'Horrible child! *Horrible* child! You've no business at all up here, do you hear me? No business at all. Now beat it! Hear me? Out!'

He blinked a few times, but he faced her, fury and all. And he rather liked 'beat it'. Sounded like the films. 'You goin' to tell me Grammy?' he asked innocently.

'I certainly shall tell your grandmother, young man! I'll tell the police, if I have to!' She was trembling slightly.

In a flash, Andrew had perceived two things: one, that she was bluffing; and two – he could almost smell it beneath the expensive manufactured scent – that despite her anger she was actually afraid of him. It gave him confidence, and he became inventive: 'Y'see, I'm only hatching me butterflies, like. All warm in t'cupboard. Grammy doesn't like 'em. Thinks they're dirty, on the clean sheets like. But they change from caterpillars in a nice silky cocoon which they eat – they eat silk, do butterflies – and then they emerge wit' their little wings all crinkled up, and then they dries out, stretch their lovely wings, all red and blue and gold, they are, like jewels, and then they fly…' (And put like that, the butterflies were as real as

[127]

if they might flutter out, at any second, from their dark mysterious birth in the linen-cupboard in a great bright shimmering cloud.) 'Beauties, they are! Red admirals and peacocks. I got a painted lady once... It's only a hobby-like. Honest.'

The blue-black eyes that stared at Lottie were anything but honest, but they were huge, the colour of ink, and engaging. She felt a sudden sense of relief wash over her.

'Sorry,' said the boy, more engagingly than ever. 'Truly, honest to God, Miss, Madam.'

'Mrs Walters. I'm not sure I shouldn't report this,' she said, glaring at him, but she spoke more quietly. 'This is my brother's – Captain Rollitt's – private apartment, you know. And you shouldn't be up here...'

''Tis me grammy's airin'-cupboard, though,' Andrew could not resist saying. And grinned, ruefully. 'Sorry, truly, Miss... Madam.'

'Oh, *honestly!*' The impossible geography of the house exasperated her. 'Now listen, you mustn't hide here any more, understand? Andrew, isn't it?' He nodded agreement. 'Because if you do, Andrew, I'm going to have to talk to my – to the Captain, aren't I?'

'S'pose so...' He hung his head. 'I wish you wouldn't tell the Captain, or Grammy. Please, Miss. Madam.'

'Mrs *Walters*. I suppose you'll get into a lot of trouble if I do...' She sighed, and he thought she was softening. She glanced briefly at his boot. Her face, sharp, like the way she spoke, and sharper with the make-up, relaxed a little.

'I will with Grammy, certain sure. She'll belt me, and me Grammy, she can belt wi' the best, no word of a lie,' he said, and he saw her bite her lip on a smile. 'You won't tell?' She had relented, palpably. From that moment, he felt an uncanny certainty that he had a power over her. (Later, it would become a confidence in his power over women that would never desert him: his young heart, criminal to its core, sang.)

'Well, just this once perhaps. But no more hiding up here, promise?' He nodded vigorously. 'Find another place for your butterflies, okay? You really must never hide up here again...' Somehow Lottie had expected a sort of nemesis, something coming to clobber this happiness she had found, and after all it was just this little lame Irish kid. She felt like crying with relief. 'Go away, now. I won't say anything.'

'And neither shall I, Mrs Walters...' He gazed up at her. Her beauty – he supposed that was what it was – the way she looked, her face, anguished him strangely. Despite this, or perhaps because of it, he badly wanted her discomposure. He could never forget the way he had seen her last. 'I mean about the last time...' Her incredible eyebrows knitted in amused puzzlement. They were a sort of dark gold colour, darker than her hair, which was illuminated by a shaft of splintered winter sunlight through the round landing window. She looked like one of the saints in the church.

'Last time?' She had light tawny eyes, like her hair. 'What do you mean, last time?' Her frown deepened again. He loved the way her expression changed; the way he could change it. 'What last time?'

'Only for the butterflies,' he said, nonchalantly, watching her face. 'Youse very beautiful in the nuddy, Mrs Walters...'

'*What?*' But now he had dodged out of her way and was gone, surprisingly agile and swift on his uneven footwear, but not before he had seen the real consternation on her face.

30

They had spent Christmas in Florence, arguing happily, and feeling delightfully free.

For Leo, there had been a loose end or two to tie up. He had sat, nursing a whiskey and soda in a dark corner of the White Horse, and watched Dean unwrap his present. Dark violet foulard silk spilled inkily from the tissue paper, and Leo saw the blue eyes widen, and then fall, and he knew he had made a mistake. His first idea – a good leather wallet with banknotes inside – would have been more appreciated after all. Of course it would. He felt foolish and rather sad. 'It's reely nice,' Dean said, not very convincingly. 'The colour, n' that. It's lovely, Cap. Thanks a million.'

'That's – um – well, that's Christmas, Dean. This – …' he produced an envelope – 'this is in the nature of goodbye and good luck…' Dean took the envelope with a gleam of hope. 'Oh,' he said, as he examined the contents. 'Vouchers?' The look of puzzlement and disappointment on the almost impossibly pretty face would have been comic if Leo had been in the mood to be amused.

'It's a course of twenty-five driving lessons, Dean. Every young chap ought to know how to drive. It's an essential skill if you ever want to – well, get anywhere.'

'Like away from the Dilly?'

'Like away from Piccadilly,' said Leo, feeling depressed. 'You will remember what we've been talking about, won't you, Dean? About your future.'

'Yeah, course I will. Look, I'm reely sorry I ain't no musician, Cap. I did try, but I ain't got an ear, not reely. It weren't you. But I might give up the idea of a group after all.'

'Perhaps that's more practical, Dean. You might consider evening classes in electrical engineering, maybe. Some sort of engineering. Let me know. I wish I were able to do more.'

'Well – life, eh? And – er – well, thanks, Cap. It's p'raps as well it ain't actual cash, reely, cos I'd just go an' spend it. You know me…' He grinned, and put the envelope in the inner pocket of his leather jacket. 'An' thanks about Aunty Et. That was real nice of yer. Much appreciated…' Despite his outward brittleness and the affectations of sophistication, Dean was at heart a true Cockney lad with a sense of family.

'She's just what we needed,' Leo assured him. 'At least, I'm sure my housekeeper thinks so…' On this score, he felt less than confident, but this was not the time or place to express his doubts.

'Aunty Etty'll be reely glad about that. She's a good ole girl, Aunty Et. Thanks a lot, Cap. Well, then. I guess this is it. Merry Christmas to you and yours…' Leo got to his feet with the help of his stick, and they shook hands awkwardly, said 'good luck' again, and Dean jaunted out of the pub, off to God knew where. Leo decided to have another whiskey and downed it in one at the bar. Glancing back briefly at the recently vacated table, he saw that the violet tie and its tissue wrapping had been left behind.

For Lottie, also, there had been loose ends: a brief, bleak and sad visit to Cambridge, sorting her belongings and those remaining things of Giles's still lodged at Gonville & Caius. This had been followed by an even bleaker luncheon in the Green Man in Trumpington with Giles's mother, who had never approved of her and, in the absence of grandchildren, was taking this opportunity to shed her daughter-in-law from the Walters family. ('I hope you know what you're going to do with your life, Charlotte. I believe it is very important that a widow should involve herself in activities that are strictly *worthwhile*, even – perhaps especially – when she is as young as you are...' 'I'm going to carry on keeping house for my injured brother, Mrs Walters...' – she had never called her mother-in-law anything else – 'until he's better and I decide what to do...') There! That ought to be *worthwhile* enough!

Then, blessed freedom. She joined Leo in Pisa, where they took a train to Florence for Christmas and on into the promising but desperately chilly New Year of 1967. Leo had received a small pension instalment from his Regiment, and they felt liberated. They spent their mornings wandering slowly over the bridges in boots and scarves, Leo increasingly agile on his bad leg with just a stick for support now. They stood staring at the freezing Arno from the Ponte Santa Trinità, or browsed and exclaimed over jewellery and gloves in the Ponte Vecchio, disappointing hopeful shop-keepers, for their funds were limited, before diving, chilled to the marrow, down into the tall, darkly forbidding Renaissance streets to drink strong coffee and grappa in little dark bars where the Gaggia machines hissed like angry dragons, and then going on to do their 'tourist duty', where they gazed, Leo leaning on his stick and sometimes on Lottie's arm, at treasures in the Bargello and the Uffizzi, and then on to eat cheap, delicious pasta or baccalà in some steamy, overheated trattoria. Then, after a sleepy afternoon in their hotel bedroom, they tried to warm themselves before meagre radiators in the tall-ceilinged lounge of the Albergo Porta Rossa, before going off in search of Florentine steaks and flasks of rough chianti for supper. They exclaimed at the cold – they were far colder than anyone ought to be in Italy, they declared – and they were dreadfully happy. 'Is it odd we've bumped into absolutely no one we know? We ought to come and live here,' Lottie said seriously one evening, wriggling her wool-clad shoulders in the snug depths of a hotel lounge chair.

'Hmmm?'

'Or we could stay on in London. You could sell up at Maxwell Road. Buy somewhere else. Or we could even rent somewhere a bit decent. We could, you know, darling...'

'What? I doubt we could afford anyhing better than Maida Vale, or perhaps Chiswick, maybe, if we tried to buy anything in London. It's getting expensive, dearest, even south of the River. Perhaps we should just stay in Fulham, at least some of the time. It is *almost* Chelsea, darling...' He still felt responsible – that Lottie needed some London amusements. His own London amusements he felt he could probably abandon for good and all, shed them like an old worn skin. He winced involuntarily. There were things he couldn't talk about, even to Lottie.

'We *could* stay in Fulham, of course... But what about Brighton? We could go to Brighton. There's the sea... Or, I know, damn it! We could go to Sarfend...'

'Idiot! Your Cockney's terrible.'

'Seriously, couldn't we come to Italy? Have a house here, anyway? It's so lovely.'

'It's certainly a thought. Lovely summers, lovely light... But we can't be too ambitious, Lottie. We're a crock and a widow, remember?'

'I wish we were richer. Aunt Ros was always so furious with Pa for going broke and losing us Anstey. Marrying Giles, I never thought I'd mind, at least not all that much...' She cradled her glass in both hands and leaned forward. 'Leo, why don't we make a bit of a plan? Tell me, what exactly is the arrangement at number forty-two? You've never really said.'

'It's quite simple. I only own the lease which incidentally is running out. Difficult to sell, and I can't afford to renew it at the moment. Ma O'Ryan lives in the basement for love if you don't count all the running around being my house-keeper for which she gets a little stipend, and she gets whatever she makes from renting the attic bedroom. It works, up to a point.'

'I see. Sounds like she does quite well, really. Leo, my dear, I've been wondering. I really think we have to get away from the O'Ryans, darling. I mean, I know she's been very good, but – ...' She bit her finger.

'Oh, dear. I know you can't bear her, can you? She has been very good to me, but I can see.'

Lottie shivered. 'Oh, but I can bear her! I mean I like her. I'm not rotting her at all. I just wish she wouldn't be so – so stand-offish with me, as if I've usurped her or something, but no! She's looked after you wonderfully well. No, it's not her. Oh God. I don't know, darling. I think, actually, it's the *boy*...' She had been true to her word, and not said anything about the linen-cupboard incident up to now. Something about that strange little exchange that had bothered her more than she could say. Those eyes. And that knowing, precocious male intelligence that had shone though them... Lottie shivered again.

Leo laughed. 'That bloody kid! He's a pain in the backside, of course, but pretty bright all the same. Plausible little wretch. Plucky, too, with his deformed foot.'

'Yes. But he snoops. I didn't want to tell you before while you were so convalescent, but I caught him in the airing-cupboard just before we came away. He said something about hatching chrysalises, but he doesn't seem the nature-loving type somehow. I don't know, Leo, I just think he's a bit creepy. He just seems to *appear*, like some sort of goblin. Yes, I know, I know, I'm being very silly...' She laughed and pulled a face. She was glad it was out. Speaking of it like this, far away in Italy, made it diminish in her mind, somehow. She *was* being silly.

'She does her best with him, you know, poor woman.'

'Why's he lame?'

'Club foot, I think. Born with it. And he was rather dumped on his grandmother. The love-child of the youngest daughter and an American airman who was married already, and who of course deserted her when he realised what his bit of fun had amounted to. The girl – she'd been nursing, first in London and then in Croydon, lots of fraternising with the American airbase – grabbed the next available USAF mechanic and married him, not saying anything about her little encumbrance, and went back to live in the US, leaving the unwanted one permanently with his grandma, where he'd been staying anyway while the flighty Miss Rosie was doing her night-shifts and what have you. The old lady's pretty stoical about it, and seems determined to bring him up properly, poor old girl.'

'I see. Poor thing. She looks so frail in some ways until you realise she's as tough as old boots. I've heard her tear that child off a strip sometimes...' Lottie was thoughtful. 'The daughter's first American must have been a Latino, or something. He's very dark...' (Those eyes, again.) 'But now he's joining mum in the States, is that true?'

'That's the plan, I gather. I only hope it works. Ma O'Ryan could do with a break, and the kid's clearly obsessed by the idea...' But he really didn't know: perhaps the husband would be reluctant to take on a new stepson, especially one like Andy O'Ryan. And there were other kids now, according to Mrs O'Ryan's rare personal confidences. Leo had been brought up to a sense of responsibility for his staff. At this moment, when all his normal responses had been so delightfully slewed by his returning health and this remarkable, wonderful new footing with Lottie, he could have cheerfully wished Mrs O'Ryan and her family concerns at the bottom of the sea; but he said, 'We can do whatever you like, dearest, but I can't just dump the O'Ryans. Besides, whatever we do, there'll always be O'Ryans of some sort or other.'

'No there won't. I can keep house and all that. I'm quite good at it. We can buy somewhere, somewhere small and manageable, a cottage perhaps in a village, and we can have a daily, or even a three-times-weekly if we're really broke.'

'Darling Lottie! Or we could simply stay.'

'I don't think we can, you know, at least not very tactfully, Leo dear. We're a bit *outré* for that, now, remember. I suppose...' She examined her hands minutely, tugged at her rings. 'I suppose that's really why I find that child so unsettling. If he really is a child, and not some sort of imp...' (Always, those *eyes*...)

'Oh, don't be daft, darling. Don't get all fey, please. He's just a precocious little brat. Perhaps he ought to be at school. Somewhere that would really shape him up. Actually, that's a damn good idea. Sort him out...not really our problem, however,' he added, watching her frown deepen. 'All right, no. Not forty-two. No more O'Ryans. Let's rent somewhere in Brighton. Or Dorset. Or Hampshire. The country – you like the country. We'll go for a village. Little Nothington under Edge where the drains won't work and there'll be a parish council for you to run and the local Rotary for me.'

'Brr! Sounds a bit sordid after all perhaps. Of course I do love the country. But I love London, too. Except when I don't. Oh dear.'

In this mood of indecision, they extended their sojourn for another week as cheaply as they could, deliberately drifting and anonymous. It was while they were huddling against the weather in a semi-deserted albergo in a walled medieval town high in the hills near Arezzo that the problem was at least partly resolved, unexpectedly. A telegram arrived, sent on late from the Porta Rossa in Florence. Aunt Rosalind had died, not, as it turned out, falling from a horse in full cry over the Wolds, but from a heart-attack following a nasty injury to the head from a falling roof tile. A sudden thick freeze delayed their departure, and they were unable to attend the funeral, which saddened them, and they comforted themselves by returning to Florence and attending a service in St Mark's English Church, and signing the book in Aunt Rosalind's memory, and then going on to the Duomo, where they lit candles. They returned to England, and sat in the draughty crumbling Hall, reminiscing in hushed voices about childhood holidays, and learned from the ancient and old fashioned Mr Lovell that Aunt Rosalind had indeed left her estate, including the tumbling pile that was Folwell Hall, entirely and absolutely, to her late sister Margaret's boy, Leofric. To Charlotte, her late sister Margaret's girl, she had left a small but significant sum of money and an antique diamond ring.

'You know what this means, apart from anything else, darling heart,' Leo said in the train to St Pancras.

'What, dearest?'

'We're rich. Or at least, we're almost rich.'

31

Mrs O'Ryan was reading the letter with difficulty while Mrs Pell was replacing brooms, mop and bucket with a great deal of unnecessary clatter in the scullery. She got very few letters, and this one was very official-looking. It was typed, and from her grandson's school, that much was clear.. *'Dear Mrs O'Ryan, It is with regret.'*... *'great concern'*... *'has not been attending'*... and there were some figures. She made out that out of a total of seventy-five school days last term, Andrew O'Ryan had attended just forty of them... *'would be very grateful if...'* and they wanted her to come to the school, in person, to see the Headmaster... Jesus, Mary and Joseph! It felt as if she was in trouble herself. If only she had someone she could ask! If only the dear Captain were here! She bit her finger. Drat that little Andy, making trouble and trouble and trouble again. The clattering stopped, and Mrs O'Ryan shoved the letter hastily into the pocket of her overall.

'Tea I suppose?' Mrs O'Ryan called from the basement kitchen – this with a customary bad grace which Mrs Pell never seemed to notice. A nosey-parker who never stopped talking in a kind of high-pitched shriek, *and* complaining non-stop, *and* still treating her as a foreigner, as dirty Irish. Oh, she was friendly enough, but you could always tell. But the Captain had hired her, and now she was doing the 'rough', as Ivy used to, but at about twice the speed, and the beds as well, and the Captain's word was Law, couldn't argue with that, and there were her knees to consider. Still, she almost missed that dopey Ivy blundering about with her slack mouth and her sullen silences. With this Mrs Pell, it was tea, tea, tea all the time, and talk about *talk*...

'Tea an' marie, eh? Don't mind if I do, Mrs O, after the mornin' I've 'ad...' She waddled through to the kitchen and sat herself down heavily with a wheezy sigh at Mrs O'Ryan's kitchen table. 'A cig, that's wot I need...' She fished for her Senior Service in the pocket of her apron. Mrs O'Ryan pushed the ashtray towards her grudgingly. A pause, while she lit a match and sucked in, coughing happily, talking through the gales of smoke. 'Well! Wouldn't let me into 'is room at first, 'e wouldn't, 'im upstairs. Yes, duck, two, ta. Stopped mindin' me figure, I 'ave. Cosy in 'ere, innit, with the boiler? Couldn't feel me feet on the bus smornin'...' She slurped her tea with relish, and bit into a biscuit. 'No. Wouldn't let me in, 'e wouldn't. Not at first. I said to 'im, I said, I gotter do the room, Mr Welham, I said. It's Mrs O's orders, that's wot I said. An' 'e said, 'e said through the door like, 'e'd got a doser the flu an' 'e was in bed. Wotcher maker that? But I hears 'im through the door, scrabblin' about, an' I shouts through, wot about the toilet rolls and yer bed? So 'e come to the door, in 'is jarmies, like, an' a right sight 'e were, an' all, an' to be fair 'e did look proper seedy, all yeller – an' 'e took the toilet rolls an' the clean sheets off of me, an' said 'e'd do it imself when 'e felt like it, would yer believe it, an' I says to 'im, I says, as yer not atcherly *in* the bed, Mr Welham, why don't yer let me do it an take the dirties down for the laundry? 'Cos Mrs O, she would't approve at all if I didn't do yer room proper, she wouldn't, I said. An' so 'e let me in...' Mrs Pell crushed out her cigarette.

'Well, that's all as it should be, Mrs Pell...' Privately, she was very glad she almost never had cause to enter Mr Welham's room these days. When he paid his rent, *he* came down to see *her*.

'Yes, but while I was strippin is sheets, like, e kind of 'overed, wantin to say summink, an' then 'e said, I ain't 'appy, Mrs P, 'e says, and *I* says, that's understandable Mr Welham, if you gotter doser the 'flu. You needster rest up an' keep warm, you do, or you'll go down with summink worse, which is wot 'appened to my Audrey's Jeff wot got the new-monia. But 'e said, 'e said – ooh, can I ave a fill-up Mrs O? Just ittin the spot this is – an' *then* 'e said, 'e said, mattererfac' 'e weren't appy 'ere, like, an' it's in stric' confidence-like, 'e says, but it all ad to do with your Andy! I'm jus tellin you, like, Mrs. O, becos I thought y'oughter know...' Mrs Pell had counted on a reaction, and she got it. She fished out another Senior Service.

Mrs O'Ryan closed her eyes and muttered something that sounded like 'Jesus-maryanjoseph'. Torn between the desire to know, and her reluctance to let such as Mrs Pell into her private family affairs, she made rather a thoughtful business of draining the pot into her own cup, jiggling the lid, and adjusting the teacosy. 'And?'

'Well, it seems 'e's bin idin', young Andy, snoopin' and stuff. Nat'rally, that Welham, he don't like it, worried about is books an' that, so 'e *says*, but if y'arsk me.'

Mrs O'Ryan muttered again. 'I'll lam the little... Is anything missin'?' she asked abruptly. The question mortified her, but she had to know.

'Oh no, Mrs O. I'm sure not. Jus' a kid's bit of a lark, like. Seems that ole Welham caught 'im in 'is cupboard, that's all. Mountains and mole 'ills! You know wot they're like that age! My Doreen's Malcolm's just your Andy's age, an' it's all spies an' that with 'im too... An' as for my nephew Dean, up to all sorts, 'e was, before he got all smart and fashion-wise...' she trailed off, thinking about her nephew Dean, who called her 'lovey' and would sometimes kiss her and give her a nice crisp ten-bob note... 'Shall I put the kettle on again?' Not waiting for an answer, she heaved herself out of her chair. 'So I says, boys will be boys, I says. S'only natural, I says. You was a boy once, wasn't you, I says, tryin' to 'umour 'im. But 'e was put out, I don't mind sayin', Mrs O. Goin' on like anythink...'

Mrs O' Ryan rubbed her temples. How many more of her young grandson's misdemeanours must she learn today? Oh blessed Mary!

'Now I blame the telly, I do,' Mrs Pell was saying from the stove. 'All them American programmes. And the films! Nuffink the same since the War, all them American GIs, nylons, dance halls... Mine you, my Aud, she 'ad the time of 'er life...' She chortled and the kettle whistled. 'Forty-four now, is Aud. 'Ere now, a fresh pot...' Plonking it down on the table, Mrs Pell sat down again, shaking her head in reminiscence. 'In fact weren't your young Andy...?' Her bird-bright eyes shone. 'That pot'll only take a mo'...' Both women stared at the teapot rather than at each other. 'Reckon she's ready – brewed not stewed, as my ole mum 'uster say!'

'I'll pour, thank ye very much, Mrs Pell,' said Mrs O'Ryan, and did so, very much on her dignity. 'S'pose ye'll want another biscuit?' She opened the tin.

'Ta, ducks. Shouldn't really... But 'e's off, ain't 'e, soon? Young Andy, off to

America?' Mrs Pell bit into another biscuit. 'Nice for 'im. New place, an 'is mum, an' school. Spose they do 'ave schools in America. Give you a bitter peace an' quiet 'n' all, eh?' Mrs Pell chuckled wheezily, then saw that Mrs O'Ryan wasn't sharing the joke. 'Though yer'll miss 'im, bound to, Mrs O. Understandable. I'm a gran'ma four times over, me, an' now young Julie into 'er first bra 'n' everythink, she is, and wantin' to put all them cosmetics on 'er face, an hairdos, an them mini-skirts, showing all they got, and these long-haired Beatles... Only thirteen, she is. An' as I says to my Aud, you gotter wotch 'em, at that age, I says... Still, all change, like wot they says at Victoria! But y'ave ter laugh, don't yer? He was in a right ole bate, was that Welham.'

'Well, Mrs Pell, if Mr Welham's got anything to say to me, he knows quite well where to find me.'

'Oh, but that's wot I *says* to 'im, Mrs O. Yer'll find Mrs O in the kitchen down-stairs, I says to 'im, I says. So don't start none of yer complaints with me. I ain't the boss, I says. Well, of course, I says, it's the Capting wot's the real boss, but yer'd better ave a word wi' Mrs O first, if it's 'er boy wot's the bother. An' that wos tellin' 'im...' Mrs Pell was evidently very pleased with herself indeed.

Mrs O'Ryan was rubbing her temples again. 'That Mister Welham, he mustn't go bothering the Captain. I won't have the Captain bein' upset, Mrs Pell...' Earli-er, she was regretting the Captain's absence; now she thanked the good Lord for just that. Curse that young Andy! She sighed, deeply enough to set Mrs Pell off again.

' 'Tween you an' me, Mrs O,' Mrs Pell dropped her voice, 'I don't think that Mr Welham is very, well, *nice,* if yer foller me meanin'. Dirty. I reckon you oughter be lookin' out for a replacement. Give 'im the old 'eave-o, like...' She nodded again, and tapped her button of a nose, which emitted smoke like a tiny dragon.

'Oh Jesus, Mary and Joseph...' said Mrs O'Ryan, shaking herself. 'Well, we'll see what happens, Mrs Pell. He pays his rent...' Her head ached. These days, she seemed to ache all over.

'Well, there's others wot'd be grateful for a nice room like that if it comes to it, Mrs O. Don't you fret. Now then, ain't the Capting come on a real treat!' Mrs Pell changed the subject. 'An' gettin' about without 'is crutches. *And* still in Italy, jus' fancy, all that sunshine! S'all right for some, ain't it, eh?'

'He's healed very well, thank the good Lord,' Mrs O'Ryan admitted stiffly. 'De-serves a good holiday, he does, to be sure...'

'Did orl right fr'imself, I reckon, though, Mrs O. Everythink laid on, like, at 'ome. Didn't ave to stop in the 'ospital for long. ...' She slurped more tea, and sucked on her cigarette. 'I mean, if yer gotter be badly, eh? 'Ome's better'n 'ospital with all them germs. Mus' be nice to be a gent an' avoid all that.'

'Well o'course, thank the Lord,' said Mrs O'Ryan quickly. 'He had Doctor Baines, didn't he now, and that's a very clever man, and he recommended that Nurse...'

'Oh, yeah. 'Er! With a name like Stockwell, or Tootin' or summink well south of the river...'

'Streatham. Nurse Streatham. An excellent nurse, she is, say what ye like.'

'Bossy ole cow, if y'arsk me…' said Mrs Pell frankly. 'A right tartar. Everythin' jus' so. 'Ow you put up with 'er, Mrs O, I dunno, I don't reely. A relief to ave 'er out of the 'ouse, I dessay. But yer mussen ferget yerself, Mrs O. Wot you didn't do for 'im, 'eaven knows. Middler the night an' ev'rythink, when Nurse weren't there…' Mrs O'Ryan was a little mollified. She nibbled her biscuit. 'Now I couldn't nurse, not fer lovenermoney,' Mrs Pell ran on, 'I couldn't truly! I was with my Aud for 'er three, and for Doreen's Malcolm, and with me poor ole Mum when she went. Cruel, that was, poor ole thing. Cryin' she were, with the pain. And our Eva wantin' to 'ave the vicar becos of 'er George wot's a sidesman in Saint Anne's at Lime'ouse, and my Mum – she could still slay yer, even at the end, an that sharp – sayin' she wouldn't entertain no man in the 'ouse at a time like this! Well, you got-ter laugh, ain't yer? Sorry, Mrs O, I know you Roamin' Cath'licks 'ave to 'ave one there an' all that, but my Mum, she'd rather die, if yer foller me, never 'avin' been religious nor nuffink really… But it was awful, it was, and lingered days, she did, pore ole love. They sent a nurse in the end, come to the 'ouse once a day, she did, thank Gawd, 'cos me Mum was that petrified of 'ospitals. But I couldn't of done it, not like that. Too much blood and pus and all the other stuff fer me. Ugh. I mean, it's one thing with little 'uns, innit, nappies n' that, but the other… Lovely cupper, this, Mrs O. Can I 'ave another fill-up? Before I go. Gotter get the thirty-eight to Aud's. It's the sales. Goin' up Oxford Street, she is…' She helped herself from the teapot without waiting for an answer. 'But I always thought 'e would recover, mind you, Mrs O, the Capting. He's got that much better, I'd reckon, and mostly thanks to you, that's wot I reckon…' Mrs Pell was a true diplomat in her way.

'Well, that's as maybe, but I was only too glad. He's a real decent gentleman, is the Captain. And thank the good Lord for these anti-bioticals, that's what I say. Medical science, Mrs Pell, is a modern miracle, it is. It was the War that done that, ye know. First the soldiers, and now us ordinary folk.'

'True enough, Mrs O. Not that we'll mention –' Mrs Pell was determined – 'a few creature comforts of a more old fashioned sort, eh? I mean,' she chortled, 'there's nuffink like a bit o'… I meanter say, wot we could tell if we chose, eh?' She dipped her head and winked. But Mrs O'Ryan stared her into a temporary silence. 'Yer muster noticed,' Mrs Pell said after an exasperated pause.

'I'm sure I don't know what you're talking about, Mrs Pell…' She was getting painfully to her feet.

Mrs Pell was determined to enjoy the rest of her tea. 'Well that sister, o' course! The glamour-girl. But 'ooster say if she was 'is sister, if yer foller me meanin'…' Bird-bright eyes interrogated across the table.

'And what in the name of the good Lord d'ye mean by that, Mrs Pell?' de-manded Mrs O' Ryan, outraged.

'Well now!' Mrs Pell tapped her tiny nose. 'A little bird tole me.'

'Mrs Pell! I'll not have that sort of talk in this house. The Captain's a gentle-man, and a gentleman's business is his own. And he pays your wages, and I'll thank you to remember it!'

'Blimey! Orl right, Mrs O, orl right. Keep yer 'air – I mean don't get in a state. But if that's the Capting's sister, then I'm the Duchess o' Kent!'

'Mrs Walters is the Captain's sister and a recent widow, poor lady, and she came to look after her brother in his hour of need as is only proper. And now if it's all the same to you, Mrs Pell, if ye've *quite* finished your tea, I have me shopping to do too…' She smoothed her nylon overall, and stomped off indignantly to get her coat and woolly hat from the pegs in the scullery.

'Right you are, Mrs O,' Mrs Pell called out equably. She slugged back the last drop in her teacup, then picked up the teapot, cups and ashtray and dealt with them smartly in the sink, her last job of the morning. 'Suit yerself, silly ole paddy cow!'she muttered under her breath. 'Ladies an' gents they may be, but you don't ave ter strip the beds of a morning, you don't.'

32

Wednesday. Market day in Putney, Mrs O'Ryan out, and Mrs Pell took her chance. To Mrs Hetty Pell, it wasn't stealing, it was perks, and there was a difference. Stealing was money. If, for instance, she'd ever dipped into Ma O'Ryan's shabby purse (that she *would* leave lying about on the table, a temptation for anybody with light fingers, silly old cow, and she ought to be grateful that she, Hetty Pell, had her pride and her standards) and helped herself to coppers – now *that* would be stealing and it would be wrong, even if it would be quite obvious where the finger of blame would point, and it wouldn't be her, but far be it from her to get a kiddy into trouble, even one like that young Andy who was a bit of a wrong 'un in Mrs Pell's opinion, and no wonder!

However, the larder was a different matter, and the scullery too – and after all, it was that Captain's property, and not Ma O'Ryan's own, and that silly old cow never knew what was in there from one moment to the next (in her last place, Mrs Pell's immediate employer had made lists.) And so it happened that Mrs Pell's capacious shopping bag might contain, on any one Wednesday, a loaf here, a jar of jam there, a bottle of Camp instant liquid coffee essence, a tin of baked beans, a packet of biscuits – the butter maries, she liked them, and the digestives – or a more practical toilet-roll or two, or a bottle of Squeez-ee. Helped Aud out, and nobody any the wiser. The trick of it was dribs and drabs, a bit at a time, nothing actually missing, not so's anyone would notice…

Wednesday, games in the afternoon which he was excused, and a good day to sag off altogether – he'd leave in the morning with his satchel and wearing what passed for school uniform, get to the top of the road, watch Mrs Pell arrive, puffing along the pavement from the bus stop, watch Grammy leave and head off in the opposite direction towards the bridge, and turn straight back again to the house to dump his bag in his bedroom and change out of his blazer. Grammy would be out for quite a while, probably popping into St Saviour's for a quick pray as she often did on her way home with the meat and the cabbages; and that fat old Mrs Pell was using the vacuum cleaner on the upper stairs, wheezing and complaining to herself, as usual. Plenty of time. Andrew O'Ryan was helping himself to the tin on the dresser where his grandmother kept the biscuits, stuffing his pockets, where not quite enough change rattled for the pictures.

The day being cold, Grammy had taken her big coat, not her mac, and in the little passage between the kitchen and the scullery where there were hooks for coats and the like, he fished, not very hopefully into the pockets of Grammy's shabby blue gabardine, finding nothing but a used hanky and a prayer card. But here was Mrs Pell's coat – a large brown woolly thing – and he fished in her pockets too. Under some old bus-tickets, he felt something heavy, familiar and metal. Two bob! That meant the bus into Town and a Hammer, maybe, rather than a silly old John Wayne at the Odeon on the Broadway… Something to spare if he could just sneak past the ticket box and into the bogs, and then dodge the usherette.

Andy listened out carefully for the whine of the vacuum – still going – and was preparing for a strategic flight out of the back door through the yard when he spotted Mrs Pell's bulging bag beneath the coat, and decided to investigate Mrs Pell's shopping for a chocolate bar. But it wasn't 'shopping' – and it didn't take a detective of any brilliance to see exactly what Mrs Pell was up to. He experienced an odd sense of outrage as he pulled a jar of Grammy's own home-made blackberry jam from under the Silver-Silk toilet rolls. He replaced the jam on the shelf in the larder and was about to replace the toilet rolls on their proper shelf alongside the packets of washing powder and the Lifebuoy soap, when he had a better idea.

It wasn't until Mrs Pell was back in her own kitchen in Lambeth, puffing happily on a Senior Service and listening to the Light Programme on the wireless and unpacking her shopping bag, that she noticed the jam was missing and that one of the toilet rolls had writing on it…

33: March 1967

'So you see, Mrs O'Ryan, there really won't be that much change to your life here, if you're quite sure you wish to stay on...' Leo had his back to her at the little table where he kept his tray of bottles, pouring sherry. Nervous, poor man, thought Mrs O Ryan. 'I may say I'm extremely relieved that you do. Mr Bollinger will take my quarters in a week or two. I think you'll find him entirely agreeable. I thought I'd keep the spare room on as my own, and then I'll be able to come and go when I need to be in Town. And – um – when the time comes, when you want to take things a bit easier, we could talk about revising the arrangement, couldn't we?'

'Revising the arrangement, sir?'

Leo coughed. 'Well, what I really mean is, should you wish to retire at any time...' He passed her a glass.

'Retire, sir?'

'Well, um, I don't mean to presume...' He coughed again. 'But you must always feel, I mean, you're not obligated in any way, Mrs O'Ryan. You – um – might want to go back to your family in Ireland...' He was beginning to babble. So hard to get it right.

'Ireland?' The old lady chuckled. 'Not me, sir! I'm a Londoner these past twenty-two years. Couldn't think of leaving the place. My Ted – that is, my son Redmond – he thinks I'm crazy o'course, but he thinks different to me. Liffey water in his veins, like...' Not, she thought rather bitterly, that I've been invited...

'Well, Mrs O'Ryan, here's to the Thames. London!'

'London...' They drank solemnly. 'And to the country, I suppose. That's very nice, surely, the fresh air, and the flower fields of Leicestershire.'

He realised she must be confused with Lincolnshire. 'Well, I'm not sure about flower fields, Mrs O'Ryan, but the country is certainly very pretty there. Seems a shame to have to sell up, in some ways.'

'I can't abide the country meself,' said Mrs O'Ryan frankly. 'But then, it was different in Ireland. Everyt'ing got better when I was wed, goin' to Town, goin' to Dublin. Not really better until London, after the War, trut' to tell...'

He was not an especially imaginative man, but Leo saw in his mind's eye mud and poverty, sick hens and (for some reason) pigs. He thought he understood some of his housekeeper's aversion, even to the point of finding blitzed and rationed London a haven... He felt a little guilty, suddenly, at how little he knew. So little he dared ask. She was saying, 'And as for taking things easy, sir, although I can't pretend my knees are what they were, work, well it keeps me goin' like to be occupied.'

'Well, here's to that! And – um – I did want to say how deeply I feel in your debt. You've been absolutely splendid, putting up with me, and nurses in and out and all that sort of thing, upsetting the household. Can't thank you enough, really.'

Mrs O'Ryan's bloodless face flushed. 'Oh, that was a real pleasure, sir. No trouble at all. And if I may say so, sir, it's a real pleasure to see you back on your feet, like.'

'It's good to be back on them, I must say. Have another spot of sherry?' Leo had been rather dreading this little interview. Now, with Mrs O'Ryan settled in his best armchair, veiny hands cradling her glass, and her still extraordinarily vivid eyes sparkling with sherry, he thought it was going better than he had dared to hope.

'Well, just a drop, maybe, thank ye, sir. It's very nice...' She watched the auburn liquid ascend in the glass as he poured. He poured himself another whiskey. 'Here's luck,' she said. 'Healt' too, the good Lord willin'...'

Her own health had been less reliable of late, but good sherry in sufficient quantity can inspire optimism, and Mrs O'Ryan was capable of looking on the bright side. A very fair man, the Captain. A good soul, and a true gentleman. And generous. She remembered to sip, not gulp. March sunshine flooded the high-ceilinged room and gave a warm amber glow to the piano. She glowed a little herself, with goodwill. Such a relief to have everything explained properly. Already, she conjured pleasant visions of the future: another proper gentleman in the Captain's old rooms, that nice Mr Bollinger...shame about seeing some of the Captain's nice furniture go – and the piano in store for the time being, he had said. She would miss it, for all it had needed such careful dusting. She would miss his music, bless the man, all those jolly jazz tunes, like the old days... But there'd be some more nice stuff coming in with the new gentleman...and she'd say goodbye and good riddance to that dirty nuisance Welham, and let his room to a nice young man, someone who'd appreciate the odd little meal, maybe... Someone in a bank, perhaps? Certainly not another nasty salesman. There would be his rent, and a little increase for her trouble. She and Andy would do very nicely for the time being. But then, she had a sudden vision of Andy hiding in the young banker's wardrobe, snooping on the stairs, annoying the Captain's friend. She shuddered a little – the bright side was acquiring a shadow... She said, 'Me and Andy'll miss you very much, sir, we will truly. And if there's anything we can do, in the packing up line, well, Andy's getting to be a good strong little feller. You've only to say the word, sir.'

'Ah, young Andy. He's off to America soon, I understand?'

'We can hope so, sir. Andy – well, it's America this, America that with him all the time these days. Tis a bit of a worry, I won't deny...' But her heart was lighter. Her son, Ted, was coming, and that was the main thing.

'Well, it seems we're all embarking on new starts one way and another, Mrs O'Ryan...'

'I'm sure I'm very happy for you, sir...' She wondered if he was getting married.

He glanced discreetly at his wristwatch. Mrs O'Ryan took the hint. She rose, a trifle unsteadily, from the depths of the chair.

'I'd better be off, sir, if youse'll excuse me. I've got chores that won't do themselves. Thank you, sir. Thank you very much...' She beamed a bright blue gaze at him, and they shook hands, a little awkwardly, and she retreated, smoothing her overall.

She was thinking, as she descended the staircase to her basement quarters, that as one worry had been lifted from her shoulders, so would another. She mumbled a 'Hail Mary' superstitiously as she went. On this occasion, however, her prayer went unanswered.

34

'So there's no chance, then, son. That's what ye's sayin'...' The old lady felt despond wash over her. They were in the basement kitchen, the mother in her sagging armchair, the son's handsome bulk awkwardly straddling a rickety dining chair, big arms folded over its back. Both nursed mugs of strong tea. The weather had turned again, and the sky was so dark with the incipient storm that there was scarcely daylight in the room, and they sat in a perverse and pervasive twilight at four in the afternoon. 'So's I'm to keep him. Oh well, if Maureen can't see her way, she can't.'

'Sorry, Mammy...' Ted O'Ryan had been sufficiently alarmed by his mother's rambling and somewhat hysterical call to have caught the ferry to Liverpool as soon as he could leave his considerable responsibilities. He had cadged a lift from the docks with a long-distance lorry to London, leaving Maureen minding the shop and all the children. He kept casting glances over his shoulder, the unfamiliar noises in the house keeping him on the alert, almost as if his large, taciturn wife might appear in person. He was unused to being, as it were, on his own, and London always made him ill at ease. But he was here for the sake of his mother, whose appearance had rather shocked him. It was as if she had shrunk. He had forgotten she was so very thin. He meant it when he said he was sorry.

'S'not your fault, son. I blame Rosie, that's who. All right for her with a new family in Rochdale, Texas, America!' She almost spat the words. 'So you've really spoke to her?'

'Long distance,' said Ted. 'An arm and a leg it cost, too. 'T'was my bill.'

'She won't speak to *me*, won't answer me letters, not properly, she won't. That's what I was tryin' to tell ye! I gets a card on me birthday, and she sent a lovely scarf, silk it is, or somethin' very like, all pinks and blues – but what good's a scarf? I just want to know what's to happen to the little feller. Rosaleen, what did she say on the long-distance?'

'She's doin' fine. She sounds very American, Mammy. You'd hardly know her voice, like someone on the filums. Hank's working for the oil company, and the babbies, Lee-anne and Hank Junior, and the new one. Scott, she's called him. She's got three now, Mammy. Teethin' the new one is, she says. Crying a lot, keepin' her awake nights, all that. But what about little Andy, I says. He'll cry a lot if he can't go to America. Little Andy's doin' fine wi' me Mammy, ain't he, says she. But he ain't so little now, I told her, and Mammy's getting old – sorry, Mammy, but I wanted to lay it on a bit thick-like – and the boy's growing into a real handful for her. Well, I can't come and get him, she says, at least not yet, not while I've got these three so small, and Hank being posted to Vietnam, now, so she says. But, she says, I know you'll do youse best until I can come an' fetch him. Youse best! D'you know what I think, Mammy? I think she'll never see her way to takin' him back. Bloody Rose,' he muttered. Loyal and defensive of his sister in front of his wife, he felt freer to give vent to his feelings now, in front of his mother.

'Well then! How fine's that? Me own daughter, and her 'is mother. She always had better things to do, did Rosaleen, right from the start...' The old lady stared grimly ahead of her and they were silent. Then she said: 'I suppose it might be that Hank, not wantin' a cuckoo in the nest. Tis understandable, son. After all, that's what your Maureen…'

'I don't *know*, Mammy. Hank might be at the back of it, of course…' This was a more comfortable thought, but having spoken to his sister, he was doubtful. 'And that's not Maureen's objection, not really. She's jus' got too much on her plate, what with five of her own, like, and the shop. She's not been so well herself.'

The old lady seemed to have sunk into a silent gloom. 'Look, you'll manage, the two of you…' said Ted, persuading himself that it was true. 'The youngster, he's a comfort to you. Sure, he is. A bit o' young life. Sure he's a bit of a mischief, don't I know, but he's good to his grammy, and you got your Captain, an' all. There's some bread in the oven, and I'll always help when I can, you know that. It'll be fine, Mammy.'

'But that's just it, Redmond! For the sake of the Lord, it's not fine!' She had half risen from her chair, and her blue eyes glared at him. She never called him 'Redmond' in the ordinary way. She stomped over to a cupboard on the wall. Grabbed a large bottle, dusted it off with her tea-towel. 'An' what with the Captain leaving, 'tis down to me to take care of everything here, and a new gentleman coming, and young Andy, now, I just can't stop him, Ted. In trouble, he is, right, left and centre. Want a drop o' Paddy in that?'

'Go on then. Cheer up, Mammy…'

'Hmph! I'd cheer up if the little divil'd give me a bit o' peace, snoopin' and spyin'… He hears stuff he shouldn't, which ain't to say he hears wrong always. But that's just the half of it!'

'Oh, come on, Mammy. 'Tis just kids' games. You take it all too serious-like.'

'But *tis* serious, Ted. Tell trut', he's nothing but trouble nowadays. In trouble at school, and with the local boys, and here, botherin' me new PG after all the trouble with the last one. Put a rat in his bed, Andy did. Don't laugh, son. 'T'aint so funny, bein' me livelihood.'

'Sorry, Mammy. I suppose the rat was dead?'

'Fresh from the trap. And he was a filt'y swine, he was, that Welham, tell trut', but what's a few fish and chip suppers smellin' the place out and a few dirty books if he paid?'

All of Ted's latent hostility to the English conjured the worst of that race in his mind when he thought of the lodger Welham and his like, and the English dirt his noble little mother had to clean up after shite bottom-feeders such as they. He thought the dead rat was a deserved punishment. 'Youse better off without him, Mammy. Filt'y beast and good riddance to him. This new one, he's better though, so ye was sayin'?'

'So far,' said Mrs O'Ryan darkly. 'Clean and decent is this young Mr Allcott. Good job in the Westminster and quiet and serious as you please. But what if Andy starts snoopin' and spyin' around *him*? What am I goin' to do, Ted?' Once again, there was defeat in her voice, and his heart sank to hear it. 'Now he's after breakin' some lad's head, did I not tell ye?'

'Ye did. I must say, I'd never have thought it of him, him bein' small and his bad foot and all. Little Andy, eh? Can't have been that serious.'

'It ain't any kind of a joke,' she said, seeing the big man chuckle. 'He *really* broke the lad's head, Ted. Pulled him off the climbing-frame. Hospital, stitches, everyt'ing Could have kilt him. *And* the other lad was a big one, great bruiser of a fat boy with a dadda in the garridge trade. Teasin' him, Andy said. About his foot and about bein' Irish.'

'Sounds like the other little divil got what he deserved,' said Ted, chuckling again. 'He lived to tell the tale, I suppose?'

'Sore head and back at school, thank the good Lord, which is more than ye can say of Andy. Saggin' off all the time now, he is, and that in spite of all the trouble after Christmas. He'll land up in court, Ted, or I shall. That headmaster, he gave me a grillin' in his office-like – told me I had to keep him under control. Anybody'd think he was goin' to send *me* before the judge and jury! Mortified, I was! I could break Andy's head for him, just thinkin' about it!'

'Poor Mammy!' Ted bit his bottom lip and stared into his tea. 'I don't suppose he was thinking of all the trouble he'd get you into. Boys don't think. Our Sean's always gettin' into scraps at school. So's little Liam, for all he's only seven. Proper little fighters, both on 'em.'

'Ted, son, ye's not *listening* to me! Don't ye understand? They'll get them social people onto me, the truancy people, ain't I after tellin' ye? Social people, here in my house! Then it'll be Borstal or one o' them approved schools. Oh, Jesusmaryanjoseph, what am I's to do, Ted?'

'I don't rightly know, Mammy, tell trut'...' He shook his head.

'I mean, *why* won't Rosaleen...?'

'Mammy, me darlin'. Face it. Rosie won't have him, Mammy.'

His mother poured more tea, and laced it liberally with the whiskey. The tea-towel twisted in her veiny hands. ''Tis my fault, Ted. He – he's only a babba, really, for all his ways. He wants his mammy. And it's America this, America that the whole time. I – I've been tellin' him he'll go soon, that Rosie'll send out for him. I thought it would help! Now, he's expectin' it. Anytime now...oh, Jesusmaryanjoseph...' The blue eyes welled, and Ted was appalled.

He was used to her sudden extravagances of language, her exaggerations to make a point. But tears, never. This tiny woman, whose towering strength had never wavered, whose indomitable, battling spirit had fed, clothed and protected four children in the Dublin slums – himself, the eldest, growing up fast but fairly steady, the man of the family after his father was dead; his brother Mickey, God rest him, always the favourite, the one with the winning ways, killed on his motorbike, crossing the border; his sister Bernadette, with the vocation, now in a teaching order in Ballylea; and Rosaleen, flighty, wilful Rosie, longing to be free of it all, kicking the Irish mud off her feet for good and all...but all of them clean, educated and strong, and all down to the strength of their mother. That she had all but defected in the end, betrayed the husband, her children's father, who had been shot down at dawn on a Dublin street by the LSF men, and gone to London to join Rosaleen, to scivvy for the bastard English, and live a new life among the enemy, a glorified scrubber for the English upper-crust...well, it scarcely mattered now. Ted was a peaceable man at heart, and this was his mother, and the wellspring of his life. He dreaded her inevitable decline.

'Oh, Mammy.'

'How's I goin' to break it to him, Ted?'

'I truly don't know, Mammy. Perhaps ye shouldn't have built up the little feller's hopes.'

'Ted. Ask Maureen again, Ted. Think about it, son. Please. He'd help in the shop, help with the stores. He's that bright, son. You don't have to tell him anything twice! Sure he's a little divil and disobedient, but he's a good little feller, and useful, too. Strong, and that sweet and innocent, sometimes, butter wouldn't melt. And his impressions, you know, take-offs of people, the telly and that, he's got a real bent for it. You should hear his Mr Wilson. Has me in tucks, sometimes. Oh, please, son. Ask your Maureen, ask her again. One more can't make that much of a difference to her. And he respects his Uncle Ted, does young Andy. He'd listen to you, learn to behave.'

'Mammy, please...' He hated the wheedling, desperate tone in her voice. 'Please. Don't ask me again. You know I can't just take him back with me. We've got five babbies at home, for the Lord's sake. And the shop. And Maureen's got the time o' life, headaches, all that. And she never liked Rosie, Maureen didn't, you know that. Not after... Anyway, it's just not possible, Mammy. I'll send as much as I can, but I can't take him...'

Mrs O' Ryan's mouth was a grim line. She wiped her eyes on her tea-towel, and Ted's wrath exploded against his sister. 'Blast bloody Rose! First in pod to a bloody Eye-tye Yank, then dumps the brat on us and then makes off with another Yank! Never gives him a second thought. Never gives *you* a second thought, Mammy. Sometimes I think my Maureen's right.'

'Aye. For all she's me own daughter...' They fell silent. Then there was a tiny noise outside the door, and it was Ted who looked up – his ears were younger than his mother's – and he caught Mrs O'Ryan's eye. 'Shh! Home from school,' she mouthed. In fact, Andrew had been home for quite some time. He had not been at school at all that afternoon. Failing to get into the Wednesday afternoon matinée at the Odeon, he had simply become cold and bored, and had slunk home, still in his grey school jacket and shorts, without his grandmother seeing, hiding in the absent Captain's quarters upstairs, until he decided to slink down to the scullery and bide his time until he could officially return. What he had overheard had nearly made him vomit with rage and disappointment.

'Come on in, Andy! Come an' say hello to yer Uncle Ted...' The big man spread his arms in welcome. Andrew looked at them both unblinking, his gabardine coat trailing on the floor.

'There, Ted. Don't he look smart in his school uniform. Least he could if he tried. Ye wants to pull them socks up, boy. And hang yer coat up. Youse a disgrace! I'll start yer tea...' She began clattering pots rather noisily to cover her discomfiture.'Come on, Andy,' said his uncle pacifically. 'Do us some of your impressions.'

35

It began as amusement after the American Dream had smashed, and it began, of all people, with Brian Tilson.

The climbing-frame incident – which really had been an accident, in as much as Andrew O'Ryan had acted on enraged impulse, and had not expected to see his tormentor tumble to the ground in quite such a dramatic fashion – had left the boy Tilson a little subdued. He had been pulled down, literally, in front of his gang of admirers, and somehow his return to school, still bandaged, had not had the inspiring effect of a returning war-wounded hero, but rather that of a fallen hero, with feet of clay. Gangs are fickle: if even the strange bog-boy with the boot and the limp could pull one such as Tilson from his pedestal, leaving him lying limp and bloody on the ground, there must be others more worthy of respect, even the bog-trotter himself. Tilson now found himself almost as much of an outcast as Andrew O'Ryan, about whom he began to have mixed feelings: bitter envy of the other boy's apparent ascendancy, and a shrewd sense that to declare out and out war would leave him with few cohorts. He watched sullenly as the standard insults of the other boys seemed to have softened to something that sounded like a grudging acceptance. The bog-boy's accent and his boot appeared to have acquired a quality of the exotic, rather than to have retained the derision Tilson had counted on before the accident. To his intense but impotent annoyance, Tilson found very few supporters in his 'get the bog-boy' campaign. Depressed and sulky, he began avoiding school, making as much capital as he could from his wounded head.

Andrew had been spending more and more of his free time – including a great many days when he should have been at school – and his pocket money at the pictures. He had plenty of pocket money these days. His financial arrangement with that miserable creep Welham had of course come to an abrupt halt after the rat-in-the-bed incident when Welham, in an expostulating rage, had left his Grammy's roof, but now there was a new lodger to spy on and there was still his grandmother's purse to raid for a sixpence here, tuppence there, but mostly there was that fat Mrs Pell's weekly shilling as well as a generous supply of pocket-money from Uncle Ted, and he felt quite rich. It was westerns that still pulled him, even if they now contained for him a sour sting, being mostly set, as he imagined, in Texas, and it was while waiting, one Wednesday afternoon, in the queue at the Fulham Broadway Odeon for a John Wayne matinée that he encountered Tilson. Both boys were alone. Fellow truants, they acknowledged one another with wary caution. Tilson was out of uniform, wearing long narrow trousers which sat rather ill on his bulky, ungainly figure, and an expensive-looking leather jacket. His hair was 'Beatle', or at least a great deal of it was combed down over his forehead, hiding his recent scar. Somehow, he managed to look a great deal older than he was, and Andrew was ashamed of his childish zip-up woolly over his grey school shorts, his long socks, and his big ungainly boot. Brian Tilson chewed gum, ostentatiously moving his fleshy jaws. He swaggered over to Andrew.

'This film's crap, kids' stuff, but then you're just a lame kid, ain't yer?' he sneered. But he lingered, hovering almost. Andrew sensed the shift of balance between them instinctively.

'Why yer seein' it then?' he countered. Andrew's new sense of malevolence to the world made Tilson almost insignificant. Tilson was large, intimidating, even; but Andrew found he didn't care, much less was afraid.

'Summink to do, innit? Gang films, they're better than this fart-arse crap. And vampires. Hammer stuff. Clint Eastwood – that's the only decent western. Bet you ain't never seen Clint Eastwood. *Fistful of Dollars, A Few Dollars More.*'

'Them's X,' said Andrew. 'Bet you ain't neither.'

'Loads o' times. I know where we can get into one now, an X,' said Tilson. 'My auntie's an usherette at the 'Ippo in Swiss Cottage. She lets me in if she can. I've seen all the Marlon Brandos, Bonds, everythink.'

'So?'

'Bond flick at the 'Ippo begins in forty minutes...' He flourished the important looking wrist watch that Mr Bartram had forbidden him to wear at school, in case it should be stolen. 'Wanna come?'

'Don't mind...'

They climbed onto a bus, rode for four stops and scarpered before the conductor could collect their fares.

'This ain't Swiss Cottage,' Andy said.

'Nah. Parson's Green, innit... C'mon. Summink to show yer!'

'What about the fil-um?'

'Shag the film. This is better. We're a bit early. Got any dosh?'

'Might have. Why?'

'Hot dog while we wait.' There was a stall wafting tempting aromas, and it was sitting on a nearby bench, companionably munching sausages and swigging Pepsi-cola from bottles, that Andrew decided to confide his dilemma to Brian Tilson. Some of it, anyway.

'Wot you need's dosh, me old china,' said Brian, slurping and burping. 'Dosh. Folding...' Brian Tilson's wider family was from the Borough and the Elephant and Castle, and Brian's version of worldly adult-speak was sprinkled with these hark-backs to this sort of old-fashioned cockney slang, peppered with the American gangster-speak he had learned at the movies.

'We all need dosh, to be sure,' Andrew said. He jingled what was left of his weekly accounting in his pocket. 'I've got enough.'

'No you ain't. 'Ow much have you got, then? Bet it ain't enough to get you to America...'

'Course it's not, stupid...' He realised he had no idea how much the fare to America might cost. 'Anyways, I'm not goin' now, am I?'

'Lissen good, pal,' said Brian the gangster. 'You need real dough...' He narrowed his eyes, became serious, lowering his voice. 'Your muvver, 'er wot's in America, maybe she don't know ow much you wants to go out there and live wiv her. Your uncle an' your gran'ma, p'raps they've jus' been kiddin' you along, like. You need dough, dosh, folding.' Tilson smiled sleepily, supremely satisfied with

[150]

his diagnosis, and sat back, stretching his arms. 'My dad's never short of a bob or two. Tell yer straight. Got 'arf the garridges in London in his pocket, 'as my ole man and me Uncle Vin.'

'How?' asked Andrew, genuinely curious, but now purturbed by the thought that his mother might want him after all.

'Simple, innit. A garridge, small outfit, farver and son, p'raps, or a couple of bruvvers, they ain't got nothing but the outfit, get me? No insurance, no nuffink. Place gets struck by lightning, goes up in a puffer smoke, that's it, curtains. Or maybe it's just a spot of bovver, like they gets a bit of trouble, nuffink too seri-ous-like, but trouble. A few winders smashed, an engine doused in creosote, that sort of stuff. An my dad, he says to em, pay me a spot of the ready, an' I'll get these bleeders off of yer backs for yer. Reg'lar sum once a week, an' they'll never come back again. Simple as that. No more trouble and everybody 'appy as a clam.'

Andrew said, 'So yer dadda's a security man?' – a remark which seemed to cause Brian Tilson so much mirth he nearly fell off the bench. 'Sort of, my son,' he said through his splutters. 'Sort of...' He wiped his mouth on his handker-chief. Andrew had been noticing too how Tilson actually *had* handkerchiefs, big, clean white ones – didn't just wipe his mouth on his leather sleeve. 'Me, I'm goin' into the fam'ly business. S'why I don't give a stuffin' cent about Gladstone Blee-din' Lane Juniors, nor the Second'ry Mod neither. S'like you goin' to America.'

'Except I ain't goin' to America,' Andrew said miserably. Then, brightening, he decided to tell Brian Tilson about the lodger Welham.

'There you go, then!' said Tilson, impressed despite himself. 'Pity about the rat. Yer should've held back, held onto 'im. But yer a natural. Think yer can squeeze any lemon for a fare to the States?'

'Eh?'

'Know anybody got any dosh? Real dosh?'

Andrew did a rapid inventory. The new lodger, a young man from the bank with a permanent sniffle was untested, and something told Andrew that, bank or no bank, Mr Allcott was not rich. Mrs Pell's shilling was the limit of her fortunes. 'Don't think so.'

'Well you gotter find some lemon that 'as and squeeze 'em, ain't yer?'

'Don't know no-one.'

'Pity. Right! Time now, I reckon. C'mon!' Tilson threw his empty bottle into a convenient bush, and Andrew did the same.

'Where're we goin'?'

'Show yer. C'mon. Quiet now. Foller me.'

'But this is the back of the men's bogs,' Andrew said eventually. 'And it stinks.'

'Shh!'

'I can't see nothing. This is boring.'

'Shhh! Wait.'

It was growing dusk, and they were hidden behind some shrubbery. Peering out, they saw some young men standing about, smoking cigarettes, waiting, curi-ously silent. They mostly wore their hair in slicked-back quiffs, and most of them sported very large ties in swirly patterns over pink or pale yellow shirts under leather jackets. They wore tight jeans, and shiny pointed shoes. They looked sharp and rather theatrically dangerous.

'Them's the queer buggers. But see that one there?' hissed Tilson into Andy's ear, pointing. 'That one's a cop.'

'How can you tell?'

'Clock the shoes. Now wait.'

The boys waited. 'Here,' whispered Tilson. 'Here's a toff punter, bet yer.'

A man in a trench coat and a trilby, apparently strolling across the Common, came level with the gents' and glanced at his wrist-watch, shook his wrist as if the watch had stopped, glanced over his shoulder. Then he went up to one of the young men, apparently asking for the correct time. A short inaudible exchange took place, and the man in the mac followed the younger man down into the subterranean green-tiled depths of Gents' Conveniences. Soon, apparently casually, the other young man – who was indeed wearing much stouter footwear than his confreres – followed too.

'Bingo! Now we get up here,' said Tilson, leading his colleague round the back of the small building. He began to scramble up some ancient ivy that provided a foothold that a boy, provided he was agile and quick, could climb with ease in order to peer through any one of the tiny bottle-glass windows that ventilated the cubicles. Tilson's bulk hampered his progress, and instead, he shoved the lighter Andy up into the branches. Andy, awkwardly supported by thick ivy trunk and Tilson's shoulder, peered through the grimy window, seeing very little, except what he thought was the Mac, standing and parting the mac, and the younger man with slicked back hair in front of him, on his knees… A loud rapping on the locked door made them both start, the older man looking stricken, and the younger one spitting, and shouting 'engaged!'

'C'mon! Scarper!' said Tilson to Andy, who needed no prompting, and half fell, half ran, and hid once again in the rancid privet. But the peering boys witnessed the police panda cars as they slunk away. On another stolen bus-ride back to Fulham, Brian Tilson instructed his pupil in the ways of the world.

'What'll happen?'

'Arrested. Sent down. That sort of filth deserve it, that's what my ole man says. Disgustin' buggers.'

'What about the posh feller in the trilby?'

'The toff? Him specially,' said Brian Tilson, with satisfaction. Thus it was that this unlikely Virgil introduced Andy to the underworld, planting, had he but known it, a seed in Andy's head that would grow roots and branches.

36

It was something to do. He got used to the routine, and once he realised it happened not just at dusk, but at midday too, he found that not only did the amusement of the parks supersede any amusement to be found at the picture houses, but that he could be home in time for Grammy getting his tea. Cheaper too, and – far more important – lucrative. His first adventures were extraordinarily successful. 'Sir...' It was always best to be polite. He'd watch, while the man in the posh mac and the hat followed the queer one into the cubicle, no need to climb the ivy, since he'd no interest in actually seeing the filth, and just wait... and then he'd follow the posh one out, catch up, and say, 'Sir...'

'Go away, sonny. I'm in a hurry.' The attempt to brush him aside.

'Oh but sir, I ain't got my bus fare home, and me Grammy's waiting...' He might at this point attempt to grab a sleeve.

This was when the man might hurry on, or might say, 'So? Look, I've...' and invariably a glance at the inevitable wrist watch, the furtive glance cast over the shoulder.

In which case...'Youse just been havin' a real good time, ain't you, sir? An' I'm a witness!'

'Fuck off, you dirty little street-arab, before I call the police.'

'Not very wise, I'd reckon, sir, in the circumstances...' The engaging grin. He was still too young to be of interest, but the grin usually did it all the same. Susceptible these geezers. Susceptible and frightened. 'Bus fare home?'

And he'd scrabble for the tossed coins as the man in the mac flapped hurriedly away.

Sentiment. Sentiment and a sort of restlessness, spring restlessness. Fatal! Leo was in London. He had a more or less regular routine: travel up to Town by train, take the tube from St Pancras to Fulham Broadway, walk the short distance to Maxwell Road, go through the household books with Mrs O'Ryan, collect any mail she had left carefully on the desk in the room that was still his, then take the bus and have lunch at his Club in Pall Mall, stay overnight, head back to Leicester next morning, collect his car from the station and drive back to Folwell Hall and Lottie. Now that old Bolly was installing himself happily in the Fulham apartment, he sometimes took late drinks with him before turning in to his bed in the spare room.

He sat now, in what had recently been his own sitting room, poring over some stockbrokers' reports, unable to make head or tail of them. Bolly would sort it out in a trice, but Bolly would not be back for hours. Outside, evening birdsong, traffic in the street below, half-heard conversations. Life going on out *there*, and this vague sense of – well, of *restlessness* (one couldn't call it anything else) and the restlessness became acute, sometimes, on these London sojourns, and now it prodded him with a certain insistence. It was a warm evening in late April. Leo suddenly made up his mind to go for a short walk...

Putney Heath. Not one of London's most beautiful public parks, but green and vividly alive at this time of year. He hesitated before he drew level with the men's conveniences. Had he really imagined that this was not where he was going? Had he now the strength to turn away, turn his back on this once and for all, as he had half promised himself he would? But here was his answer: an exotic young man in an extravagantly-patterned tie stepping out of the shrubbery, a young man whose blond hair and slender shoulders reminded him so poignantly of someone that he murmured 'Dean' not quite inaudibly.

'Dean ain't here. I'm Ashley. But you can call me Dean, if that's what you want. I'm flexible...' The tart's smile that never got as far as the eyes; the assessing look, taking in the quality of the hat, the shoes, the light macintosh. And of course, close up, this Ashley could never have been Dean, but Leo, restless and now resistless, allowed himself to be led down the tiled steps...

'Scuse me, mister, sir...I ain't got me bus fare and I want to go home.'

'Not now. I'm in a hurry. And he was. He hurried away from his shame as much as from the persistent voice behind him, as fast as his lame leg would allow. Child beggars! He suddenly longed for Lottie, and his train north, longed to not have to see Bolly in all his cheerful simplicity.

The voice – Irish, unbroken – wheedled on, closer. 'What's yer hurry, sir? Youse had a real good time back there, didn't yer?'

Leo made a fractional pause, felt the bile in his throat, made to hurry on, but now a tugging at his sleeve made him wheel round angrily. 'Look, just –'

'Sainted Jesus Christ! Captain Rollitt!' said Andrew. Leo was speechless, pan-icked into sudden immobility.

'Andrew,' he said, finding his voice. 'What a surprise. Well, now, I suppose we're both headed in the same direction, aren't we?'

'That's for you to say, sir.' Andrew had recovered some of his composure.

'And I say that we are.' Leo had recovered too. Lame boy hurried alongside the lame man, who covered ground with surprising speed, towards Maxwell Road.

Now, in the course of a highly unpleasant little interview, Leo was grateful for his soldier's training. It had not been hard to learn that the boy had actually seen nothing, bar an exchange of words between a hatted stranger – himself – and the young man he referred to as the 'queer bugger'. Badly rattled but keeping his nerve, he discerned that although the boy was far from innocent – criminal to his core, in Leo's view – he was fairly ignorant. He was also slightly pathetic in his desperation.

'Let's get this straight, Andrew. You want me to pay your fare out to America to join your mother, in return for...what, exactly?'

'Me not telling about you and that queer bugger in the toilets. Or –' the boy's eyes lit up suddenly – 'about you going to bed with that lady what ain't really your sister...' Another serious jolt which almost unmanned him. But threat produced a lucid logic in Leo, and it quickly came to him that not only had the boy grasped the wrong end of the stick, as it were, but that it constituted a rather complete refutation of the charge as stated. He reminded himself that the youngster on the carpet in front of him was a mere child, even though the thought that, somehow, this benighted urchin must have witnessed some of his most preciously private moments with Lottie, made him feel slightly sick. He lit a cigarette and paused before he spoke.

'Andrew,' he said slowly. 'I realise how much you want to go to America, but while it isn't a crime to use a public lavatory, or to exchange words with another member of the public, or even for a man to go to bed with a woman in his own house, what you are doing, potentially is. Is that the life you want?'

'I don't understand, sir.'

Leo sighed. 'It seems you are in the habit of snooping and then going up to complete strangers and making accusations and demanding that they give you money. Now you are attempting to do the same with me. You know what this is, don't you, Andrew? It's attempted blackmail. Demanding money with menaces. These are crimes. I suggest, Andrew, that you will end up in prison if you continue in this way.'

'Can't go to prison, can I? I'm a minor.'

'I see. An answer for everything. Well, let me tell you, my lad, that there are plenty of detention centres for youngsters who commit crimes. They aren't pleasant places, as I fear very much you will find out, sooner or later.'

'What yer goin to do then, sir? I still reckon you've got worries of yer own. I've seen the police arresting queers outside the gents' toilets in the parks...' The boy stuck obstinately to his guns.

'Have you, now? Andrew, I wonder... Do you know who I am?' It was time to pull rank and let the boy's imagination do the rest. 'I mean what I do for a living?' he said, as the boy looked puzzled.

'The Army, I s'pose. As yer a Captain.'

'There are a lot of branches of the Army, Andrew. Now then, I can't say any more, but you leave the arresting to me, okay?' He forced a grin. 'And no more snooping. And let me remind you, Andrew, that the United States of America doesn't let people in if they have a criminal record. That's their law over there. Did you know that?'

Andrew looked at the carpet.

'Now then,' said Leo, standing up. 'I suggest, Andrew, that you concentrate on school from now on. You go up to the seniors in the autumn, don't you?'

The boy nodded so miserably that had Leo been less put out, he would have patted him on the shoulder. 'Off you go, then. We don't have to say anything more about this. Concentrate on school, and make your grandmother proud of you.'

After the boy had gone, Leo poured himself a large tumblerful of Bolly's scotch, thinking furiously, and it wasn't until the following morning that he managed to see Mrs O'Ryan and ascertain, definitively, that Andrew's mother in America simply didn't want him. It was fairly plain, too, that Andrew's grandmother couldn't cope with him either. 'I think, Mrs O'Ryan, that we might consider a school for young Andrew.'

'Well, he's off to big school in September, sir. The secondary modern, they call it, though between you and me, sir, it'll be a miracle if he actually stays there.

Saggin – that is, playin' truant all the time now, is Andy. I'm at me wit's end, sir, I truly am, the good Lord help me!'

'Perhaps we can work out some solution, Mrs O'Ryan.'

The sour taste in Leo's mouth only began to subside as his train trundled him northwards from St Pancras, and he forced his mind back to drains, gutterings, and the rat problem in the stables. He had convinced Mrs O'Ryan that a boarding school for young Andrew was probably the answer, and had convinced her, finally, over her voluble protestations, that he, personally, would bear the expense. It was a solution. The best solution. The lad was bright after all – probably too bright, and God alone knew what he might amount to – but Camfield, small, but not too small, and strict, but not too strict, would provide the boy with a foundation and some much needed discipline. Get him out of his grandmother's hair…get him out of his own hair at the same time, yet put him where Leo could keep an eye on him… The only problem was, he would infinitely prefer it if the boy would somehow decide that this was the answer for himself, rather than be dragooned, as it were, kicking and screaming… So important to do the right thing… How very complicated life was sometimes…

A much faster train hurtled by in the same direction, jolting Leo from an uneasy snooze, overtaking at a furious pace – as events, as it turned out, were about to do.

37

The probate machinery had ground slowly. The task of clearing up at Folwell Hall was, as these things tend to be, a mixed bag, for while there were treasures to discover, there were also some horrors. A mountain of old clothes and soft furnishings heaped into a corner had become home to a large colony of rats, and Lottie had shrieked as a large grey creature scurried over her shoe – she could not help herself – and felt embarrassed to have betrayed such weakness in front of one of the men. A once excellent saddle was rotted beyond repair, dripping with wet fungus. Water had poured into a disused upper bedroom wrecking an ancient hanging tapestry, and in the 'Hogarth Room', many of the prints had suffered, splotched with damp, the frames crumbling and wormy. There was foul-smelling mould almost everywhere, worse now the weather was gradually warming. It rained, incessantly, and the roof leaked a lake into the once handsome drawing room.

Lottie and Leo, with the help of various 'muscle' mostly in the form of the Henrys' nephews and grandsons, sorted, shifted, and made bonfires. Men from salerooms with pencils tucked behind their ears trooped round, assessing; an expert from Christie's came and sneered knowledgably at the French nudes; a local auction house had been more positive about the silver. Builders and plumbers came to do estimates for the drains; viewings were arranged with agents. Leo's leg was mending well, but he still tired easily, and it was Lottie, in wellingtons, rolled up sleeves and a large duster round her head, who actually got down to tackle the physical labour. It was only practical to stay at the Hall – to actually live on the premises while they worked, and they worked vigorously, from morning to night. Their conversation consisted mostly of practical matters, such as whether or not to keep the giant oval Georgian table in the dining room, and what to do about the horse and Aunt Rosalind's ancient Hillman.

However, there was a conversation that they were avoiding. The fact was that while Lottie saw the whole operation in terms of getting it done and arranging a suitable sale, Leo was beginning to feel more and more at home. Already he had established himself as a regular in the Rose & Crown for his pre-luncheon whisky and soda and had been approached by a chap on the local Bench. He had begun making tentative inquiries about hedging, ditching and the roof, doing rough sums in a notebook. The renovations would be extensive and costly, but perhaps they could be financed gradually – just possibly (and this was one of his brighter ideas, and he hugged it to himself for the time being) just possibly with the help of the National Trust... There would have to be open days, teas, suitable parking, some sort of public lavatory – but why not? The more he turned the idea over in his mind, the more optimistic he felt. They would do the place up, not grandly, but suitably, rescue the Adam fireplace, refurbish the kitchen, make some more convenient bathrooms... Lottie would supervise the gardens, revive the roses, mend the topiary. They could perhaps revive the concerts, even the outdoor Shakespeare... And he could put all of his old anxieties behind him, enjoy rather than dread his enforced retirement, become – and this was another thought he enjoyed as a sort of private ironic joke – ensquired at the Hall. He and Lottie, growing old together, growing roses... He would acquire a dog, a Jack Russell, maybe, or a labrador. As it was, the Henrys' ancient cocker spaniel followed him on his perambulations round the grounds, and he would stare out, with a sense of quiet satisfaction, from the vantage at the edge of the budding wood at the outlying villages nestled in the rolling country where winter had softened into spring... Glorious riding country! He doubted he would have the physical confidence to actually hunt again, but he imagined a horse in the stables, on the premises. Something quiet. Maybe even bring old Nimrod home for a gentle retirement... The season was ending now. The sound of distant hunting horns made him feel positively sentimental.

Meanwhile Lottie was working with greater and greater fervour. She was not a venal woman, rather the reverse, but nevertheless her thoughts were concerned with expediency and – simply – with money. She regarded the Hall – what was left of it after swingeing death taxes – purely as a material asset, currency. It represented a passport to the true freedom that she and Leo could buy. Far from feeling at home at the Hall, she had begun to feel bugged by it. On a practical level there was the chilly, sticky damp. There was nowhere in the house where she could feel warm and comfortable, where her breath did not show. Even in her bed, which despite hot-water bottles and Leo's warm, pyjama-clad embraces, Aunt Rosalind's ancient linen always felt vaguely slimy on her skin, and there was the constant, pervasive smell of paraffin and mould which somehow seemed to be ingrained in the fabric of everything. Perversely, she almost welcomed this discomfort. It meant that she could not allow herself to just sog into somewhere, *faute de mieux,* a place that would do as home for want of somewhere that felt real. As for sentiment – the family connection to the Hall, the place where assorted young Rollitts and Bullivants and Dearborns had played and gone almost feral during summer holidays was, for her, more than simply over – it was something that felt actively redundant, spent. The last thing she wished to do was revive the place as a museum for memories.

Aunt Rosalind's lonely, stoical and increasingly squalid old age was all too pathetically apparent the more she poked and delved into rooms unused for years. Now, her one thought was to get the place sold into the care of others, allow the grand old place a new lease of life before it fell down. If she could be sure that this was Leo's driving concern too, she would have been uncomplicatedly content simply to get on with the job and get it over. As it was, she was no longer so certain. She watched him, happily limping off with his stick to 'inspect the estate' (always said in irony, but an irony that was not – she felt now – entirely sincere) followed by the ancient and smelly Spike to some far corner of the grounds, and her heart sank. She knew him far too well not to know what was going through his head, and it irritated and alarmed her. Couldn't he see that even if they both desired with a single mind to turn the Hall into their home, even if the money could be found to do the sort of repairs and renovations the place required to be habitable at all, that as things were this would simply be out of the question?

Couldn't he see that for them to go on living as they did – and they currently occupied Aunt Rosalind's bedroom and Uncle George's dressing-room, an arrangement that caused no comment, since these were the only two habitable bedrooms – ruled out living where they had been known since childhood? Their chosen life had a certain inevitable subterfuge knitted into it.

All the time these days, Lottie felt as if a wasps' nest had taken up residence in her guts. She felt oppressed by the Henrys, who had agreed to stay on for this difficult, transitory period for the sake of their late employer, but who, she was sure, regarded herself and Leo as 'Londoners', unused to the ways that had gone on time out of mind. And there was the Village, agog to know if Captain Rollitt and his widowed sister were going to rescue the 'poor old Hall' and somehow reconstruct the good old days when dear old Lady Bullivant kept a decent stable, a welcome table, ran fetes for the Church, and where chamber music concerts in the Adam room and theatre troupes in the maze had amused people of cultivation from far and wide…

Lottie kept her own counsel. She dreaded seeing Leo's face fall, but he would surely see sense for himself in the end. She had also decided that Leo would be far more likely to respond to a *fait accompli* than to argument, and had therefore kept Mr Armitage's most recent visit, arranged during one of Leo's visits to Town, a secret.

One can keep secrets from one's nearest and dearest, but not from an English country village. Moreover, secrets of the kind that involve visits by 'city men' in dark suits and large, smooth Rovers tend to get expanded and inflated in the most improbable ways. It was Mrs Jenkinson, who kept the livery stable where Aunt Rosalind's elderly gelding was lodged, who provided the catalyst for the private family discussion that Lottie had been avoiding.

She was poring over some accounts at the dining table, breakfast barely finished, and Leo was draining his coffee before doing his 'rounds', when old Mrs Henry had come in unceremoniously. 'I'm so sorry, Mrs Walters – I only just heard the bell go, and…'

'Helloo-oo!' A spare, muscular woman with short iron grey hair, wearing jodhpurs and riding boots was close on her heels. Audrey Jenkinson had a certain local reputation: not for nothing did the Village call her 'Radio Folville'. She strode in after Mrs Henry, bringing with her a pungent odour of horse which is either delightful or nauseating, depending on one's point of view. 'I'm completely out of order, Charlotte,' she fluted. 'And so's your telephone, did you know? That's why I'm here. Oh, Leo! So sorry. Didn't realise you were here. Tell me to go away if I'm a nuisance.'

'No, no – not at all, Audrey. The phone gets affected by damp, I'm afraid. I was just off, anyway. Have some coffee. Oh, Mrs Henry, could you – er?' Mrs Henry was hovering. Mrs Jenkinson promptly sat down, and Mrs Henry snatched up the coffee pot with an audible 'humph' – not her fault if visitors just burst in without a decent warning, but she had her standards and she was put out.

'What is it, Audrey? Is something wrong with Nimrod?' Lottie frowned. She hated this sense that they were somehow open to all comers at any time of day. It was as though the Hall was village property.

[159]

'Nimrod's as fit as a flea, ' said Audrey Jenkinson. 'He's an old boy, of course, but he likes to be hacked about. Wendy takes him out every morning, and that idiot locum of Craven's has just filed his teeth.'

'Oh dear – do we owe you something?' The vet's bills were something that Lottie had not foreseen, and she was poised on the brink of a conversation with Audrey about the venerable Nimrod's future.

'No, no, we'll talk about that later, Charlotte. No – I've just dashed over impromptu. I wanted to quash this rumour!'

In spite of herself, Lottie felt her insides sink. She was jumpy as hell, and it probably showed. 'What rumour?' She glanced at Leo, but his face was smoothly untroubled. 'Rumour, Audrey?' he said cheerfully. 'Ah – more coffee. Thanks, Mrs H. Tell us, Audrey, do.'

'Well! Yes, thanks, Charlotte, two please… Thing is, I saw Edie Bloxham in Kirk's yesterday morning, and she told me she'd spoken to somebody, old Miss Sibley, I think, and she'd told her you were selling the Hall to a pop star. Of course, I told her she must be mistaken. Dear Edgar's old biddies *will* gossip and get the wrong end of the stick. Edie said Armitage had come with some people last week in very flashy cars. I suppose her spy must have been talking to Mrs Henry, but I said that you'd had a lot of people looking at poor Rosalind's paintings, but as for selling the Hall to a long-haired pop music person! Oh dear, do say it isn't true. It would be *so* awful! Lovely coffee.'

'A pop star? Of course it's not true, Audrey,' Leo said. 'What an idea!'

'Oh!' Idiotic relief washed over Lottie. She even laughed a little. 'Absolutely!'

'Hurrah! I can tell Edie it's all bosh, can I?

'You can reassure the Vicarage that there won't be any Rolling Stones at the Hall. Nothing's decided yet. Is it, Lottie?'

'Not yet, no. We are on Armitage's books – he brings people from time to time.'

'Oh – so you are still proposing to sell,' said Mrs Jenkinson, looking crestfallen.

'We're still thinking about it. It's still very early days, Audrey – we – we're still doing sums, aren't we, Leo? This is – would be – a pretty enormous project, you know. Anyway, I promise you we won't be letting the Hall go to the Beatles or Adam Faith…' Lottie wished the woman would just go.

'No fear,' Leo said.

Mrs Jenkinson persisted. 'But I suppose you might have to sell to *somebody!* Oh, what a dreadful *pity!* We'd all *so* hoped that you might – well, decide to stay on, Leo. This would be such a perfect *family* house, wouldn't it?' She gave Leo a look that would once have been described as 'arch'. The whole of Folwell Village, and indeed many villages for miles around, had learned of Leo's broken engagement, and the pet local occupation in recent weeks had been dusting off suitably marriageable daughters, granddaughters and nieces for the newly eligible bachelor. Leo no longer found it amusing.

'I'm afraid selling up has always been on the cards, Audrey. If we do sell, we promise it will be to someone who'll be, you know, suitable,' Leo said.

'Well, I still think it would be a terrible shame!' said Audrey Jenkinson.

'I agree,' said Leo heartily. 'Fingers crossed, eh?'

'Now!' Mrs Jenkinson stood up. 'I'm in your way! I'd better get on with my morning. I've had that bay animal of the Breretons lame for the last week. I'll be in touch about old Nimrod, Charlotte. Morning, Leo! You must both come over for drinks or something very soon. Roger and I thought you'd like to meet the Staffords. They're out at Surley Weston, you know, and their second daughter's just back from Switzerland. The poor girl's bored to death with all of us old fogeys. Her name's Esmé, and she's very musical, I gather. Sings.'

'Good God! FF with a vengeance! I wish people wouldn't just burst in like that.'

'No. Ghastly. I say, Lottie? Pop stars? Last week?' Leo's raised eyebrows would have been comic in other circumstances. 'What's going on, dearest?'

'Well, of course it's not pop stars! I simply forgot, Leo, darling. I meant to tell you, but it slipped my mind, because it wasn't really significant. Just Armitage being a bit zealous. He brought some people round while you were away. Now, everyone seems to have turned it into a sort of wild surmise.'

'Evidently.'

'It's nothing to get excited about. People want to see it, naturally. Then they decide it's far too much of a ruin. But – well, that's really our problem, darling...' She took a deep breath. '*We* can't afford to put it right. This place just gobbles money. The roof alone.'

'Maybe. But, listen, Lottie. I've been thinking, and I wonder if it's wise to sell so cheaply. We can do it slowly, bit by bit. We'll find the funds. I've got one or two little ideas up my sleeve. And I think – well, I mean, I think we might be happy here if we gave it a chance. It's – well, it's really rather lovely here, Lottie. Isn't it?'

'I'm not denying it's lovely, Leo...' She was actually hating it more and more. 'But – look, darling, we can't stay, for obvious reasons, I'd have thought.'

'If we could find the funds, I really don't see why not. .'

'Don't you? Don't you *really*?' Her exasperation flared. 'How do you imagine we'd go on? Honestly?'

'Well, I thought we'd begin by liquidating the assets – the silver, this table, the punch bowl, all the obvious museum pieces. And then I thought I'd have a word with Somerville at the Trust. If we could interest them, they'd do the sums, probably take on the whole show, with us in it...or at least go half and half. I need to find out precisely how it works. But if it could work, Lottie, just think, darling!'

'Oh, Leo...' Lottie rubbed her eyes between her thumb and forefinger. 'I don't just mean funds, for heaven's sake!'

'It just seems, well, such a pity to let it go. As La Jenkinson said.'

'She's trying to marry you off to the musical Esmé Stafford! Honestly, there's an entrenched feudalism about this place that gives me the creeps.'

'Aren't you over-reacting a bit, dearie? Look, at least consider the idea? Please?'

'I think if we get a serious offer we have to consider *that*, Leo!' His obtuseness alarmed her horribly.

It marked a moment in their lives: this was the first real battle of wills since their childhoods, and it repeated an old pattern. Lottie looked likely to win it, as

[161]

she always had. And Leo, stubborn beneath the affable exterior, agreed with her and went underground.

It was the next morning's post that produced the crunch.

'Leo? Oh, darling, do listen, please…' She couldn't quite keep the excitement out of her voice. 'We've had an offer! Somebody wants to buy the Hall for twenty-seven thousand pounds! Just think, Leo – this is riches! Look…'

'It is the Rolling Stones or someone then,' he said, taking the letter.

'Idiot! No, not as bad as that. But – oh dear. I know you're not going to like this, darling, and God knows what the village will think. Somebody wants to open a country house hotel.'

He read, and his frown deepened. 'Oh no…oh, hell, *no*, Lottie!'

'Darling, please do listen to me. It's twenty-seven *thousand*, Leo! It's only a company like that that can afford these old places now. If we accept, we can go away. Buy somewhere in Italy, maybe. Go away and be free…Oh, please, Leo!'

He got up and stared out at the dilapidated terrace. 'You mean free to pretend. Yes, I suppose it must come to that…' The life of pretence he had constructed in his mind was of a somewhat different order, and it was poised to collapse.

'And whatever did you imagine we'd have to go on doing here? For God's sake, Leo, be a bit realistic. If this – this life, together, that we've chosen to live – if it matters at all to you, you surely must know we have to pretend somewhere! We have to go away where people don't remember us as children and pretend to be husband and wife or something. Hell, I don't mind being your mistress. But we can't go on here as we are with everyone prying and trying to marry you off and casting me in the role of Miss Murdstone or – or Dorothy Wordsworth, or someone. It won't work! It's reckless, crazy. Surely you *see*?'

'Oh, Lottie… We could live at opposite ends of the house, I mean officially. It's nobody's business but ours, darling.'

'Leo! God…you really *don't* see, do you? What about the Henrys? Or anyone else we employ? This is a *village*, for heaven's sake! Everybody talks. We – we could end up in jail, put into a mental home, forced apart forever. Please, Leo. I'm begging you! See *sense*…' She was almost in tears. 'It's madness, Leo. Pure madness. God, sometimes, I think you're away with the bloody fairies! Oh!' She choked down a sob into her handkerchief.

He grimaced and crossed the room and took her hand. 'Don't cry, Lottie, dearest, please. I suppose, you see – I mean – I do tend to live on the edge, a bit. I'm used to – risks.'

'Well I'm *not*!'

'We'll work something out. Shh, darling, please.'

'Yes! Shh, darling! Thank God Mrs Henry's deaf! I suppose you think we'd get away with it because, and I quote, you're not the marrying kind? That's what they all say in London, and it's true, isn't it, Leo? Well? Isn't it?'

'Lottie…'

'You need to marry someone properly, Leo. Cover your back. Find someone suitably understanding and live your – your other life on the side. That's what you'd been planning, wasn't it? A sort of rusticated double life. Your country seat and your London diversions. Ha!' She snorted back tears, still feeling slightly hysterical. 'It's not a bad idea. It just can't be with me, that's all. That's two double lives, Leo, and it wouldn't work. Oh *hell*. I just wish to God this had never happened, that's all...' Her face crumpled.

'Oh, Lottie...' He was almost in tears himself. 'Please, please don't say *that*...' He stroked a tear down her cheek.

'The Hall, this place. I meant this place. It's confused everything so much. I know how much it means to you. And I'm so *sorry*... Oh, God, darling, whatever are we going to do? I don't want to stop – *this* – not if you don't.'

'No! Oh, please, no...' He took her in his arms. 'I've been so unfair, darling. You – you're the only person I can imagine actually *loving*, you see...and it's so wonderful with you, dearest. But. Oh God. I – I have to be honest with you, darling, because it isn't fair otherwise. I may still go on being – well, a bit risky. I'll try not to. I have been trying. It's all pretty squalid.'

She wiped her eyes and blew her nose. 'I don't mind that, Leo. Truly. I mean, I've thought about it, and I don't. It's – it's sort of part of you.'

'Lottie...'

'I love you so much. Let's just please go somewhere safer.'

He nodded. 'Yes. You're quite right. I do see that we have to...' And, remembering his recent interview with the O'Ryan boy, he did see. All too clearly. 'Italy?'

'They say all that's easier in Italy, too,' said Lottie, through a watery smile.

38

Hubert Bollinger, arranging some books and gramphone records into what had been Leo Rollitt's shelves, answered a frantic knocking on the door.

'My dear Mrs O'Ryan! Whatever is the matter?'

''Tis…tis my Andy,' sobbed the old lady. 'He's…he's…'

'Tell me, dear lady, please. Look, come in, do. Sit down. Whatever's happened?' He steered her to a chair, and she sat, sniffing into her tea-towel while he looked on, much at a loss.

'I want to speak to the Captain,' gulped Mrs O'Ryan. 'As soon as possible. Oh, sir! Oh, jesusmaryandjoseph!'

'We'll ring him right away, Mrs O'Ryan. Never you fear. Now, do please tell me what's happened to Andy. Something's very wrong. No – wait. Let's pour you a drink, shall we? Here. I've only got scotch, I'm afraid. Now then. Drink this and tell me.'

'Oh God, I'm so sorry, sir,' gasped Mrs O'Ryan. 'What you must think of me – oh, Holy Mary!'

'Mrs O'Ryan? Do tell me if you can. It might help,' said Bollinger rather helplessly. The large and friendly stockbroker who, it was rumoured, could be savagery itself on the 'Change, was fazed entirely by any woman's tears.

'Andy – my grandson – he's – he's been *arrested*!'

'Arrested? Lord, Mrs O'Ryan, thank God for that! I thought you were going to tell me he was dead!'

'He might as well be, sir,' cried Mrs O'Ryan, passionately. 'He's in a cell down at the Police! Oh, Lord, whatever's going to happen?'

'Let's get hold of old Leo at once,' said Bollinger practically, picking up the telephone. 'He'll know what to do…'

39

'You do know what this means, don't you, Andrew,' said Leo sternly.

'I think so, Captain Rollitt, sir,' said Andrew O'Ryan, looking at the carpet, mostly because his grandmother's piercing eyes were on him.

'Well?'

'I'm not going to prison, but you're sending me away to school...'

'Yes – well, that's about the sum of it. I've also paid your fine. That's my part of the bargain.'

'Say thank you to the Captain, boy, for the Lord's sakes. Ye'd have been in handcuffs still had it not been for him, ain't that right, sir? Say thank you properly and mind your manners...'

'Thank you, Captain Rollitt,' said Andrew, standing awkwardly to attention on his asymmetrical footwear, his eyes unwavering. He wore his school uniform, complete with tie. It was the closest thing to smart clothes he had, but it had the effect of making him appear very young indeed – something, Leo was reflecting, that might have had a considerable impact on the Magistrate.

'That's better,' said the boy's grandmother. 'It's far more than you deserve, boy. We're just so grateful, sir. We can't thank you enough, can we, Andy?' Mrs O'Ryan in her best black coat, a hat with a straggly feather that bobbed every time she spoke, and a gash of red lipstick on her bloodless mouth had rather made the most of her brief appearance in Court, vouching for the good character of her errant grandson with a volubility that the Magistrate had had eventually to quell. Now, the three of them stood rather ill at ease in what had once been the Captain's sitting room, from which Mr Bollinger had made himself tactfully absent. 'Ye'd have been in such trouble, Andy, but for the Captain!' But sometimes, it seemed to her, the good Lord sent blessings in disguise, and she would say so to Father Coffey this very evening.

'Mrs O'Ryan – I think maybe it would be best if I could have a word with Andrew on his own.'

'Of course, of course, sir.' The old lady bobbed and so did her hat, and she tottered off a little painfully in her best shoes, leaving her grandson with the Captain.

'All right, Andrew. We'd better talk about your part of the bargain, hadn't we?' said Leo once the old lady had gone. 'Do you have any idea what that is?'

'Not to break glass and spray paint over the new school, sir?' Now that his grandmother had left the room, he seemed suddenly more confident and somehow older. For a boy who that very morning had stood in a Court of Justice, flanked by two policemen and facing a Magistrate on a charge of wilful damage and vandalism, he looked and sounded entirely unhumbled, staring boldly into Leo's face, even a trace of sly humour in the inky eyes. Leo resisted an urge to slap him.

'Andrew, I shall be receiving regular reports on your progress. As your sponsor, I'm entitled to that. I've saved your bacon, Andrew. You've got a second chance. And in return...well, in return, don't let me down, that clear?'

'All clear, sir. I mean, I ain't got much choice, have I?'

'No, Andrew. You haven't. Except to make the very best you can of it and stay out of trouble. Obey the masters. Read. Learn things. Work hard and pass your exams. And –' Leo suddenly felt exhausted by the catechism and paused. 'Andrew, I want to ask you a question. It was that other lad, the Tilson boy, who actually did most of the damage at the school, wasn't it? Come on, boy. You can tell me. You can't be tried for the same crime twice. I'm just interested in why – well, in why you shielded him. It seems to me to be – well, unnecessarily noble, since he was to blame at least as much as you.'

'I put him up to it, sir. It was me. My idea...' It had been, up to a point. Tilson's father's protection racket had provided the germ. Tilson's recent beating from the headmaster for getting 'above himself' had produced the spur. The rest had been a matter of rudimentary breaking and entering with a can of red spray paint.

'I see, I see. Or I think I do.' Leo scratched his chin and frowned. 'You're telling me that because this Tilson youngster acted under your instruction, you felt you had to take responsibility for the whole show yourself? Is that really true? My God, boy!' Leo was gazing at his protégé with new eyes. 'I actually think that was rather fine of you, Andrew. Not to – er – snitch. On a pal.'

'Yeah, well, maybe, sir. But fact is, sir, his dad's a big cheese round here – a sort of crime-boss, if yer foller me. If I'd snitched, I'd've been dead meat, sir.'

'Ah,' said Leo. 'I see.' And, to his consternation, he actually did.

There were bustling sounds behind the door, and Lottie came in, breathless and triumphant, laden with parcels and carrier bags. She was up in Town for the sales, staying with her friend Alison Porter, who ran an antique shop in the King's Road.

'Dearest! Whew! I've virtually bought up Peter Jones and Marshall & Snelgrove *and* Selfridges! Can I have a drink? Oh! Sorry – you're busy. I didn't realise. Can I just dump these things here, or shall I bung them in your room?'

'Come in, my dear. Andrew and I have been discussing business. But he's just off to join his grandmother downstairs for some lunch, I don't doubt. Right, Andrew? Say how do you do to Mrs Walters, Andrew.'

'How d'ye do, Mrs Walters,' Andrew said, with slightly exaggerated formality, his eyes meeting hers. She felt her mood descend suddenly.

'Hullo, Andrew.'

'Andrew's just going,' Leo said, giving Andrew a nod of dismissal. 'Good lad...' And Andrew left the room, winking slyly and privately at Lottie as he did so.

'Oh, God, darling. I'd forgotten this morning was the court case. I'm sorry to have just barged. How did it go?'

'Very well on the whole. G and T? I certainly need one.'

'I take it he's not been locked up,' Lottie said. 'Since he's still here. Cheeri-bloody-oh.'

'Cheeri-bloody. No. On the whole, it went very well. I managed to insert myself between that boy and a dreary fate, thank God. Old Ma O'Ryan enjoyed herself enormously. Best coat and hat, and called the magistrate 'your worship'.

It was old Foxley. He took it all with a pinch of salt. Anyway, we got let off with a fine, a severe caution and – well, um.'

'My, my! Well, I hope he's worth it. What have you done? Paid his fine, I suppose.'

'It was a bit more complicated than that, darling. I've had to vouch for him. I'm sending him to school, Lottie. I'm sure it's the best thing. I've – well, I've more or less agreed to be his guardian.'

'His *guardian*? Leo! Honestly, how could you? A little hooligan like that! If you want my opinion, that boy belongs in a home for delinquents. He *is* a delinquent! Oh, Leo, *honestly*!'

'He certainly would be if he had ended up in some sort of detention this morning. That's no place for a bright boy, Lottie. He'd just learn how to be a criminal. And worse. No – trust me, dearest. I'm sure this is the best thing. Poor lad. His mother in the States doesn't want him. It's rather pathetic, sad.'

'I'm not surprised they don't want him in America! They've got enough low-life there already.'

'Lottie!'

'Sorry. I'm sure it's very sad about his mother. But basically this means we've got him in our lives now, haven't we? I wonder sometimes if you can see beyond the nose on your face, Leo. He's a perfectly horrible child! I don't know why you're doing this. It's crazy.'

'Is it? Is it crazy, Lottie, to want to – well, to make a difference? I think I *can* make a difference. Don't let's fight, please, darling heart.'

'Sorry.' Lottie bit her lip. 'You're too good, Leo darling. You collect lame ducks. You always did. Remember Hoyden?'

'Hoyden! Poor old Hoyden. She was actually a lovely bitch, darling, just a bit temperamental. She obeyed me.'

'And nobody else, Leo. Which was why, if you remember, she had to be destroyed after she practically severed Johnny Barkby's hand.'

'Yes. I wasn't there, remember? I was at school…' They both sat silent, remembering the Hoyden incident. They had been at Folwell for the holidays. Hoyden had been the runt of the litter of a local farmer's collie pups, kicked out to fend for herself, left, so Leo had claimed, to die. Finding the bedraggled stray half starved and injured in the woods, Leo had taken pity and fed and nursed it, and the little dog had rewarded him with a terrible devotion. The problem occurred when Leo had had to return to school. Hoyden was unmanagable, pining and whining incessantly, and then, banished to the stables, became vicious, literally biting the hand that fed her. Lottie had been staying with their aunt and uncle when the garden boy had been rushed to the cottage hospital, his face white, his hand pouring blood. She had also witnessed her brother's anguish when he returned home to the news that Hoyden had been shot, and Uncle George's stern assertion that he should have cared more about the wounded Barkby than the fate of a mad dog. She had found Leo sobbing in the stables, mourning his foundling, inconsolable. It was one of the very few times he had cast her away from him, told her to go. Now, she wished she had not brought the subject up.

[167]

'Sorry, darling. I'm just a bit – you know – jumpy.' This was an understatement. For some reason she could scarcely explain to herself, let alone to Leo, the thought of the O'Ryan boy in their lives gave her a horrible feeling of foreboding.

She would have felt far worse had she heard Andrew O'Ryan's footsteps sneaking away from the door and murmuring 'bitch, bitch, lovely bitch' as he stomped down the stairs. As it was, she heard nothing but the sweet tinkling of crushed ice in their glasses.

Part IV

40: Last year in Washington DC

'You've been following me about absolutely all day. Who the hell are you?' Veronica Dearborn rounded on the man at the bar. She had had enough gin and tonic to embolden her, and besides, this ghastly gig was supposed to be in her honour – well, hers amongst others. She felt she had every right to ask.

Through the lunch and the speeches and the prizes, he'd been there, on and off all the time, distinctive in his rather scruffy black leather jacket and the shades. A reporter, obviously. She would have to get used to those in a new way, after having been followed about so much by them before. But this one seemed aloof from the rest, and he didn't carry an obvious camera, and he wasn't writing things. He just seemed to be staring at her, trying – perhaps this was her paranoid imagination – to catch her eye. His own were half-hidden behind the dark glasses – overdone indoors, surely – which lent the thing as the day wore on an ambiguity that she found more and more puzzling. It had got so that (very annoyingly) she was actually looking for *him*. A space in the crowd, and she found herself trying to locate him, if only to establish him in place so she could forget him. But, strangely, he seemed to be capable of being everywhere at once. Just when she thought she had spotted him on the mezzanine floor behind a chrome banister in a gaggle of reporters with cameras, suddenly here he was at her side downstairs by a drinks and nibbles buffet, close enough to witness that silly little scene when the waiter had taken her respectfully by the elbow: 'The celebrity table is right over there ma'am, and you don' have to serve yourself. We'll be right there…' 'That's right, ma'am! This trough's for the reporter piggies,' said the man in black.

The voice wasn't American, so far as she could tell, but neither was it exactly English. She'd barely given him a glance, and retreated chastened, unversed in the protocol, and waited for her lunch, talking to the Armenian author on her left, whose famous and much-reviewed political novel she hadn't read (which caused her a terrible moment of panic, in which she tried and failed to remember a synopsis, let alone anything else he had written.) Fortunately for Veronica, he soon became deeply engaged in conversation with the person on his other side, and Veronica turned with relief to the woman on her right – no 'boy, girl' *placements* here – a golden blonde, thin beyond belief in a tailored trouser-suit of cream linen, a Ms Granby-Getz, who had recently produced a work on female sexuality that had had caused such a stir that Veronica could almost believe that she *had* read it. Beside these comparative giants, her own book seemed paltry, almost fraudulent, despite the 'Best Debut Non-Fiction Award' it had won.

She stared at the lobster coleslaw on her plate and toyed with her wine glass, which was empty again. Ms Granby-Getz was drinking mineral water, she noticed, and waved the waiter away when he materialised, napkin-wrapped bottles poised. Veronica's 'Yes, please, white,' clashed with Ms Granby-Getz's strident

'No thanks!', but the waiter filled Veronica's glass anyway, much to her relief. 'Now I see that you drink,' said the Granby-Getz woman accusingly. 'I'm AA...'

'Oh dear,' Veronica said. 'How awful!'

'Not at all. Not. At. All,' intoned Ms Granby-Getz. 'Going AA was the best thing I ever did. I feel liberated. Once again, I'm in control of my mind. And my bah-dy,' she added, staring pointedly at Veronica, and at Veronica's drink, which was half way between the table and her lips.

'Oh,' said Veronica, feeling suddenly huge and more depressed than ever, putting the glass down, untouched.

'And so will you, when you take that little step and stop. For good...' Ms Granby-Getz took a delicate sip from her Perrier, and began forking into her Waldorf salad. Veronica tried, and failed, to imagine Ms Granby-Getz's intimate interview technique.

'One day, maybe,' she said, taking a smaller sip than she wanted to. 'I mean, I don't think I have a problem with alcohol. I just like wine. Too much sometimes. It makes me put on weight...' Already she seemed to be bursting out of the new mustard moiré-silk tunic and rust linen-silk trousers she had so recently bought, and tucked her napkin firmly into her over-large bosom. She always felt awkward at these sort of occasions, and now, because she was one of the celebrities, she felt even worse.

'Uh-uh...' Ms Granby-Getz's artfully gilded head nodded up and down. 'That's what we all say, honey. We all say that, and look at us! Slaves to the stuff. Bad medicine, that's what that is. Give it up. Stop now. Say to yourself, Vanessa – sorry, I realise I don't know you at all well – call me Cornelia – but you have to say to yourself, Vanessa, this is bad medicine. A no-no. And stop. I can see you're a woman of enormous strength. You could, you know...'

'Yes. Yes, I could, I suppose...' It was the word 'enormous' that did it. Veronica suddenly felt blessed rebellion rise and took a liberal slug from her glass. 'But I don't think I want to, and actually, Cornelia, I call myself Veronica. You can too, if you like. Poor thing. You must have been through such hell being an alcoholic. I really am so sorry...' Which, mercifully, was when the Armenian writer on her other side burst into gales of rich laughter, prompted by his neighbour, and he turned to her and said companionably, 'Have you met Mr Richard Dorchester? He's an expert on the sex life of the lobster.'

'Julie? Excuse me, Julie?' Coffee was being served, and it was apparently the moment at which guests got up and mingled. Julie Knight was the Visitors' Co-ordinator, and Veronica spotted her chic, shingled, platinum head at the special executives' table, which some of the executives had deserted in order to smoke on the veranda outside.

'Hi, Veronica,' said Julie, squeezing Veronica's hand. 'Have some coffee. I thought your speech was just wonderful. Everything okay?'

'Thank you. Yes, marvellous,' said Veronica without enthusiasm. 'Nice lunch. Lovely. Julie, tell me – that man over there...' She pointed. 'Who is he? Do you know?' But the man in black had vanished. 'Oh. He was there. Just a moment ago. He's in sunglasses, black leather jacket.'

[170]

'Sunglasses, black leather jacket,' repeated Julie Knight. 'No, I don't see him. Sorry. Do you have a problem?'

'No, no problem. I just – I thought I knew him from somewhere. Probably seeing things...'

'Oh, I expect he's with one of the magazines. Don't worry. They're all over the place.'

'Yes, I suppose so. Though he looks more like a sort of gangster.'

'*Really*?' Julie Knight said, raising an eloquent eyebrow. 'I shouldn't think there are *too* many of those at a publishing convention in Washington, would you, dear?'

'I expect I'm being silly. Too much of this lovely wine...'

'Good. That's what it's for,' Julie Knight cooed. 'You have a nice afternoon nap, now, dear. You can find your room okay?'

Oh God, Veronica thought. The woman thinks I'm *pissed*... 'Fine, thank you,' she said, trying to sound austere, but probably sounding merely rude. How she longed to escape this appalling gathering!

'Or the driver's booked to take a party up to the Capitol and the Monument if you want to join them in a half hour or so,' continued Julie Knight. 'We assemble for cocktails and supper down here at six-thirty.'

'Thank you...' Supper at six-thirty! The waist band of her trousers felt horribly tight already, and her head was swimming a bit. Now all she wanted to do was put her feet up before she made even more of a fool of herself. But the man in black was on her mind. She couldn't swear he'd not been among the small crowd at the elevators that conveyed them, swiftly, noiselessly, up twelve floors. When the doors swished open, she had hurried to her room, turning to see if he had followed. The plushly carpeted corridor was empty. It was only while she was inserting the card – with difficulty – into the slot in the door that she thought she caught a glimpse of a black clad figure vanishing into another doorway...

Round two. Here we go again. But Veronica felt better for her rest, hating the occasion slightly less than before. She could use a cocktail – a proper one, a nice big G&T to brace the mini-bar one she had already had during her shower with the CNN news on the room's TV. She was dressed in a flowing kaftan, a deceptively simple creation that hid most of her bulky figure, exaggerated her height, and she sailed up to the bar with the impressive dignity of a galleon. And there he was, large as life, drinking a glass of hospitality fizz, and virtually reaching across her to pop an olive into his mouth from a silver bowl. That was when she challenged him. '...Who the hell are you? I suppose you're a reporter. Report away. What do you want to know?'

'Are you always this combative, Miss Dearborn?' asked the man. Not American. Scots? She couldn't place the accent.

'No,' she said. 'I just don't like being followed about. How do you know my name?'

She had deliberately left her stupid conference tag behind in her room.

'Ahhh...' The man tapped his nose. 'Homework, my dear Miss Dearborn. Or do you prefer Mizz?' He was of middling height, fairly slim, with thinning curly dark hair. His naturally olivey complexion – Mediterranean? Spanish? – was of that pallid, almost pasty hue that suggested he spent most of his time indoors. Out of the sun, anyway. She put him in his early fifties, probably older, but his clothes and demeanour, not to mention the dark glasses which he still wore, suggested rock-musician more than gangster. One of those eternal youths who refuse to grow old, gracefully or otherwise.

'I don't think I care. But you still haven't explained anything, Mr –?'

'Todd. People call me Todd. At your service…' He made a mock bow.

'How do you do. So, what's this about?'

'Simple. I'm a fan. I enjoyed your book. I even said so in print. Would you care for another of those or something stronger?'

'Oh! You're *that* Todd! A. O. Todd, the one who said such nice things about it in the *LRB*…or was it the *New York Review*? Gosh! What a surprise. Gin and tonic, please…' She suddenly felt very silly.

'There. You'd not thought of that, had you? Shall we sit?' He steered her over to a nearby island with a semi-circular plush bench and a drinks table. She noticed he walked with a limp. 'You had me down for some kind of wierdo psychopath, didn't you? Glad to put the record straight. Cheers!'

'Cheers. Actually,' Veronica said, 'I thought you were a gangster. How awful's that? Sorry.'

'You know, Miss Dearborn, your face really lights up when you smile like that…' He was sitting close enough for her to catch a glimpse of his eyes behind the dark lenses. He had one of those sculpted mouths, with lines deeply etched from nose to chin. She was aware she was staring.

'Oh! Um, it was nice that you liked my book…' Deeply suspicious of anything like flirting, she hastily tried to turn the subject. 'I mean, I know perfectly well why it got all this attention. It wasn't – isn't – all *that* good.'

'You're being far too modest, Miss Dearborn. *Too Big To Cry* is very good. A few *longeurs*, maybe, and your urgent use of the present tense when discussing things very much in the past gets a trifle confusing, but these are details, unimportant. And I was, of course, fascinated by its subject matter.'

'Oh dear. So is everybody. That's why I'm here, really. That and the fact that the Americans can't get enough of the English aristocracy. I don't kid myself. At least that's what's accounted for most of the sales. Anyway, you were very kind about it.'

'Kindness, believe me, Miss Dearborn, is something nobody accuses me of.'

'So why?' She was aware of his eyes again, glad of the dark glasses, a little confused.

'Because…' He sucked his lower lip and looked down at his hands and spread them – pale, well-made hands with square, capable looking fingers, and very clean except for suspicions of nicotine and ink – choosing his words. 'Because,' he said carefully, 'I think you sustained all that excoriating anger very well. Because your prose borders on the eloquent. And subtle. You allowed your characters to reveal themselves, that was the truly subtle touch. But you spared nobody, not even yourself, which is what saves it from being a victim book, if you know what I'm saying, and that gives it all a splendid ring of truth. And…and because I hadn't read a memoir quite so candid, or quite so – what's the word ? – vituperative before. Especially one that mostly concerns people who are still alive. As I think I wrote in that review – it was in the *Independent*, by the way – "if this doesn't make the author's family choke on its breakfast, it'll be because they're all too busy trying to make her choke on hers".'

'I remember. I was frightfully chuffed by what you said. Oh, God!'

'And did they? Try to assassinate you? Libel suits? What happened? I really want to know.'

'Oh! Well, no, no libel suits. It was about me, you see, really, and I was the only actual criminal. Someone at my publishers warned that there could be a defamation thing, but no-one has bothered. It's beneath their contempt, and anyway they'd always run the risk of keeping it all in the public eye for longer than it need. They – .they're not very pleased, if that makes you any happier. My sister would cheerfully poison my coffee, on the grounds, she says, that I've embarrassed her illustrious husband. He's a politician, the Cabinet, but you probably know that. Actually, that was all a bit unfortunate. The book came out the very week he was trying to get some bill or other passed about muzzling the press, arguments about what constituted the public interest, all that. I'm afraid I laughed a bit…' She was laughing a bit now, relaxing. His eyes behind the dark glasses (an eye complaint?) were gazing intently at her.

'And? Have an olive.'

'Thanks. I'd better nibble something or I'll disgrace myself over this ghastly supper. And – well, let's see. My brother stopped speaking to me entirely, not that he's really spoken to me for years. He's in Africa most of the time. As for my mother, well – she just responded in typical fashion, madly giving interviews all over the place, telling everyone how *pleased* she was that *darling* Veronica has had such a *thrilling* success, and how she wishes me all the luck in the world. That sort of thing. It's Mummy's version of the pre-emptive strike. She's very good at it. She manages to come across as sweetly noble every time. Her friends have been pretty vile, though – saying all the things she couldn't, as it were. I've had hate-mail, all that sort of stuff. Even some dog-shit through the door.'

'Nasty.'

'Nothing I couldn't have expected, and as I didn't try to eat it for breakfast, I didn't choke on it,' said Veronica, taking down most of her drink at a gulp. 'They were bound to react like that, weren't they? I take full responsibility…'

The man called Todd summoned a waiter. 'You still hate her?'

'You mean, was all this catharsis sufficient to kiss and make up? Not on your life, Mr Todd.'

'Just Todd, please.'

'Todd. For what it's worth, Todd, I still think she's the biggest hypocrite I've ever met, and – well, sort of worthless. On the other hand, if I'm being entirely honest…' She paused, frowning.

'Yes? It's all very interesting, Miss Dearborn. I'm fascinated. Do go on.'

'Oh dear. I'm not sure I should. Sorry, it's not you. It's just that this is exactly the sort of interview I keep trying to avoid...' The fresh drinks appeared, and some rather more substantial cocktail snacks, which Veronica bit into gratefully.

'This is not an interview, Miss Dearborn. Okay? This is private. If you want to do some sort of interview at some point, fine. We can arrange it. In the meantime, just between ourselves, okay? You were about to be entirely honest. About the relationship with Mummy.'

'Yes. God, I mean I never *talk* about this normally. Well, it's as if the book... I mean, it wasn't intended to be cathartic, an exercise in mental health – although it is perfectly true that my cue came from some trick-cyclist in the prison hospital – I got a bit depressed. But I mean, it was always intended as a *book*. I enjoyed writing it. Began to feel my way as a writer, you know? But now it's out of me, so to speak, now it's done, well, life has to go on, doesn't it? Mummy's just Mummy. She won't ever change. Perhaps I sort of accept her better, or at least accept that she was the Mummy-card I was dealt in life. I certainly intended to sock her in the teeth, and whether she admits it or not, I succeeded. But – well – I'm a writer now, aren't I?'

'You sure are, Miss Dearborn.'

'Please. Veronica.'

'Veronica... And so, Veronica, you – no! Let me guess. You've got another project on the boil, isn't that so?'

'Yes...' Veronica frowned. 'How do you know?'

'Writers write, Veronica. It was predictable. Can you tell me what the next one's about? A novel, maybe?'

'Hell, no!'

'Woosh! That was vehement, Veronica. Not a novel, then...' He pronounced 'novel' as 'navvil'.

'You're Irish,' she said.

'Only up to a point, Veronica. Go on. This new book. Not a novel, you say?'

'No, I can't write fiction. At least not yet. I feel – oh dear. You see – Todd – that I'd only be capable of telling just the one story, and that would be hellishly boring, wouldn't it? No, my next is going to be a life, you know, a biography. I've begun it already.'

'Well, good for you! Who's the lucky party, or is that top secret?'

'No secret at all. Guy called Sir Henry Cuffe. He was secretary to...'

'To the Earl of Essex! And a spy for m'Lord Burleigh? Ah, the son. Robert Cecil. Got him! Interesting piece of work, if I remember correctly, this Cuffe. Nasty. Sort of home-grown Machiavelli.'

'Oh wow! It's so amazing to meet someone who's ever even heard of him, you know? But he wasn't just nasty. I mean, not so much nasty as just thoroughly malcontented. Clever, brilliant, even, and heartily sick of his superiors purloining his ideas and passing them off as their own. I thought he'd be fun. Interesting. So's the way Machiavelli got distorted. I got all fired up about those Elizabethan malcontents when I was at university.'

[174]

'So did I, Veronica, and I'll tell you something…'

'Everyone!' fluted a familiar voice. 'Please everyone, if the VIPs, that is the prize-winners, would mind taking their places at the supper tables, you will all be served very shortly. The Press Buffet is open for everyone else. Ah, Ms Dearborn, ready for your supper? Grand! Ah! I see you found him, your gangster, eh?' She gave the man called Todd a dazzling smile. 'Now then, this way everyone. Yes, this way, Mr Katachurian…and Ms Bayliss, Mr Dorchester…' Julie Knight beckoned her flock towards the waiting tables. Veronica rose a little unsteadily.

'Oh God, I suppose I've got to go through with this. What a bloody bore. I don't suppose I can just come and feed at your table can I?'

'Uh-uh. Not VIPs with the Press, alas. Think of it as the price of fame, dear Miss Dearborn. Veronica…' Todd took her hand in his. 'And in any case, I have an appointment. I have to leave this merry gathering. This has been a real pleasure. Can we meet in London?'

'London? Er –of course, if you'd like. Oh God, she's calling again. Look, here's my email…' She scribbled almost illegibly on the pad she kept in her bag, tore off the page and gave it to him. 'Thank you, Todd… Um, goodbye.'

'A presto, surely? Fellow-travellers are rare, Veronica. Take care now.'

She spent the supper hour a little distracted. He had not given her his number. Still, he had hers. And what had he meant by 'fellow travellers'? Difficult, now, not to cast about the vast chrome and red carpeted lounge for a glimpse of him again…

'Sit down, please, make yourself comfortable. You will excuse me not getting up. Selina! What do you drink? Whiskey? Brandy? Or are you TT? Nearly everybody is. If I could still give dinner parties, which I don't, not any more, let me tell you there'd have to be a table for the vegans, a table for the allergy-sufferers, and a tiny table for those who still enjoy meat and a smoke with the cognac. I'm a minority, and soon I shan't even be that. Selina!'

A tiny dusky-skinned maid in a neat little uniform trots in with a tray. She looks like a ballerina: neat legs and smooth dark hair in a thick coil behind her well-shaped little head. In an understated way, and like everything else I have seen in this house, she is exquisite. Mostly, I'm simply aware of the overpowering heat: except that we're in a glass-fronted drawing room overlooking the Chesapeke Bay, and there isn't an orchid in sight, I might have stepped into *The Big Sleep*. I can feel dampness at the back of my neck, my shirt sticking to me. 'Do take off your jacket,' says my host. 'I haven't got any proper blood in my veins any more. It was good of you to come in person. Selina, give my visitor a drink. Or do you prefer coffee at this time of day? I've frankly forgotten what time civilized people do things, Mr Todd.'

Surprised? Of course you're not. I get everywhere, and my kind, if I have a kind, is legion.

'Whiskey's fine,' I say. My host's facial surgery has contorted his natural expression into a curious, unmoving grimace, the lips large in his face and blue-ish, the perma-tanned skin stretched taut over the fine old bones, quite a lot of hair still, very white. A tiny old man who could probably pass for seventy at a suitable distance, but who is actually a great deal older, Giacomo Ginelli sits in an armchair bolstered with several cushions, swathed in a blue cashmere rug from the waist down under which peep impeccably polished brown brogue loafers. He wears a thick Harris-tweed jacket over a cashmere pullover, and round his skinny neck is a soft silk cravat in a very recognizable pattern. If he weren't so obviously ill, he would still be handsome. I am beginning to sweat as if I'm in a sauna and I remove my battered leather jacket gladly, aware the the lining is coming apart. He is too polite to stare.

The maid hands me a generous measure of an aged Talisker. I breathe it before I drink it, aware of my host's eyes on me, the slight contortion of his mouth that passes for a smile. Then she hands a large, opaque green glass goblet to the old man – something steaming and smelling powerfully of peppermint. His eyes, black and fierce, bore into mine. 'This disgusting stuff is all I can have now. *Salute.*'

'Thank you. *Salute.* It's very good of you to give me your time, sir.'

'Time! As if I didn't have enough of that on my hands now. And no. Not good of me. Bad of me. By the time you reach my age, one should be above such things as petty revenge. I am not, it seems. I pondered your letter for a very long time, I may say, young man. I wondered, after all this time, is it worth it? Is it *vale la pena?* But that rattlesnake whore, famous now, all these years she rankles me. I've decided to give you the story. Before I do, however, I want to make clear certain conditions. My brother is dead. He is beyond earthly reach. Nothing we say can hurt him personally, is that understood? *Capisce?*'

'*Ho capito. Senz'altro, signor Ginelli.*'

'*Va bene.* But the business, Famiglia Ginelli, it is alive and well. Nothing must hurt the reputation of the business, *capisce?*'

'Fine by me, sir.'

'Good. You can do as you wish with what I am about to tell you, provided you can assure me of that. You understand, Mr Todd? I am not a traitor.'

I tell him again that I understand, feeling my collar, waiting while the old boy sips and breathes noisily.

'My stupid, vainglorious brother! My brother Giorgio – he was my twin, you understand? He was my other half. But we were not identical, biologically or otherwise. He was – well, he was weak. He had this weakness. For women. I never did, you understand? *Capice?*' His voice is harshly transatlantic, as if he's swallowed gravel; but his intonation becomes more and more Italian the more he remembers.

'Uh-uh.'

'He had this other weakness. For money. No. That's not quite true. He had this weakness for what money represents. And this combination, women and money, it was lethal. His fault. His great fault, *il povero* Giorgio. For me, it was only the family name, it was only la Famglia Ginelli, and the magnificent, perfect things we made, made to order, for only the very, very rich. Six months, sometimes, it took, to make a bag, to make a trunk. Six months! Our silks were the finest from Lucca; our skins, crocodile, zebra, leopard – not something to boast about now, but they were imported from all over the world. Cashmere, woven only in Scotland. The finest, you understand. Only the best, the very best! We named one of our most famous designs, a travelling bag, after one of the greatest stars in the world, a princess, no less! Ahh, you are too young, my friend. These days, it is all mass-production in China and logos, if you please, logos! Everything worn on the outside like a stupid badge, not like the old days when you could see – *see* – from the very workmanship... Boh! Our father, he would turn in his grave if he only knew what became of us...'

The old man closes his eyes, silent for so long that for a moment I think he has actually nodded off. I stare about the room, at the extraordinary picture-window and the great broad river. There are framed Rembrandt drawings on the walls, a Severini, Sheraton tables, porcelain vases you actually wouldn't mind owning, and a small Bechstein piano, covered in framed portraits of the great and the good, or at least the rich and the famous, including the princess in question.

'He sold us out!' The old boy suddenly springs to life. 'My brother Giorgio! Oh of course, I'm not naive. Times changed. We had to change. Oh, how can you understand! We came from nothing once, our family. We were first *contadini*, then *artigiani*, artisans you will say, but we were the very best. Toscani DOC! Giorgio and me we learned our trade at the workbenches in Scandicci, Italy, from the age of fourteen. We were experts, exclusive experts, and everything was made by us, ourselves, and by the workers we had trained to pay minute attention to every tiny detail, every stitch. The leather was chosen by us, the designs made by me, the business run by Giorgio and our father who oversaw everything, this little business just outside of Florence, which was one of the greatest names in exclusive luxury. And then, suddenly, we have decisions to make. My father is dead, and we are still a family business. Giorgio he is married to Grazia, who is our cousin, and also a Ginelli. I am the number one designer of our bags and our trunks, and now we have the scarves and belts, the wallets, the shoes. Famiglia Ginelli, known all over the world, and so few who can afford to have the discreet stamp on their luggage. And now Giorgio, he sells out our majority share to a large corporation, a corporation that includes Vuitton, Christian Dior. He persuaded me. We're a big name, but we are a small business, and after the war, we struggle. This corporation, it can make us so much bigger. We keep our name, we still produce the luxury goods in Florence, the family divides its time between Italy and the United States. It is not such a sacrifice. Now we are nearly as rich as some of our clients, my friend, and our turnover triples, quadruples. Some of our production, the lesser lines, you understand, goes to Mauritius, to Hong Kong, and we have outlets, flagship stores in New York, in Chicago, later in Las Vegas – that was Giorgio's brain-child. I leave the business side to Giorgio, he knows what he is doing, I think. The Famiglia Ginelli label, it is like before but business is so much better. And if Giorgio wants to spend his pocket-money on yachts and dice and women, that is his own business. La Grazia she is comfortable in Italy. She lives in all the comfort she wants and she has her own weakness – for *la Chiesa*, for priests. Their kids attend exclusive schools and universities in America where they learn how to be businessmen, not craftsmen. Good, the whiskey, eh? It is exclusive too.'

'Excellent…superb…' I'm not lying. 'Do go on, sir. This is fascinating.'

He sips his peppermint concoction without relish. 'Giorgio, he lived the life of the playboy. It's okay – he can afford it. Girls, models mostly, minor actresses; yachts in Sausalito, and on Lake Tahoe, and he's often in Vegas, gambling. His new friends are Hollywood stars, businessmen with bad reputations, and he gets into the news too often, the gossip-papers. I like to live quietly, Mr Todd, and it grieves me that he is throwing himself about, making himself the fool. But – well, I am not my brother's keeper! I say to myself, *al fondo*, Giorgio knows what he is doing. And then…' He looks up, his chalky, perfectly manicured fingers drum for a moment on the arm of his chair. 'And then,' he says to the ceiling, 'my brother falls in love.'

'Ah.'

'Yes! In love! I suppose that is what one must call it. Even one of the shrewdest business brains I have ever known is not immune. It is a form of madness. Selina!' The little maid reappears on softly-slippered feet as if from nowhere. 'Give Mr Todd another whiskey. And some of those cheese relishes. I forget, Mr Todd, that other people require sustaining. These days I live on air… Thank you, Selina. That will be all for now. This woman, Mr Todd. Aah, I could see how it was

[178]

from the beginning. My brother, by now he is what, sixty-three, sixty-four. He is slowing up, a little, and he has lived too well, he has a paunch, he has a bad heart, and this girl, she is twenty-six, or maybe thirty. She is beautiful, undoubtedly, but she is nothing so very special. She is not talented, she is not Faye Dunaway, not Michelle Pfeiffer. But she has a certain – allure, let us say. Her talent is that of the *putana*! And frankly, man to man, my friend, she obviously knows better than most exactly what will please my brother. But this is madness. Giorgio had this weakness for women, like I said. In the old days, he was quite incapable of fidelity, not just to his wife but to anyone! The difference between one girl and the next is not much – blonde, brunette, redhead – he's like the child in the toy-shop. He amuses himself, he gets bored, he finds a new toy. Boh! That was my brother! He was good to be seen with, was Giorgio. Glamorous. Rich. But he was a businessman, and he had his priorities right. Women were his little hobby, but he was always sane, always right in his head. Then, with this woman, it was – *uno colpo di testa*, as we might say. Suddenly, all is her, her, her, and she is worthless! He won't marry her. Even Giorgio won't stoop so low as that, give poor Grazia the elbow, but he sets *her* up, gives her paintings, an original Lartigue, a Dali, a minor Picasso, a Maximillien Luce…he doesn't even *like* art, not Giorgio, but he knows its value. So does she, and on the quiet, she sells them, banking her spoils. He gives her fabulous jewellery which she wears once, and then off she goes to the bank with that. He gives her a little villa in the Bahamas, a love-nest for both of them, he thinks, discreet, out of the way! Boh! And she carries and wears her exclusive Famiglia Ginelli bags and scarves like trophies. He trades off money and jewels that should have gone to his children, and soon, he is not so rich. The business, that was safe enough, partly because so much of it no longer belonged to us. But Giorgio had sole power over his personal fortune, and within three years, my friend, he dissipated the whole lot. This woman, she had the mentality of the whore. And she is a nothing, a nobody! Thinks she is grand because her *babbo* is a minor White House official. She took him for every available cent! Please, drink your whiskey and I will join you in spirit. I grow angry…' The old man breathes wheezily, his nostrils dilating. His eyes when he gazes back at me are very angry indeed, black pinpoints staring out of the unnaturally smooth, perma-tanned face.

I drink, gingerly, and bite into a cheese relish. The combination of whiskey and the hot room begins to make me feel slightly faint. 'So what happened?'

'What happened? Why, she broke him! Broke his balls, broke him at the bank and broke him in spirit. It was inevitable. I don't suppose she ever pretended to be faithful to Giorgio, but there are protocols of these things. She began seeing some young jerk, some pop-star, a two-bit crooner with long hair and leather jeans, being photographed at cocaine-parties, at opening nights with minor film stars. She took this gigolo to the very house my brother had given her in the Bahamas, and because this little asshole's got a fan-following, appears in the teenage press, there's photos of them there, too, cavorting on a beach, topless in the sea… Giorgio can't ignore it any longer. He won't blow her out, but he gives her an ultimatum: give him up, come back, or.'

'Or?'

'Or nothing…' The old boy sighs like a death-rattle. 'What could he threaten? He couldn't take back what he had given her. No, it's her that's doing the threatening. Get a divorce and marry me, she's suggesting, and Giorgio he's in torment, not only because it's the one way to get her back, but because that way, if she were his wife, he gets to regain some control of her spending. But he can't do this thing to Grazia, to his moral conscience. He's a tortured man. It is a stale-mate. And then, Giorgio, suddenly he falls sick…*porca miseria!*' The old man gulps some more peppermint potion and stares stonily ahead. 'When he died…my brother Giorgio…when he was dying of a stroke in the hospital, he was calling her name. The end is near. I am there. So are his sons, and so is Grazia, and yet he calls for her, who is absent, who has robbed him of so much. Grazia is a good woman, too good if you understand me. She said to me, perhaps we should try to find her, this woman who has been her humiliation for more than five years. Grazia, always too full of prayers and forgiveness! His sons, they are horrified. I myself am horrified. We go out into the anteroom to argue, but Grazia picks up the telephone. At a time like this, we cannot argue with Grazia. And that woman, that little rattlesnake whore, she laughs. Laughs! I can hear it now, like metal, *fiorini* over the wire… She is about to catch a plane to California. And anyway, we are too late. The nurse comes and takes the arm of Grazia, and Giorgio in his bed with the priest saying the last blessing, and he gasps and he dies. Drink, drink, my friend. Another! Selina!'

'No thanks all the same, sir. This is just fine…' We sit in silence while he catches his breath, the gracefully cat-like Selina hovering discreetly over her master. 'You said there was evidence,' I prompt after an interval. The old boy's breathing gets more steady under the bulky herringbone.

'Yes. Evidence. Pass Mr Todd those envelopes, Selina.'

I flick through ten or so large black and white prints of an aging, glamorous, white-haired and vaguely familiar geezer in bermudas and shades being entertained aboard a yacht by a young and very recognizable Louise wearing nothing but a g-string, and try to mask my disappointment. Faces nice and clear, but nothing untoward, nothing more pornographic than an old copy of *Playboy*. 'These are old press photos, sir. I don't suppose she'd like to have them splashed about in the *News of the World*, but it's not very much. I'd hoped for some – well, harder evidence.'

The old boy smiles like a reptile. 'Open the second envelope, Mr Todd. I copied only the relevant portions…' More photos, in colour this time, and of pictures, fine art in frames, and another of a very fine pearl and ruby choker with earrings to match. There is some printed matter, a copy of the late Giorgio Ginelli's will, or part of it – the part that itemises specific material bequests. I read in silence, concentrating, while the sharp old eyes watch me intently.

'You see? You see the significance?'

I sigh. 'I think so, sir – this appears to leave various paintings and these rather glamorous baubles solely and absolutely to his sons, Arturo and Giancarlo. I imagine under United States law, they are still entitled to them if this will hasn't been revoked by a deed of gift or something. But I'm only guessing. I'm no expert, I'm afraid, Signor Ginelli.'

'Under Italian law, it is very, very difficult to leave one's fortunes to anyone other than family, my friend. As Giorgio's executor, it was my concern to see these things properly distributed. It was only after his death that we realised they were missing... There is no doubt at all about where and how they went. What more do you need?'

'Signor Ginelli,' I say carefully, 'I'm just a humble journalist, but I think this might be more complicated than you realise. Even if your nephews are entitled to these things or their value, this smacks of a very long and expensive court battle to me. You'd need to prove theft. I'm sorry, sir. You need to consult an expert.'

The old man makes a sound I interpret as laughter. '*Madonnina!* You think I have not? My friend, I'm not asking you to track down stolen art treasure and jewels! I'm not interested in either the goods or the money, and my nephews are rich enough anyway, and shits in their own ways, both of them. But they were happy enough for old Uncle Giacomo to pursue this if it amuses him. No! I want something else. All I want you to do is to put the fear of God into *her...*' He laughs again, softly, nodding his head up and down like a grotesque marionette. 'You say she is a British celebrity these days, this fuck-monster rattlesnake whore? An angel of children's charities and divorcing a rich celebrity husband?' The old man's eyes are very bright. I've already surmised there is more than just peppermint in the goblet.

'That's about it, sir.'

'I think you have enough there to do as I request. At the very least she will have to consult a lawyer, one who may not be discreet. She will probably have to ask this husband for the money. She is not clever... and she will panic. The press will no doubt enjoy the story...' He delicately examines his diamond pinkie ring. 'I'm a very sick man, my friend. Before I die, I should like to see her *suffer– Capisce?* It's a family thing.'

I tell him I understand perfectly, accept another small Talisker only half reluctantly while we talk business.

42: London, Spring Bank Holiday Last Year

'That was great, man. No, I totally mean it. Care for a pint?'

'Yeah, okay, thanks. Nice of you. It's only a hobby.'

'No, you're really good. A decent drummer makes a band, I reckon. Did you ever think of going professional?'

'Well, not really. I was in this band at uni that got paid a bit, but we just did party gigs. Fun stuff, you know. Nowadays I've hardly got time, but I join the lads when I can. I like these Beatles evenings, even though it was all before my mother was born, just about… Cheers! Thirsty work, on that stage. I'm Gavin when I'm not being Ringo, by the way. Mind if I remove the wig?'

'Go for it, Gavin. Cheers. No, I mean it, the band's okay, but you're *good*. You could do better than this lot, I reckon. I know what I'm talking about…' Gavin's new companion, an odd-looking individual with a round face like an elderly child's under a pork-pie hat worn over unfashionably long wispy hair, and wearing a battered white leather jacket, tight white jeans tucked into desert-boots – an outfit that did nothing to disguise a spreading waistline – fished out a card from his pocket and flipped it onto the bar. 'Call me Lion.'

'Lion Barley…great name! And you're a talent-scout! Stone me! What brings you here to Tooting Bec?'

'Scouting,' said Lion Barley.

'Wait a minute. Why's that name so familiar?'

Barley grinned coyly, showing expensive dental work somewhat marred by tobacco stains, and waited.

'Got it! You used to be the front man with that LifeBoyz band. Had a number one with a cover of 'Lady Be Good'. Blimey! My band at uni did our own cover of that song back in…well, some time ago. It was a great act, LifeBoyz. All that nice close-harmony stuff. We had fun getting it right. You lot were great! But blimey, must be what? Ten years ago now, easy. And you did that ad, didn't you, when you went solo – all those girls screaming onto the runway just to bite your chocolate bar! Crikey, that takes you back… Oh, shit, sorry. I mean…' Gavin couldn't help staring at Barley's face, and then smothered his curiosity in his pint of lager.

'Hey, man. Less of the anno domini. But yes, I've done it, smoked it, drunk it, shagged it and spent it…and now I'm doing my bit to help others do the same. Once in the business it gets addictive, totally in the blood. Like another?'

'My turn. But they're packing up here now. They're pretty quick off the mark once the last set's finished. Like to get everybody out by one-thirty…' Behind the bar, glasses were being cleared into washing-up machines, the staff pointedly ignoring the punters nearest the counter. A couple of men dismantled band equipment while the piped music was turned down and the conversations of the thinning crowd became more audible.

'Uni, eh? What did you study?'

'Law. Property, mostly. Nothing exciting.'

'So you're now tied to a desk all day, sorting out mortgages?'

'Not exactly. Actually, I've got a job most people would kill for, I suppose...'

A Paul McCartney look-alike, very unlike up close and without the wig, tapped Gavin on the shoulder. 'Next week then, mate? Don't desert us, will you? You're our main attraction now.'

'Sod off, Garry,' said Gavin good-naturedly.

'He's a famous telly star these days,' said the man called Garry, winking broadly at Lion Barley. 'No kidding.'

'See you next week, mate. God, I'm starving. Look, nice to meet you, Lion , but I'd better be headed home. My mum leaves me a dinner out on band nights. Thanks for the beer. I'll return the favour next Saturday if you're down this way again.'

'Hey, not so fast,' said Lion Barley. 'What about hitting Town? Fancy a curry?'

'Yeah, okay. There's a good one just up the road...' Suddenly, as well as being very hungry, Gavin felt deflated at the idea of going straight back to his mum's house and his boyhood bedroom just up the road. 'It doesn't close till three.'

'Oh, come on, man. There's this great place just off Gerrard Street. Let's grab a cab to the West End...' He punched numbers into his cell phone. 'So – what did the Macca would-be mean about being a telly star?' Lion asked as they crossed the river.

'Well, I – um.'

'No, wait! Oh shit, man!' Lion Barley smote his forehead so hard his hat almost fell off. 'I should have seen when you took Ringo off. You're that lawyer guy on that Jerry Fairbrother show. *Sort It!* Big Fair Brother looking after you, all that crap. It's a good show. Watch it all the time. Might need old Jerry one day, never know. Well, bugger me! You won't be needing a drumming assignment with Duffy's backing band, then. Shame.'

'Actually, you know, Lion,' Gavin confided to his new friend over the chicken tandoori and a third pint of larger. 'If you're really serious about professional drumming, I would like to know more. This job of mine – well, it mightn't be much more stable than – well...'

'A nineties boy band?'

'Yeah. No offence, but it's a cruel world. Shows like *Sort It!* come and go. Drumming might be better than a mortgage broker's office. And I don't kid myself I'm just the new boy.' Gavin had listened to the inside story – as told by Lion Barley – of Lion Barley's career: the young hopefuls, the talent show prize, the tyrant manager, the hit single, the hit album, the groupies, the on-off relationship with the super-model Silvie Snape, the famous chocolate ad, and the infamous drugs bust in the US – a set-up, pure and simple – and the tax frame-up by the tyrant manager which had toppled it. This had been followed by Lion's successful new career with a new dynamic agency, how he had dodged the tax-man to keep his apartment on the river, the parties... Lion Barley seemed to have an inexhaustible supply of gossip and anecdote, indeed seemed to be inexhaustible entirely, nibbling at a popadom, eating very little of the curry and speaking as if he had told the story many, many times.

Now, tired as he was and suppressing an unbidden yawn, Gavin felt like imparting some insider information of his own. 'Like I'm new to this, the show, still feeling my feet. But it sails a bit close to the wind sometimes, and I'm speaking as a lawyer, Lion. Look, this is top secret. I mean real confidential stuff. I shouldn't be telling a soul, but – hey, you're not some sort of undercover journo or anything, are you?'

'Come on, man. I can hardly write my own name. But go on. This is totally interesting. Hang on…' Barley fished in his pocket for his mobile, which he laid on the table in front of him. 'Sorry, man. Expecting a message. Go on. I met that Jerry Fairbrother once or twice on the talent show circuit. Okay sort of guy. Must be good to work with…'

'Yeah. He's great. No mega-star crap, sense of humour. And doing the show's fun, you know? Keeps me on my legal toes, and the studio stuff's interesting if you don't count the snooty women, but, well – that goes with the territory. But – I shouldn't be saying anything, but I've got a feeling that the show might just be on the brink of a bit of a scandal.'

'Get away! Oh, you mean Fairbrother's marriage to that Louise woman, all that shit?'

'No. I mean, yeah, that too. But this is something else. And apart from whoever's at the bottom of it, the only one who knows is me.'

'Wow, man. Tell me! What sort of stuff's going down in the squeaky-clean offices of *Sort It!*?'

'It's quite a relief to get this off my chest, in fact, Lion,' said Gavin, and proceeded to do so.

'I shouldn't be doing this!' Gavin giggled. 'Thank God you're not a journo, Lion. I'm supposed to be a lawyer!' The thought suddenly struck him as hilarious. In the men's room, before they headed out for Soho, Gavin snorted his first ever line of coke through a rolled fiver on a wash-basin, while Lion stood by, guarding the door and happily padding messages into his mobile.

At five in the morning, Lion Barley tipped his new friend into a black cab from the Night Garden in Greek Street, a trendy little club where Gavin had learned how to stay awake, drink cocktails with crazy suggestive names, sweetly rebuff the flirtatious female advances of what was evidently a sort of fan-club: partly out of an old-fashioned respect for his host, and partly out of a certain knowledge that he would disgrace himself. Towards dawn, he had passed out quietly at a plush table. 'Take him to Tooting,' Lion told the cabbie. 'If he pukes, this should cover it.'

43

A gaggle of nurses, trying to be discreet, admitted Jerry into Ben's room and hung on in the corridor discussing, doubtless, the etiquette of asking for Jerry's autograph.

'You look as happy as Larry, you old bugger,' said Jerry. 'Hi, Horst…' Ben Young was propped up on pillows, his hospital bed strewn with books, magazines and a laptop. Horst hastily turned off the television suspended in a corner and stood up, tall, blond and somewhat older than his smooth features suggested, to shake hands with that Teutonic formality that had never altered in his relations with Jerry for more than a decade.

'Hi Jerry. Good holidays?'

'Not bad, Horst, thanks. Plenty of swimming,' Jerry smiled. The holiday had been a disaster.

'You look fit. Well, I'll leave you two to discuss show-business. I'm for some real coffee.'

'Won't get it here, gawdelpus,' Ben said. 'All they serve is pap and cats' piss. Not brought any beer, have you, Jerry? No? Gawdelpus, more flowers and fruit. Thanks. And a book – ah, Rupert Everett. I've been meaning to read this. Great. Well, sit down, Jer. Forgive the mess. The maids'll be in to clear me up soon. They're darlings but they bully me something merciless. You look worse than me. Sit down, for gawd's sakes. Tell Uncle Ben.'

'Oh, nothing to tell, really. La Bastide would have been fine except that my lady wife insisted on coming accompanied by a waiting press to tell the world what a happy family we are when she has anything to do with it. The usual.'

'Bad. Want to see my scar?'

'Not much. You're looking better than I expected, Ben.'

'I'll live, or so the quacks in here tell me. Be out this time next week. So. How *is* show-business?'

Jerry gave Ben the latest gossip, including the transfer of Ben's replacement. 'Lynne's doing her nut. Says she wasn't properly consulted. There's a cat-fight scheduled for the next series, I'll bet. Makes for a rather unpleasant atmosphere. We all miss you, Ben.'

'Poor Lynne. Not that it's my biz any longer. That sinewy Armstrong dame – I thought she'd get it. Knows her job, but a real martinet. Not my choice, but then I wasn't consulted either, was I? Still, onwards and upwards, eh? Gawdelpus! Any more funny mail?'

'Odd ones. Still no actual demand, and still no proper contact number. But the last one concerned *Sort It!*. Hinted there was something wrong with programme funds – specifically, money paid out illicitly to individuals. To keep a certain story afloat.'

'Do you know anything about that? Dodgy deals?'

'No! Not a thing, truly. But then how would I?'

'I'd keep it that way if I was you, Jer. Keep squeaky clean, which in this game means ignorant. S.E.P. stands for Somebody Else's Problem. Got it?' Jerry nodded unhappily. He was beginning to feel battered, and was supremely aware that he was here to cheer the patient, not bang on about his own troubles.

'How's little Suzy?'

'Oh, you know. Busy. She's fine. Being very tactful with La Belle Armstrong…' Jerry didn't quite meet Ben's shrewd gaze.

'Good,' said Ben. 'She probably won't have to for much longer. Uncle Ben's been pulling some strings.'

'You're supposed to be resting, Ben.'

'And dying of boredom, apparently, gawdelpus. Don't you worry about me, Jer. You take care of yourself. Flick a switch, will you? There's some Formula One on.'

44

Dear Ms Harrison
A certain middle-eastern client of yours might be very interested to learn where the
funds to do up a certain Canonbury property came from. Suggest you investigate!
Naturally, I can't reveal my sources, but a trip to Television Mansions might be
indicated? Buona fortuna, babe…

'Suzy, who sent this?' Jerry appeared suddenly in the glass door-way, leaning on
the jamb, papers in his hand.

'Jerry! Welcome back! How's Ben? Have you seen him?' Suzy hastily shoved
the compact and the lipstick into the drawer of her desk.

'Ben's doing fine. Demanding beer and bacon sandwiches. Giving the hospital
hell. They'll only let him eat soup and salad, apparently, and beer is a no-no…'
Jerry was smiling, but Suzy thought he looked ill at ease. His holiday with Louise
and the children in France didn't seem to have improved his morale, and she
didn't know whether to be glad or sorry. 'Suzy, this story. Who sent it?'

'Which one?'

'This, er, this hit and run accident thing.'

'Oh, that. Yes, well, I thought you might be interested. I know it's a bit of a long
shot, but it intrigued me. This elderly couple want help tracking the guy that hit
their son on his bike in Italy. It's more than twenty years ago, but I wondered if
we might have ago. They had almost given up and then they got a lead recently.
They hired a bilingual lawyer through the Consul who checked the Carabinieri's
records. There was a witness, apparently. A local farmer came forward at the time
to say a big Mercedes saloon with foreign plates came speeding passed his truck
on the morning it must have happened. These poor parents hope that that was
the vehicle that caused the accident, so they can sort of close it, poor old things.
Their son was killed, and they're pretty convinced he didn't just run into a ravine
by mistake. So are the police, apparently. It's an open file. Skid marks, all that…'

'I have *read* that, Suzy. It's all here…' He sounded uncharacteristically impatient. 'I take it the farmer didn't remember the number?'

'They say not. I guess they'd have traced it, the Italian police. The farmer
thought there were two people in the car, and it was a black soft-top model.
Non-Italian plates, but no other ID. That's it.'

'No ID. I see. So this kid. On the bike. You're saying he was a Brit?'

'Yes. He wasn't found for a couple of days. It must have been pretty awful.'

'Ghastly. But I can't think why you think it's a suitable story for us, Suzy. It's
years old and we're not likely to be able to find out more than the Italian police,
are we?'

'Perhaps not. But I thought we might just air it as an appeal. It might jog another memory. The car was unusual. Even if we don't get anywhere, it's a touching story. Someone with a bad conscience might even own up…' Suzy saw Jerry's
hands were shaking slightly. 'You okay, Jerry?'

'Yeah, fine. Bit of a late night fuelled with too much caffeine. I think we can't pursue this, Suzy. Sorry. Um…how did it come? This inquiry? Could I see it?'

'No problem. It was a snail-mail. A Mr and Mrs Todd, staying in London at the moment but normally resident in Spain…' She sifted through a pile of paper-work and passed him the letter, a longish handwritten screed in a semi-educated hand on the letterhead of a well-known budget chain hotel. A recent date. It was marked in Suzy's red biro: 'SM/LB cc JF'.

'I see you've already passed it on to Lynne.'

'Of course. As always.'

'Yes. Look, love, it would be good – that is, I'd be grateful if sometimes I could have a chance to look at things first. Before Lynne.'

'But you weren't here, Jerry. Is something wrong?'

'No! No, of course not. Okay. If she gives her okay, you can chase it, I suppose. We've got a meeting in Lynne's office later, haven't we?'

'Yes. This afternoon, four-thirty…'

'About?'

' It's Mr Mehmet Mehmet's lawyer…'

'Who?'

'Mehmet Mehmet. Landlord in the Canonbury squat case. The place has just been broken into, over the Bank Holiday. I left a memo for you – you've probably not seen it. Someone pierced a pipe, damage to the new bathrooms we screened for the last series. It looks like deliberate sabotage. That's why the lawyer's here, I think. Trying to prevent us from leaping to obvious conclusions.'

'Oh, Christ. The whole team, I take it? I'm not going to be thrown to the lions all by myself, am I?'

'Don't worry, Jerry. We'll all be right behind you…' She grinned at him, but the muscles of her face hurt in the effort.

'Great. Look, I've got to slide out on some errands this morning. Field everything, will you, love?' He smiled at her then, but it was his public smile, and her heart sank further.

'Sure, Jerry.'

'What's his name? This lawyer? I'd better know.'

'Harrison. And it's not he, it's she. A Ms Jayne Harrison with a 'y'. She's incredibly rude, according to Lynne.'

'Oh God. Look, thanks. I'll be back. Plenty of time…' He glanced at his watch.

'Fine. Drink after the meeting?' she heard herself add, although she had sworn to herself she would not. But the glass door had closed and she watched his re-fracted image retreat through the striated glass.

The desk telephone rang. 'Suzy Merritt,' she said brightly into it.

'Suzy? Hello, I'm Tina Gladwyn, Deirdre Watkiss's secretary. If you could spare a moment this morning, could you come up to Deirde's office?'

Suzy was finding it difficult to concentrate on what Gavin Macavity was say-ing. Her recent impromptu interview with Deirdre Watkiss in the *Round Britain* office had had the effect of lifting her spirits to such an extent she had to force her eyes onto the small screen.

'I still don't understand what this means, Gavin.'

'I'll explain if you'll let me. It's fairly simple – almost stupidly so. No, hang on, hang on, I don't mean you. It's meant to be a bit cryptic, but a hi-tec kid could solve it with a bit of insider-knowledge. These codes, see? This column. These represent the show's 'cases', okay? And this column here represents expenditure. Not programming costs, as such, but expenses paid to individuals, et cetera, like for filming in people's houses, interviews and so on. You could almost call it petty cash. And this column is dates. But look at this figure here – and this one. Notice anything?'

'No. Oh, wait.'

'Got it?'

'Yes – at least I think so. The figures are fairly small, but they keep occurring against the same code. Am I right?'

'More or less. The codes vary a bit in fact, look. This one is virtually the same as this, but for 'C' and 'D'. Agree?'

'I still don't understand, Gavin. And my phone's ringing. And we've got a meeting in about fifteen minutes. The Canonbury squat case.'

'Wait, please, love – Suzy. This is all very relevant, believe me. The thing is, Miss Merritt – Suzy – that this code, or this series of codes, represents these Canonbury Squatters. These figures – here, this column – now these represent sums that have been paid out to individuals in the case over the past year or so, and they add up rather amazingly. To nearly a hundred and eighty grand in fact. And I've got a fair suspicion there's a lot more...' Gavin's one idea since his recent indiscretion was to pass on the information as fast as if it had been a ticking bomb. Now he had, he relaxed a little.

Suzy heard the ringing stop. 'But Gavin, this is classified information! How in hell did you get hold of this?'

'Just punched buttons, Miss Merritt – Suzy. They told me to familiarize myself with everything on *Sort It!* and that's what I've done. Now I need your advice. What do I do with this?'

'Nothing! I mean, it obviously has a perfectly reasonable explanation. Leave it with me. I'll query it with Lynne. I'm sure they didn't mean for you to go hacking into this stuff, Gavin. You must have had an authorized code to get into it. Who gave it to you?'

'Nobody. Honest, love, Suzy. It's a piece of p – cake – when you know how. Even so, it's as well to know what the opposition could throw at us, ain't it?'

'I don't *know*. Look, just leave it with me for the moment, okay? Don't discuss it with anyone. Not yet. Oh, God, come on. We're going to be late.'

The atmosphere round Lynne Berry's conference table was rapidly turning ugly, and Suzy was jolted into the immediate present.

'Frankly,' Jayne Harrison was saying in harsh tones, 'it's plain to me this would have been a straight-forward case of trespass and eviction if you lot hadn't stuck your oar in. And I don't understand what all this squit's about anyway...' She was in her late thirties, wearing jeans, a denim jacket, and a very aggressive expression. 'I mean, what is this? Are you a public service or are you reality TV for a start?'

'We're both, Ms Harrison,' said Lynne Berry firmly. 'I take it you're familiar with *Sort It!*? Okay. Well, as you know, the programme attempts to sort out people's legal problems. Strictly civil cases, like your client's, nothing criminal. People write in, contact us, and with the help of our team of legal experts we advise them on how to proceed. Consumer affairs meets conciliation meets –'

'Meets show business,' interrupted Ms Harrison. 'I mean, who does he think *he* is?' She pointed at Jerry rudely. 'He's no lawyer, unless I'm very much mistaken!'

'Indeed I'm not,' said Jerry heartily. 'Not nearly clever enough. I'm just a humble presenter. I rely on my team...' He grinned cheerfully round the table: at Lynne, and took in Emma, making notes at her side; at Natalie and Gavin, who had so far kept silence, and at Suzy, who gave him a brief smile.

'But you get to choose the stories or whatever, don't you?'

'Well, naturally. Up to a point. I mean, we have to make a –'

'Mr Fairbrother has a veto, certainly,' Lynne Berry said. 'That is, an editorial veto on the programme itself. But the expert team reviews each story, and then we make a team decision. As the programme's producer, I have the final say. We do have a great many inquiries every week, Ms Harrison. We have to decide which of them is likely to –'

'Boost the ratings. Capture the popular imagination,' interrupted Jayne Harrison again. 'Get an entirely unfair exposure on public television, in other words. It bloody *stinks*.'

'An exposure, certainly, Ms Harrison,' said Lynne Berry, 'but why unfair? Surely not, if it's in the public interest.'

'Not unfair? Not *unfair*? The whole thing's decided on telegenics, for a start. If this was a case of some kids from the wrong side of the tracks shitting in buckets and lighting themselves with candles, you wouldn't want to run it, would you? No. Exactly. Your clients are a bunch of articulate, white middle-class university-graduates with – *apparently* – a flair for DIY, and your programme follows them through a wrecks-to-riches job on a house that doesn't actually belong to them, hinting that my client, a member of an ethnic minority, has a criminal background and is therefore acting criminally now. You've prejudiced his case to evict them, while this precious quartet has acquired a fan-following. He gets pilloried on your show because it makes for good television. This is not only sick, it's almost certainly illegal. I'm reporting you and your programme to the CRE, as well as encouraging him to sue the programme for defamation. It's a bloody disgrace!'

'Please sit down, Ms Harrison,' said Lynne patiently. 'This has absolutely nothing to do with Mr Mehmet's ethnic background, let's be entirely clear about that. We can appreciate that as his legal representative you are bound to leave no stone unturned in defending his cause, but the fact remains that we are very confident that Mr Mehmet has left it too late to simply evict these people and reclaim his property. He left a house in central London to virtually fall down. He couldn't be contacted, despite our clients' best efforts to do so, and his lawyers – not you, obviously, Ms Harrison – refused to have any dialogue with them. Then he reappears with an eviction order, having put the property on the market. Mr Pyke, Ms Falmouth, Miss Kypri and Mr Singh,' she emphasized the last two names, 'have every right to object. The law is complicated, as I'm sure you know, Ms Harrison, but we are checking our facts scrupulously. I have to say that our clients do seem to have a serious case, isn't that so, Natalie?'

'Yes, they do,' said Natalie North. 'There seems to be quite a lot going for their claim, at least as far as a legitimate tenancy goes.'

'And who are you again?' inquired Ms Harrison unpleasantly.

'I'm Natalie North, and I represent the Citizen's Advice Bureau. Let's see...' She consulted an impressive bundle of notes. 'There has been continuous occupation for over five years and a genuine effort to contact the original owner. They were always prepared to pay Mr Mehmet a proper rent, had he acknowledged the tenancy, which he did not. They've paid the Council Tax in their own names. I really think there's every chance the law would find in their favour, certainly to allow them to stay, and either block an impending sale, or insist on these people having entitlement as sitting tenants. Their rights in the matter look fairly secure, I'm afraid, Ms Harrison.'

'So what about my client's rights in the matter? This is still his property we're talking about, I might remind you!'

'So far, Ms Harrison,' said Lynne.

'You just don't get it, do you? All right. Let me put it another way,' said Jayne Harrison. 'First, you're not denying you're on their side? Helping them to win this case with all the might of popular TV?'

'They came to us, Ms Harrison. We will help them as far as we can.'

'And how far is far, Mrs Berry? Huh?'

'I'm sorry? I don't understand.'

'Let me be entirely plain, then. I came here this afternoon to make it perfectly clear to you that you cannot run this flood-disaster episode. It's entirely biased. And unless you want to see your precious show sued for libel and taken off the air, you'll drop this story pronto. Like today.'

'Oh really, Ms Harrison, that is out of the question,' said Lynne briskly. 'We are profiling a legitimate human-interest story that closely follows the legal ramifications in a complicated case and of course we hope all this can be settled out of court. So much more civilized, not to say cheaper for all concerned. As for this unfortunate new development, we're bound to follow it up since it has happened. We plan to simply report it – as the press has already. To ignore it would be ridiculous not to say impossible. There is no reason to drop the episode, I can assure you.'

'Oh *really?* You say your programme, your *human-interest story*, no less, gets involved in nothing criminal? Right? Then tell me, okay? Do you deny you've relied on a regular bulletin about the renovations at the Canonbury property?' Jayne Harrison was on her feet again, opening a folder. 'A roof-job, followed by a damp-course and new floors... interviews with builders, site managers, the

[191]

Borough engineer… not to mention your clients in boiler-suits installing a kitchen and doing their own tiling and grouting in brand new bathrooms?'

'Well there's nothing criminal in fitting cookers and doing up bathrooms, let me say…' A small titter went round the table.

'It depends on who's been paying for them, I'd have thought. As it stands, your programme seems to be suggesting that these illegal occupants stand to get a free house, a house with a market value of – let's see, eight hundred thousand plus – because they have significantly contributed to the property's value themselves. That is what you're suggesting?'

'It could be a factor, as I have said, Ms Harrison, but it is in fact beside the point in terms –'

'A factor! Well, suppose these renovations do have a material significance for the outcome of the case, and it can be proved that they were bankrolled by this programme as part of your services? I think that would put an altogether different slant on matters, don't you?'

Jerry Fairbrother was too professional to look startled, but he shot a look at Suzy, nevertheless. Suzy glanced at Gavin, who was looking innocently at the ceiling. Lynne sighed, concentrating on Ms Harrison.

'That is completely beyond the brief of this meeting, I'm afraid, Ms Harrison,' she said. 'If your client wants to file an official complaint against the programme for any reason whatever, that's up to him, and he would have to take it up with the appropriate authority. Now, I'm afraid we're running over time and we must wrap this up for the time being. I'm sorry…' She began to gather up papers.

'So you're not denying it!' cried Ms Harrison. 'Well, that speaks volumes. And we've got proof – you wait!'

'I don't think this is getting us anywhere, Ms Harrison. I'm not trying to obstruct you in any way, but I can't comment any further. Now, if you don't mind, Ms Harrison, we are all very busy people and we have a great deal of work to do.'

'Crap! This is serious. Your programme, this sham justice, well it's about to hit the skids, believe me. You've bankrolled your clients at the expense of mine and I'll –'

'Ms Harrison, please, for the last time.'

'Frankly, I wouldn't be surprised if you hadn't flooded the place yourselves just to continue a storyline!'

Gavin spoke. 'Whooa, Mizz Harrison, please. Naow, naow. Hang on a mo! Let's not run ahead of ourselves, start making – um – suggestions we can't prove, eh? But I agree with you, Ms Harrison. Wilful damage, that's a very serious charge and you should pursue it. It's okay, folks…' Gavin Macavity was grinning, and he cast a sly wink at Lynne, whose mouth opened and shut on a suppressed gasp. 'But let's look at it from the other way up shall we? I mean, on the face of it, the timing – I mean frankly it *could* look as if your client had simply bided his time until he thought the property was worth reclaiming, and decided to try to cash in, now couldn't it? The place was falling down, condemned. Now, putting aside that it's famous for starters, a court of law would be bound to take the fact that it's virtually a different house now into account, regardless of how our clients financed the renovations. As for this recent nasty flooding accident, well, on the face of it, that's –'

'Beside the point, thank you, Gavin,' said Lynne, glaring.

'Not necessarily, Mizz Berry, if you'll excuse me saying so. But leaving that aside for a minute, let's just revise, shall we? The *a priori* position, if you'll 'scuse me getting a bit technical, is as follows. It's all down in case law, Mizz Harrison. In England and Wales, adverse possession has been governed by section 15 of the Limitation Act 1980, since 1 May 1981, if I remember rightly. The limitation period for the adverse possession – squatting, in friendlier terms – is twelve years under Section Fifteen point one section five. It's all there, you can check. After this twelve year period the title of the original owner is extinguished. But – this is the rub – a court of Civil Law can intervene well before that time-period and, to be honest, Mizz Harrison, if I was a betting man, I'd say a person in Mr Mehmet's shoes would be just as likely to lose as win in this case well before the time's up, in a court of Civil Law, that is, because even before twelve years is up, the adverse possessor still might become the person with the best title to the land, entitled to maintain an Action in Trespass against anyone who might seek to dispossess him. See? That's what your client's trying to do now, right? Dispossess our squatters, clients. Frankly, if I was him, I'd agree to a tenancy and forget the sale. He's got a hugely improved property and a set of model tenants. Thing is, you see –' he continued with a certain impressive authority, and they were all agog now, as he had not consulted a single note – 'well, now, unless he were to try to forcibly eject them, or, well, otherwise ruin the property, make things difficult, flood the basement, make their life generally impossible – this is only theoretical, you understand, Mizz Harrison – he would remain at least on the right side of the other Law, the Old Bailey kind. Only hypothetically speaking, Mizz Harrison...' Macavity grinned.

'My client has done no such thing!' cried the outraged Ms Harrison.

'I never said he had, Mizz Harrison. Now did I?'

'Are you aiming to add defamation to the other things my client can level at this programme?'

'Of course not, Ms Harrison,' said Lynne Berry hurriedly. 'Mr Macavity was simply outlining a scenario. Strictly hypothetical. But I do think you will find that your client may – conditional on any ruling, obviously – but he may be compelled in law to forfeit his rights to sell this property until legal ownership has been established. I really do suggest...'

'Brrr,' said Suzy in the lift to Jerry as they made their way back to their offices. 'Do you think Gavin's just commited kami-kasi?' She was standing uncomfortably close to him, felt his breath on her neck, wanted to melt into him, stopped herself. 'I mean, he obviously touched a nerve, about property damage and all that, didn't he? And that Harrison woman sort of folded, but it was *so* off the script. I hope he's not got himself into real trouble. He's a bit of a rogue element, is Gavin.'

'Hmm. If I know Lynne,' Jerry said into her ear, 'he'll be promoted.'

'You're not serious!'

'I am too! Here we are. Don't worry, Suzy. That sort of thing happens all the time. Lawyers waving their briefcases. Bright kid, that Gavin. Now then. I've got a hot date with another lawyer. Hold the fort, darling, will you?'

'Sure. Of course.'

'Good girl. Have a nice evening…' He kissed her lightly on the forehead. 'Sorry I'm so tied up, sweetie. See you tomorrow.'

'Sure,' she said again. Through the glass partition, she watched him grab his jacket, check for keys; his face almost stern, pre-occupied with something wholly outside of anything to do with her. Within moments, he was gone.

In the relative privacy of her glass office, Suzy stared blankly ahead of her, her eyes pricking with unshed tears. Then her mind switched back to her meeting with Deirdre Watkiss earlier that day. Perhaps things might work out for the best, after all. Damn it, she'd show him! Bollocks to him!

Jerry Fairbrother, indeed on his way to see a lawyer, took one of the studio's cars and gave an address near to Lincoln's Inn. The traffic was bad, and he gave up staring out of the window. The driver was mercifully morose: so often he had to listen to a full resumè of how the man had answered the *Big Quiz* questions to the £250,000 mark from his own armchair.

These hints about *Sort It!* funding the Canonbury renovations… Depressing to realise how very little he knew about the things going on under his own nose, going on with his name on them. Worse, *somebody knew*. His anonymous correspondent, who had presumably primed Mehmet's harridan lawyer… It was looking horribly likely that his correspondent was under his nose also, otherwise how in hell – ? And now this other ghastly thing. He was beginning to feel physically ill. He pulled from his trouser pocket Suzy's careful synopsis of the hit and run story he had purloined from Emma's in-tray. Christ, was he jumpy! Mustn't panic. A coincidence. A stupid, rogue coincidence. Things he'd thought buried, forgotten forever… He shivered.

'Sorry, Mr Fairbrother – you cold? I'll turn the air-con down. I enjoyed the show on Saturday. I got that one right about Tutunkahmun, and the one about John Lennon. My missus, she keeps threatening to write in and nominate me, but me, I couldn't cope with the stage-fright. John Lennon got stage-fright, just fancy. Uster throw up back stage, so I read.'

Jerry Fairbrother sighed. Life, it seemed, was returning to normal. Or what passed for normal nowadays.

45

'Angus, I'm very sorry. I know you're doing an almost impossible job, but we can't carry on like this…' Jerry's plate was almost untouched. An early supper – albeit in a very quiet and anonymous lawyers' eatery in Chancery Lane where the food was old-fashioned and excellent – had been Angus Tremain's idea. On the whole, Jerry would have far preferred this conversation to take place in Angus's office. Angus, on the other hand, was evidently hungry, tucking into his steak and kidney pie with gusto.

'Like what?' Tremain spoke with his mouth full and waved his fork. 'As I see it, Jerry, you two simply need to come to a basic agreement and then we can fine-tune the details. That's what I'm for, but I can't do anything until you've both met each other half way. Money and property, obviously, and the children. Charlie being a somewhat separate issue.'

'Charlie *is* a separate issue, Angus. Literally. Louise is not his mother. That doesn't seem to stop her wanting to cart him off to the United States with the rest of the family.'

'Look, I think we can mediate on Charlie, Jerry. I think Louise would play, if we put it to her fair and square.'

'Fair and *square* ?'

'She did legally adopt him, remember.'

How could he forget? All those touching photo-sessions ten years ago: Louise with the toddler Charlie on her pregnant lap in *Hello!* and *Okay!* and *The Daily Mail*, playing happy families. Jerry suddenly felt so angry he could have pushed the table over. 'Jesus! You just don't get it, do you, Angus? I don't want – can't bear – …' He felt his throat constrict, saw a waiter glance in their direction and lowered his voice, tried to steady himself. 'I don't want to lose the girls either. These are my *children*! They're not bargaining counters, for Christ's sake! Look, Angus, this isn't working out. You working for both of us, I mean. I'd hoped that someone impartial, a mediator, would be better than two lots of lawyers battling it out, but I was wrong. I need someone on my side, Angus…' He avoided saying that he no longer believed in the impartiality.

'I have been doing my best,' said Tremain, clearly put out. 'It's not exactly easy being a professional pig in the middle, you know. Louise, as we know, can be a touch – um, volatile.'

'Volatile? My God, Angus. I'm trying to be entirely level with you, and I can't, not really, because you're working for her as well. But I will say this. She's having me followed. Did you know?'

Tremain frowned, a smooth and professional frown, as he mopped his plate with a knob of bread roll. 'That's bad, Jerry. No, for what it's worth, I didn't know. But – well – we can't put it past her, can we? She's pulling out the stops now, trying to find proof of anything that will boost her case. As it were. It's – um – sorry. It's fairly common knowledge that there might be something to find, Jerry.'

'Angus – look. This isn't really about infidelities, mine or hers. It's about armament. Weapons. I have a pretty shrewd idea she's seeing someone too, but I just can't be fished to have her tracked, that's all. Perhaps I should.' In fact, Jerry had been wondering if Louise were not seeing Angus himself, but the lawyer's face gave nothing away. Perhaps there was nothing to give.

'Maybe. Sort of *quid pro quo*. A counterblast,' Angus began on a pudding.

'Oh, dear God. This is all getting so very *ugly*. All because, apparently, she hates me so much she wants everything. Not just half, not just joint custody of the children. She wants to – to *destroy* me, Angus, as you must know. I'm going to have to fight her, because I don't have a choice. And I'm afraid this means that from now on, you work exclusively for her. If that's what you want. I need to find someone to fight my corner, work for me alone. I'm sorry, Angus. It's nothing personal.'

'I know, Jerry. I understand. Fact is, one can only mediate so far, and only between people who are at least prepared to talk to each other even if only through a third party. If you want me to recommend somebody, I can help. If not – well, I can only wish you all the very best. Coffee? Brandy?'

'Thanks, yes to both.'

'To be honest, Jerry, I'd be just as happy if you two were to kiss and make up. On a personal level, anyway. Conciliation's much more in my line than warfare, believe me. Cheers!'

'Cheers. Not a snowball in hell's chance of that, I fear. But it's friendly of you, Angus. Appreciated.'

On his way back to Wimbledon, Jerry almost wished he had told Angus more about his anonymous menace, if only just to see a reaction. If the letters were Louise's doing, she presumably would not have confided as much in Angus. Unless Angus were in it with her. And this, he had to admit, was looking less and less likely, unless Angus was a superb liar. Perhaps he was. Round and round in paranoid circles. Jerry felt very lonely, friendless and suddenly afraid.

46

'How was America?'

'American.'

'Suit yourself, sourpuss. That stupid Lion Barley rang. Says he's been trying to get you,' said Angel. 'And I did that little job you wanted, exactly as you said, copied it all out.'

'Good. Bravo. Well done. Unless there are any serious hostages to fortune, everything can keep. I've got jet-lag, Angel. I've got to sleep.' Drex stumbled towards his bedroom, but his progress was arrested by the image on the huge TV screen.

...London landlord, businessman Mehmet Mehmet, is planning to sue the popular consumer affairs cum legal mediation show, Sort It!, *following the broadcast last night. Mr Mehmet owns the property in Canonbury Square where the progress of the four squatting residents has become compulsive viewing for Sort It!'s regular audience, and where a recent break-in resulted in considerable damage to the property. Mr Mehmet is attempting to have the squatters evicted. Earlier today, Tom Nugent spoke to Mr Mehmet's legal representative, Jayne Harrison...* Cut to interview: *'No doubt at all. The programme is biased in the extreme, and implicated my client...No, true, they didn't actually accuse Mr Mehmet, but implications can be libellous. You can be sure that Mr Mehmet has a case, he's going to stand his ground and fight the programme through the courts...sorry, at this stage I have no further comment...'* Back to anchor: *The* Sort It! *producers were not available for comment today, but we will bring you the lastest on that story as soon as we hear more. Now, we go over to the Fayre Trade charity fashion show which opened this afternoon at O_2, where a glittering array of fashion-conscious celebrities have been gathering in support of environmentally-friendly fabrics and production. This thousand pound a ticket event is intended to promote awareness of the exploitation and waste of the 'wear it for a day then throw it away' budget clothing industry and raise money for the thousands of ill-paid clothing machinists in China and the Far East, many of them children under sixteen, and convert the fashion-world to timeless styles that last made from ethically produced fabrics in factories which pay proper wages to employees. Jane Phillpot spoke to some of the celebrities as they arrived.* Cut to O_2: *'I'm like this is really, really important? Oh, yeah, I'm definitely a supporter. Like the stuff's really great, and it helps save the planet, yeah? I'll be wearing stuff like this forever...'* Miss Silvie Snape twirls for the camera in baggy white pima cotton pants and a natural-dyed indigo top. Jane Phillpot: *'Thank you, Sylvie. Supermodel Sylvie Snape. And now I can see interior designer Louise Fairbrother, well-known for her fashion sense and for her support of children's charities...'* Louise Fairbrother emerges from a limousine, wearing an elegant linen kaftan dress, slit to the knee, in a shade of pale lemon. *'Oh, but I support this one hundred per cent. We just have to be a bit aware, you know? The point of fashion is looking good, but we have to feel good in our clothes in every sense. Like not plundering the planet, you know, and not exploiting people. The idea that little children work a fourteen*

hour day in Asian factories and live in dormitories miles away from their families just to put clothes on our backs in the West is really disgraceful. I know we can do something. I'm making a speech later.'

'Jesus Christ, Angel. Turn that crap off.'

47

'Enter hero, stage left, through french window. Hullo, you! Why the back stairs? I've been listening for the bell...' She looks up from her typing, removes her specs, smiles.

'Surprise,' I say, and kiss her forehead briefly. 'How's Sir Henry?'

'Fine. Horrible. Delightfully horrible. Just let me finish this para, will you... Why don't you pour us a drink? It's all in the kitchen. Don't feed Grimbles. He's had his supper.'

I go through, find the fixings, including lemon, ready sliced in the fridge, and pour – one for me, one for her, not too strong. The cat Greymalkin, a rather beautiful creature, very dark blue-grey, follows me and rubs against my legs, purring expectantly. She has been so pleased that the animal seems to like me.

The kitchen is a sort of annexe to Veronica's sitting-room-cum-studio through an elegant little archway. How very different it all is! She has made a pretty little courtyard of the old backyard; a large and rather deluxe bathroom of the old scullery. I bring the drinks and she stops work, happy to see me.

'*Slàinte...*' She's even learning a smattering of Irish.

This is a very different woman these days. She wears a loose linen shirt over demins, and has lost a great deal of weight. Good bones in a longish face; a smile that is quietly radiant. She is almost beautiful. Beautiful, intelligent...and maybe, at last, happy in herself. Todd, I reflect wryly, is a lucky man. '*Slàinte,*' I say.

'I've done some lemon chicken pasta and a salad. Do you think perhaps it's warm enough to eat outside?' The courtyard has a cast-iron victorian table and chairs in a leafy bower, where this evening the wisteria is wafting its pungent scent, and a climbing rose, deep red, all pouting buds, is about to do its stuff and burst into flower.

'Why not,' I say, stretching out in a comfortable armchair. Todd has his feet well under the table here, the jammy bastard. The cat jumps heavily onto my lap. I stroke him absently and he purrs.

'So, how's the John Marston life?' This is the book Todd is currently reviewing.

'Heavy going, I'll admit. Badly written, really. Very well researched and all that, but presented so turgidly you constantly want to put it down.'

'That's a shame. God, I hope I don't make the same mistake with Sir Henry. There's quite a lot of dates and what happened when, and everybody skips those. But I really do object to those biographies where the writer sort of makes it up as they go along, don't you? You know, lots of guessed-at psychology and made-up conversations, mostly anachronistic. It might be more fun but it never seems fair. I'm such a tyro at this game, really. Sir Henry will probably turn out to be a complete turkey.'

'Don't worry so much, Veronica. You can write. This guy's primarily a re-searcher, and a good one, but no feel for prose. I shall have to say so, I fear.'

'Poor sod,' she laughs. 'You'll probably cripple his career.'

'Only as a writer maybe. He'll go back to the lecture-theatre where he un-doubtedly belongs. In fact, he only gets animated when he talks about the actual works.'

We banter on, talking shop. It's still all quite new, this, and there's still a feel-ing-the-way kind of embarrassment hovering on the edges... and something that could almost be called joy somewhere at the centre. Later, over a bottle of good-ish Waitrose Orvieto, the remains of the pasta salad still on the table, and our smoke wafting into the wisteria-scented air, some Billy Strayhorn snaking seduc-tively through the french windows from the battered stero in the sitting-room, she touches my hand.

'I'm so glad this happened, Todd... I never thought it would. I mean ever again, for me...'

'Neither did I,' I answer truthfully. It was inevitable, however. A meeting over drinks in London after that Washington gig, ostensibly about an interview, fol-lowed by dinner, followed, in fact, by a chaste farewell on her doorstep... You can't rush Veronica. But then there was another dinner, followed by an interlude of quite extraordinary passion. On both sides. For a pair of battered grown-ups who have driven round the block more than enough times, we didn't do badly at all.

I like Veronica. I mean I really like her. Her mind has that unsentimental fibrous quality I find entirely refreshing; her wit is acerbic, her politics iconoclas-tic, her manner a mixture of deliberately charmless pugnacity, even cynicism, punctuated by moments of sudden, sunny warmth, as if she has opened a blind. And she opens her lovely, large, warm body with a generosity and enthusiasm that takes the breath away. Todd's a lucky man, as I say. He's captivated; even feeling a little reckless.

Later, in Veronica's big comfortable bed in the room where my grandmother used to sleep on lumpy horsehair, our limbs still entwined and our bodies still sweetly sticky, I lie reflecting. If this weren't a different life, if I hadn't mapped out something else, maybe...

'Todd?'

'Veronica. Call me Andrew.'

'All right. Why? Andrew?'

'Because it is my name.'

48: October 1973

Uncle and nephew stood awkwardly together, watching the departure of the coffin through the front door. They were alone in the house where so lately the mortal remains of Grammy O'Ryan had lain in state in the front parlour, fussed over in hushed tones by neighbours, by members of the Roman Catholic Church of St.Saviour and the priest, new since Andrew's childhood, a muscular young man with a London accent called Father Spelman who had assured them of a good send off for the old lady on the following day and had left, crossing himself on the threshold almost as an after-thought as the undertakers' men had placed the coffin, now sealed, onto the trolley and wheeled it into the waiting van.

'Well, that's it then,' said Uncle Ted. 'Till tomorrow that is…' He sounded tired. He had grown more grizzled since Andrew had last seen him, and acquired a belly. 'Maureen and the kids will be here in the morning. And Bernie. She'll be stopping with the Sisters in Brompton, so she tells me. You've met your aunt Bernie I suppose, Andy? She's a teacher.'

'I thought she was a nun.'

'She's both, she is, Bernie. She belongs to a teaching order.'

'Oh. Will – will my mother be coming?'

'I don't know, Andy. Haven't heard back from her. Have you?'

'No. I'm not in touch with her.' He had written once, from school, to the address in Rochdale, Texas, America. He had not received a reply.

In the dark kitchen, the two of them sat at the table, awkward and embarrassed, as if the ghost of the old lady might at any moment appear to open the biscuit tin, pour tea. It was Andrew who suggested a glass of her favourite tipple. Ted got the bottle from its familiar cupboard and poured a liberal measure of Paddy whiskey for each of them.

'You've grown so, young feller,' Uncle Ted said, raising his glass. 'Here's to her, eh? May the good Lord bless her poor soul. Grand lady, she was, and no mistaking. Grand lady…' He blew his nose and drank deeply. 'She'd a been that proud of you now. School, and grown so tall and fine.'

'I want to ask you something, Uncle Ted. About my mother and –'

Ted was growing sentimental. 'She always loved you, you know.'

'My mother?'

'No, your grandmother, may the good Lord rest her. There was a woman for ye. Askin' for ye, she was, at the end. Did ye know?'

'I did mean to come. I was too late. School…' This was a lie. Andrew had deliberately avoided a last meeting with his dying grandmother. He felt a sudden rush of shame, and something else. A sense of loss.

'Ahh, yes. School. In the country down in Somerset. Doin' well there, are ye? Ye certainly looks smart enough, young Andy. Hardly recognized ye, I didn't. No, she'd have been proud enough, for all she didn't approve of fancy schools and fancy ways.'

'Ain't got no fancy ways, Uncle Ted.' But he had to fish for the accent to say it. Perhaps he had acquired 'fancy ways'.

'No? Well, maybe not. But youse'll go far, I reckon. She'd have wanted that. So long as you remember to make her always proud of ye, ye'll not go far wrong. Poor Mammy, poor ol' lady...' Ted looked as if he was about to weep.

'Uncle Ted?'

'Yes, son?'

'Who was my father?'

Ted blew his nose. 'That's all in the past, young feller. Best leave it there, eh?'

'You mean you don't know?'

'No. That is, Rosie – well, it was Rosie's business. At the time.'

'You mean she didn't know? Was she really that much of a whore?'

'Andy!'

'Well?'

'Andy, did your Grammy never tell ye?'

'No. She'd never talk about it. Look, I'm almost eighteen. I want to know what you know. I think I – well – deserve to know.'

Ted gave his nephew an assessing look, drank some more of his whiskey, looked vaguely about the kitchen. Sighed.

'Tell me about my father, Uncle Ted,' prompted Andrew, gently. Inside, he was as clenched as a claw.

Ted O'Ryan sighed again, deeply. 'Not much to tell, son. That's t'trut', honest to God. Ye mustn't blame Rosie – yer mammy – not too much, son. She truly believed he'd marry her. She wasn't really a little tart, just more high spirited, and easily led. Lovely girl, she was, too. Ye could understand, like, the way the men went for her...red hair, she's got, like a halo...at least she did have, when she was young...' When Andrew tried to imagine his mother, the vision of that other redhead, Lottie Walters, always got in the way...

'Did you meet him? My father?'

'No, son. Truly, I didn't. Mammy – your grammy – she met him. Just the once, I think. She didn't approve, not on yer life.'

'Why?'

'Instinct, son. A woman's instinct. And a mother's. This man'll hurt my little Rosaleen, she thought, and she was right enough there. Turns out he was married, back in America. When Rosie told him she was expecting, well – off he went, back to the States, and she never heard hide nor hair more, no not hide nor hair.'

'Which is when Rosie dumped me on Grammy and ran off with another Yank. Hank the Yank, right?'

'Ye's very harsh, son. Doesn't do to be too harsh.'

'Unless it's the bastard English,' Andrew said, grinning suddenly. 'At least my father wasn't English. Say...can I have another of those?'

'S'pose so, Andy, now yer all grown up. Not too much, mind. Big day tomorrow...' He poured a liberal slug into both their glasses. Andrew raised his.

[202]

'Death and agony to the bastard English,' he said. 'At least I'm not an English bastard. What was his name? Did you know that?'

'Antonio. That was his name. He was a Wop, Eye-talian. She called him Tony, Rosie did. Tony. I don't rightly remember his surname, except it was like Bellows, or Ballard, maybe… It's all the past, son. Your Grammy, she was yer real family, and don't you forget it. And that Captain Rollitt might be bastard English, but he was good enough to your Grammy, and he got you out of a hole. He'll be here tomorrow for the funeral, I daresay. He writes a nice letter.'

Andrew was not listening. 'Bellows…it couldn't have been that if he was Italian. Bello, maybe. That means beautiful in Italian…or war, in Latin. I like it…'

There was a nice turn out at the church, as Uncle Ted commented later. Afterwards, round the graveside in the enormous cemetery, the crowd had diminished somewhat, a huddled little group in the cold, watching as the mortal remains of Grammy O'Ryan went underground in its neat pine coffin. Ted, somberly dressed as befitted the chief mourner, was flanked by his large wife Maureen and their assorted children, the two older sons now as tall as Ted, and Aunt 'Sister' Bernadette was there too, dressed oddly, Andrew thought, in clothes that were too short for a nun: a black raincoat that only reached her bony knees, with her black stockings and stout black shoes beneath. She wore a nun's veil, short again, like a sort of headscarf, and she held a black umbrella against the spotting rain. Her face was white and puffy-looking – she looked at least ten years older than Ted, although he knew for a fact she was two years younger. Behind them, at a respectful distance, stood Captain Rollitt in a trenchcoat and a hat. Beside him, weeping into a large hankie, was stout old Mrs Pell in a navy coat that strained over her amble bosom, and beside her were the two girls who had latterly done the 'rough' at number forty-two. Both wore black PVC raincoats. One was Mrs Pell's niece, Sharon, a weaselly-looking blonde of about twenty-two with exaggerated eye make-up and strange teeth, and who stared rudely at Andrew, who stood deliberately a little way off from the rest, feeling awkward in his gabardine mac and his school uniform, observing. The coffin was lowered slowly into the ground on ropes by the cemetery staff, men in boiler-suits and ill-assorted jackets, straining not so much under the tiny weight as the sticky black slitheriness of the ground from all the recent rain. The priest, the cheerful Father Spelman, swung the censer and muttered prayers that sounded out of place, and threw in a handful of dirt which hit the coffin with an audible splotch. Ted solemnly followed suit, throwing in some soil, wiping his hands on his trousers; Maureen shushed the youngest of her brood; Sister Bernadette crossed herself; the Captain bowed his head; Mrs Pell choked a sob; Sharon stuck her tongue out at Andrew, and he realised she was flirting. The ceremony was more or less over. Rain began to fall, heavily. Ted was shaking hands awkwardly with Father Spelman, thanking the men, having a brief discussion with one of the undertakers who was indicating the waiting black cars. Andrew looked away, across the seeming miles of neat graves blurred in the now teeming rain and saw a figure crossing them, a woman teetering awkwardly in heels, boots with long heels, twisting her ankles, picking her way towards them. She had on a dark red coat, and on a fuzz of frizzy reddish hair she wore a dark red beret; as she moved closer, he saw her eyes: vivid blue as Grammy O'Ryan's had been. Andrew felt his stomach lurch.

'Good Lord Jesus Christ,' said Ted, who was leading the forlorn party from the graveside to the gravel sweep and the cars. He stopped in his tracks. 'Oh Godalmighty! *Rosaleen!*'

'Ted, oh Ted!'

'You mis-timed it as usual, Rosie,' Ted muttered. And then he clasped his sister in his big arms, almost pulling her off her feet in the long-heeled boots.

'The cars will go back to Maxwell Road,' cried Maureen, taking charge. 'I'm after puttin' on a bit of a spread, just in case. Come on, Hetty,' she said to Mrs Pell, who was staring round-eyed at Ted and the strange woman in his arms. 'Let's get up there, shall we? Hello, stranger,' she said sourly to Rosaleen as she passed. 'A bad penny always turns up. Don't keep Ted, now – we've got things to manage. Now, where's that young Andy? Captain Rollitt – you must join us now, you who was so good to the mother-in-law. 'Tis your house, after all, and the Irish know how to serve a decent drink. Well, if you're really sure, Captain Rollitt. 'T'was real good of you to come, like, and beautiful flowers. Appreciated. Father Spelman, you'll take a drop in her honour to be sure.'

Maureen O'Ryan shepherded the party into the waiting cars, leaving Ted and Rosaleen standing awkwardly, getting wet.

'Rosie, I don't know.'

'It's all right, Ted.' The voice had a strange twang – Dublin overlaid with Texas. 'I'm not coming to spoil your party. I just couldn't not…well, you know. Poor little Mammy, I just couldn't not…' Her blue eyes began to stream as she glanced back through the rain to where men were covering the coffin with fresh earth.

'You might have paid her more attention when she was still with us,' Ted mumbled.

'Oh, Ted. I'd no idea she was so sick.'

'None of us had, Rosaleen. Always kept her troubles to herself, did Mammy. How long you over for, anyways? Are you by yerself? How are you managing?'

'Hank paid my fare over, Ted. He's in Texas with the kids. I'm not stoppin'. I'm flying back tomorrow. I just wanted to come, Ted. Couldn't not.'

'We're getting soaked, Rosie. Get in the car, for the Lord's sakes before we drown. Come back with us, Rosie. See the house where she lived. It's still full of her.' He held open the door of his hired Cortina.

'I can't, Ted. I'm going back to Shirley's in Seven Sisters. We were nurses to-gether. She's puttin' me up. Maureen can't abide me – don't make us go through it, Ted. Please. And I've nothing to say to Bernie – she's in another world. I've done what I came here to do…' She pressed a handkerchief to her eyes.

'Not altogether you haven't, Rosie. There's something you left behind, remem-ber?' Ted cast about the nearby trees for Andrew. 'He must have gone back in one of the cars. Come and meet him, Rosie. Your son. You'd be so proud. He's a public schoolboy, now. Mammy did a wonderful job, you know. He's a very bright lad. He'll be going on to a university.'

'Oh God, Ted! No, no! Please, Ted, I can't. It's all in the past! Please, Ted. Don't...' She was twisting out of his grasp, sobbing.

'So why did you come then? Go on, why did you come? For the good Lord's sakes, Rosie. You musta known he'd be here.'

A black cab swished up onto the wet gravel. 'Here's my taxi. I've got to go, Ted. I'm sorry. Tell them all I'm just so sorry...'

'Rosaleen!'

Andrew, still sheltering behind a tree and staring after the departing cars, started at the touch on his sleeve. 'Oh, it's you, sir.'

'Yes, it's me. Can I drop you anywhere? It is getting rather wet.'

'No thanks. All the same. I'll stay here.'

'Andrew. Please come out of the rain. Let's go for a whiskey. Beer if you prefer. You'd like that, wouldn't you?'

'You mean really for a whiskey in a pub, and not to number forty-two?'

'No, not to number forty-two. They'll do perfectly well without us, eh? And I can do better than a pub. Come on, young man.'

In a squashy leather chair in the lounge of Leo's club, his raincoat having been borne off by one of the staff to get dry, Andrew sipped a fine old malt and began to feel warm. There was a plate of cheese biscuits and some small pieces of a good meat pie in crumbly pastry.

'Cheeri-bloody-o,' said Leo. He was aware that the lad was shivering. 'You don't have to talk if you don't want to. Just drink up and get a grip on yourself. Funerals are always depressing.'

'Thanks, sir.' His mother's face – so much older, more raddled than it had been in his dreams, filled his thoughts. And she was here, in London, on her way by taxi to – he had not really caught it. Out of his life, anyway. Again.

'Less of the sir, at a time like this. Come on. Drink up. And eat some of these things. A bit of a shock, eh?' Andrew realised the Captain was referring to his grandmother.

'Not really, sir – Captain Rollitt. She was very ill. I just wish I'd gone up to see her.'

'That's very natural, Andrew. But she would have understood, you know. Been proud. I – I've been proud of you, too, Andrew. You've been doing very well.' It was true. Andrew's school reports had been little short of excellent. 'It's been, well, it's been a pleasure to sponsor you, Andrew. Some time, not now necessarily, we need to discuss your future. What you're going to do next, all that. Have you any ideas?'

Other people showed their stuff to their mothers. Or their fathers. Or even their grandmothers. The whiskey and the warmth and the presence of this benign, understanding human being almost lured him into a vulnerability to which he was naturally resistant. Rollitt looked thinner and a little older, but otherwise much the same. In the comfortable cigar and leather-smelling atmosphere of the club, Andrew felt almost fond of him, and in that strange dislocation of mind – caused by the recent vision of his mother, and the knotted sense of profound

[205]

curiosity and an even more profound anger the sight of her had left – he pushed aside the thought that the secret knowledge he held over Lottie Walters, and fully intended to use, would also affect his benefactor. It had not taken super-detection to work it out. A few reference works in the school library had provided *Walters, Giles R., b.1928 academic, poet, Fellow Gonville & Caius, Cantab., 1958– 1966. d 1966, m 1962 Charlotte Anne Rollitt, d. of the Hon C. P. W. Rollitt;* and *Rollitt, Leofric, b.1930 Capt. 7th Lancers, DSO, s. of the Hon. C. P. W. Rollitt;* and *Rollitt, the Hon. Charles P. W., d. 1959, stockbroker, Lloyd's of London, m. Margaret Enid Dearborn, d 1957 d. of Edmund Dearborn, 4th Baron Fitzrivers…issue Charlotte Anne (b.1928) and Leofric (b.1930)…* However unlikely it seemed (and of course 'Mrs Walters' *could* be an impersonation – he mustn't discount this possibility) Charlotte Anne and the woman the Captain called 'Lottie' must be one and the same. It followed that this toff, this big noise in the Special Branch who had more-or-less adopted him, was, however improbably, shagging his own sister – but to Andrew, who was sisterless, and had not as yet shagged anybody as such, if one did not count the odd erotic encounter with school tart Freddy Hayes-Pilsborough in the senior showers, it appeared less odd, *per se*, than it might have to anyone else. What was much more odd, as his growing adult intelligence informed him, was the *risk…* Rollitt's eyes, kindly interrogative, smiled with genuine interest.

'I – I think I want to be a journalist, sir. Captain Rollitt. I like writing. And reading. And I'm keen on Shakespeare. And Webster. My year-master thinks I ought to apply to university to read English Literature. It'll depend on my A-levels.' The whiskey warmed him.

'You certainly write an amusing letter, Andrew. I enjoy them. They have a certain – flair…' And indeed, Andrew's sporadic letters to the Captain were intended to amuse: mostly descriptive character portraits of boys and masters, not necessarily always truthful, but this was scarcely their point. They gave the impression, for instance, of a boy well-integrated with his fellows, in the thick of school life and school activites, rather than revealing the aloof and lonely character of the writer; but the literal-minded Leo Rollitt read them and chuckled, and took them at face-value, as it was intended he should. It was true that Andrew had long since passed the stage of being ragged and bullied: nowadays, his school-fellows called him 'The Oddity' (others, more waggish, called him 'O'Ditty') and tended to leave him to himself, but a more sophisticated faction and a number of masters had recognized his talents. When he had been persuaded to play Richard of Gloucester at the end of last term, and he had deliberately parodied his deformed foot, the boys had begun to treat him with that totemism that amounts to affection, and masters had acknowledged 'style' and something they put down to 'courage'.

'Thank you, Captain Rollitt…'

'Well, that's splendid, Andrew. I'll back you. You can count on it. And if the A-levels don't quite work out, we can talk about some sort of training, can't we?'

'I'm, well, I'm very grateful, Captain Rollitt…' A steward came up noiselessly and said something in an undertone about the 'young gentleman's coat'.

'Seems your mac's dry, Andrew. What are you going to do now? Join the family in Fulham?'

'No – no fear, Captain Rollitt. I've got my stuff. I thought I'd go to Foyles bookshop before they close and then to Paddington to get the train back to school. It's the middle of term, you see...' They were making their way to the foyer cloakroom, where Andrew's gabardine mac was duly handed over. Outside, it drizzled insistently, dirtily, and the pavements looked greasy.

'Very well, Andrew. You obviously know what you're doing. Here...' Leo fished in his hip pocket and produced a note. 'Better get a cab in this.'

'That's far too generous, sir,' said Andrew. 'Thank you.'

'Not at all, my boy. Buy a good book or two. And eat some supper.' They shook hands awkwardly, and Andrew turned up his collar and stepped out onto the oily pavement. Leo stared after him, filled with a vague nostalgia and those pleasant thoughts one has when one feels one has made a serious difference for the better in a life less comfortable than one's own.

49

'Do you know about flights to the USA?' Andrew had bought books in Foyles, and it was almost pure impulse that took him into the travel agency virtually next door, but he had formed a plan.

Behind the desk, a youngish woman with a supercilious expression looked up through dark-rimmed spectacles and saw a schoolboy. 'Of course. Now where would *you* want to go?' If she had added 'sonny', she could not have been more rude.

'I don't – that is – that is a friend of mine is flying out to Texas tomorrow. I want to – to catch him, to give him an urgent message. I need to know the airport and the times.'

'Okay…' The woman took down a large folder and flipped through some print-ed matter that might have been a timetable on a huge scale. 'That'll be Heathrow, to Dallas Fort Worth at five-fifty-five. BOAC. It's the only one tomorrow. Pan-Am flies the day after to New York.'

'I don't want New York. Five-fifty-five. Good, thanks. I've plenty of time to catch him, then…' The thin-faced schoolboy with the limp, the strange eyes, and an accent that could be Irish struck her as odd.

'That's five-fifty-five in the morning,' she added, sighing.

'Oh…oh, well, yes of course. Thank you.'

When you have just a matter of hours in London and nowhere to stay, you can do as you said, get a train from Paddington back to school. Or you can do the other thing. Andrew's pocket money – his carefully counted allowance, together with Captain Leo's handsome twenty – was more than enough to buy him supper in a Wimpey after his book-purchases, and then, he supposed, he would make his way to Heathrow and wait.

He sat down at a formica table and waited for his Wimpey-burger, chips and glass of coca-cola. Beside him was his overnight bag, now weighted down with books. He had bought postcards in Foyles, and a large envelope at a nearby sta-tioner. He took out a pen. 'He capers nimbly…', he wrote in block capitals on the back of a lurid line drawing of Richard the Third – Foyles stocked a collection of theatrical studies – and put this, together with a paperback Revels Series copy of Ford's 'Tis Pity She's a Whore into the envelope, addressing it to Mrs C. A. Walters, c/o 42 Maxwell Road… This was something he had been planning to do for some time from the anonymity of London, but it was a long shot, one which said more about his new-found erudition than it did about his deep-running grudge against the would-be recipient, and as he caught the last post in a nearby Post Office in Regent Street, saw the clerk paste on the stamps and collected his change, he felt a stab of adolescent futility. The rain had abated, and he simply wandered in the deepening dusk, rehearsing in his mind what he would say to his mother when he found her…

'Fancy a nice time, sweetheart?' Two girls, one bottle-blonde in a very short black PVC mac who could have been Sharon Pell's double, and another, smaller, younger, a red-head, emerged from a gloomy doorway and barred his way. 'Real nice time. Just a fiver. Take your pick. We're both available!' They giggled. It took him a moment to realise what was being offered.

'Oh...'

The red-haired girl stared at him under a street light. 'Oh, shit, forget it! He's just a kid, Jackie. Ain't yer?' She could not have been more than seventeen herself.

'Leave me alone,' said Andrew.

'Coo – quite the little toff, ain't he?' said the blonde. 'Miserable as sin, too. Been to a funeral, or summink, mate?'

'Yes, since you ask. Please let me get by.' The blonde one had her hand on his sleeve, feeling the fabric. Her red nails were chipped and she smelled powerfully of unpleasantly strong scent.

'Yais, since you arsk! Get that, Georgie? Eton, is it? Or 'Arrer?'

The girl Georgie gave him a look that could have been friendly. 'Shut yer gob, Jackie. Let him alone. Sorry, mate. Our mistake.' The blonde girl addressed as Jackie had spotted another possible punter and immediately lost interest. Andrew suddenly made up his mind. 'How much did you say?' he said to the red-head.

'Five quid. Ten for the whole works. I gotter room, too...'

So it was that Andrew O'Ryan, on the day of his grandmother's funeral, popped his cherry, as his schoolfellows would have put it, under the skillful and even tender guidance of a red-headed young prostitute called Georgie in a shabby bed and breakfast hotel where she apparently lived and plied her trade on a bed that was normally home to about fifteen teddy-bears and who had apparently liked the experience sufficiently to throw in an 'extra' for 'love'. By the time he got to Heathrow on a dawn bus – his financial resouces having dwindled too low to afford a taxi, and his mind filled inevitably with this initiation into the mysteries of muliebrity and he stared at the crowd of departing travellers trundling their bags under the coldly watchful eyes of uniformed airport officials from the barrier. He thought he caught a glimpse of a dark red coat and a beret perched on a frizz of reddish hair vanishing round a corner. Part of him wanted to call after her. Part of him felt nothing but relief that he could not.

50

That same evening, the night after the funeral of Mrs O'Ryan, Leo too was at something of a loose end. He put through a long distance call and spoke to Lottie in Florence from the telephone booth in the foyer of the Club and she sounded happy. Always, he worried for Lottie's happiness. His grand schemes for Folwell had long since fallen through – the Trust had become lately wary of gifts they could not afford to maintain. In order for them to consider taking Folwell on at all, Leo would have had to sell all he owned to provide even part of the upkeep fund the Trust would have demanded, and while he could have retained a right to live in it, the Trust would have demanded a rent. Even so, Leo had wavered, and it had led to an inevitable tussle: 'No, Leo, I'm not plunging my tiny capital and Giles's royalties into this crazy scheme!' Lottie had cried. There had been no moving her. She had been adamant, and in truth, after a lengthy exchange of letters with his friend on the Board of the Trust, it was clear they could not raise nearly enough in any case. Leo had been disappointed, but he had faced up to the inevitable. Lottie, for her part, was relieved that the matter was out of her hands, and not merely down to her own obstinacy. She had even allowed herself to shed a tear along with an immense burden when Folwell Hall became the property of Country Breaks Ltd.

Now they had become somewhat nomadic – a life that seemed to suit them very well. They had a rented apartment in central Florence, where Lottie had got herself involved with the British Institute library, helping in the art-history section. She had her eye on a dilapidated farmhouse between Florence and Siena. They had melted into a sort of nebulous anonymity, and their peculiar privacy had begun to feel secure, so much so that neither of them – as far as Leo could tell – gave it much thought any longer. Their London sojourns were less frequent than formerly, but they tended to stay for longer, he at his Club or at Maxwell Road; she with friends, catching up.

Now, having come up to Town impromptu for Mrs O'Ryan's funeral, he was on his own, and now that the O'Ryan tenure of number forty-two had finally ended, he had much to do. He must wait, of course, until the O'Ryan family funeral gathering – for them it was presumably a 'wake' – was over, but then he must go back and sort things, speak to that very pleasant son, Redmond O'Ryan, Andrew's uncle Ted, and make sure that they had any of the old lady's belongings they wanted to remove. Then? He might, of course, put the house on the market. There was still a young tenant in the attic. Perhaps he was Redmond's responsibility now. Bolly's fortunes had revived, and Bolly was now living at an address in St James's. The Fulham place was still handy. Nothing, Leo decided, need be done in any hurry. His room at the Club was booked for another week. He could, as far as it went, relax. After a modest supper in the Club dining room, he took himself for a wander…

The Black Bull had changed beyond recognition. Once one of those quiet oases of good beer and good sandwiches that were fast disappearing altogether from central London, it was now a brash and rowdy venue for the young. If it hadn't just started once again to pelt with rain, Leo would have not got past the threshold. As it was, he shook the drops from his umbrella, and sat in the quietest corner he could find with a Bell's and soda and did the only thing possible in such a place: trying to ignore the colossal din – conversation shrieked and yelled above the racket of David Bowie or whoever it was – he watched his fellow customers, reflecting that the 'young', no matter how outlandishly dressed and made up, no matter how long or absurdly dyed their hair, were always somehow beautiful, even the fatter, spottier ones. It was simply Youth... His thoughts strayed errantly to particular aspects of youthful beauty, and he felt himself grow nostalgic. He pulled himself up rather sharply. The law had changed, but so had Leo, up to a point. For one thing, he really did have a job, of sorts, with the Special Branch – a roving brief concerned with cells of Italian terrorists and the passing of information to England. While this was pretty much a sinecure – there was little political violence to trouble the ancient hauteur of Florence, and he was far more occupied giving private music lessons and the odd lecture at the Institute – he had far too great a sense of responsibility to chuck the whole thing for an embarrassing and squalid episode on home soil.

Now, a particular crowd of young people who had just burst in and were loudly ordering drinks in braying voices, changing their orders, confusing the barman, joshing each other, calling each other names and slapping each other with boisterous affection, attracted Leo's attention. It seemed to be somebody's birthday. They mostly had long hair – the young men's hair seemed especially glossy and well-cared for – and they were more or less of a recognizable stamp. In Leo's parents' day, they would have been 'Bright Young Things'. In these class-confused days, they could be almost anyone – Leo's money would have been on some sort of a theatre group – but they were probably no more nor less than a bunch of nicely brought up private school kids out on a jag. Or a rave-up. Having a party, anyway. It was hard not to feel hopelessly old-fashioned, out of things. Leo's own youth – born at the advent of a War, and made to attend the sort of schools that had taken cricket and military training very seriously – had been stern in the extreme, and the 'teenager' phenomenon had yet to be invented. He looked at these peace-time young and felt not so much envy as longing. Many of his own contemporaries – the military types at the Club, for instance – had turned into premature old codgers, reactionary moralists, old before their time. Leo could so easily have become such himself. As it was, he would far rather be here, observing, reflecting. He wondered if he might fight his way to the bar and order another Bell's...

'Leo?' The tall, rather bulky young woman wearing dark purple lipstick and a lot of pale make-up on a rather formless face had separated from her group of friends, barged through the crowd to his table and sat herself down. 'I knew it was you!' Her voice was a gruff contralto, with a patrician tone which affected cockney could not disguise. Her hair was dyed a rather unbecoming but undeniably dramatic black. He frowned, puzzled.

'I'm sorry, do I?' She knew him. It followed that he ought to know her.

[211]

'I'm Veronica. Your cousin. Second cousin, or is it once removed? Anyway, I'm Hugh Dearborn's daughter, or I would be if he wasn't dead as a dodo, but his father and your mother were sisters, I mean siblings. You're Leo Rollitt. I'm Veronica Dearborn. And I'm horribly pissed, but it is my birthday. We've not met for about a hundred years. I saw you, just sitting there, and I thought, that's not Leslie Howard! Bloody hell, that's Leo. That's bloody Leo!'

'Good God!' He looked at her more closely. Yes. This girl – and good Lord, what a girl, a girl squeezed into shiny black trousers, silver boots and a sparkly top that showed an alarming expanse of ample cleavage – was, must be, Veronica, the second child of that ill-fated marriage between poor old cousin Hugh and Anabel Trent. There had been a son, and then Veronica, and then another child, he seemed to remember, by the Callington man she ran off with. Anabel, a noted beauty, had made rather a habit of marriage – and divorce. 'Yes, I see. Good Lord, Veronica. What a – a splendid coincidence. Um – would you like a drink?'

'Yes, but I'm going to get you one. It's whisk and sod, isn't it, by the look of things? Piers!' She shrieked above the din, and a tall, very good-looking young man with rippling fair hair turned towards them. 'Lovely Piers! Get me a – Bell's? – yah, Bell's and soda, and another of those Bull-Blasters for me, there's a petal! My tab! It's my birthday,' she explained to Leo again. 'Do help me celebrate. This is hysterical, meeting you like this. What a complete gas! I've not seen you since I was about this high.'

'And now it's your –' he guessed – 'eighteenth birthday?'

'Right on, Cuz! Eighteen. The key of the door. Well anyway, Dad's trust-fund...'

'Well – um – happy birthday, Veronica. I – I should never have recognized you, I'm afraid. It's clever of you to recognize me...' He racked his memory for the time he had last seen her. 'How are you? Apart from celebrating?'

'I'm fantastic! I come into this f – socking great allowance today, and it's no holds barred. I'm going to enjoy myself for once. Oh, marvy, Piers, ta. Piers, this is my cousin, Leo Rollitt. I'm going to persuade him to join us at the Piggery! Leo, Piers Prescott. He's at school with Jamie, my brother – or he was. We're all leaving, aren't we, Piers? Except. Ex-*cept*...' She lowered her voice to a stage-whisper, 'Piers is going to Oxford because he's much, much cleverer than he looks...'

The young man shook hands with Leo who half stood, and said, 'Later at the Piggery, then,' and smiled, but glanced back to the roistering group at the bar. 'Great. See you in a bit. Happy bidet, Vee,' he added, kissing the top of her head.

'He's not my beau,' said Veronica. 'Unfortunately...' She stared after him with naked longing. Back at the bar, Piers had slung an arm round the shoulders of a girl whose blonde hair almost reached her waist. 'Piers's girls are always so fuck-ing *thin*... Sorry, Leo. Look, this is great meeting you like this. Do come on with us to the Piggery. It's a club. A gas. Jamie's going to join us.' Veronica had taken after heavy-set Hugh, rather than chic, slender Anabel. In his present reflective, mellow, theatre-audience mood, Leo found himself feeling rather sorry for her.

'This is very kind, Veronica, but I fear I might be a little out of place.' Leo coughed. 'I take it you're not off to university yourself, my dear,' he said.

'Not bloody likely. Mummy wants me to enrol for some art-history thing in Italy, but I'm resisting it so far. I'm just going to have a good bloody time!'

'Well, I wish you all the luck in the world, Veronica. Cheeri-bloody-o!'

'Wow, that was old Aunt Ros Bullivant, wasn't it? 'Cheeri-bloody-o'. I remember going to Folwell at least once, Mummy, Daddy, Jamie and me…Lucie wasn't born then. I was sick. Someone called Mrs Henry held a big pan for me and I puked my head off. Kids are always being sick, aren't they? I'm never going to have bloody kids. And how's Lottie? I haven't seen her since her wedding to that poet and I was really small then. I was sick at the wedding, too – that big party in some Cambridge college. I'd had too much cake and trifle, and Jamie dared me to drink champagne. She was amazing, Lottie. So pretty. She wore gold and not white, and I remember Mummy going 'tut', but she would, the hypocritical cow! She didn't have kids, did she? Lottie? What happened to her after Giles Walters smashed himself up? Did she get married again?'

'No…no she didn't. She's mostly in Italy these days. In Florence. Art was always rather her thing, you know. I'm there quite a bit myself now. You know, Veronica, if you change your mind about art history, I'm sure Lottie would be delighted to see you.' It just slipped out, this vague invitation. He was by no means sure that Lottie would be 'delighted'. He coughed again.

Veronica pulled a face as if considering. 'Oh. Well, you never know – I mean Florence might be cool, and you're there too. It might be a gas – you know, nice to know people. I'm just so anti-Mummy at the moment, I can't quite bear to agree,' said Veronica frankly. 'Say, hang *on*!' Suddenly Veronica began to laugh, and prodded him on the arm. 'You know – God, this is so hysterical – someone – it might have been Mummy, actually – told me *the* craziest story…'

'Story?'

'Yah…it's probably completely insane. Someone said you were in Italy and Lottie was pretending to be your wife, so's you didn't have to come out – I mean, admit to being gay. Sorry!'

Leo suddenly felt prickles on the back of his neck.

'Did they now? Well, Veronica, my dear, if you'll pardon my sounding very rude, if that story came via your mother, I'd say it was typical.'

'Oh yah, absolutely,' said Veronica, not at all put out. 'She's terrible, isn't she? Scandals are her hobby. I'd hate her if she wasn't my mother. I almost hate her anyway. She certainly hates me. So it's not true then? I mean, if it is true, it doesn't matter. Nobody minds about queers these days, do they? Only Mummy's generation and that's just sheer hypocrisy. Oops – sorry, that's your generation, too – I didn't mean…' Veronica's face had gone rather red under the white make-up.

'I know what you meant, Veronica. Don't worry. Look – I think your friends are trying to hail your attention.' To his relief this was the case. Declining another slightly less enthusiastic invitation to the Piggery, and scribbling down the address of his Club, he submitted to a rapturous kiss that left a smear of bruise-coloured lipstick on his cheek, and watched them clatter out of the pub, a noisy, whooping bunch of young people who now made him feel very tired. Very soon afterwards, he stepped alone into the street himself, and after the intense fug of the bar, the rain on his face felt positively balmy.

[213]

51: Spring, 1974

'Well, now, that's splendid,' Leo murmured. He was sitting in a shaft of sunlight at the table in their tiny, dark apartment opposite the Museo Bargello in Florence, reading a letter. Lottie came in with more post.

'What's splendid, darling?' Her voice had that breezy, slightly brittle quality that meant she was put out, something that Leo noted in some interior of his consciousness.

'Oh, just the O'Ryan boy. Andrew. He's been offered a university place. East Anglia.'

'Well I never...' If the 'O'Ryan boy' was not exactly a taboo subject between them, Leo tended not to discuss him with Lottie. 'That must be very satisfying.'

'It is rather. It will all depend on the A-level results. You were wrong about him, darling. He's doing very well indeed. Now what about yours? Anything of interest for you?'

'It depends on what you mean. There are two things. We – that is it was addressed to me but I think it means to include you – we've had a letter from poor Hugh's daughter, Veronica. Says she met you in London before Christmas. I wish you'd said.'

'Oh! Good Lord! I'm sure I did tell you, darling. What does she say?'

'She says she's coming to Florence to do an art-history and Italian course here at the Institute...wants to know if I can meet her. She doesn't exactly say so, but I rather think she'd like us to put her up. I wish you had told me, Leo. This could be very awkward.'

'Let's see it...' He took the letter, which was written in lurid purple ink and read. 'No, darling. She's not angling to stay. I expect she just wants a friendly face or two when she comes. We can't put her up anyway – we don't have space for ourselves here let alone a guest. We might help her find somewhere, though, mightn't we?'

'The Institute has its own accommodation arrangements, Leo,' Lottie said sharply. 'And I don't like it. I foresee – complications.' She gave an audible shiver. 'And I'll swear you didn't say anything about meeting her.'

'I did, you know, darling...' He had, in fact, but he had made so light of the encounter that it probably had not registered. 'Oh, Lottie darling, don't worry. She – she's a rather nice kid. Quite a lot the looks of poor old Hugh, in fact. I think we should try to make her welcome, feel at home. It can't have been easy for her, Hugh's death, all that. And I can only imagine what it must be like having Anabel for a mother. Try and be a bit charitable. She's our cousin.'

'*Exactly*! Honestly, Leo, I think you must be as blind as a bat. You really don't see, do you?'

'I see that you are over-reacting a bit, Lottie darling. You live here, she knows I stay here quite often. There's nothing strange or out of the ordinary. I really don't see the problem. She doesn't have to come and poke into the bedroom or anything. We could meet her for lunch, and you could make sure she's got com-

fortable quarters, that sort of thing. Come *on*, Lottie. We can't skulk forever...'
But he was remembering, uncomfortably, the things Veronica had told him her
mother had said.

'I am not *skulking!*'

'Darling, don't shout, please.'

'Sorry. Maybe you're right. It would be nice to be nice to poor Hugh's daughter. I get a bit – jumpy, that's all. Just when one begins to feel a bit less nervous.
There's something else. I – I've been sent this book.' His eyes had strayed back to
his correspondence.

'Leo... please.'

'Sorry, my dear – what is it? Barbara Robshawe's thing on Austen?'

'No. Leo, please listen for a moment. This is something else. It's a play. Jacobean, I think. I just wanted to know how did it come? You brought it back with the
other post from London.'

'Well, then it came to the Club. Or forty-two. Didn't you order it?'

'No. It's a bit mysterious.'

'Probably just a book club making a mistake. They do it all the time. Chuck it
if you don't want it, darling. Give it to the Institute Library...'

'This isn't a book club, Leo. It was sent privately. There's...there's a message.
Look...' She thrust the postcard in front of him. It was a line-drawing of Cleop-
atra in a barge, waving a fan.

'Hmph. "Age cannot wither her, nor custom stale her infinite variety," eh? You
must have an anonymous admirer, darling. Someone at Cambridge, maybe?'

'It was posted in London, not that that means anything. Leo, darling – I –
don't think this is an admirer. I think this is weird. This is the second one I've had
in less than six months. The same book. And there was a postcard with that one,
too. *Richard the Third.* And the – the title's so nasty.' He could see how agitated
she was.

'Hmm. *'Tis Pity She's a Whore*... Yes. I agree, darling. It is a bit nasty. Always
hated that Jacobean stuff myself. Nasty, crude, melodramatic. Chuck it...'

'You don't think – well, that it's some sort of *message?*'

'Oh darling. Come on, don't get into a state. Chuck it, I would. Chuck it and
forget it.'

'All right. Perhaps that's best. The bin this time, maybe. I gave the first one to
the Library. I don't suppose they want a second!' A brittle little laugh. 'But – well,
if it's not a book-club, who could it be?' In fact, she had her own thoughts on this
one, and tried to dismiss them as merely paranoid.

'Hmmm?'

'Oh, nothing, darling. Do you think it's too early for a pre-lunch G & T?'

Lottie did not throw the book away. She tried to read it, and found it heavy
going. She had got herself into what Leo would call one of her 'states'. Leo had
gone out, and Lottie had a sudden impulse.

'Barbara? Barbara Robshawe?'

'Speaking. Who is this?'

'Barbara, it's Lottie, Lottie Walters. I hope this isn't a bad moment.'

'Lottie, my dear! Good Lord – wherever are you ringing from? Are you in England?'

'Not – not at the moment. I'm still in Florence. I'm partly ringing to thank you for *Jane*…so kind of you. I'm loving it. Thank you so much for sending it.'

'Not at all, my dear. I'm glad you're enjoying it. I'm just glad to get it off the stocks, so to speak. I've begun the *Letters* – now that's much more like hard work. You should have written, you silly girl. This call must be costing a fortune. How are you, my dear?'

'Oh, gainfully employed…sorting out the art history section of the British Institute library…and I really will write properly with all my news about the farmhouse. I'm planning a rose-garden. Barbara – I'd better keep this brief – can I ask you a question?'

'Of course. Anything – unless it's about plants, because everything I touch dies as you know. Tell me.'

'Well…Do you know anything about John Ford's play *'Tis Pity She's a Whore?*'

'A bit,' answered Doctor Barbara Robshawe. 'It's not exactly my bag. If you really want to know, you'd need to ask David, but he's dining in College this evening. I'm only a humble Janeite. Why, my dear?'

'Oh…I…well, I – it's not really important. It's just that I've been asked to this play in London, some old friends of Giles's, as a matter of fact, and I thought I'd better bone up.'

'I see. Well, as far as I recall, it's about a brother and sister who commit incest and who aren't a bit ashamed and both get murdered. Very Jacobean and lurid, but quite fun. I could ask David to write and give you all the low-down.'

'Oh.'

'Lottie? Are you still there?'

'Yes… No, that's fine, Barbara. Thank you. Thanks very much. Please don't trouble David.'

Her hand was trembling as she put the telephone down. Lottie gazed again at the book, and flung it against the wall, and felt instantly embarrassed, as one does by gestures of sheer futility. She wanted to cry out. She wished Leo was in the apartment with her. She was glad he was not. She could not get the O'Ryan boy out of her mind. She wondered if she were not going slightly crazy. She went to the tiny kitchen, opened the fridge and washed down three aspirin with a triple gin with very little tonic in it.

Part V

52: Silly Season Last Year

Arise, Sir Jerry! The much-loved TV personality and radio broadcaster Jerry Fairbrother has collected a knighthood from the Queen at Buckingham Palace. As well as hosting a number of consumer affairs programmes over the years on radio and television, and being a frequent guest judge on TV talent-spotting shows, Christmas specials in aid of children's charities, and compère on the last three Royal Command Variety shows, the veteran former actor and writer of satirical comedy presents the highly popular Big Quiz, *which he took over from Miles Stanton five years ago. The show attracts an estimated nine million viewers each week, and is said to be favourite viewing of Her Majesty and Prince Philip. Fairbrother also heads the ground-breaking consumer legal affairs show* Sort It!, *famous for its exposures of corrupt local councils, housing associations, faulty weights and measures and property scams on the Continent. The programme has recently been at the centre of a legal wrangle of its own after the disgruntled owner of the show's long-running Canonbury Squatters saga presented an unsuccessful libel suit last month. 'All sorted now,' said Sir Jerry, proudly displaying his KB medal.*

Born in Hatton, Cambridgeshire, the son of a local solicitor, Sir Jerry read English and Drama at East Anglia University, and with student colleagues went on to become part of the Scrape the Barrel *alternative comedy team in the late seventies, before co-writing and co-starring in the off-beat and often foul-mouthed Channel Four series* Plug & Socket. *Mainstream success and a shedding of the 'bad boy' image followed in the early 80s with the consumer-aware* Earthwatch *which he co-wrote with J. J. Webster of* Read All About It *and* It Pays to Advertise *fame. For many years he has been a familiar voice on breakfast radio, presenting the 'Smallprint' slot on the on the* Jilly Tantram Show *and got the consumer-issues bug badly. Had he ever wanted to be a lawyer? 'No fear! Not nearly clever enough. Actually, I really always wanted to be a serious actor,' Sir Jerry smiles ruefully, 'but there were too many lines.'*

Now Sir Jerry's line is 'Thank you very much, Ma'am.'

Drex was moodily picking out butts from the ashtray and lighting them, reading the BBC news on the internet on his laptop.

'Now who's being disgusting?' Angel said.

'Yesterday's long stub is today's smoke, Angel.'

'You're still disgusting. Anyone'd think you were broke. Have one of mine, for God's sake. Bloody Norah!'

'And who pays for those, may I ask?'

'All right, mardy-arse, suit yourself. Oh, you've seen the news, then? That Fairbrother's a Knight of the Garter and everything.'

'Not the Garter, pillock, that's just for diplomats. Or is that St Michael and St George? Oh, hell, why should you know? Anyway, he's a Knight, a sir… Arise, Sir Jerry, for thou art a total twat.'

'Whatever he is, he's in a bit of bother.'

'No he isn't. You're well out of date. It's sorted, as he said. The programme producers've had to justify a bit of under-the-table dealing, but they're claiming that they merely acted as guarantors on a loan, not gave out the dosh themselves, which is bollocks, but as that Rachman character withdrew his libel suit – doubtless he was worried that his less than squeaky history would appeal to the ladies and gentlemen of the Press – *Sort It!* will survive, and so will Sir Jerry. For the time being. He won't in the end. Nobody does, sooner or later.'

But it seemed that Her Majesty had been busy. 'Sir Dominic' was quoted on the topic of GM crops following an outburst from his royal patron, and a small column in the 'celebrities' section quoted 'Lady Fairbrother' speaking at a charity bash for third-world child victims of AIDS.

Drex swore softly.

53

I get hacked off when nothing much happens. Time, I think, to stir up a bit of shit from under the straw. Time, in short, for a visit to Kinseyder's stinking kennel. And to work a metaphor, as the man said, I'm bringing bones.

The Kinseyder office at the *Mercury* operates under the editorial aegis of one Thomas Oliver Wragg, known in *Mercury* circles inevitably if unwittily as the 'Toe-Rag' but one can't blame them. This is an impressively grotesque individual with all the personal charm and finesse of an outsize troll, a permanent sneer on fullish lips pulled back over large and crooked teeth, and a figure strongly reminiscent of Yogi Bear: it's as if some force of gravity has somehow drawn all of his considerable bulk away from his rather insignificant shoulders and down to his backside. Unprepossessing. He also has one of those glandular problems that produce a powerful corporeal odour, which he tries unsuccessfully to mitigate with cologne and room-deodorants. For this reason among others, I appear in person as little as possible in the Toe-Rag's office, but sometimes these *tête-à-tête* parleys are unavoidable. In an outer office, his secretary, a bottle-blonde bit of vinegar he calls 'Sunshine', has made me some strong coffee.

'We can run this one, I suppose. Up to a point,' he says, while I drink espresso, willing myself to ignore the nauseating admixture of chemical vanilla and odeur de Wragg. 'You'll have to tone it down, because all we've got is a portion of a will that may have been revoked and some barely recognizable photos of two people on a boat, and your 'source' isn't prepared to give us a proper story. We can't just start making accusations of theft.'

'Bollocks. Crap. The whole column is devoted to hint and suggestion. It's not as if we haven't sailed close to the wind before.'

'Not in a recession we haven't.' It occurs to me that Wragg is fearful for his job. Smug bastards deserve all the unsettling they get. I rejoice silently. 'One, this is probably perfectly legit, and we'll be farting into the wind. Two, if the paintings and the jewels and what have you were actually given to her, we don't have a leg to stand on, except a wages of sin story. Couple of column inches at most.'

'Fair enough,' I say. 'Slip her a couple of inches.'

'Very funny.'

'Come on, Wragg. She's big news – especially as she's doing a Princess Di act at the moment. Say, now. Suppose I could find you a tape of her chatting up a hit-man? Planning to bump off our recent celebrity Knight?'

'You mean one you haven't faked up in your own living room?' Wragg's default mode is scorn. 'You've got above yourself, Bello, like you did with the drunken ramblings of that so-called whistle-blower on *Sort It!*' I take this abuse because I can see from a glint in the piggy eyes that he's taken the hit-man bait, even if he won't admit it to me.

'It was a good story and it rattled a lot of chains,' I say. 'It's not as if burden of proof is the business of this godforsaken column...' It was frustrating: that near-exposure of the *Sort It!* shenanegans prompted Mehmet to withdraw – in effect it played into *Sort It!*'s hands. Win some, lose some. You have to be a bit philosphical.

'Good luck, Bello…' Wragg leans back in his chair. It's one of those big black leather semi-rocking jobs on springs. His weight nearly tips him backwards. He bounces back. It is almost funny. 'End of conversation. If I were you, I'd come up with something good and printable quite soon…' He makes a decapitation gesture under a larger than usual sneer. 'I'll keep this on file, I suppose, but I'd say you're losing your touch. Sunshine!'

'Sunshine' slouches in, takes the photographs from him, and slouches away wordlessly to the scanner in her own room. They say that Wragg applied successfully to Mensa, that he is a priapic womanizer in private life, that he once played a sweet and tuneful guitar, and that he was born above an abattoir. Only the last I can believe. Only the hell-rending squeals of throat-slit piglets in his formative years could possibly account for him. I open a packet of chewing-gum – in the absence of a cig, only strong menthol can help me through the next few inevitable minutes in the stygian atmosphere of his office – and I spread the real reason for my visit on the table.

'What's this? I have a meeting in less than five minutes…'

I watch his fat face undergo some changes as he sifts the photos. The perma-sneer vanishes. 'Christ!' he murmurs. 'Sunshine!' he yells. 'Who took these?' he asks me.

'You know better than to ask me that, Wragg,' I say. 'You recognize the main protagonist, I gather. Now, if you don't mind, I'll be going…' I start to gather up the prints. 'These belong to me,' I remind him.

'Yes, of course – no! Wait. Don't go. Sunshine! Wait, Bello. We need to talk business. Sit down.'

54

'Angel – haven't you got anything to amuse yourself with?'

'Maybe. What're you reading, anyway?' Angel peers over Drex's shoulder.

'Mind your own bloody business and fuck off, will you? I'm waiting for a call.'

'My, my, we are in a strop. The *Sun*? Ay-oop! Not your usual style. Who's the babe? Looks sort of old fashioned, like Ursula Andress or someone in an old Bond...'

'She's Fairbrother's bit of trouble and strife. Recognise her?'

'Coo-er, so it is. Who's the old bloke?'

'Angel, please kindly vanish. Like fuck off. Like now...'

'Hnnn, hnnn!' But Angel prances away and makes himself scarce, leaving Drex to pour his own scotch and peruse the papers...

Oh, Lady Louise! Nice, nice speech at the NSPCC dinner! All those deprived kiddies can rest in their truckle beds assured that you, for one, are on their side. What a credit you are to Sir Jerry! So good to know that the wages of sin – the famous playboy's yacht and all the jewellery and pictures salted away in Swiss banks, not to mention the bijou island residence in the Caribbean – are long consigned to the (oh, sooo-o) interesting past, eh? But perhaps the Ginellis are on the point of staking an old claim? Watch this space...

I answer the phone on the fifth ring.

'Yes, I've seen it, ...' I say wearily. I'm resigned to the inevitable hysterics. The pictures don't amount to squit, of course, or at least not much squit, but they're recognizable enough to dent a skin-thin reputation. For a public avid to blame the woman trying to ruin their precious Sir Jerry, Lulu's 'interesting' past doesn't entirely square with the image that she'd most like to project now: all charity, children and noble suffering, and of course this is all grist to the mill. As for the Ginelli litigation hint, this is a bit more serious, and she's a bit upset, naturally.

'That piece of spite in Kinseyder!' shrieks Louise. 'This is going to ruin me! They've got it all wrong. What does it mean about the Ginellis' old claim? I don't owe them a cent! This is outrageous! And why *now*?'

'Search me, *bimba mia*. You're news at the moment, dollink. I did warn you about hostages to fortune, no?'

'It's so *unfair*,' she wails. 'Those Ginelli boys are total bastards. Giorgio's sons. They always hated me, the pricks. Now I'm just made to look like some gold-digging whore, and it wasn't a bit like that. Not one bit. The press have distorted everything! Giorgio and I were close at one time. In love. He gave me things. It's not a *crime*!'

'No. And, Lulu-babe, this isn't a great big deal,' I soothe. 'It's years ago. Ghosts of boyfriends past – or in this case, sugar-daddies. Nobody's perfect. The timing's a bit awkward for you, I admit, but it's nothing you can't ride out. Don't worry. *Sta' tranquila!*'

Indeciperable obscenities down the line.

'Louise. All we've got here is just these very tame shots of you sharing some quality-time with an elderly gent on a boat and a suggestion he might have – well, overpaid for services rendered. Get it in perspective. Anyone could have dug them up – they're in what's called the public domain, babe. These are old press photos. Someone was bound to hit on them sooner or later with the amount of publicity your impending divorce has been getting, let's face it. Call it the price of notoriety. Forget it. Trust me.'

More obscenities. Lulu is in a tremendous bate. I decide I've had enough, and pretend to hear someone in the background. 'Yeah, okay. Coming! Louise, sweet-ie, I've got to go. Business. Call me later, okay? Sorry…' I click the call off.

Later, of course, she calls again.

'I've had… had a message…' She sounds tremulous, scared. 'Can you come over? To Fulham? Now?'

It's two in the afternoon, and I don't have another appointment for another couple of hours or so. There are good reasons why I don't fancy going to Fulham however. 'That's a bit awkward, Louise. Can you make the Riverside office – say in about an hour?'

'Why not Fulham? I'm here!' I can almost hear her stamping her foot. The word 'brat' was invented for people like Lulu. Unfortunate in a child, tolerable if tiresome in a beautiful chick, and very, very unbecoming in an aging woman. If Louise is wise, she'll adapt her act before she acquires wrinkles and a dowager's hump.

'Just being cautious, dollink. You know, what you pay me for. I'd come away from Fulham, if I were you. Truly, I think it might be – *safer.*' I can't help it. It's irrestistible. 'Come to the Riverside. Better all round. *Brava!*'

'Ohmigod!' I hear her gulp. As well she might.

So I ring Lion and fix it, and in due course, Lulu turns up, dressed in jogging gear and shades, which is her idea of a disguise.

'Somebody sent me this!' She removes the shades, and it's obvious she has actually been crying. 'In the mail. It came to – to Fulham. I thought you might be able to – to, you know, detect something, tell me what it all *means.*' This babe's belief in my powers is truly flattering.

She gives me a brown envelope with a shaking hand. I remove an A4 size photocopy of some typescript and a couple of black and white prints from the envelope. 'This one appeared in the *Merc* this morning,' I say. 'And the *Sun.* How long did you say you've had these?'

'Just this afternoon. Lunchtime I guess. Veronica must have left it out for me. I don't know when it came. Look, there's no stamp. No date. Just my name. Oh, God! It means they've been to the house…to *Fulham!* Someone *knows.*'

'It looks very like it. But even so, this is stale, babe. It's already hit the press. It's a reminder, maybe, but no more. Ease up, I would.'

'Ease up? They've tracked me to Fulham, for Chrissakes! And look at the other thing! I don't understand at *all*! It seems to be a portion of Giorgio's will. Look at the back of it, for God's sakes!'

[222]

'Aah!' Someone has scrawled in an elegant, old-fashioned and somehow for-eign-looking hand: '*Maledetto, putanacia! Muori! Die, rattle-snake whore!*'

'It's mad, Louise. Mad and melodramatic. There's no demand, for a start.'

'I *know!* This is just the beginning. Oh, *Jesus!*' I've never seen Lulu so rattled. I mean, she looks shit-scared. 'At first I thought it was Jerry. Do you think it *is* Jerry? Trying to scare me? He might have got someone tracking my movements. Is this just one of his back-handers?'

I pretend to consider. 'Seems a bit unlikely somehow. Unlikely he would have got hold of this, for a start, if it's genuine, that is.'

'Ohmigod. Somebody wants to kill me! They know where I go! The Ginellis, Giorgio's sons. They – they're *Italian*, for Chrissakes. And they're out to get me! Oh, Christ! They've got the Mafia on to me! 'Maledetto' does mean curse, doesn't it?' Her voice is a horrified whisper.

'Yep. Sure does, babe. But I really wouldn't get too hysterical, if I were you. They're not demanding anything, except possibly the paintings and the pearl necklace thing. I suppose you don't still have them?'

Her hands fly to her neck as if checking. 'No! They were *presents* goddam it! They were *mine!* He gave them to me! I sold them when I was – was in *need*. He never said that he wanted them back! I was broke. I needed *money*.'

'Hmm,' I say, enjoying myself. 'Then you married old Jerry, didn't you? Look, it's possible it's a fake. Anyone could have written this, after all. We can't rule Jerry out, I suppose. How *is* old Jerry these days?'

'You ought to know that better than I do!' Lulu shrieks. 'What the fuck have you been doing, losing leads on him?'

'He's fizzled, dollink. Faded out. Living the clean life, apparently. Not my fault if he's decided to see sense rather than the pretty assistant.'

'He would! Bastard!' She's been pacing about, staring at the river through the picture window. Now she sits down in one of Lion's leather cube chairs and faces me, still sniffing a bit. 'Jerry! Shit, he's – he 's gone so stange, these days. He's not at all like himself… it's *weird!*'

'I expect it's the strain,' I say.

'I still think it's him! I think Jerry's working with the Ginellis! Oh, *God!*'

'Lulu, *bimba*… er… I've been making those inquiries, the ones you asked about.'

'You mean –?'

I draw an imaginary gun, aim and fire. At her head.

'*Jesus Christ*! Drop all that for God's sakes! I can't afford to be – to be – oh, holy *shit!*' The poor girl's losing her grip.

I hold out a hand. I can hardly resist her when she's like this, vulnerable, trem-bling. 'Come to bed, *tata mia*.' Lion's guest-room is at my disposal.

'I can't – I'm too wound up, antsy.'

'I've got you safe, babe. Come on to bed.'

More reluctantly than usual, she does.

'Better?'

'Uh-uh.'

[223]

'*Brava!*' I kiss the tip of her nose. 'You know, dollink.'

'Mmm?'

'You're not going to like this, but I'd really be inclined to make things up with old Jerry if I were you. Heal the breach, if you get me.'

'You cannot be *serious!*'

'Oh, but I am. Think about it. With a united front, you can ride this out. I think this present crisis calls for some staunch family values.'

'What? You've got to be *kidding!*'

'Just think about it, babe. Remember your hero Charles the Second and Catherine of Braganza?'

'Who?'

'His wife. He was shagging anything that moved and your heroine Lady Castlemaine was getting uppity and ambitious. But when push came to shove and they were after poor old Catherine's Roman Catholic guts, if you recall, he shielded her.'

55

It was the sort of news that exploded, briefly overtaking and displacing the economic crisis, global warming, Afghanistan, Iraq, a senior banker about to be hauled before the courts and an exciting new Open champion. It relegated the latest health bulletin of a cancer-stricken soap star to the inside pages, together with the marital problems of a certain well-known television personality. The picture was banned almost at once – but of course it got a massive coverage on what nowadays passes for the underground press. Push the right buttons, and you'll get the whole show if you're quick about it. But the story couldn't be suppressed, and the headlines, from the *Times*'s factual 'Dominic Mann in Brothel Scandal', to the *Mail*'s explicit 'Mann Exposed as SM Slave', to the *Sun*'s gleeful if illiterate 'Bottom's Up' – they all ran it one way or the other, although it was the *Mercury* ('Hit it, Mann, Hit it!') which had had the scoop and broken the story, picture and all, suitably cropped. It was this that had captured the butterfly attention of Louise Fairbrother, flicking through the papers for news that concerned herself in her bedroom in Wimbledon, where she was almost confined, being now too paranoid to venture forth except when accompanied by a phalanx of reporters on public display. This Dominic Mann had nothing to do with her, but the headlines were too lurid to ignore, and she became so absorbed that she didn't bother with the post, didn't sift the stack of mail in the handsome hallway, did not see the jiffy bag with no stamp and the neat lower-case lettering in felt pen, didn't see it, pick it up or examine its contents until several hours later... By which time – by four o'clock, in fact – the news exploded again, this time with the report that royal aide Sir Dominic Mann had gassed himself in his Berkshire garage.

'Bloody Norah,' said Angel. 'That's that perve from Polluty-Cough's! Done himself in, has he?'

'Angel, kindly fuck off. I'm trying to watch something.' *And now Afghanistan...* 'Bugger!'

'It'll be back at six. Or try Sky. Here's your tea.'

'What? Oh, cheers!'

'Beautiful?'

'What *now*, Angel?'

'I want to ask you something. No, look at me. You did that, didn't you?'

'Did what?'

'Killed him. Made him kill himself.'

'Oh, yeah. Sure. I frog-marched him into his garage in Hambleden or wherever it is under the nose of his wife, sealed the draught from under the electric automatic doors, sat him in his car, shoved a hose from the exhaust pipe up his mouth and a clothespeg on his nose and turned on the ignition in the Range Rover, while he just lay there like a comatose dog. Course I did, Angel. Like I can be in two places at once. Now, will you please vanish?' Drex was actually thrilled. He wanted to enjoy the moment in private.

'I didn't mean literally-like.'

'Stop pouting, stop trying to be clever, and fuck off or at least shut the fuck up.'

'You underestimate me, Drex,' Angel said, standing his ground. 'And – well, you're beginning to worry me.'

'Worry you? I can't see why. Any time now, Polutikowski's going to come unstuck, like I promised you.'

'I mean, you scare me.'

'Oh, buck up! Come on, little Angel-mine. Frankly, you're beginning to make me feel like Doctor Frankenstein. Work that one out, if you're feeling sophisticated. Now will you please leave me in peace?' He began to flick channels.

'Oh, very scary! I suppose you knew this one at uni too.'

There is no comment from the Palace at this stage concerning the death of Sir Dominic Mann, the newly knighted royal aide who was found dead earlier today at his home. Foul play is not suspected, and police are not looking for...

'The proper word is 'university', and, as it happens, I knew this specimen at school.'

'School! Puh! I hated school. Everyone called me 'gaylord' and I spent most of my time bunking off down the pool hall.'

'Playing pool?'

'Well, sort of. More like fishing, really,' Angel giggled.

'Did you learn anything?'

'Fuck off! Did you?'

'I learnt a great many valuable lessons, actually.'

'But didn't you hate it?'

'Some of the time, Angel. Some of the time. With a vengeance.'

56: January 1969

Lights out, Junior Wing, Percy House, Camfield School, Somerset…

'Just stop calling me Bogger. I mean it.'

'He wants us to stop calling him Bogger, Fleas.'

'So he does, Woodlouse.'

'So we can't keep on calling him 'Bogger', can we, Fleas? Not if he doesn't like it.'

'Yes we bloody well can, Woodlouse. I mean, why not?'

'Well – sharing a room and all that. And it's not his fault he's Irish. Or a bit of a barbarian, come to that. I mean to say.'

'It's not our fault they pushed him into our dorm, come to that, Woodlouse.'

'Not his fault, either, Fleas. Be reasonable. And don't forget he's L A M E…' This last spelt out in a stage-whisper.

'S'pose not. Puh! It was still going to be better without him. And his accent really stinks, Woodlouse. I can't understand an effing word he says.'

'Oh shut up, Fleas, and stop being a twat. Look, Bogger – shit, sorry – what is your name?'

'O'Ryan.'

'Okay. O'Ryan. Look – O'Ryan. I'll explain. Him – he's Fleas, right, because his name's Freestone. Freestone, freebags full, flea bags, fleas – get it? And me, I'm Woodhouse, woodlouse? That one was too easy. But everybody does it here in Percy. Peter Warren's Bunny, of course, and Alexander Carter's Farter, and Chris Bell's Dinger, which's why we call him Dong, though…' The two boys were suddenly consumed in snorting giggles.

'What's funny?'

'Well, Dinger Bell's dong…oh, never mind. Don't think we can make anything out of O'Ryan, can we, Fleas?'

'P'raps not. O'Ryan… Pryin', tryin', cryin'…maybe not. What about his first name? What's your first name, Bogger?'

'Don't call him that. It's not polite…' More sniggers. 'Sorry, Bog – O'Ryan. What's your Christian name?'

'Andrew.'

'Andrew, Andrew…' said the boy called Fleas. 'I'm quite good at this. I'll have to think. Andrew…Andy Pandy…Android… Ah! Got it! Andrex! Bogroll – get it? Bog-Roll! Andrex bogroll! He can be Andrex!'

'Andrex,' sniggered the boy called Woodlouse into his pillows. 'G'night, Andrex!'

'Fuck that, you miserable cunt!'

'D'you hear him, Woodlouse? "Fock thot you mis'rible cont." What language does he speak, pray?'

It happened in what seemed like a single moment. The small room was arranged in ship-like bunks, the boy Fleas on top of Andrew O'Ryan's bunk, and the boy Woodlouse's divided from O'Ryan's by a night table. Andrew reached and grabbed the pyjama'd leg of the boy Fleas, and pulled him from his bed. He smashed his teeth on the ladder before he fell to the ground with a terrible yowl. The boy Woodlouse leapt from his bed on the other side and grappled O'Ryan over the moaning body of Fleas. Fleas, recovering, aimed a vicious punch at O'Ryan's groin, but caught Woodlouse's shin instead. More terrible yowls. 'You fucking Irish bastard – I'll –' 'No, I'll – I'll…!' 'You fucking swine!' 'You moron, it's *me!*' 'I'll fuckin' get the both of youse…' 'Ow, fuck, you've killed me, you cunt.'

'What, in the name of anything holy, is going on in here?' said a stately voice from outside the door.

'Oh shit, you've done it now, you fucking Irish prat. Here's Dreadlock!'

'Shhhh!' Fleas and Woodlouse scrambled for their beds, Woodlouse rubbing his shin. 'Get back into bed, Bogger, you bloody prat,' hissed the boy Fleas to O'Ryan. 'Who's Dreadlock?' asked O'Ryan. 'Robin Medlock – Dreadlock. Duty prefect. Soccer A team striker. He's okay.'

'Better than the Neanderthal.'

'A thousand times.'

'Who's?'

'Shhhhh! Get into bed, you stupid *prat!*'

'Well?' Silence. 'I'm coming in.' The dressing-gown clad figure loomed huge in the shaft of light from the corridor. Cigarette smoke billowed into the room. 'Well?' said the figure again.

'Nothing. Nothing, honest. A bit of a scrap that's all, Dreddy…'

'Yeah, really, nothing. It's a new boy. He was in Campion last term. We were just…'

'Honest, Dreddy, nothing. We'll be quiet now.'

'And someone's not in bed!' A large hand grabbed hold of Andrew O'Ryan's shoulder. 'And who are you?'

'I'm O'Ryan. I'm new. I was just…'

'Hmmm. Well, get into bed at once, O'Ryan. And you two – leave him alone, okay? I said, *okay?*'

'Okay, Dreddy.'

'So shut up. Now.'

'Okay, Dreddy. Sorry.'

'Playing with the second years, Robbie? I thought you had a mind above such things,' drawled another voice. The big sixth-former had been joined by another slighter figure, also in a dressing-gown, also smoking.

'I've got duty roster, worse luck,' said the young man now addressed as Robbie. 'And I'm supposed to be finishing an essay for the Crowe.'

'Okay. Why don't you leave this to me? Let's see, who've we got here? Freestone, Woodhouse and – well, then, now. A newbug. Who's this insect?'

'O'Ryan,' Andrew said. '…sir,' he added, and the other two boys sniggered behind their sheets. 'You don't say "sir" to prefects,' hissed the boy Woodhouse.

'Shut up, Woodhouse. My God, O'Royn, sorr, but that's quoit a brogue ye have t'ere, I t'ink! These two little bleeders showing you the Percy ropes, eh? Eh?' He gave Andrew's ear a vicious tweak. Andrew stood facing him, unblinking. 'Eh? It's only polite to answer when you're spoken to, O'Ryan.'

'I thought it was a rhetorical question,' replied Andrew. 'Sir.'

'You did, did you? A *rhetorical* question no less. Begorra, bejabers! I expect you t'ink yer very clever, don't you, O'*Royn*? Fucking hell, answer me, will you?' This second prefect still had hold of Andrew's ear, and now he twisted it again, very sharply. Andrew's eyes, watering involuntarily, continued to stare at him. 'Fucking *hell!*' said the prefect, letting go of the ear and slapping Andrew's face instead. Andrew backed awkwardly onto his bed, dodging the ladder.

'Dom...'

'My God! See this!' the one called Dom cried. He was a thin, whippy-looking youth of about seventeen, his cruel good-looking face marred by serious acne. 'It's lame – look! Look at its foot! It's a goat! God, that's just gross!'

'Hell, Dom – leave it out,' said the prefect they called Dreadlock. 'Come away, for God's sake. Now you lot, lights out and belt up or it's detentions all round. Come on, Dom...' He pulled at the other young man's sleeve.

'I don't,' said the prefect addressed as Dom, showing his teeth, 'tolerate *attitude*, especially in little lame bog-crawlers like this one. I mean, are they letting in total riff-raff, or what? You haven't seen the last of me, *O'Royn*, believe me.'

'Oh, come *on*, Dom!' The door closed.

'You're just soft, Robbie. These little bleeders need to be kept in line.' Their voices faded down the corridor with their footsteps. Three young boys listened in silence.

'Strewth,' said the boy Woodhouse, after an interval. He turned on a torch, beamed it at O'Ryan's face. 'You just don't do that to the Neanderthal, Andrex. You'd better learn.'

'He'll learn, all right,' said the boy Freestone, sounding pleased at the prospect.

'Why do you call him Neanderthal?' inquired the boy O'Ryan.

'Because his name's Mann.'

'Oh, I see,' said O'Ryan, seeing. 'It's not exactly witty, is it?' The Neanderthal's method of chastisement may have been violent – and O'Ryan's slapped face was smarting badly and his ear stung – but it had all the suggestion of anything but primitive.

'So? Being witty won't get you very far here,' said Freestone, sulkily. 'Perhaps they're witty in Ireland, Woodlouse. What do you reckon? Oh begorra, Paddy, that's so-o witty to be sure, to be sure.' He giggled stupidly. 'I say, I say, I say, what did the Irishman say to the Frenchman?'

'Shut up, Fleas. Look O'Ryan, this is for your own good. Neanderthal Mann's a serious sadist,' said Woodhouse, earnestly. 'He's a killer, the Neanderthal. He means it. You haven't heard the last.'

'No in-*deed*,' said Freestone. 'By the way, I feel a biggy coming on.'

'Too much information, Fleas! Take no notice of tossy upstairs,' whispered Woodhouse, turning off the torch. 'Listen, Andrex, I thought that was pretty impressive, I did. You facing out the Neanderthal. But it's true – oh for God's sake, do it in silence, you gorilla! He won't forgive you, and he's a sort of shark.'

'Is he now,' murmured Andrew O'Ryan, as the bunk above him shuddered to a halt. 'Well, we'll just see, won't we?'

It was inevitable, and it happened a week later. Junior baths, supervised by the large, florid, aproned woman known as Matron Percy. The harsh light, the chilly tiles, the row of basins, all chatter subdued in the frantic cleaning of teeth… Ten basins in all, shared between twenty-five boys, queueing. The new boy, of course, was last, and Matron Percy had her hands full, shepherding her young charges into their rooms, when Dominic Mann strolled up, leaned on the door-jamb, watching the operation.

'Evening, Matron.'

'Oh, hullo Dominic. I'd forgotten it was you on duty. Almost all done. Perhaps you could help young Master O'Ryan to bed when he's finished?'

'A real pleasure, Matron. You can count on me.'

'Thank you, dear. Come on, you two – off to bed,' said Matron Percy to Freestone and Woodhouse, who were waiting, pyjama-clad, clutching towels and wash-kits. 'You're done. Now!'

'Please, Matron, can we wait for Andrex – O'Ryan? He rooms with us,' said Freestone.

'No you can't. He'll be along shortly. You both go to your room.' She bustled out, shooing several boys in front of her, including Woodhouse, but the boy Freestone slunk behind, hung back in the corridor, peeping through the door, watching…

Dominic Mann ignored the boy brushing his teeth at the basin and slid into one of the lavatory cubicles. Timing perfectly the moment when the tap stopped running, Mann emerged on silent feet, grabbed Andrew's arms from behind and pulled them up behind his shoulder-blades in a neat and paralysing full nelson, frog-marched him into the cubicle he had just vacated and, holding Andrew's wrists with one hand in a wiry grip, slid his other arm across the boy's middle and folded him over, as easily and as neatly as a piece of card. In seconds, O'Ryan's head was in the lavatory bowl.

'Now, you vile little shit – or should I say shoite? Eat it! Eat it, you little piece of excrement! You think you can give me crap! Well, here's some for you!'

Andrew's face – his mouth, his nose – entered the foulness: the pale green urine, a large sausage-shaped turd. He gagged and struggled, but Mann's hand was an impossible weight on his skull, pushing him down. Acrid fluid entered his nostrils. He was helpless. And for a brief moment he thought he might literally drown, forced to suck up Dominic Mann's effluent into his lungs… He used all his young strength to heave himself backwards, push the bigger weight away, tried to cry out. Then his sudden pinkish puke curdled with the green, the brown…

'Oh dear, dear! Our supper. Rice pudding and jam, by the look of things. What a shame. Now apologise.' Mann pulled the boy's head up above the mess by his curly hair. 'Apologise,' he hissed again.

'Never!' cried Andrew, his head half-turned. A stream of vomit splashed onto Mann's white shirt, egged over the belt of his trousers.

'Why, you revolting little –'

'Master Freestone, you should be in bed! I told you ages ago! Now then, all

[230]

well in here?' Matron Percy – his saviour, had O'Ryan known it – bustled into the bathroom. 'Have we finished our chores?'

Mann skipped smartly out of the cubicle, and Andrew was released. 'Fine now, Matron,' Andrew heard Dominic Mann say smoothly, only slightly out of breath. Andrew, suddenly released, fell backwards. 'I'm afraid young O'Ryan has been a bit sick… we didn't quite make it to the lav.'

'Oh dear, poor old thing. Never you mind now, Dominic. I'll see to him. Oh dear, look at your poor shirt! That's the nice one your mother sent from India, isn't it? He must have been poorly, poor little lad. Take it off at once, dear! I'll see it gets into the laundry. Goodness me, what a nasty mess!'

Andrew straightened himself, wiped his mouth and flushed the lavatory, emerged from the cubicle. 'Here he is! All better, Andrew?'

'I'm okay now, thank you, Matron,' he said faintly.

'Not going to be sick again?'

Andrew shook his head.

'No san for you tonight then, let's hope. Let me feel your forehead… no, no fever, that's the main thing. Far too early in the term for flu bugs! Too much pudding, probably, knowing you youngsters. Nothing nasty on your pyjamas? No? Well that was lucky. Now then, thank Dominic for being so kind and taking care of you, and off you pop to bed. I'll see you settled in just a minute. Give me that poor shirt at once, Dominic, and you'd better go back to Senior Percy and have a shower, dear…' Mann's fastidious fingers began to undo the buttons. 'Say thank you, Andrew.'

Andrew O'Ryan stared up at his enemy. 'Thank you, Dominic, for taking care of me so kindly. I shall never forget it as long as I live,' Andrew said formally, fixing Mann with his unblinking, inky stare.

'Well, isn't that a nice little speech, and said in such a lovely lilting voice,' said Matron Percy, beaming. Dominic Mann turned and left. Meanwhile, Fleas had hopped back to his sleeping quarters and was telling Woodlouse all about it, and it was with a new respect that Andrex was greeted back into their shared room.

57: Last Summer

'Darling, I'm so sorry. You don't want me to?'

'No! No, thank you.'

'But – ?'

'Jerry, stop. Please. I'm not in the mood either. Not any more.'

'Oh, darling, I am so sorry...' Jerry turned onto his back in the semi-dark of the curtained room, wishing he still smoked. The assignation had been intended to amuse, create a diversion from his teeming troubles, even to revive a flagging interest. He, perfectly legitimately, heading off to his Barbican bolt-hole after a working lunch; she, joining him in the late afternoon, Friday casual with a brief-case, simply letting herself in with the key he had given her... But he was almost grateful that his treacherous body had let him down.

'It's over, isn't it?'

'Oh Suzy! Love, I'm sorry. It's not usually like this, you know that.'

'I know. That's not what I meant. It just *is* – I can sense it. So can you. Obviously.'

'The odd – the odd failure can happen any time. I'm sorry. Too much on my mind, I guess. Oh, darling, try and understand a little. I'm not – things are a bit... I really don't want to cause you unnecessary pain, Suzy.'

'Unnecessary!'

'I'm more than aware that I've made things very difficult for you, love. You've had to work for me, all the subterfuge... But it's been...this has been – well, it's been the nicest thing to happen to me in a very long while, Suzy. Don't ever forget that, please. Try not to think of me as a shit. Please.'

'Past tenses! Wow!' It might have been a giggle or a sob, and she compressed her lips and screwed up her eyes, willing the tears not to fall. 'So it is over. No. I don't think of you as a shit, Jerry. Just a little boy in a sweet-shop.' The tears ran anyway.

'Oh, God. I have been a shit. Don't cry. Look, darling – Suzy – I want you to know that I'll do anything to help you in your career. It's not fair that... Well – I mean I can help, or at least I'll try. I can pull strings. You've been absolutely the best PA I've ever had, and I mean to say so, Suzy, properly, in the right quarters.'

'Don't make it even worse, Jerry.' She was actually laughing now, a harsh, brittle, ironic sound, uncharacteristic. She was also getting out of bed, and when he looked up at her, she had pulled on the jeans and thrown on the sweat-shirt top she'd arrived in, and was scraping her hair into a clip. 'You don't have to do anything, as a matter of fact, Jerry. I was going to tell you next week, but now's good enough. I'm resigning. I've already told Lynne.'

'Suzy?'

'Yes, I'm sorry, Jerry. I've enjoyed *Sort It!* no end, but I'm going to be joining *Round Britain* as an anchor presenter. I've been head-hunted. It's official.'

58

'Ay-oop, Lady Louise! Get a load of this. A voice, rather high, with a strong region-al accent, Northern British, she thinks, gives way to a pause, a crackle, and then another voice. A voice she knows intimately, in spite of the distortions: 'I suppose you mean I might have him killed. Rubbed out. Of course I've thought about it, believe me...' Crackly pause. 'You're not shocked? Of course I've thought about it. But I thought it was a bit drastic. Anyway, I don't know any of the right people. You can't just look hit men up in the Yellow Pages. Can you?' Another pause. 'Do you? Know people, I mean?' Pause. 'How much? Theoretically?' Pause. 'Perhaps it's too much of a risk...I mean I – one – would be in their power for one thing. And it is a bit well, extreme. Silly, maybe. No. It's absurd, isn't it?' A laugh, her own. Then: 'No – yes. Okay. Do it, then. Inquire. Whatever it is I do, I've got to do it first.' Then the first voice, impossible to tell if it was male or female: 'Oo-er...Nasty, nasty. You'll be hearing further.'

A moment of frozen hysteria. Then she plays the thing over again. Is there enough to incriminate her? She does not know, and feels too panicked to consider the matter rationally. It is recognizably her own voice. She remembers the conversa-tion, the who, the where. Frantically, Louise punches 'call' into her mobile. The number rings and rings before cutting out, inviting her to leave a voice-message. No! She punches in a text. 'Call me!' Adds 'PLEASE' in capitals. Flings the CD into the bin along with used tissues, bits of cotton wool. Fishes it out. It is far too big to flush down the lavatory pan. She is about to stamp on it with the heel of her velvet mule shoe. No point. This is a copy, and there will be others. The brown envelope, addressed simply to her – lady fairbrother – in lower-case let-ters printed in felt-tip, lies on her dressing-table. Thinks again, furiously. Buries the disc at the bottom of her bag. Takes it out, buries it at the back of a drawer containing underwear. Runs to the bottom of the top-floor stairs. 'Dorota!' she shrieks. 'Dorota!'

The children are all at school. Perhaps Dorota is out too. She listens intently. She can hear some noises downstairs – Mrs Wylie in the kitchen, probably. She takes big, deep breaths. Forces herself to calm down. 'Dorota?' Her voice is a sing-song now. Sounds from upstairs, where the children sleep and where Dor-ota has her own self-contained bed-sitting-room. She is damned, she thinks, if she will actually go up and knock on Dorota's door, and clutches the bannister to prevent herself from running upstairs. 'Dorota?'

'Did you call me, Madam?' The girl appears, dressed in jeans and a bright em-erald sweater. 'I am tidying the rooms of the girls. You want something?'

'Yes, Dorota. Will you come down here for a moment?'

'Of course, Madam.' There is something in the way this girl says 'Madam' (she has always refused to address her as 'Louise', although she happily calls Jerry 'Mr Jerry') and in her demeanour generally, which grates on Louise. There is an insolence she cannot put her finger on, although Dorota is careful always to be correct, polite. She feels her irritation rise, but as at this moment Louise wants Dorota to be as cooperative as possible, she softens her tone as much as her agitation will allow.

'Dorota, I'm sorry to interrupt your morning. It's nothing really – me being very silly, I guess. Did you bring in the mail this morning?'

'Of course, Madam. As I always do.'

'And did you see the mailman?'

'I never see the postman, Madam. He is always too coinciding with the school-run, and he leaves all the post in the box by the gate. As usual, on my return, I collect it and bring it in the house. I have the key.'

'So you didn't see who brought this?' Louise produces the jiffy-bag.

'No, Madam.' Eyes, ice-blue, free of make-up; eyes which might be defiant, challenging, or merely honest. Eyes which do not like her, seem to despise her.

'It – well, it's just a little weird, that's all. It didn't come through the ordinary mail, I guess. No stamps. Do you remember any others like it?'

'Perhaps, Madam – one or two. But you see, I only check to see if there is anything for myself, and then I just bring everything in the house as Mister Jerry has asked me to. I do not examine it.' No mistaking the challenge now. It is as if Louise were accusing the girl of something.

'Thank you, Dorota. That's quite right. But this – this envelope – it was with the rest, this morning, as far as you know? I mean, it didn't arrive later, or anything?'

'No, Madam. There has been nothing else so far. I brought the post after I took the children to the schools. I can look again now, if you wish.'

'No! I mean no, that's okay, Dorota. Don't bother. Jerry's so famous that we get some stupid things come to the house.' She even manages a casual little laugh.

'Not to the house, now, Madam,' says Dorota, ever literal-minded. 'Not since Mister Jerry had the electric gate twenty-four-seven. Always, there is no-one admitted into the drive and the letters come always to the gate.'

'Yes. And there are the cameras too…' She murmurs this almost to herself. 'Thank you, Dorota. That will be all. I'll get my husband to check.'

When Dorota has gone back upstairs, Louise, her heart pounding, extracts the disc from its hiding place. She realises that in her haste she will have obliterated any finger-prints, and swears. Then she realises that, in the ordinary way, she could never present this thing as evidence. Bile rises in her throat, and she almost throws up. Then she obeys her first instinct – she tries to pulverise it – it is surprisingly resilient – under her heel, and then in frustrated rage, snatches it up and snaps it into pieces, cutting her hand, cursing, puts the splintered plastic mess into the bin, drips blood onto the fluffy white rug. Runs her hand under the cold water in the bathroom…watches her own blood run down the white porcelain…finds a band-aid and applies it, shakily. Then she tries the number again, the one she tried to ring before. The same invitation to leave a message. She pauses over Angus's number, decides against it. For now. Then, while her bath is running, holding her head in her hands, rocking herself with fear, she sits on the edge of the bed and tries to think straight.

[234]

59

It was the next communication that decided her. It had been slid under her bedroom door, written on a torn out page of a school exercise-book, and enclosed in a white envelope that was simply addressed to 'Louise'. There was no doubt, this time, of the identity of the author.

I HATE you. I would rather be eaten alive by sharks than go ANYWHERE with you. If you make me go to America I will kill myself first and tell the Daily Mail. *I hope you die in a horrible accident. I hope this makes you afraid and gives you nightmares every night. Signed: Your ENEMY!!!*

A soft tapping at the door. He barely registered it. He was listening to a Beatles anthology CD and playing a word-game on the computer – you had to fill in as many words in a bare couple of minutes from the first three given letters and not make more than three words of the same letter-length. It was more difficult and tactical than it looked, not merely a matter of thinking of words. It was absorbing, a welcome distraction from the notes he was composing, the draft of an official letter to the light entertainment controller, the man ultimately in charge of *Sort It!* and *Step on UP.* This had not been an easy decision, and the outraged voice of his agent, Shelley Tasker, was still ringing in his ears. 'But Jerry!' she had cried. 'Think of your *career!*' 'I'm thinking about more than that, Shelley. I'm thinking about my life.' Shelley had retired for all but a handful of favourite clients. She had taken it personally.

The tap became a little louder. 'Jerry? Can I come in?'

'Louise! I'd no idea you were here! Good grief!' Jerry snapped off the computer and turned the music down. He was disconcerted – she so seldom sought him out, and his den was almost never penetrated by anyone else except Charlie. 'I thought you were out.'

'No. I'm here.' She was wearing a long gathered robe in soft lemon and sage swirls he remembered buying her in Ibiza several years ago. Her dark golden hair fell over her shoulders, and her face was almost naked. It was still lovely.

'Come in, do! Do you – would you like a drink?' Suddenly, he felt he had to play host. Felt awkward. His own glass of red wine was at his elbow. He remembered she hardly drank. 'There's some Perrier, or there's some Alsace white. Very light, Alsatian, but it doesn't bite, you might say, or some of of that Gaillac Perlé – you liked that – I can get it from the cellar in a jiffy.' He was blathering.

'I'll have some of whatever you're having, if it's nice.' She seemed unusually subdued.

'Sure – of course. Look, sit down...' She sat. He poured. She was part guest, part intruder, and there was a certain novelty. 'Here. This red is actually rather fine, I think, very smooth... Well?' She sipped, cautiously, watching him, and he watched her. They were almost like strangers, but not, and he trusted her so little.

'It's lovely, Jerry. French?'

'*Oui, madame.* Buzet.'

'Boozy, huh?' Her eyes gazed up at him from under her lashes, mournfully flirtatious.

'Not very.' He grinned, but bells jangled in his head. 'I brought a couple of cases over after Easter. I rather enjoy it. It ought to be dinner-party fare, but, well, it doesn't keep.' He went to refill his own glass.

'It's good. Very smooth as you say. Jerry? Jerry – about La Bastide. And dinner parties...' She was watching his back, large and solid in its big blue casual shirt. 'Jerry?'

When he turned, he saw that that her face was cast down and that she was biting her underlip. She was never this submissive. His heart hardened. 'Why have you come, Louise?'

'We – we have to talk, Jerry. I – I got this. This morning...' She passed him the envelope with a hand that trembled slightly. He took out the contents. Read the careful, still childish lettering: half joined-on, half print.

'But it's Charlie! Charlie. *Christ*, Louise!'

'I know. It's horrible. Ha – has he said anything? Charlie? To you?'

'I'd no idea he was quite this troubled if that's what you mean! Oh, God. Dorota said he'd been having nightmares, wet his bed a couple of times. Bloody hell, Louise! Poor *kid*.'

'I *know!*'

'I was afraid something like this would happen. Shit!'

'We have to do something, Jerry. I –'

'Damn it! This is *your* shit, Louise. Threatening to drag the kid to America!'

'You're – you're right to be angry. Oh, Jerry, Jerry – where and why have we gone so *wrong*?' She looked up with anguished eyes into his face.

'We? Are you *serious*?' He had rounded on her, Charlie's letter still in his hand. She realised he was furious, his jaw working. She shrank back instinctively.

'Oh, Jerry, don't! I'm so – so *sorry*! I mean *poor* little Charlie, poor baby!'

'*Sorry*? You're sorry? Louise – words – words *fail* me. You poison this house, create an atmosphere of threat and loathing and – and – *stink* – and you turn my kid into a nervous wreck! Talking about killing himself! When did you last talk to him properly, eh? Talk to 'poor little Charlie'? Eh?'

'He – he won't let me talk to him, Jerry. He's so – so *hostile*. He only ever confides in Dorota if he confides in anyone at all. It's so impossible now.'

'And you're surprised? Jesus Christ!'

'Jerry. Please! I – I'm so, so *sorry*...' Her tear-filled eyes left him entirely unmoved.

'Am I expected to believe you? That a pathetic letter from a troubled child you don't even like let alone love has moved your heart? I don't think you've got a heart, Louise. I did once. I was wrong. I am as anxious as you are to see this business finished, believe me. Louise... look, this won't work. I don't know what your game is, but it's far too late. Perhaps when you've finished your wine.'

'Jerry – Listen to me, please. Don't just send me away. I came down to talk to you. We have to *talk*. Everything's gotten so *crazy*, Jerry! And it's not as if you've been perfect. This isn't just me! You and that girl. I was so sick of being humiliated. Nobody just kicks me *over*, Jerry! I – I had a lot of anger to deal with. I just wanted to go back to the States, go home, take the kids, live quiet and be…'

'You'll take the kids away over my dead body, Louise. I'll fight you all the way and I don't care what it costs. I've sacked Angus Tremain as he's probably told you. He can work for you, but I've put a stop to all this mediation mularkey. You wanted war, and now you've got it. I suggest you get on with your packing and fight your lawsuit and make up your mind to leave – alone. You'll stand to get quite a decent whack out of it. Angus will see to that, especially now he's only got your corner to fight. As far as I'm concerned I'd be happy to pay you to just go.'

'Oh *God,* Jerry! Jerry, *please.* I – I don't blame you for feeling sceptical, for re-acting this way. I think – I think I've just been wanting to punish you, and all the time I've been just hurting *myself*… Oh, Jerry, I'm sorry. So sorry. Truly.'

'So now you think I've learnt my lesson, suffered enough, is that it? That Charlie's suffered enough?'

She sniffed and wiped her eyes. 'We've *both* suffered, Jerry. And of course the children are suffering, too. I've been thinking very seriously about all sorts of stuff, Jerry. I really do want to try again, if you, well if you…' Her eyes were huge, luminous. 'But I do realise you've probably got other plans. I suppose you want to get married.'

'*Married*?'

'The girl at the studios. I don't even know her name. Is it very serious?'

'Suzy. She's called Suzy. And it's over. It was never very serious, if you mean would I marry her after we divorce. She's a very nice kid. Sweet, gentle. A bit of a novelty for me lately. But frankly, Louise, I think you've put me off marriage for life.'

'Oh, Jerry, Jerry!'

'You should have been an actress, Louise. You do the humility bit quite nicely when you want to, don't you?' He gazed at her dispassionately. 'Frankly I think there's something you're not telling me.'

'That's not *fair*, Jerry! I'm being as straight as I know *how!*'

'Louise, you must think I'm a fool. I do read the papers, you know, watch Sky.'

'You mean Giorgio? But that was years before I met you, Jerry. You can't mean…'

'Don't be dumb, Louise. I don't mean the fact that you had a rich old boyfriend who gave you the …works, although God alone knows how you think you can plead poverty. No. I mean it's just obvious that the press has been mangling you, and now it looks as if you stand to lose most of the public sympathy you ever had, despite all this charity circuit farce. You've done your best to throw broadsides at me, at my career, and they've started to ricochet. I suppose trying to patch up our marriage is your idea of damage-limitation, like you tried it in La Bastide, and invited the press to the party. Well, isn't it?'

'Jerry! Oh, Jerry, how can you *say* that?'

'You mean I sound cynical? Oh, my dear, you could run an advanced course in cynicism. You don't want *me*. Which means something very bad must have happened. What is it? You might as well tell me.'

[237]

She twisted her fingers, ringless apart from her wedding band, gulped and chewed her lips into a grimace that could never be quite ugly on such a nicely-arranged face. But the face had gone very white. She really was in the grip of some powerful emotion, and he realised suddenly what it was.

'You're scared, aren't you? Seriously scared!' He could not help himself; the thought gave him a certain satisfaction.

She nodded, gulped wine on a sob. 'Yes.'

'Then tell me. Just don't pretend this is something it isn't.'

'You're so *mean*, Jerry! Oh, God. I'll tell you. I've been having – getting – hate-mail, Jerry. I mean, real *hate*-mail. Not just Charlie.'

'Oh. Is that all? I'd have thought it goes with the territory.'

'Jerry, you don't *understand*...' Her voice was a whisper. 'Someone is threatening to *kill* me.'

'Then you must tell the police. Report it.'

'No, Jerry, *no*! I can't – not yet. It might make things worse. I might have to. I don't know. I think I know who it is, and I'm *scared*, goddamn it! Scared! It – it sometimes comes to the house. To this *house*, Jerry – someone delivers it anonymously, not the ordinary mail. They actually come here, within a few metres of us! Oh, my *God!*'

'So our friend has got to you, too, has he?'

'What?'

'Oh, I get hate mail all the time. It comes here and it comes to the studios. Forget it or report it. That's what I do. Frankly, I thought mine were from you. I still do, for what it's worth. You, or someone working for you. Look, Louise. I've got an early morning tomorrow – interview with Isobel Archer on Radio Four. I've got to go to bed. We've got security gates and close-circuit, and I'll get Johnson to organize a twenty-four hour watch if you're that paranoid. The way I see it, if I can live with it, then so can you.'

'Jerry!' She stood up and suddenly threw herself into his arms. 'Oh, Jerry! It's *not* me! How *could* you believe that? Someone's – someone's attacking us both, Jerry, if it's true you're getting them too!'

'Louise – look, go to bed. Please. Nothing will happen tonight. Try not to get hysterical. It doesn't help.' He took her forearms and firmly held her away from him. 'Go away, Louise. Please just go away. We might talk some more tomorrow. Later, okay?'

With that she had to be content, and on a reluctant sob and a last silent imploring appeal, big tearful eyes staring into his face, she went, closing the door softly behind her. Jerry glanced at the draft of his resignation letter, deleted it, began another to Shelley Tasker, and deleted that. Then he went to bed, feeling exhausted, but sleep came fitfully and only after a long time. He had been so convinced that somehow Louise was at the back of his 'funny mail', as Ben Young called it; and to imagine it was Louise somehow kept it in bounds, contained, provided a nasty but perfectly adequate explanation. Now, Louise's histrionics notwithstanding, he was not at all so certain – she had seemed so genuinely bewildered – and the uncertainty polluted his sleep until the alarm woke him at five-thirty.

60

'Have you ever really wanted to kill someone?' Veronica strokes my face in the dark with a gentle finger. I've been telling her an edited version of my life. Truth and lies

'Yes,' I reply, truthfully. 'Haven't you?'

She has been telling me more about herself. Also suitably edited, I imagine.

'Yes. One of the warders at Holloway. I could have killed her without mercy, if I'd had the means. I'd have got life, of course, but at the time I didn't care much. I'd have gone to the scaffold or the chair or something if they'd offered it. Life was pretty bloody. But I didn't really mean that sort of thing. She was just uncompli-catedly vile. Enjoyed tormenting me for being a – well, a privileged druggy with a handle and a sentence… I meant… something else.'

Veronica and I have a lot in common. Jug, for a start. Vile mothers for another. 'Tell me.'

'My mamma. She used to call me 'the changeling' because I was big and ugly. I used to lie in bed – you know, as a kid, small – and I'd plot ways of killing her. Making her eat foxgloves or something poisonous. Stabbing her with a stolen kitchen-knife, running some nylon thread across the top of the stairs and watch her break her neck. And then I'd think – no. Killing her's too easy. I just really wanted to see her suffer, and then realise it was me, and then apologise. I suppose I just wanted her to love me. Pathetic, isn't it?'

'Not really.' Soft breathing. I run my hand over her shoulder. 'And then?'

'Well, nothing. I knew she would never see the point, just try to have me locked up. Then of course I did get locked up…that wasn't her fault, of course, at least not directly… And the book made her suffer up to a point. She hated it, and it made her squirm. But then – well, nothing. She'd never apologise, because she was far too busy being beautiful and shallow, and justifying everything. I blamed her so much for my father's death. I wanted to hurt her for him as much as for me. But I think – I think I mean that once I realised that I was so much cleverer than she is – it all seemed so wretchedly futile. I could never make her suffer what I'd suffered, because to do that, she'd have had to have been me… Oh, hell – does that make any sense?'

'Yes.'

'Andrew…' Her soft breath on my face.

'Yes?'

'Well, only that I don't want to kill anyone anymore. I'm too happy.'

At this moment, lying beside her, my fingers interlacing with hers, her warm thigh on mine, I want so much to be able to say the same.

61: 1986 'Outside...'

A crimson coat and a matching crimson beret, colours clashing resoundingly with frizzy coppery curls, elusive, disappearing into a taxi, round a corner, forever disappearing round a corner.

The man Todd – that is what it said on his passport – landed at Dallas Fort Worth with one aim in mind. He bought a local map, took a bus west towards Irving and got off at Inwood. He had breakfast in an old-fashioned diner, where the slovenly woman behind the counter addressed him as 'stranger', and the other customers, big men in denims and check shirts, eyed him suspiciously over their coffees and giant plates of waffles and bacon and talked in subdued tones mostly, he thought, about him. He asked the woman about car-hire.

'Better talk to Frank. Frank! Stranger wants a word about autos.'

Frank owned the gas-station next door where he kept some tourers for hire. 'Fifty dollars down, three days, bring her back full, okay, stranger? Say, you okay with that boot? She got a clutch, ain't she?'

'I'll manage. Thanks.'

Frank made a photocopy of Todd's licence at the back of a scruffy office and led him outside to a dilapidated Ford Granada. 'English, huh. Goin' anywheres partic'lar, stranger?'

'Rochdale. Is it far?'

'T'ain't far, exactly, stranger. But there ain't nothing doin' in Rochdale. Unless y'here specially...' The man Frank was squinting in the sunlight, sizing him up.

'Vacation. I want to look up some cousins of mine. The MacBains.'

Frank eyed the man Todd as if he did not believe him. 'MacBains, huh?'

'Yes. Know them?'

'That would depend,' the man said, spitting onto the tarmac, 'on which Mac-Bains y'mean. Could be a hundred a' more MacBains here'bouts. Say, fella – y'ain't the press are ya? The papers?'

'No. Should I be?' Some internal antenna twitched. He watched the man's face.

'Well, I believe ya, fella! Like I said, a hundred MacBains here'bouts.' The man Frank gave Todd a sly wink.

The man Todd got into the car and drove.

'Welcome to Rochdale.' It was impossible to tell where Harrison ended and Rochdale began. Both sides of the road had towering plastic signs like giant cocktail swirlers advertising burgers, drive-ins, motels... Downtown was just the same, a strip, but busier. Las Colinas Drive started smart from the turn off at Main Street, and became shabbier as he proceeded west. Number Two Thousand Five was a small, squat, low-slung modern bungalow building with a flat roof and aerial antennae set off the street behind dusty pines with no apparent boundaries at the front between it an its neighbours. A dog behind a fence in the next door backyard barked hysterically, throwing itself at the netting. He rang the bell. Varnish was peeling on the front door and at the window the blind was drawn. The place seemed deserted, but he thought he heard television voices from inside. He rang again and waited. A woman's disembodied voice from the next door house screamed at the dog, which kept up its lunatic noise. All my life, he thought, I have waited for this moment. He rang again. Waited.

He pressed his ear to the door. Heard soft, shuffling footsteps, and the drawing of bolts. Stood back as the door opened by a crack, a door on a chain. An elderly black woman in a checked overall appeared at the crack, eyed him. 'Huh?'

'Good afternoon. Does Rosaleen MacBain live here?'

'Who wants to know?'

'My name's Todd. I've got a message for her. From England.'

'She ain't here. And you ain't welcome.'

'Does she still live here?'

'None of your goddam business, stranger.'

'What about the husband? Hank MacBain? They live here, don't they?'

'You mean y'aint *heard*?'

'No,' said the man Todd. He took out a twenty dollar note and let the woman get a good sniff at it. 'I'd be grateful to know more, Ma'am.'

She eyed the twenty. 'Now I *knows* you's the goddam papers,' she said contemptuously. 'We don't need no bribes...' She started to press the door closed.

He put the note away. 'Sorry, ma'am. My mistake. Forgive me. I – I've just come in from England. If I could just have a word with Mrs MacBain...' He removed his sunglasses, and his eyes briefly met hers.

She held the door ajar. 'You *isn't* the papers?'

'No. I'm family. Truly. From England. I've just got in. Came up from Dallas this morning. I'd be very grateful to have a moment of your time. Please?'

'Since it happened, there's been papermen on the door-step, non-stop. Junior said to not let anyone in. Guess they'll tell you up at the Precinc' all ya wants to know, up back on Main Street, just ask for Dep'ty Frazer.'

'Please, I've come a very long way...' The heat was sweltering, beating down on his head, the back of his neck. 'Please, Mrs – ?'

'Mrs Jackson. Ya *sounds* English enough, I guess. Wesley!' She yelled over her shoulder. 'Wes!'

'Mrs Jackson, is – er – Junior here?'

'No way, no how. Ain't nobody here. Jus' me and Wesley, lookin' after the place. Wes! Wes! Shut off that goddam game!'

'Okay, Maw.' Suddenly a very large young man wearing a singlet and shorts loomed up behind the old woman, blocking all the light in the dim passage. 'He *says* he's family,' the old woman said succinctly. 'What d'ya say y'name is again?'

'Todd. Todd O'Ryan. Rosaleen MacBain's my – my aunt.'

'Ant, huh? She was called O'Ryan. Says he ain't heard,' she added to the enormous Wesley, who was staring, chewing gum like cud. 'Reckon he should go up an' see Dep'ty Frazer at the Precinc', that's what I say, if he wants the story.'

'Best let him in, Maw. I reckon so. He gonna frazzle sure out there.'

Under the beating sun outside, the man Todd indeed felt as if he might melt.

It was cooler – slightly – in the kitchen, and there was a screeky ceiling fan which pushed the stale air around. At the plain formica table, Todd removed his jacket and drank lemonade with ice gratefully. Once Mrs Jackson had decided to trust his credentials, she fussed over him, offered him rice-cakes with honey, and as much lemonade as he could drink. Wesley padded back to some inner sanctum to watch his game. He kept the volume down, however, and Todd had the impression that the apparently slow and lumbering Wesley would be on his feet in a second if he scented trouble in the kitchen. The old woman's story came jerkily, in bits. He had to piece it together.

'So Hank MacBain followed my – aunt – and her lover to the Crossways Motel at Inwood, and he shot them…and now he's in jail pending trial. And the lover is in hospital with multiple shot-wounds and he'll be the chief prosecution witness if and when he's well enough to talk. And my – my aunt Rosaleen is dead.' His thoughts were rioting. 'Yes. I see.'

'T'ain't a pretty story, Misser Todd. T'ain't up to me to judge people. I's jus' sorry for the sufferin',' said Mrs Jackson. 'I's real sorry, son. T'ain't pretty, no it ain't. It's Hank I feels sorry for, truly. I's worked for him since Junior was knee high. He'll go down, Hank, that's for certain-sure. Vietnam veteran, he is. My ole man, my young Wesley's pappy, they fought in the same platoon. Killed in sixty-nine, an' Wes only jus' stop' suckin', jus' before they was due home. Makes ya doubt the Lord. Hank's leg was all shot up. Did okay on the rigs after, did Hank, bein' an engineer, but he always had this temper. That crazy goddam Asian war! If they wasn't killed, they was wrecked. An' I ain't judgin', Misser Todd, and she was your ant, but that Rosie MacBain was enough to put the devil into a man.'

'I see. What about Junior? And the other kids, my – my cousins?' He hardly knew what he said. There was a new image now, a woman, red-haired, freckled doubtless as much on her naked body as on her face, a face contorted first in joyous ecstasy, then in horror, as the gimcrack motel door burst open and the shots shattered through her.

'Ain't kids no more, Misser Todd. Junior, he got kids of his own. Lives down in Harrison, wife, job with the Insurance. And Lee-Anne, she's on the airlines, gonna marry a pilot, or so Junior said.'

'What about Scott?' It was Scott, the new baby, who had finally displaced him. Maybe. Who could tell?

'Scottie? Too bright for his good, I say. Went to school, run off and went to the bad. Don't like to say this, Misser Todd, she bein' your own ant, n'all, but he took after his maw, I reckons. Went out west, California, joined one of them crazy hippie communes, so Junior says. Kinda disappeared. Say, now, maybe if you's got the time you might try an' find him. Tell him his Pappy's in big bad trouble, tell him to pray.'

'I will try,' said Todd on the doorstep, not meaning it, putting his thin white hand in Wesley's enormous black one, and submitting to a hug from Mrs Jackson, who wiped a tear on her overall as he climbed into the oven-like Ford, and watched him drive away forever from Rochdale, Texas, America.

[242]

62: Later, 1986

'Shelley Tasker recommended you. That is, she recommended Mike Coates. I'd rather hoped to see Mr Coates in person...' Drex was sitting in a dark office just off Grafton Street. That he was there at all indicated hope of a sort. On the other hand, it would have been lunch if the news had been at all good. The young man sitting behind the desk – a bit younger than himself, thin, bespectacled, a certain businesslike briskness belied by an obvious naïvety of the world – smiled a professional smile.

'Ahh, yes. Shelley Tasker. Well, Mr Coates passed this on to me. I've read it, Mr Bello. It's very good. Excellent, in fact. You write with a great deal of – verve. And style. The dialogue is great. But I don't think it quite works as it is. Not as it stands. I'm sorry. If you'd be prepared to consider some – er – modifications, we might – erm...'

'Modifications. Like what?'

'Erm, now. That's a good question. You see, basically, erm, basically – I loved *Plug & Socket*, by the way. Basically –' Young Adam Forster felt acutely uncomfortable. Here he was, in a position of unaccustomed power over someone whose work he had admired since he was a schoolboy, and he was turning it down. Moreover, there was something about the man – the shades, the unblinking eyes behind them – that he found distinctly disconcerting. He was rather cursing his senior colleague for this ordeal by fire.

'Basically?'

Forster took a breath. 'Basically, as it stands, *Jug* is far too dark, far too – well – druggy. We can't fly in the face of popular appeal, you know.'

'So you're not going to take it.'

'Not as it stands, no. Not for a popular comedy TV script. This is hardly *Porridge* after all. Basically, like I say, if you'd be prepared to consider, well, lightening it up?' The young Forster had an unconscious habit of cracking his knuckles.

'If I lighten it up, it would *be Porridge* with treacle on it. It's been done. This is meant to be darker. And it's not comedy, as such. This is satire.'

'I realise that. But it's my job to consider markets, I'm afraid. Look – Mr Bello – I did have one idea. If you were in effect to *darken* it – I mean, remove the obvious elements of comic absurdity altogether – we might run it by someone as a one-off. A late night drama, maybe. But I still think we can't have the hero, effectively, as a drug criminal. The world has – erm – well, changed its attitudes a bit. Erm - since – I mean...' It was no secret that Drex Bello had recently been in jail. Forster felt himself grow hot. 'I'm really sorry. I just don't think we could get anyone to buy it. The issues are a bit complicated. It appears to be knocking the penal system and endorsing crime. Ronnie Barker can get away with it, because his character is an old-fashioned cuddly burglar and it's all sort of cloud-cuckoo anyway. This is too – well, realistic. If you see what I mean.'

'I suppose I ought to be grateful you just said that,' said Bello, getting up. 'Well – thanks anyway.'

63: 1987, 88, 89...

What next, Veronica? They'd probably call it depression now. I'd call it being seriously pissed off and aimless. Also fairly broke. Drift. Deal a bit, quietly, professionally, sometimes with the Whisper, sometimes on my own. Mostly keep my nose clean. Submit a couple of successful band reviews to rock-music mags. Use this as an excuse to go and see the little Lion in action in Hammersmith. My protégé, in a way, but managed now by one Jake Durphry, the friend of a friend, who'd snapped him up after that spectacular win on *Step on UP* when it was Fairbrother's vote that had swung it. A red-letter day for Durphry, no doubt about that. This was the summer that Lion and the Boys were making it: a big hit under their belt with the TV winner, a number two in the British charts, a bullet in the American ones, and an album deal, complete with a single version of 'White Christmas' and 'Winter Wonderland' in rocked-up close-harmony, ready for the sentiment-market come December. Whatever could one say? In some ways, I felt responsible. 'Synthetic' was my adjective, I remember, but it was seriously hard to ignore the fainting, shrieking teenies; even harder not to refute, vigorously, the buzz-notion that these clean-looking, cocky young twerps with tight trousers, nice voices and no original material were the 'new Beatles'. An equally anodyne girl-band with a personalities gimmick was having the same effect: role models for an aimless generation. Enough to depress anybody. Wrote a scathing review of a book called *The Scene* for another rock-music mag. Got commissioned to do another similar hatchet job on a bad Stones biography...collected some sparse royalties from *Plug & Socket* re-runs...rewrote *Jug* as a novel. Watched the rejection-slips heap up. Watched TV and Fairbrother's relentless rocket to the middle of the road. Felt quietly sick. Went to see Gwil Jones as Laertes in *Hamlet* at the Young Vic – he was seriously good and, not being an actor, I felt genuinely happy for his success. Got hugged and kissed warmly backstage by a lot of Gwil's luvvie crowd, who were thrilled, apparently, to meet the silent member of the *Puke & Soddit* team. Got involved with a girl called Cindy who worked in the publicity department of a well-known *prêt-à-porter* fashion-house: a light-hearted affair, by which I mean there was no real heart in it at all...

So Cindy and I were having a post-gig drink on the South Bank, watching the river, like you do. Not much conversation, not even about the band we had just seen – a mediocre post-punk outfit that I was supposed to be reviewing. I was scribbling the odd note. Cindy wasn't the conversational type, and I wasn't feeling remotely chatty myself. It was enough that she was well-turned out, good-looking, good-tempered, compliant, and sufficiently incurious and self-contained not to ask questions. Dim-witted? Possibly. She liked doing nice things to my body in the privacy of her neat, sweet-smelling little flat in Pimlico, and she never wanted to *talk*. As far as I was concerned, this was one of her greatest assets, seriously restful. After four months, I had no idea who she really was, where she was born, whether she had sisters and brothers, whether she cared if Thatcher got in again, whether she had any dreams beyond doing herself up perfectly and using her work as a sort of showcase. She knew even less about me, except for *Plug & Socket* and my association with little Lion Barley, although I remained tactful about exactly how I had met him. And she could bend right over, from the vertical, and touch her toes, hold her foot at a right-angle like a robotic ballerina, holding a pose for seemingly ever, like one of those human sculpture acts… She was also squeaky-clean, as far as it was possible to tell. She never objected to my excesses, but she never asked to join me, and on my Cindy evenings, it was simply better for me to be as sober and sensible as she. She had met the Whisper once, by accident – it would never have been my doing, that – and he styled her 'Robot Woman'. He was pretty robotic himself, but he had a point: if one could have constructed a perfect humanoid female, Cindy would probably have been the result. She laughed carefully; I had never seen her weep; her orgasms (if that is what they were) were expressed in tidy little gasps of controlled breath.

Like I said, there we were, not saying much, an island of more or less companionable silence sitting at a picnic table in the teeming hubbub of a popular pub-garden on a balmy night in London in July. Suddenly louder voices, and she recognized a group of people who had wandered out. She waved. 'Drex – scuse me a minute, okay? That's Silvie and Carrie – back in a mo!' She weaved through the crowd, a tall, dark-haired chick with a big wide vacant smile and superb teeth, wearing black patterned tights and a black leather mini-skirt over very impressive legs which drew admiring eyes, and I felt nothing. Absolutely nothing. She could have vanished forever. I continued to stare at the river. The boats chugging. The runnels of oily foam behind them. The reflected lights in the black water. I suppose I had been vaguely aware of the promenaders below: holiday-makers, tourists, concert-goers, the constant background chatter. He spotted me before I spotted him.

'Andrew?'

'Yeah. My God!'

'I thought it was you. May I sit down?' He had his customary stick. He sat down on the wooden bench. He was hatless, and he looked older – greying, thinner. He ordered a pint of bitter from a passing waitress and offered me another. I accepted. He had been, he explained, to a production of *Cosi Fan Tutti*.

'You should have been in touch, Andrew.'

'I didn't like to, sir.'

'Less of the "sir".' By now it was a private joke. He smiled with genuine warmth, and something knocked in my frozen heart. It was good to see him. I owed him a great deal, after all, and he had always had the grace never to remind me. 'Why not, Andrew?'

I looked out over the river. 'Shame, I suppose. Leo.'

'I see. Unnecessary, really. I wish they'd just make it legal like gin, although one does hear of some rather frightful things. You didn't hear me say that, by the way…' The ghost of a twinkle. He had sent the odd book while I was in jail. Manners demanded I send brief notes of thanks. Since I had been out, I had avoided contact. 'What are you doing now?'

I told him. An edited version, anyway.

'I have followed some of your – er – work. I can't pretend to have liked that comedy about the two young men you did, but I gather it was very successful.'

'It's history, Leo. So is success, it seems. What about you?' I was not especially interested. I knew vaguely that there was a farmhouse in Italy. That he and the woman who might or might not be his sister presented chamber music concerts in a rose-garden. I had long since given up sending her cryptic messages in Jacobean play texts. Frankly, I couldn't have cared less now.

'I – um – I was very sorry to hear about – um – the tragedy in the United States. I would have written to you, but I didn't know how to find you. How appalling!'

'I never knew her,' I said, and we went silent.

Suddenly, we were surrounded by Cindy and these girl mates she had met. They sat down, a lively chattering flutter of scented femininity, all flamboyantly dressed, all slightly louder and more on display than the circumstances demanded. I was reminded of one of those plays in the round, in which actors emerge from the audience, as if by accident. I also realised that this was Cindy's natural home. I had never seen her so animated. I introduced her to Leo simply as 'Cindy Patterson' and let him draw his own conclusions when she briefly touched my hand. Cindy began introducing everybody else: Elvie, Carrie, Stevie… One of them, a smallish girl in a drapey silver-grey frock over rose-pink tights and Minnie Mouse platform sandals was familiar, from the papers at least, and remarkable, in that she was several inches shorter than her tall friends despite the footwear. She wriggled up next to me, budging me along the wooden bench as if she had known me all her life. 'And this,' Cindy announced, looking sublimely happy, 'is Silvie. Silvie Snape…' It all snapped into place. Silvie Snape, the teenage fashion model who had made *Vogue* and was being hailed as the new Twiggy in all the Sunday sups, tipped to displace Claudia, Naomi, et al, as queen of the catwalk. 'This is Drex Bello.' I said a general hello. Cindy whispered something into Silvie's ear, and Silvie said 'Wow!' and wriggled up closer. More drinks arrived, glamorous ones, daquiris, mojitas, margheritas… big frosted glasses with coloured plastic straws. Girls, very, very glamorous girls, sucking, giggling, winking at each other. Leo seemed boyishly chuffed to be in the midst of all this pulchritude, and I couldn't help being rather amused.

Silvie said to me in an intimate whisper, 'I've heard all about you! And I wanna meet *him*.' Mockney voice. A face that you couldn't exactly pin down: it was undoubtedly pretty, but you'd forget it in a second. The complexion was very young, poreless, and close up it was obvious there was almost no make-up on it. It was only her eyes – bluey-grey, almond-shaped, vividly alive with intelligence and mischief – that were compelling, and now they were focused, full beam, on me.

'Who?' I asked.

'Why *Lion*, stupid! Lion Barley! Cindy's been telling me everything! I've got like this gigantic mega crush, you know? I'm like I can't breathe! I've only seen him on stage, and you – you're actually his manager, and I'm like, wow!'

'Cindy's been exaggerating, I fear,' I said. 'I'm not his manager.'

'But you discovered him! It's like common knowledge!'

'It's true I knew him before he hit the big time, recognised his talents, all that.'

'Will you introduce me? Pleee-ease?'

I saw Leo watching us. 'I promise,' I said, 'to invite you to a lovely party, and you shall meet the lovely Lion in person. There.'

'Wow, that'd be *bliss*! Do *you* know Lion Barley?' she asked Leo, giving him the same full-on treatment she'd been giving me. 'Sorry – didn't catch your name... Wow! You know you look just like Leslie Howard in *Gone With The Wind*.'

'Leo Rollitt.' He smiled politely and looked a little non-plussed, as well he might.

'Leo prefers Mozart.'

'Oh! Well, there's this really *lush* boy-band – LifeBoyz – but Lion's the only one who counts, ain't that right, Drex? They won this TV talent thing, and now they're really hot to trot. On TV all the time *and* a number one! You *must* have heard of him!'

'Leo's mostly in Italy these days,' I explained. 'Don't suppose he sees much English TV, do you, Leo?'

'Andrew is right. Very rarely, I'm afraid. The news, sometimes. I'm rather out of touch with things, my dear. Silvia, isn't it?'

'Ooh, get your *voice*! Silvie, just call me Silvie.' I could see that young Silvie Snape was a serious little operator. She obviously thought she was in the presence of Somebody – and Leo was pure 'gent' from his thinning fairish hair and smoothly shaved chin to his well-made shoes. Obviously he was nothing to do with show-business, but equally obviously he was a friend of mine, and she did not know quite what to make of him. It was all highly amusing. 'Tell me about yourself,' she said, leaning across the table and giving him the whole of her vivid attention. 'What do you do? In Italy?'

'Let's see now...' Leo was amused too, playing her game. 'I play piano for fun. Classics, but Cole Porter and Gershwin, sometimes. I used to give lessons.'

'Wow! Do you do concerts?'

'Every now and again. Very quiet affairs, mostly. Just friends, nothing grand.'

'Is your piano grand? I mean, have you got a lovely grand piano?'

'I have a small Bechstein.'

'Coo...*lush*.' Leo could have told her his piano was a small Bentley. The effect was just as galvanic. Silvie was mesmerised. 'What about your house? Is it near Tuscany?'

'In Tuscany, as a matter of fact, my dear,' said Leo. 'Between Florence and Siena.'

'Wow! And big grand gardens? Roses? Jasmine 'n' stuff, lemons, all that?'

'Jasmine and lemons,' agreed Leo solemnly. 'We have to bring the lemons in in the winter, because it gets too cold. There's a sort of brick and glass conservatory where the lemon vases go in the winter-time.'

'Wow... Have you got a pool n' stuff?'

'Not yet. I can't afford a pool, my dear. Not rich enough, I'm afraid.'

'Go on!' said Silvie in frank and comic disbelief. 'Are you open? To the public?'

'We sometimes open to the public,' Leo said. 'There's an organization a bit like the British National Trust, and they run tours round places of interest. And we have concerts in the garden sometimes, too. Small orchestras, singers and so on.'

'Mozart,' said Silvie with a grin. She was flirting outrageously.

'Mozart. And Bach and Schubert.' He was flirting too, in his dry way.

'Wow,' said Silvie again. 'I just love Italy. We're off to Milan for the shows in September. Say – do roses flower in September?'

'Yes,' said Leo. 'Rather well, very often. August is too hot, but they get a sort of second wind when it's a bit cooler. Are you interested in gardens, my dear?'

'Very, right this minute,' said Silvie. Then a peculiar little frown crossed her smooth little brow. 'Hang on, Leo! Cindy! Cind!' Cindy looked up from what was obviously an hilarious conversation with Elvie, Stevie and co. 'Cind! Come here! Lissen!' Cindy, summoned, got up. 'Guess what!' said Silvie without preamble, grabbing Cindy's arm. 'This lovely guy here – Leo Roland – sorry, Rollitt. I'm useless at names. He has got this fabulous Italian garden with roses, lemons, jasmine, the lot!'

Leo looked politely non-plussed again. Smiled at Cindy, who also went 'Oh. Wow!'

'Lemme explain, Leo! I'm a model, okay? We want to do this really special shoot for the spring stuff, and the colours are all rose pastels and lemon. We're looking for a garden, right Cindy? It can't be England, cos it always pours, and we'd got somewhere lined up near Milan, but they've just let us down, a real bummer. But if we could do it in your garden instead – then that would be perfect, wouldn't it? What'd you say, Cind?'

'Better talk to Elvie,' Cindy said. 'Elvie's locations,' she added, rushing back to where Elvie and Stevie were receiving another tray of exotic drinks. Silvie dashed off after her, and the girls all went into an excited huddle, chattering, pointing.

'Have you any idea what this might be about?' Leo said to me, *sotto voce*. He still looked amused. That was what was endearing about Leo – this ability to be a spectator on the world, have fun with it in his dry buttoned-up way, without judging or condemning it. 'What's a shoot? They don't mean hunting, do they?'

'I have a feeling,' I said, 'that they might try to persuade you to allow them to photograph some fashion models in your Tuscan garden.'

'You're joking!'

'No, I'm serious. It would all take about three days, and they'll pay you a stack. If you could bear the disruption, I'd think about it. And don't let them sell you short.'

'But I haven't the faintest idea how much to charge. And that's even if – I mean, it wouldn't be entirely up to me. A garden magazine came and did a – well, a write-up, took some nice photos. But they didn't pay us, or at least not much.'

'These will,' I assured him. 'They'll mention a figure. My advice would be to stick out and double it.'

'Oh dear God. We – I shouldn't want any adverse publicity.'

'I think they wouldn't need to mention the location at all if you didn't want them to. This would be all about young fashion styles with your garden as a backdrop. But you could probably afford the swimming pool.'

'Well, well! I think you had better be my manager, Andrew.'

So it was that, a couple of months later, a tribe of fashion models, photographers, and an entourage of publicists that included yours truly as Cindy's escort along for the ride, with an *arrière pensée* to ensure fair play and good behaviour and, if I am to be entirely honest, with motives of sheer base curiosity – turned up *en masse* in Leo's delightful rose-garden in the Chianti Valley.

64: La Casa del Ruscello, September 1989

'Darling, I *know* they're paying us a small fortune. It's very welcome. But *they* aren't exactly. I don't want to have to entertain them. I don't want to *see* them, even! Sorry.'

'Lottie, dearest. They arrange their own catering, and they'll all be gone by Saturday. You could always just go to Florence for a few days and avoid them all.'

'I could, Leo dear, but I'm just terrified the garden will be damaged. Umberto found cigarette butts everywhere this morning, fussing about his lawn. And Marisa told me they'd been really uproarious in town last night. This is our local reputation, dear, for heaven's sake. Everyone's so quiet and conservative, and we've landed them all with a bunch of wild young things from London, demanding entertainment at all hours, as if they were in Milan or Venice. Bianca was positively sniffy this morning. I can't possibly just desert the ship, can I?'

'You could, dear, if you were prepared to trust me not to make a cock-up of things. I have to say that I trust that director man, Travis. I've shown him everything, where not to tread, et cetera, and he seems to perfectly understand. These are professionals, Lottie. They do these photo-sessions all the time.'

'Well, I'm not going and that's that. Besides, we have Tilda and Marcus coming for lunch tomorrow. I tried to put them off until this is all over, but you know what Tilda's like – she can't wait to have a gawp at the side-show.'

'Oh dear. Typical! Never mind, darling. I'm sure everything will be all right...'

But he was not at all sure. In fact, Leo was a little put out. Having persuaded Lottie that three or four days' disruption – not, after all, very much more disruption than the summer music festivals created at any one time – was worth the truly amazing sum that they had been offered for the use of their garden, the stables, the outside lavatories, and the *limonaio* for the costumes, he had now begun to have doubts of his own. For one thing, although the little Silvie girl was as cheekily charming as she had been when he had first met her, he felt instinctively that her rock-star boyfriend spelt potential trouble. High as a kite on benzedrine or cocaine, if Leo knew anything about such things, and here solely for the party, and while he had relied on Andrew to vouch for everybody's good behaviour, he had kept guiltily quiet about Andrew's involvement, and, as far as he knew, Andrew was still in London. Perhaps just as well. Lottie seemed so very much better these days, but it was always a fragile stability. He had very much hoped to persuade Lottie to go to Florence.

Lottie's curiosity got the better of her. Leaving Marisa to put the finishing touches to lunch, Lottie went out with a basket and secateurs to cut some roses for the table. She rounded the corner past the box maze, and almost tripped over a snake of black wiring, said 'Damn!' and someone said 'Shhh!' without turning round. She beheld an extraordinary sight: in front of the pergola, on a low platform draped with fake lawn and bestrewn with roses and rose petals, posed three young women dressed in houri pants in exotically subtle pastel colours ≠ mauve, apricot, buff yellow, baby pink – and little, floaty, subtly beaded jackets under which they appeared to be wearing nothing at all. One lay prone on her stomach, legs in the air, propped on an elbow; a middle one who was probably the famous Silvie Snape, the one Leo had not stopped talking about for weeks, was standing up, hand on hip with her eyes on the sky, and a third girl was on her knees looking up at her. A variation on the Three Graces.

Their upper bodies were draped in some sort of diaphanous gauzy fabric, which fluttered and swam in a breeze which was caused, Lottie saw, by a man with a very large electric fan. Another man behind a large and impressive camera said, 'Okay, okay, hold this one, okay, smile a bit, Silvie…now to camera, and Carrie…great, lovey, okay, keep the wind turning, Jon, nice and gentle.' Suddenly, a real gust of wind blew the gauze across the face of the kneeling girl, the middle girl laughed, the pose broke suddenly, and the photographer swore loudly. 'Shit! I might have enough, but we might have to do this again, kiddies. Take five and stretch, and don't smudge anything, and mind the gauze with those heels, for Chrissakes!' He became aware of Lottie's presence. 'Yes?' he asked, impatiently.

A thin young woman with short bright blonde hair and wearing workman-like jeans and a red tee-shirt said, 'Hang on, Vic,' and rushed over to Lottie. 'It's Mrs Rollitt, isn't it? I'm Elvie. Elvie Lawson. Locations! This place is just fabulous, Mrs Rollitt! And we're just so happy you and your husband decided to let us do this here. We're all a bit tied up right now, I'm afraid. Um, is there anything special?'

'No, no. Not really. I just wanted to cut some roses, but it looks like you've beaten me to it.'

'Very carefully, Mrs Rollitt, I promise. Mr Rollitt said we could use some for the sets. That pale apricoty one on the arch is so lovely. It smells fabulous, too. What is it?'

'The one on the pergola? 'Lady Hillingdon'. It is attractive, isn't it? It does very well here. Er, I take it I could cut two or three of these 'Reine Victorias' without disrupting the scene too much…' She indicated a bed where some mauvy-pink shrub roses bloomed vigorously in tight little scrolls amid their companion lavenders.

'Of course, Mrs Rollitt! We'd like to use this as a backdrop for another shot quite soon. If we could. These are so gorgeous too, aren't they?'

'I shan't take many,' said Lottie, and began to clip. 'I hope you're all comfortable – in the town, everything.'

'It's all fantastic, Mrs Rollitt. Everybody's so friendly and sweet.'

'It's all a bit quiet round here – I'm afraid we tend to keep country hours.' She hoped the girl would take the hint. 'I suppose you'll be going on all day, will you? Photographing?'

'We'll go on as long as the right light holds, Mrs Rollitt, but that's really up to Vic – Mr Travis.'

'Ah, yes. It's just that I've got some people for lunch.'

'Oh dear, I'm afraid we're invading you so badly.'

'No, no. Actually I was wondering if we could invade you – come and see you at work later this afternoon. We'll be very discreet, I promise. My guests are just curious to see what's going on.'

'Oh! Well, I'm sure that will be fine, Mrs Rollitt. I'll square it with Vic, don't worry. Oh – they're beginning again. I'm needed! Sorry!' With that the girl Elvie sprinted off, and Lottie continued to snip – six roses on long stems and a lot of lavender.

'Now why,' thought Lottie as she made her way back to the house, 'do I feel like I'm the intruder?'

Tilda and Marcus Grantley were a lively elderly American couple who lived a few miles away and who were staunch supporters of the music circuit and the local gardening club. Marcus was something of an expert on wine – the Grantleys had a thriving vineyard – and lunch that day was a jolly, informal affair on the loggia which went on into the late sunny afternoon accompanied by some very impressive bottles.

'I still want to see what they're up to,' said Tilda Grantley. 'Hell, am I jealous! If these people want to use another garden anytime, it's our turn next!'

'Don't look at me, Tilda – this was all Leo's doing. He has all these glamorous young friends in London.'

'Lottie, really! Well, let's go and see, shall we, before the light goes?'

The party, only slightly unsteady on its feet, made its way down to the rose garden where, to Tilda Grantley's lament, nothing was happening except a couple of young men in jeans tidying away some coils of electric wiring and the fake wind machine. Leo hailed one of them. 'Finished for the day? We were hoping to catch you in action.'

'Fraid so, Mr Rollitt. Light's not right. Just clearing up. Back in the morning early if it doesn't fog over.'

'Fine. Don't forget to lock the byre when you leave.'

'Righty-ho, Mr Rollitt. No worries.'

'I'm just so *disappointed*,' said Tilda Grantley. 'Never mind! You'll give me their address, my dear,' she said to Lottie, 'and we can have them next, perhaps in the spring? They seem very neat and careful, I must say.'

'I promise we'll share them,' Lottie said, laughing. 'Would you like to come back in for some coffee?'

'Better ask Marcus. He's doing the driving.' Leo and Marcus had gone into a huddle over some caterpillars, and Tilda went to join them. 'We'd love some coffee,' Tilda called, after a brief conference.

'I'm going to show them where we might put the pool, darling. Now, Marcus, the real problem is going to be adequate shade.'

'Fine,' said Lottie. 'Come up when you're ready.'

Impulse made her check up on the stables on her way back to the house. There was a trestle-table set up in the big byre, on which various bags – personal stuff and equipment – sat among what was obviously the remains of people's snack lunches and some filled ashtrays, but apart from this inevitable debris, everything looked organized and businesslike – just as it normally did when the young chamber orchestra people were here – and Lottie, feeling mellowed by wine and cheered by the orderly appearance of things, made her way back towards the house, past the various vehicles still parked in the courtyard. Voices, male, in one of the vans. Angry voices. 'Fuck this up, Barley, and I'll see you finished! And tell that snakey little tramp the same. Christ alive! I'm going back to town! These people matter, okay? Just keep this shit out of here!' A man emerged, limped down the steps of the van. A youngish man all in black, wearing dark glasses and an expression of pure fury. So furious was he that he did not see the slender middle-aged woman with the fading chestnut hair emerging from the byre and almost collided with her, actually grasped her shoulders to stop them falling into one another.

'Christ, I'm so sorry!'

'You almost knocked me *over!*' Lottie said. 'Who the hell are you? I suppose you're with this fashion photographing thing.'

'Yes. I'm terribly sorry… Clumsy.' A modulated voice, vaguely London vowels with a tinge of Irish, perhaps… inky eyes beneath the glasses. 'You're not hurt at all, Mrs Walters?'

'No, no, I'm fine. Oh! You just called me –' She saw his built-up boot. Looked again at his face. 'Oh…' The world swam.

'Whooa! Perhaps you'd better sit down, Mrs Walters. Here.' She sank onto a bench. 'Don't worry now. That's it, deep breaths.' He held her head down. 'Better?'

Lottie looked up at him with a face blanched of colour and an expression of frozen terror. Then she got to her feet and bolted.

Leo led the Grantleys back into the house, via the outdoor steps to the loggia where they had recently eaten lunch, and where Marisa had cleared the table.

'We'll take our coffee in the sitting room, shall we? Getting a bit nippy. Lottie!'

He went through to the kitchen. Marisa was wiping her hands on a tea-towel. '*Vado via, Signor Rollitt. Ho finito qui. Tutte bene?*'

'*Benissimo. Molte grazie, Marisa,*' said Leo in his careful Italian. '*Un' pranzo ottimo, comè sempre – la Signora non cè?*'

'*No, Signor Rollitt. Cè caffè sulla stufa – è pronto. Va bene?*'

'*Benissimo, Marisa.*' The tray was prepared with four small cups, sugar and spoons, and there was a small jug of cream. Marisa or possibly Lottie had thought of the Americans.

He carried the tray through to the sitting room and served his guests. 'A spot of brandy, Marcus? Grappa?'

'Better not, my dear boy. We have to get home in one piece. We'll just have coffee and then we'd better go, okay, Tilda? Excellent lunch, by the way.'

'Indeed – your Marisa is a perfect treasure. Or was it Lottie's doing?'

'A bit of a joint effort, I think, Tilda. I wonder where she's got to.'

'Little girls' room, probably. Speaking of which…' Tilda got up.

'Seriously, Leo,' Marcus said when his wife had gone. 'Tilda disagrees, because she loves wisteria, but if you're thinking of real shade, you need trees, not vine plants. There's an ornamental mulberry – you can clip it, pollard it – and its roots don't suck all the goodness out of the ground like conifers. I'll send you the info – or better still, come and take a good look at ours.'

'They sound just the job if we could transplant big enough ones,' Leo said.

'That nursery Vivaio Balestri will. I'll let you have their number. They'll deliver and plant. It'll cost, of course, but who wants to wait for saplings?' Voices.

'Ah – Lottie, darling. Marcus was just saying –' But Tilda came into the room alone.

'Oh. Isn't Lottie with you, Tilda? I thought I heard you speaking.'

'No – I was saying my farewells to Marisa. She just went home.'

'Oh. How odd.'

'Isn't Marisa just darling? You're so lucky to have her! My, my, how late it's gotten! My dear,' she said to her husband. 'We'd better be on our way. I must just say goodbye to Lottie before we go.'

'Yes. Where can she have got to?' There had been a time, when Lottie was a lot less happy, when she would simply vanish from a table and go to bed. He had imagined those days were passed, remembered her cheerful face in the garden. A cloud passed over his mind. 'Back in a moment.'

'She was fine, wasn't she?' whispered Tilda Grantley to her husband. 'I mean not too –?'

'So far as I know.'

'I mean, she seemed perfectly herself. We'd better just creep away.'

'Wait, Tilda.'

Leo checked the kitchen again, the downstairs bathroom, the winter dining room, the music room, the study... 'Lottie!' he called softly. He went as fast has he was able upstairs. 'Lottie! Darling – Tilda and Marcus are just leaving, dear...' He checked the upstairs bathroom. Opened the door of the main bedroom, half expecting to find her stretched out on the bed. But the bed was just as Marisa had left it that morning, tidily made, and Lottie's shoes neatly placed under the painted Venetian wardrobe. His dressing room, the first floor spare rooms, he called up the attic stairs.

'Well, Lottie seems to have vanished,' he said, re-entering the sitting room slightly out of breath. 'Can't seem to find her anywhere.'

'Now don't you disturb her, Leo. She's probably resting. We'll just tootle away, and you give her our love.'

'I know she'd have wanted to see you before you go,' Leo said, a strange dark panic beginning to grip him.

'She might be outside still, talking to one of those young men,' said Marcus. 'Let's check, shall we?'

They went out into the courtyard where the light had almost faded. The byre was locked, the vans had gone, and so had the hired Fiat Uno belonging to the photographer. The Grantleys' big Saab stood next to Leo's Range Rover. 'Her car's not here. Oh God!'

'You sure?' Marcus Grantley's gravelly New York voice sounded serious.

'Yes. Her Panda – little dark blue thing – it was here. You squeezed in next to it, remember?'

'Hmm. Could she have put it round the back?' They checked. No Panda. 'Oh my God,' Leo said again.

'My, oh my! What on earth can have happened?'

'Bit mysterious. Are you sure you've checked the whole house, Leo?'

'I didn't go up to the attic rooms. But where's her car? It was here, I swear it was here.'

Back in the house, and after Marcus and Leo had checked the attics, Marcus said, 'We have to be logical. Seems she's driven away. Where would she have gone?'

'I suppose to Florence, to the apartment. But this is just – well, so unlike her...' He saw the look pass between the Grantleys. 'She's been so very much better these days. Oh dear God!'

'What I want to know is, why would she have just left without telling anyone? She wasn't upset. Whatever can have *happened?*' said Tilda.

Marcus Grantley was practical. 'All we know is that she's been gone – what? How long do you estimate, Leo? Forty-five minutes? An hour? The Florence apartment's got a telephone, I take it.'

'Yes.'

'Then let's try it, shall we? If that's where she's gone, she'll be there by now.'

'If she can find somewhere to park,' said Leo, trying to smile.

They tried the Florence number. No answer. They sat round the kitchen table. Leo tried the number again. 'Look, do please go on home. I can manage this. I'll ring and let you know.'

'Nonsense! I'm not going anywhere until this is all happily solved, isn't that right, Marcus?'

'Sure. We'll stay, Leo. Let's get this mystery cleared up, eh?'

'Thanks, Marcus. I know! I'll try the Albergo Medici in town. That's where most of this crew are staying.'

'Okay. Good plan. I'm going to check the gardens. Got a flashlight?'

'A torch? There's one in the cloakroom. And I'll put the floodlights on. But it's her car, you see. I'm sure she's not *here.*'

'Still best to check.'

'Be careful, Marky.'

'Travis? Victor Travis? This is Leo Rollitt...yes...sorry to disturb you, but my wife isn't there with you people at the hotel by any chance, is she? No? No, no matter. She just popped out and I need to get hold of her. Yes, please – ask her to ring.'

'Now don't you worry, Leo. She'll be fine. Let me make some more coffee.' Tilda got up and began clattering about, rinsing cups, hunting for coffee.

'I'll do it, Tilda. I know where everything is.' He got up, began mechanically to empty coffee dregs into a bin, fill a coffee percolator at the sink. Something wormy and hollow sat in the depths of his guts.

'Have you got a concierge or somebody, you know, someone with a key to the Florence apartment?'

'Yes. The landlady Signora Ghezzi. She lives below.'

'Perhaps you might give her a call.'

Marcus came in from the gardens. 'Nothing, I'm afraid, Leo.'

'Leo's just ringing the concierge in Florence. Oh my, oh my!'

Signora Ghezzi's thick Florentine accent: '*Shi...s hubito, Shignore... un attimino...*' Pause. Tilda poured the coffee, putting milk into Leo's, but he was too anxious to care.

[255]

'She's not there. Mrs Ghezzi's just been up to see. She says she'll let me know.'

'Leo, old man. We might wait, what, another half hour, and then we'd perhaps better report this. Lottie might be in difficulties.'

'Oh God.'

'I keep telling him not to worry so much,' said Tilda, but Marcus Grantley looked unhappy.

They called the local Carabinieri. 'Lottie will be furious if this is all a mare's nest,' said Leo, repeating the licence number of Lottie's car into the telephone, repeating the procedure with the Polizie Stradale.

'Better safe than sorry, old boy,' Marcus said.

It was Marcus who answered the door to two Carabinieri officers a fretful couple of hours later.

'Leo, Leo, old man... I'm afraid it's bad news. Seems there's been an accident...' But Leo already knew from Marcus's face.

65

'You're not coming back then,' Cindy said. She sounded neither surprised nor especially upset, although her face was suitably grave. The modelling crew had finished their work in the Boboli Gardens in Florence after the tragic news of Mrs Rollitt's death on the autostrada had made it impossible to continue in the Rollitts' rose-garden, and nearly everybody, including Barley and the Snape girl had gone back to London. On the day of the funeral, the lounge of Pisa airport had provided an impromptu photo-opportunity for the two young rising stars, and this glamorous young couple had been splashed over most of the Italian dailies and shown on the TV news, drinking prosecco, climbing into a plane, waving to a crowd. The show must go on.

'No. Not yet, anyway,' I said.

'I have to get back to work,' Cindy said. 'Will you be in touch? When you're back in London?' The fact she felt she needed to ask spoke volumes in itself. We were standing awkwardly together on a teeming railway platform in Florence.

'Perhaps. I don't know. I mean I don't know when I'll be back.'

'I'm really sorry, Drex. About your friends. I expect he'll be glad of your company now, poor man.'

I nodded bleakly. I knew I could never see Leo Rollitt again.

A guard shouted and blew a whistle. 'That's my train about to leave. Well, goodbye, Drex, and good luck.' She pecked me on the cheek. I was glad I had not broken her heart. Perhaps she hadn't a heart to break… She clambered up steep metal steps into a carriage, I helped shove her travelling bag on after her, and that was the last I ever saw of her.

Me? I went to Rome and drifted. Then I went to Venice and drifted some more.

66

29/7/1990

Esteemed Madame La Signora Tasker

It is with the greatest regret that I must tell you the sad news of the death of Mister De Bello who was recently staying in my guest-house here in Treviso. He was taken gravely ill while he was staying with us, and sadly died later in the hospital. I claimed your address and name from his documents, and I would be in gratitude to you if you would send to me the address of his family so that I can send his personal belongings. It is solely the one bag. Because of very warm weather here his funerale was very short time after death and he rests in the cimitero here.

With distinct salutes and in much consolation for your friend,

Lombardi Andrea,
Albergo I Tre Rei
Via Castellone 56
Treviso…

'I don't know what to make of it, kiddo. De Bello must mean Drex, mustn't it? But the number doesn't seem to exist. I tried.'

'I suppose there's the police,' said Jerry, reading the letter again. A thick, good paper, printed letterhead, careful typescript, decent attempt at formal English. A sprawling, illegible signature. 'Or the Consulate. They are bound to have been informed, I suppose. It's weird, I grant. I'd have thought they'd have to repatriate the body of a foreign national. Maybe not. Hell. And I'm not even sure Drex had a family, as such. There was an uncle in Ireland, I believe. And there was some sort of guardian once, I think. Perhaps it's not our business. Poor old Drex.'

'Yes,' Shelley said. 'Strange he should have put my address on his papers. I mean, I've not seen or heard of him for yonks. He wrote and I recommended an agent for some script he'd written after he came out of jail, but I've not actually seen him since *Plug & Socket* went phutt. Poor boy! I suppose it was drugs.'

'Very likely, I'm afraid. Somehow, old Drex was always pressing the self-destruct button.'

'Do you think we should inform the press? Put in some sort of short obit?'

'Maybe, if we get some sort of proper confirmation. For now I think we stay out of it, Shelley. The Consulate will find the uncle, bound to.'

'Yeah, I guess so. Brr. I felt as if a goose had walked over my grave when I got it. Poor talented, screwed-up boy.'

'Yes. He was brilliant, in his way, Shelley. Some people just can't hack it, you know. It's very sad.'

'Yeah. But these things happen, kiddo. Life, eh? Now! Let's talk of something more cheering, shall we? How do you feel about consumer affairs?'

'Consumer affairs? You mean like *Watchdog*, that kind of thing?' Jerry's attention snapped back to the immediate present.

'Yes – except this is breakfast radio, not television. Radio Four.'

'Oh. Sounds a bit tame.'

'It's Jilly Tantram.'

'Jilly Tantram? God, you're joking, aren't you? She eats broken glass for breakfast by all accounts.'

'Well, now she wants to eat you, kid.' Shelley Tasker's diamante specs glinted wickedly.

'And you advise this, do you, Shelley?'

'I do, Jerry. Widens your audience. Important now that *Step on UP* is taking a break. There aren't any strings, unless you count getting up at four in the morning. The research team's all in place. All you have to do is present the 'Smallprint' slot and ensure continuity. You have a nice friendly voice and you can sound authoritative. And there's something to be said for the older market, you know.'

'The grannies.'

'Don't knock em! And don't knock radio. You don't want to be constantly identified with the 'yoof' thing, Jerry, or with television necessarily. This is a good move. Promise.'

'Okay, Shelley. You're the boss. You've never given me bad advice. But if Ms Tantram lives up to her name I'll roundly curse you.'

'Nonsense, Jerry-mine. You'll charm the pants off her,' said Shelley Tasker, with unconscious crudity and remarkable prescience.

36-39 Pall Mall, SW1
September 10, 1990

My dear Mr Fairbrother
It is with deep regret that I must tell you of the death, earlier this year in Italy, of your friend and colleague, Andrew O'Ryan, also known, I believe, in the sphere of the theatre and television, by a stage name: 'Drex Bello'. Perhaps this sad news has reached you already, and I fear that only now am I able to catch up with necessary correspondence, having been for some time in Africa on official business.

I had known Andrew since he was a small boy, and for many years acted as his guardian and sponsor. I can only say how very sad I feel at the thought of this young and talented life cut so short. He spoke of you very often in high regard. On sorting through his few worldly effects, I came across the enclosed, and felt sure you would like to have it as a memento.

Yours very sincerely,
Leo. E. Rollitt

The photograph, a colour portrait eight-by-ten, showed a crowd of young people in a restaurant. Jerry himself was in the centre, flanked by Chloe Cunningham, Gwilym Jones, Marie Oldroyd, Drex and several others. Everyone looked hilariously happy, doubtless very drunk. He himself looked slightly bemused – he had been, he remembered, pretty much smashed – staring upwards rather than to camera. Now he stared at the photo for a long time, wincing at the memory. On the back was a rough diagram and the initials, in Drex's crabbed handwriting, of the members of the gathering, and a caption: *'Il Bistrot', London, 1982. Before the bombshells*. Little comments accompanied the intitials. He was especially struck by the comment against his own: *JF – gazing star-wards*. He felt an unwonted pricking at the back of his eyeballs. Then he put the photograph into the back of a drawer in his desk, where it joined many such photographic records of his past, and made a note in his diary to acknowledge this Leo E. Rollitt's letter, racking his brains a little, trying to remember if he had ever met him.

If Captain Leo Rollitt was surprised by a short, hand-written missive on a BBC letterhead from a Jeremy Fairbrother, expressing thanks for a photograph, and regrets that Andrew O'Ryan was dead, it was a surprise that barely filtered through the fug of his depression. He had sent no such letter, no such photograph. And apparently, according to Bolly, this Jeremy Fairstead, no, Fairbrother, was a television personality. There had been a mistake. It hardly mattered, except that it was very sad if it was true that poor Andrew O'Ryan was dead too. The world was a vile, cruel place, and everyone Leo had ever cared for was dead, or so it seemed.

67: 1994

'*Leo?* Leo Rollitt?'

Veronica had been cursing silently in the supermarket queue. Her sense of awkwardness and vulnerability in a big, brightly-lit crowded space and her anxiety, never far from the surface, her impulse to escape, to be altogether elsewhere, were things she was learning to deal with, but supermarkets and shopping malls could still root her to the spot in a wave of sudden, irrational panic. There was also the sheer drag of everything, the whining child behind her, apparently determined to eat an unpaid-for packet of crisps and the irate mother's loud unpleasant threats; the surliness of the slow and sloppy girl on the till, who looked as if she was hating every minute of her job (and who could blame her?) and the other empty checkout tills where one extra cashier would have mended everybody's temper considerably, and now to top it all, the elderly man in front of her who had dropped his change on the floor and was scrabbling awkwardly for rolling coins in the narrow aisle, cursing under his breath, banging his head as he got up from his painful stoop, now dropping his wallet, saying sorry to the surly girl who just looked stupidly up to heaven, and to the waiting queue of impatient shoppers who greeted his apology with mulish ill-humour. It was then she thought she recognized him. Her own very few purchases – two bottles of wine, a bottle of gin, a ready-meal of spaghetti bolognese and a packet of cigarettes – went through the process fairly quickly, and when she emerged, the man was still there, loading his two plastic bags into one of those canvas shopping carts on wheels, putting his wallet away in the interior of his macintosh, regaining a soldierly bearing despite his stoop, adjusting his scarf, grimly preparing himself for the outdoors. Very gently she touched his sleeve.

'Leo?'

'I'm sorry? Do I know you?'

'I'm Veronica. Your cousin, Veronica Dearborn.'

'My God.'

'Well,' he said over the large gin and tonic he had insisted on buying her in the Woolpack pub just down the road. 'This is all most jolly.'

'Cheeri-bloody,' said Veronica, raising her glass. 'Thanks, Leo. This is very nice of you.'

'You are most welcome, my dear. Ah, yes, cheery-bloody. And I must thank you for your very kind letter, my dear. I'm afraid I probably didn't answer it. Very remiss of me. Everything was all a bit....'

He had aged, in the way paper ages. His face had a look of parchment now, as if each taut smile might etch another network of fine lines. His hair, what was left of it, had turned a dull sandy white. He looked rather ill.

'Nonsense. I was the one being remiss. I would have written ages before, only I didn't even hear about Lottie until several months after. I was – well, I was away. Otherwise I'd have been in touch very much sooner. I just sent a note to your

Club and hoped for the best. And you did answer – you sent me a cutting of poor Lottie's obit. I was so very sorry, Leo. It must have been so dreadful.'

'It was.' He gazed into the depths of his gin.

'Where are you these days?'

'Oh, here and there. I mostly roost at the Club, and I've still got the house here in Fulham. You must be local too.'

'Yes. I've got a – a place in Colderidge Road. I rent it.'

'Coleridge Road? My dear girl, we are virtually neighbours!'

'I wish we weren't. Sorry. I mean, the room in the house where I'm living belongs to Mummy's latest husband. Gilbert Wardley-Hill. He's a – a sort of Rachman, amongst other things, but the sun shines out of his whats's-name, and this is Mummy's idea of generosity. I insist on paying rent, just to be independent, make a stand. Idiotic, really. I just can't quite bear – well, to be beholden, if that makes sense.'

To Leo, remembering Veronica's mother Anabel, it made perfect sense. He had met the ghastly Wardley-Hill man: classic cars, big business, a theatre 'angel', and a total pill, as Lottie might have said. He had to remind himself that the tall, gaunt young woman in black jeans and a dirty black sweater with unbecoming cropped hair in front of him was his own cousin, his cousin Hugh's daughter. When had he last seen her? Aged eighteen when she came to study Italian in Florence, and at sporadic intervals since, and then not at all, for many years.Must be in her thirties now. Late thirties, even. From the look of her – one mustn't pry – it seemed as if she had been through the mill. That court case – things were coming back to him as if through thick fog – had caused quite a stir, not least because of Veronica's involvement. The Buckley boy had died, he remembered. And yes, surely it was Lottie who had told him that Veronica had been 'sent down'.

'It's very good to see you, Veronica, after all this time. What – what are you doing now?'

'I'll be perfectly candid, Leo. I came out of prison less than six months ago. All this liberation is still very strange. But that's why I couldn't come to Lottie's funeral or anything. If you don't want to sit next to a convicted criminal, I'll quite understand.'

'My dear girl! Nonsense! I expect you'd like a refresher?'

'Love one. But I say, Leo, they do food here. Let's have some lunch and a glass of wine, shall we? On me. Mummy's not ripping me off that badly…' To Veronica, Leo looked half starved, and an aroma of microwaved pies suddenly made her feel violently hungry. She also found his company surprisingly restful.

'I'm afraid these pies aren't too good, ' Leo said. 'Gluey. I should have taken you to a proper restaurant, my dear. Don't think very straight these days, I'm afraid.'

Veronica said, 'Frankly, after Holloway, this is *haute cuisine*! There's still a novelty in real food. Sorry. I know I'm a pig. It was all so ghastly. But it's over. I'm trying to pick up pieces. But tell me about you.' She was pleased to see he was eating. 'Do you still stay in Italy sometimes?'

[262]

'No!' Too vehement. He forced a wry smile. 'Almost never. I let the house through agents. I mostly prefer to be here.' He could not confess to her how Italy now had become such an anathema. After Lottie's death, he had bolted back to his familiar London warrens, poking his head above ground every so often, feeling sick and ill. Sometimes the short walk to the local shops felt like an impossible voyage. Sitting here with Veronica was the first normal social occasion he had enjoyed in many weeks. His old friend Hubert Bollinger had remarried, and the happy pair had set themselves the task of pairing Leo off – there were dinner-parties with a spare widow or divorcèe – and Leo had begun to invent excuses. There were things he could never tell Bolly.

Perhaps it was the second glass of wine, or maybe it was the satisfied interior feeling after a square meal topped off by a slice of apple-pie and cream, but Leo suddenly found himself saying, 'Veronica, I have an idea. Don't just discount it. Think about it.'

'Blimey! This sounds serious. Do tell.'

'You mightn't like it.'

'I probably shan't care.' Veronica had been savaged in jail and had grown a carapace as a result. This was one of the first gentle conversations she had had since her release. 'Tell me anyway,' she said.

'Well, I mostly let the Fulham house. I'm afraid it's a bit scruffy, probably not suitable at all really, but one of my tenants is leaving. He's off to South Africa. I've not found a replacement. I wonder if – I mean, if living *chez* Wardley-Hill is really bugging you, perhaps you might like to have a look round?'

'Yes! Yes, yes, yes!' She looked better today, wearing a nice orange scarf over the apparently customary black, and she had bothered with her face, and done something with her hair. She looked less stark, less unhappy. He poured her another gin and tonic. They had inspected the basement apartment and now they sat in the rooms where Leo had lived for many years, rooms he had vacated for Bolly once when he and Lottie had made off for Italy. It was still the one place he could call home, his bolt-hole. He had never, in all this time, been able to quite give it up.

'You think you could make yourself comfortable?'

'It's lovely, Leo. Really, just the ticket. I'd love to move in downstairs. But I am going to do battle with you over this rent business.'

'Very well, my dear. You can pay me a peppercorn, if it makes you feel better. But this is not a gift, Veronica. If you would be prepared to manage the cleaning staff and the rents in the attic, keep the books, all that, I think a small flat in exchange is more than fair. I actually need someone to do this for me.'

'Okay, but I still think I'm getting the best end of the bargain. Cheeri-bloody!'

'The future.'

'And you'll be upstairs. How nice.'

'Not all the time, Veronica. I'm pretty superannuated, but there's a – well, an assignment. I'm going to be travelling a fair bit now. If I accept.'

'Hush-hush?'

[263]

'Something like that. Nothing very exciting, just absurd European bureaucracy. But it really would be good to know you'll be holding the fort. I'd be very happy for you to – well, make it yours. I'd – well, I'd like to think you had a home here.'

'I honestly can't think of anything nicer, Leo. I'll put some plants in the back yard, and maybe a bench to sit on…and I know just exactly where I'll put my desk, everything. I'm trying to write a book. Now I'm going to write my fingers off! How amazingly lucky for me.' Her face, when it brightened, was distinguished rather than beautiful – it could never be that – but it was warm and intelligent, and he felt an uprush of fondness for her. It had been a very long time since he had felt he had made any difference to anybody.

'This isn't luck, my dear, unless you count our chance meeting in the Spar or whatever it calls itself. I think it's a seriously good idea.' He got up from his chair, gazed out of the window. 'This has cheered me more than I can say.'

'I'm so pleased, dear Leo.' Veronica too felt flooded with warmth. This was civilization, in a way that she had for so long had to learn to do without. 'Would you mind very much if I had a kitten? They won't let me, in Coleridge Road.'

'A kitten? Why ever not! I rather like cats. You can have anything you like to make you feel at home. A dog if you want to.'

'I think it's not really fair to have dogs in town. Anyway, I prefer cats. Oh, Leo! All of a sudden the sun's come out. Sorry! Too much gin.'

He was still staring out of the window. 'I don't know how to put this, exactly. Um, there are a number of ghosts here, Veronica. I rather hope that your new life here will put them to rest.'

'Ghosts?'

'Not actual ghosts. Don't worry, my dear. The place isn't haunted. No…there was a child here once. He – he was the little delinquent grandson of my Irish housekeeper. They had the basement rooms once. Impertinent little devil. Going to the bad. I – I did what I could for him. I sent him to a decent school to save him from going into detention – it seemed like the best thing at the time. One never knows, you see, Veronica, whether interference is a good thing or not, does one? One just has to trust one's instincts, the decent ones, that is, and hope for the best. Lottie always thought it was mad of me. Maybe she was right. She often was.'

'Poor Lottie.'

'Yes. I – I miss her so terribly, my dear. Lottie…The boy's dead now too, by all accounts.'

'You loved her very much, didn't you?'

'Yes. It's difficult to explain.'

'You don't need to, Leo dear.' She almost got up, almost put her arm round him. Arrested herself. 'Well, the future, eh? Cheeri-bloody!'

Part VI

68: Last Year, Autumn

He had been curious to see, so she took him on a tour of the house. In the middle apartment, he had glanced discreetly at the Escher beetles in the master bedroom. 'Dear God,' was all he said, giving nothing away.

'I was thinking of selling this eventually. Or a long-term let. At the moment, it's more or less empty, except for a friend of mine who uses it occasionally. She's an interior designer. Well, sort of. She did this, as a matter of fact. I've never liked it much, but it's supposed to be snazzy.'

'It's certainly different,' said Andrew Todd.

They wandered into the sitting-room: a lot of chrome angularity, greenish-white walls and bold abstract oils on canvas, a single green-grey and cream geometric rug on the coir-matting floor, bold black and pale green cushions on plain ecru sofas. A large, low, chrome and glass table. Lamps with angular coloured glass shades. Long silk-screened window-blinds in a wispy design of grasses.

'I had to insist on this hemp stuff. You can hear every footstep otherwise. Not exactly cosy, is it?'

'No.' Andrew gazed round the room, so recently familiar. Now for some reason it was a vivid picture of himself and Leo Rollitt that surfaced. 'It's good, but it might have been better left as a sort of post-Victorian clutter – Persian rugs and a baby grand piano in lightish wood with lots of photographs on it, rust-coloured velvet curtains, standard lamp with a Liberty shade…and an old chaise-longue thing. Maybe.'

Veronica looked at him strangely. 'Come and see upstairs,' she said.

She unlocked the glossy racing-green door at the top of the narrow stair-case. 'I have to keep the passageways strictly utility. No point in integrating the place. The last tenants have just left. I'm advertising for some new ones – more students, perhaps. I can't hear them from the basement.'

The attic apartment was comfortably but plainly furnished, modern IKEA-style utility. More coir-matting. The narrow iron bed where Welham the PG had slept and the old-fashioned oak wardrobe that had once hidden a grubby little boy had gone, replaced by a double divan and a built-in closet along the wall. A door that never existed before led into a bathroom.

'No lino,' Andrew remarked.

'Not any more, no.'

When they returned to her basement sitting-room, she poured glasses of red wine. An aroma of beef casserole wafted from the oven. This was a late Sunday morning; he had stayed overnight and Sunday lunch had become something of a ritual. She had gone silent, doing something at the stove, frowning. Then she said, 'Is it true the Irish have second sight?'

'As true as leprechauns hoard gold.' He wrapped his arms round her from behind, nuzzled her hair.

'Mmm, Andrew, I'm trying to be serious. There's either something slightly uncanny about this, or you knew this house intimately once. That would be the rational explanation.'

'And you don't believe in leprechauns?'

'Frankly, no. Come clean, Andrew. You came here long ago, didn't you? Stop evading, and stop that, or these beans will boil over.'

'Pax. Okay, I had been meaning to tell you. I used to live here, when I was small. This was my home once. My bedroom was your closet under the back stairs.'

'Good grief. So –'

'My grandmother was your cousin Leo Rollitt's housekeeper.'

'So you were 'the O'Ryan boy', the boy in the basement! God, Andrew. Hell, that is fairly uncanny, actually. My *God!* It is a bit weird, you have to admit! So you knew him, you knew poor old Leo?'

'Yes. I was in trouble and he rescued me. I'm eternally grateful to him, in a way. And it certainly wasn't his fault I got into trouble again.'

'I think he wondered if he hadn't done you a disservice after all – plucking you from your own world and transplanting you. He was a good man, Leo. I became very fond of him. He sort of rescued me too, after my release, and maybe I sort of rescued him, a bit. He was terribly lonely after his sister died. They were practically joined at the hip. He believed you were dead, did you know that?'

'We… we lost touch. I was sad to read about him. Stroke, wasn't it?'

'No. Heart. Out somewhere in Africa. Actually, I think it broke. Hearts do, sometimes.'

'I will try not to break yours, Veronica. I'm not the man you think I am, maybe.'

'No, I realise that.' She kissed him softly. 'You're a leprechaun.'

South Ken Brothel Boss Arrested! Drugs Squad uncovers cocaine cache in safe: private club owner denies involvement.

The gracious building in the mostly residential Somerville Gardens, South Kensington is once again in the spotlight after being the .focus of a media frenzy earlier this year when royal aide Sir Dominic Mann, who later committed suicide, was caught in flagrante in a private 'cabaret and buffet' club run by Hungarian national Laszlo Palutikowski. Police seized 5kg of the Class A drug – said to have a street value of around £50,000 – from a private office on the premises after an anyomous tip-off. Kinseyder understands that Mr Palutikowski will be granted bail pending trial later this month, and that in the meantime, the club has been closed down while the boys in blue serge are investigating the boys and girls in pink satin. Horrified local residents, mostly respectable knights' widows and other blameless members of the upper echelons of polite society, have been forced into the public eye once again...

'You got him! Oh, you got him!' Angel is beside himself. 'You're fuckin' wonderful! Here!' He passes me a glass of single malt, and I see he has taken a drop for himself. He doesn't, as a rule. 'Cheers!' He insists on clinking glasses.

'Cheers. I did bugger all.'

'You could be a bit happier. Bloody Norah! Say, I hope Laurie got out of it okay.'

'If you're worried about your little colleagues, they'll all have scattered by now, if they've got any sense. Then they'll find another Palutikowsi. It's the way of the world.'

'Stop being so mardy! They might find someone like you!'

'They should be so lucky.'

'But there's nobody like you, Beautiful.' He tries to kiss me, but I resist. Angel has put on weight since he stopped doing the hard stuff. Pity. All he does is watch TV now we've installed Sky. That and smoke dope and munch biscuits. He's healthier, heavier, and far, far less interesting. Now, he slots a DVD into the machine and some familiar music begins to play.

'Your appetite for total crap is so depressing, Angel.'

'This isn't total crap. It's called *The Husband of the Bride*. I recorded it last night, while you were out on the tiles.'

'Oh. And you've just got to watch it all over again, have you?'

'I fell asleep. C'mon. Watch it. I'll make some tea to go with the scotch.'

'I don't want any bleeding tea. And I've seen it before. A million times.' I have, too.

'Suit yourself, mardy-arse. It's got that girl in it – that Marie Oldroyd, the one in *Plug & Socket* – the one you knew at uni. She's dead good.'

'She's also dead, Angel.'

'What? You're kidding!'

'Nope. Dead as earth. Look her up on Wiki.'

'Hadn't thought of that. Coo, what a shame. She can't have been very old. That's a real pity, that is, lovely girl like that. Shame. Bloody eck!'

'She's not a girl, Angel. She was an actress who was a minor star in a crap comedy film that appealed to the Americans which was made before you were born. And old enough to be your mother.'

70: About five years ago

Her eyelids, twin bruises in her little sallow face, flutter open and closed, as if she doesn't know whether she's asleep or awake or somewhere in between. She has told me a long, long story, and it's exhausted her. I wait as she lies back, flopped livid against the white pillows, listening to her sick breathing, wishing we were both anywhere but here. But it's strangely peaceful, too; tranquil, as if we have all the time in the world. From the very comfortable armchair in her over-heated little room I stare out of the window at the snowy grounds. Snow, clean and white, snow settled on neat clipped evergreen hedges on what is normally a lawn and now a compact Christmas winterscape waiting for snowmen and kids with sledges, except it's February, and this is a hospice for the dying.

She rouses a little, rousing me. Where has she been? Do the dying flit in some hinterland between here and the hereafter? I've never really believed it. We're like chalk marks on a pavement in the rain. She's being smudged, obliterated, rubbed out.

'Drex?'

'Still here, Marie.' I suddenly have an impulse to hold her hand, hold onto her. I resist. 'Why did you tell me all this?'

'I've never told anyone before.'

'Marie, I don't believe you.' I'm grateful for something rational. 'You've told this countless times. To psychiatrists, to counsellors. You must have.' The story, it had the ring of a tale told many times.

'Oh, yeah, well of course I've told people about *it*. I've just never said *who* like.'

'Oh.' My thoughts riot a bit. 'So why – why me? Why now? All right, skip the now.'

'You're an old friend. It's – it's so good you're here, Drex.' Marie's beauty has vanished. Her hair, all that lovely long silvery hair, which had been later cropped close to her head in boyish spikes, turned pink, turned blue – is now a sort of pale yellowish fuzz, what's left of it. Her eyes are pits, her face peaky and yellow-white, her little body a scrap in the bed. Her death-bed. Yet, despite the tubes and drips and the ominous plastic bag, filling steadily with some unspeakable morbid sludge, half-hidden beneath the crisp drape of the sheet, she still has some luminous quality, something alive and vital.

'I still don't really understand why you wanted to see me. Of all people.'

'Reason not the need, as the man said.' She cracks a little smile, a smile to smite the ungodly, and I wince. I remember writing sketches with her, and the spangles in her hair, her fairy feet in satin ballet-shoes, fairy wings, the thin, gravel-sharp little Yorkshire voice doing the parody of Ariel.

'I haven't got too much time, Drex, you know? I was so hoping you'd come. I've been, well, waiting. Hanging on, like. It's taken quite a lot of will-power. I never had much of that did I?' She smiles again, a rictus of blue lips in the blanched face. I turn away, stare out of the window again. 'But Janice found you.'

'Yes. Your sister found me.' With disconcerting ease and an effective lack of subtlety: 'Marie is ill and needs to see Drex. Urgent. Please contact Janice...' must have gone out to every A. O'Ryan and every Bello in the London white pages as well as the small ads in *Loot, Time Out* and *Metro*. She must have paid a fortune in stamps, and a great many A. O'Ryans and Bellos would have been puzzled. A long shot that might have missed. But it didn't.

'She's wonderful, my sister.' Marie takes up a plastic cup of water from the side-table in a shaky little hand and swallows with difficulty. 'Completely different from me. I've not told her about, well, Italy. I kept this to myself always, but now... Well, it explains a bit why I left him, why I couldn't bear to see him. Why I fucked up so completely, maybe. It's haunted me, like, so much. And somehow I know it's on his conscience too, like. He – we – should have stayed and reported it, didn't have the bottle.'

'This belongs with a priest, Marie, not with me,' I say. I'm not sure why.

'Drex. You've only hated him because of me. Please don't, not any more, not after all this time. I've forgiven him. He's a poor soul.'

'He's not a poor soul. He's a self-serving git, Marie. A two-faced, two-timing git. He'd have dumped you in time. I didn't blame you for catching his rising star, I just hated the way he dumped *me*.' Ironic, her pleading his cause, and for all the wrong reasons. But I believe her. I can imagine her backing off, unable to look at him without thinking about it. I remember her trembling when she came to see me in jail all those years ago. I'd thought she was just over-dramatising, but now, after what she's told me, it makes sense: the fear had been real.

'He's just, well, weak. You know? A bit of a coward. Ambitious. We all were, you know. Even you, remember?' She smiles another tiny wan smile.

I remember. 'Yeah, well. You do know he pinched my stuff, don't you? Pinched the stuff that would have been the third *Plug & Socket* series and rolled it into that thing he did with Webster. All the guest cameos, the lot. But it was the tone. He pinched the *tone*, he used my words – as if my being in jail sort of meant I didn't exist anymore. And then all that squeaky-clean condescending moralist crap in the papers. I almost puked. I was going to smash him for that.' Now, because of Marie's confession, I can. Does she imagine – can she know – the enormity of what it was she has just given me?

'But you didn't.'

'No.'

''Cos life's too short?' She's trying to prop herself up on her elbow, wriggling feebly free of the snaking plastic tubing bandaged into her forearm, dripping morphine and whatever else is keeping her pain-free, infection-free, just about alive. She pauses, getting her breath back. For the very, very sick, everything, the smallest movement, is an effort. I wait, helpless.

'No. Because I'm waiting. I think he thinks I'm dead. He's in for a bit of a surprise.' I'm only telling her this because she will be dead too, any time soon.

'After all this time? That's – that's so – so *soul-destroying*, Drex. You should have taken him to court for plagiarism or something at the time. But to *wait*.'

'Lawsuits are a bit awkward from behind bars, sweetie. By the time I got out, I'd made other plans.'

[270]

'Look, don't hurt him, please. I've got a special reason for asking.' She sinks down on the pillows again. 'I'm about to ask you a death-bed favour.' A tragic little giggle, a tiny sound like a battered toy concertina.

'Tell me.'

Her eyes are still very, very blue. Now they are bright with tears. 'It's – it's Marty.'

'And who is Marty?' I ask, back at the window, staring at the grounds, the snow on the distant moors.

'That's why I wanted you to come.' A tiny, painful sob. 'Marty's my little boy. My son. I never told Jerry I was pregnant when I left him. Not after everything. I tried to abort him, and when that failed – well, I took something. I wanted to die. I nearly did die. Then it was too late for an abortion. They had me committed, and I was in hospital for a long time, and Marty was born, just a tiny scrap. He was only four pounds and something. I couldn't even feed him, and even if I could've they said my milk would be bad for him. Polluted, they said...' She pauses, takes some heaving breaths. 'They would have put him in care, but Mam and Dad stepped in, looked after him for a bit. I – I went into rehab, stayed clean for a long time. I was always going to try to have him back, but he was settled. He stayed on with them in York. I went back to London. Crazy days. Lots of really bad stuff, you know. Good stuff too. I got that part, remember? In *The Husband of the Bride.*'

'I remember.' How could I forget? A seriously important ingenue role in a British indie comedy that enjoyed a successful enough run here but which took the US by storm. Suddenly Marie was famous and sought-after: her dream come true. I went to see that movie about eight times in an Italian cinema, subtitles. Bought the vid and watched it over and over, wore it out doing 'replay' for her scenes, just for that triangular Tinkerbell smile, those eyes, that squeaky Yorkshire voice. It lasted about a year – all the fame and interviews and exposure. She never had another offer like that. A bad TV sit-com that flopped, some guest roles on both sides of the Atlantic. And there were the meltdowns, the public screaming fits, the rumours of 'eating disorders', that she was 'difficult', that she was 'neurotic', that she was impossible, unprofessional, and addicted... It was, of course, a familiar story among many similar. Marie sank without trace.

Marie reaches feebly for the water again. I try to help. 'Don't, Drex, please. I can do it. When it all went tits-up, my career, I sort of lost touch with everyone. My parents – they just thought I was bad news, you know? Bad for Marty, like. They never told him about me. He went on living with them, went to school. They've brought him up, been good to him, done their best but they – well, they're fairly primitive, Drex. Neat little council house, you know, not a book in the place? They couldn't believe it when I got a place at uni. That was for like other people, you know? Perhaps that's where I went so wrong, trying to be someone else.' I watch her in silence, the weak little gasping breaths. 'My parents – they're getting so old now. They were fairly old when they had me. Janice was far more like a proper daughter of theirs. Worked as a hotel cashier then got married to a motor mechanic and gave them real grandchildren, like.' Her eyes close. 'Nobody wants to tell me, Drex, but I know. I just know that Marty's run away. He's almost grown up now, and he's been very wild, and he must have been such a trial for them, but he's so young too. He's my little angel, and he's all alone… I want you to find him, Drex. You can. It's what you do, like, isn't it, finding people? Janice said. So…' Breaths uneven, rasping. 'I want you to find my angel. Take care of him, for me, if you ever loved me. That's why I asked you to come. Mystery solved…' She swallows painfully. '*Please!*'

'Marie, God! You must know I'm hardly suitable guardian material, for Christ's sake. It wouldn't be a good idea. Besides, surely Jerry is the most obvious person. If anybody's responsible for this – for Marty – he is.'

'P'raps. But too complicated. Jerry's married. There's a family. But I want him to know, and I want him to look after Marty financially, like. You can tell him. I can leave everything with you. You'll know best what to do.' Her eyelids are drooping again, and there's a very long silence. Then she murmurs, 'I was afraid of you for a bit, once, like… not any more, Drex.' And she smiles again, tears sliding down her ckeeks. And something twists inside me.

'*Marie!*' I can't help it. I'm on my knees, suddenly, beside the bed, her tiny, bird-thin hand in mine, at my lips. She gently tugs it away.

'Not yet! Don't get all theatrical. Stand up, Drex, please! Look, here's Karen. Hello, Karen.'

A solid, capable-looking young woman wearing a green tracksuit type of garment and soft white clog shoes has entered silently, gives me a brief smile, goes to check drips, bags, equipment by the sick bed, places a capable-looking hand on Marie's waxy forehead. 'You can stay just as long as you like, Mr Bello.'

But very soon after that I leave, making a promise I know I probably won't keep. And very soon after that – three days later, in fact – Janice telephones to say that Marie has slipped away, as she puts it, in the night.

71: Autumn Last Year

In his *Sort It!* office, Jerry sifted his post and print-outs. In the outer office, Suzy Merritt was inducting the new recruit, Debbie – a young woman on secondment from the *Round Britain* offices to where Suzy herself would shortly depart for good. This girl was used to studio routine, and the handover promised to be a smooth and easy matter. Not that he cared especially any more, although it amused him, a little, to see that Lynne had picked someone very unlikely to appeal to his weaknesses. Up-date on the disabled child, now installed in a new house with her mother; an imperial weights and measures climb-down by a Midlands town council; an interesting-sounding case in Cornwall where a private landlord had given a prospective tenant a key to an empty flat, and then changed his mind and the lock at the last minute, leaving the tenant on the doorstep with a removals van. This one had been ticked with the initials 'GM'. Jerry buzzed the outer office. 'Suzy? Oh, sorry. Debbie. Could you ask Gavin to spare me a moment this morning, please?' An A4 envelope, marked 'personal, private & confidential', still sealed. He frowned and slit it…

I can understand the mentality of the hit and run driver.

Can't you, a bit? You're on your way, say, to the airport, to keep a date; an interview, let's call it an interview. It's important enough to give you that little buzz in your guts. You can't afford to screw up, but you're confident, and the message at the albergo was very encouraging, so you've gladly packed your bags, cut your holiday short. And here you are bowling happily along with the top down, along this good straight glinting road, a dark empty sweep of tarmac through endless fields and hills and bloated blackening sunflowers; cypress trees dotted on the skyline, views of distant mountains, warm dry breeze on your face. No traffic in sight, and so you open the throttle, enjoying the sensation, going quite a bit faster than the limit, but not more than a comfortable cruising-speed for this babe – this near-silent machine needs no encouragement. You're whistling softly, maybe, or going dum-dum-dum to the car-stereo, to the soundtrack of the private movie in your head, to the mood of the early morning. And if you keep this pace, keep the adrenaline up, you'll be in plenty of time, you won't be late, you'll get there, and you'll shine. It's a mood-thing as much as anything. In this mood, you can fly. The car is big, powerful, a quiet surge of serious engineering under your hands and feet, under your lightest touch. It's a moment, almost blissful, to lose yourself in. You're not so much driving the car as dancing with it, skimming the smooth surface of the empty sparkling road. You overtake one of those little 'Ape' three-wheelers that the local farmers drive. You feel like waving to him as you sweep past. The road is still all yours, and on you go.

But now, very suddenly, it bends, sharply – this is Europe – and you take the corner too fast, apply the brake and change down a little too late, annoyed with yourself, feel the inevitable lurch. The girl at your side gasps – you've almost forgotten her presence – as the car's back wheels swing and the suspension takes the strain. But suddenly – like that! – something's happened. You saw the black and white chevron strip, but you didn't see the bike. It was a flash, a jazz in the corner of your eye; you hardly felt the clunk on the Merc's robust bodywork as you hit it. It could have been a bird, a clod of earth in the road thrown up by your tyre, a small animal. Perhaps you clipped the chevrons themselves. But you're not thinking this, it takes nanoseconds. 'Christ, what was that?' you murmur, sobered. But the girl screams, 'Stop! Oh, stop, for God's sake, stop! You hit him, you hit him!' What? You stamp on the brake with a sickening screech, slam into reverse, squeal back up the road, back to the bend, halt with a jolt, ghastly sick feeling in your stomach, the world suddenly upside down, disrupted, curdled. But there's nothing there. A nightmare, a fantasm on an empty road. Here's the corner, mountains to the left with little towns nestling in crevices. Toy towns with toy bell-towers, olive trees, cypresses, the constant chirring of crickets under the hot morning sky; the steep forested bank to the right, and somewhere below, a small dry river-bed, the smell of wild thyme. You begin to thank God, and discover that you are shaking, that your legs feel weak under your weight.

But the girl, who has leapt from the car, is up by the chevrons, searching, trying to see, craning over. You fear she will fall, and in sudden panic, vertigo by proxy, you rush and grab her shoulder, pull her away, but she screams, and screams, twists wildly in your grip, pointing and screaming, unable to say a coherent word, and then suddenly she crumples to the ground, her head in her hands. You, balanced with one hand on the guard rail, peer over, see what she has seen, the mangled little wreck of limbs and light metallic tubing thirty, forty feet down the wooded bank, bright synthetic blues and yellows, with something dark and red and wholly organic seeping into the clumps of wild thyme in the rock crevices. A wheel still spins, folded improbably over the man's body. You make out what must be his head, the turtle-shaped helmet twisted at an impossible angle. She moans, the girl, her hand clamped to her mouth as if she's about to throw up, her eyes bulging with horror, unable to look, unable to look away. You swallow, you grab her arm and yank her to her feet, haul her, support her, back to the car, bundle her in. 'We have to call someone... we have to get help... help...' She is still barely coherent, hysterical. 'Marie! We can't do anything. He – he's dead...' Your voice doesn't sound like your own. Hers is a horror-struck whisper. 'You – you don't know! We have to get an ambulance, the police! He might be still alive!' 'You saw his head...' you murmur grimly and gun the ignition, pull out onto the road. She leans over the side and vomits.

You drive, slowly this time and in silence. She wipes her face on a tissue and hiccups quietly. You're trying to think, but no proper thoughts will come. All you really feel – and you do know this is crazy, but it's true, nevertheless – all you can feel is the loss of your mood, all that wonderful exhilaration. All you want to do is spin back the seconds, the bend taken smoothly, the guy still safely on his bike, safely passed, safely past. Now, a car passes in the opposite direction, towards that bend. The driver won't see anything. There's nothing to see...

More vehicles. You're entering a town. Houses, gardens, dusty pollarded trees beside a pavement, a petrol station, shops, the old centre, antique buildings with peeling green shutters. Signs, black on yellow: alberghi, ristoranti; white on brown, an ancient monument, a shrine; another, black on white, with the little emblem: Carabinieri. 'Turn left, quick, turn left...the police...' But you keep going. 'We can't do

[274]

anything,,' you repeat. Now, you're as rational as a machine. 'Really. Nothing. Just endless forms, reports, bureaucracy. The language problem will be hell – no! No, sweetie, honestly, no,' you say as she protests. 'The poor guy's dead.' You've convinced yourself, and if you're right (and you probably are) then the form-filling, the endless waiting, the inevitable interrogation, the detention – her as well as you – the court, the sentences, at best the fines, the publicity, the disgrace – these cannot possibly help him now. Can't help him. He misjudged the corner. He fell, felt a moment's unspeakable terror as he went over. 'But we killed him,' she sobs, but you drive on.

'Hi, Jerry – you asked for me. Blimey, you okay, Jerry? You look as if you've seen a ghost!'

'No, no – I'm fine, Gavin. Er – some shares of mine have just gone down the pan, that's all. I...'

'Happy days, eh? You wanted to see me. Is it this poor bugger stranded in Padstow with a van full of stuff?'

'Yes – yes, it is. This is a runner, Gavin. Get all the details, will you? Give them to Lynne. We'll want to interview this guy, and the landlord if we can get him. I take it that handing over a key constitutes a contract?'

'To all intents and purposes, yes – but we need to check the details. Difficult, if nothing's in writing, but not impossible. Specially if there was a witness. Locksmith's the obvious. I'm on to it now. Say, you sure you're okay, Jerry?'

'Fine, bit of a late night, that's all.' He forced a rueful grin. 'Ask Suzy to spare me a minute, will you?'

'Don't you mean Debbie?'

'No, I mean Suzy.'

'Okay. She's around somewhere. Blimey, we're about to be in a minority, ain't we? This one's another ball-breaker like the Armstrong.' He winked and grinned.

'Your political incorrectness is very refreshing as always, Gavin. No, I mean it.'

'Hi, Suzy – sorry to interrupt you. I know you're busy. Er – Debbie doing okay, is she?'

'She'll be fine. She's a seasoned show secretary. She's very efficient. Was there anything special, Jerry?'

'Yep. Suzy, you remember that case earlier in the year, the old couple whose son was killed in Italy? Did you ever speak to them?'

'No, no. I'm sure I didn't. I just sent the standard refusal – that unfortunately it wasn't a suitable story for us. It's all on file. Is there a problem, Jerry?'

'No! No problem. They – they seem to have written me another reminder, that's all. Private and personal. I'll bin it.'

'Are you all right, Jerry?'

'Yes. Just very tired. Bit of a headache. Look love, could you be a sweetie and send me in some decent coffee?'

'Of course, Jerry. I'll send Debbie in with some at once. Paracetamol?'

When Debbie knocked a few moments later bearing a tray, she surprised her new boss with his head in his hands.

72: A Year Or Two Ago

Sometimes things happen only by the purest accident, and that was how I found Marty.

I wasn't looking. Marie had breathed her last a long time before. In fact, I had other things on my mind entirely.

That execrable little worm Lion Barley and I were waiting for the Man, the Whisper; talking business, or trying to, in an undertone, in code, perched on chrome stools with plush purple seats in a fairly septic little club called 'La Pooche', one of those newish floor-show-cum-disco joints just off Oxford Street that isn't exactly Soho and sounds far more novel than it is, and would doubtless vanish tomorrow. Cheaply gimmicky, cheap altogether unless you counted the entrance charge and the bar-prices, trying too hard, and shunned by anyone who considered himself part of the in-crowd – anonymity guaranteed, therefore. But I was jittery anyway. A neon-lit cut-out of a cutesy cartoon poodle with a lolling pink tongue and wearing a pink bow dominated the back of the bar, which served pink drinks and left a lot to be desired. The day-glo décor – pink, naturally – was migraine-inducing, and I was wearing shades. Apparently, this venue was Barley's instruction from the Whisper. 'It's all so camp in here – one more weirdo more or less won't make any difference.'

'Thanks a bunch,' I said, sourly.

But he had a point, up to a point. When in doubt, my friend, if you have anything to hide, go public. Preferably, go with the habitual hiders, the ones absorbed in disguise, subsumed in Town's black holes. They won't be able to tell you from the real thing; no questions, no challenge. At least, that's the idea. Personally, I prefer a station-yard, say, or the Park in the dark, or some very anonymous quietish pub, but there are always shadows… And of course there are the parties, the sort of gatherings where the hundreds of guests are so off their faces that one person more or less, one dodgy delivery into a jacket pocket, one palmed roll of notes – these can pass unnoticed. But walls have ears, and eyes, and lenses. So do rings, wrist-watches and mobiles. I should know. Anonymity, if I can say so without sounding unduly paranoid, is never guaranteed. If they're watching, they can see and hear, know what I mean?

Some of the clientele – the regulars, fairly obviously – were in a sort of nostalgia uniform, either got up as Village People or as bikers. But this was very much post-AIDS hysteria, and the atmosphere was brittle, inauthentic, a travesty of the old days – less sin than synthetic, and somehow unjolly, forced. There were some obvious tourists, too, seeing London; a group of Japanese businessmen in suits getting systematically and solemnly drunk on vodka shots and strong lager, saying 'kanpai' loudly in unison without smiling, gawping at the freak-show. The place was smallish, crowded and hot, and I was feeling deeply uncomfortable, exposed and claustrophobic. I hoped we were blending into the background and feared that we probably weren't. Lion, whose days as a boy-band star were long since over, wasn't helping much, since he couldn't help expecting to be recognised, forever tossing back his thinning mane and striking attitudes.

'All right, so where is he?' I said, sipping my whisky. It was a decentish single malt, an aged Macallan, which I'd stuck out for in favour of a 'pink slink'. As long as a place keeps a good bar, that's okay with me, and at nearly four quid a shot, it had *better* be good.

We had been waiting for the Whisper for fifty minutes, maybe an hour, and I was growing testy. We had entered to pounding retro seventies disco, Donna Summer and the Bee Gees, boys in designer-shorts and teeshirts break-dancing on the miniature dance-floor for the delight of older punters in tight white jeans and vests, or black leathers and Village People caps, all gym-toned-and-tanned pecs and biceps, tattoos of doves and angels, teeth gleaming, irridescent as their tee-shirts in the lighting. After Frankie Goes To Hollywood – there was no end to the nostalgia here – had had them all squirming balletically over each other – these guys know how to make a show, give them that – well, all this had then cleared away for the floor show proper, and a general thirsty zoom towards the bar: voices sounding suddenly unnaturally loud in the lull, piped Freddie in the background: 'Take Another Little Piece of My Heart.' I generously bought Lion Barley another expensive, disgusting-looking cocktail that looked like diluted nail-varnish. I wanted Barley's help, and everything has a price, and I was keeping my temper, just. Louder Freddie now – the pulsing thrust of 'Give. Me. Somebody. to Ler-erve.' Some pink gauze parted and a troupe of lithe male dancers came cartwheeling onto a small raised podium, in spangles, pink of course – crotches bulging, thigh-muscles and abdomens like anatomical diagrams. General enthusiastic applause. In its tired way it had a sort of innocence. My perch was in view of the doors and the bogs and the bouncers. I watched, waiting for the Whisper, wishing I didn't have to, working on some serious retirement plans.

'He'll be along,' Lion said. 'Chill, man. We can wait. Enjoy the show. It's not bad.'

'Didn't think all this was your scene.' There was a notable absence of girls.

'It's not, man! Not like that. Come on!' He gave me a macho sort of punch in the arm. 'But this cabaret's really good, man…' (Lion will be calling his geriatric nurses 'man', should he live so long.) 'There's usually a good drag act, Madame Danae, comedian and raconteur. I used to know him. Real name's Dave Pottle. He's supposed to be on tonight. Relax!'

It was twelve-fifteen. 'For fuck's sakes! I'm not here for theatrical edification.' I was carrying a wad – I mean serious folding, and almost none of it mine. I wanted to hand it over, get the deal, get it over. Lion felt the same way, up to a point – he wouldn't get his share until the deal was done, and the Lion's share was to be partly in kind. His red-rimmed nostrils twitched at the prospect, but he seemed far too cool for comfort, a chemical cool with a low combustion level. I regarded this specimen with extreme distaste.

A couple of older guys dressed in homage to Freddie – white singlet vests and zapata moustaches – hit the bar next to us, refused pink slinks, ordered lagers, eyed Lion up, clocked me, decided they wouldn't bother, decided that the lovely Lion was taken. I gave him a proprietorial look, even patted his hand as I decided they weren't the Bill. My nerves subsided. A little. I tell you, it'd have been marginally funny if I hadn't had this bulge pressed into my side under my jacket, hadn't been waiting for The Whisper, who was about to walk in, also loaded, to join us. My nerves returned, in spades. Lion's eyes were on the floorshow, where some more dancers of indeterminate sex in fishnets and tutus had joined the others, kicking their heels to a can-can, laughing, going 'whoop!' as they flounced their frills, jiggled their little tails – to be fair, it was all quite professionally put together. Worth watching, even, if one weren't strictly on business. Lion Barley, he never could distinguish the difference, and that made him more than a bit of a liability, but he had his uses. He could go where I couldn't.

'I've got a little job for you, Lion,' I began to say in an undertone, leaning close. 'Something else,' I told him what it was, having to talk low and close to his ear, doubtless compounding any impression we had made as an item.

'Okay? Got that?' The dance-routine had finished.

'Sure. Got it. And I really do get this audition for my trouble?'

I'd counted on this, of course – Lion's heart being in his work, I mean. 'This all depends, Barley. If you don't fuck up, expose yourself, or me...'

'Oh yeah, man. Sure. I know that.' He gave me a look: sly, slightly flirtatious, thoroughly nauseating. 'Usual terms will have to be upped,' he said, sipping at his cocktail and looking up at me through artificially darkened lashes.

'Why?'

'Risk. He's got minders.'

'Fewer than most, actually. If you fuck up, all that will happen is that you'll be mistaken for some nuisance celebrity stalker and you won't have a job, with me or anyone else. Get it?'

Lion pouted. 'I might just be totally recognized as myself!' He liked to think that he could 'return', like Norma Desmond, and didn't like to be reminded that it would take quite a lot of leverage for that to happen in any form at all.

'So make sure you're not. It's called 'undercover'. Okay?'

'Okay, Drex. Spy stuff. I get it...' He looked like a kid playing a game.

'You owe me, Barley. Remember?' I clasped his wrist and squeezed it, very, very hard, just in case he thought I was joking. Barley winced and – give him his due – didn't cry out. 'Okay? Especially if you want the family viewing stuff.'

Barley pouted again. I could grass him like that, and he knew it. The PA roared with feedback, and I looked round automatically, releasing my grip. A compère in a penguin suit and a pink dickie-bow: 'And now, Gentlemen, Ladies, however you style yourselves.' (little giggle) 'Friends, Friends of Dorothy, Friends of La Poochette! Without further introduction, can we welcome La Belle *Mitzi!*' And that's when I almost fell off my bar stool.

'Mitzi', a tiny, leggy thing with spiky rainbow hair, extravagant earrings, a silver tu-tu that fluffed out round her tiny rump, legs encased in sparkly tights, pirouetted onto the little raised podium. Little heart-shaped face, a perfect little triangular mouth. She looked about twelve. A karaoke piano intro, and the little creature bowed, grinned, and began to sing, in a little, reedy, perfectly pitched voice: 'I'm Just A Gal Who Can't Say No' with a phalanx of ballerinos doing mimed obscenities behind her. Then they left the stage, the spotlight dimmed, and 'As Long As He Needs Me' fluted into the sudden hush. We were in for yet more hard-core nostalgia. Remember? Late eighties? Freddie Mercury recently dead; Kenny Everett a vivid legend, memorials held at St Mary's Paddington every day of the week. Now, couples clutched each other, clutched other couples, swaying in mass sentiment. There was something so 'good old days' about the whole thing, I could have puked. There wasn't a dry eye in the house when Mitzi finished her number. She bowed again under the spotlight which caught the frosty glitter in the polychrome hair, and sashayed away, the crowd roaring for more. She ran on again, little feet in spangly ballet-shoes. 'Judy Garland!' shrieked someone in the audience, and she began again: 'Somewhere over the rainbow.'

'Man...shit...' Breathy voice suddenly between Lion and me; reek of garlic and a powerful, not altogether pleasant scent, like frangipani in a closet of old shoes. It was Chris The Whisper, in the customary economic undertone that gave him his name. A walking trade-mark, this Whisper – he hadn't changed since the days of HMP Stonethwaite: the grubby linen suit, jacket open, a gold talisman hanging into a hollow, sallow, hairless chest; loafers, no socks, and under the greasy brown fedora hat, the large nose, the stove-in cheeks, the more or less invisible eyes. I was struck again by his wraith-like quality. He is tiny, insubstantial, and somehow looks as if he made a pact concerning his soul a long time ago, and has been forced to walk the earth in this guise ever after. God knows where The Whisper is from. I've never known. His very high, taut cheekbones under the hat suggest the Slav; his greenish-olivey pallor, the Hispanic. Chris is probably not his name, but then again maybe it is: Kris, or Cristofero or maybe just plain old English Christopher; and there was doubtless a surname, a patronymic once, Diaz, or da Luiz, or Jablonski, even Smith, but long ago 'The Whisper' took over, and The Whisper is what he is, or was, since he now seems to have vanished altogether... Lion greeted him with theatrical extravagance: an air-kiss aimed at both cheeks. In as much as The Whisper registers any emotion at all, he looked vaguely embarrassed.

The Whisper and I greeted each other with that perfunctory cordiality that has nothing to do with joy in each other's company. We both knew why we were there and wanted to get it over, as fast as possible, without drawing attention to ourselves. He had all the looks of a man ill at ease trying to look like he wasn't in any particular hurry. I offered him a drink for form's sake and he declined. 'Let's leave. Not here...' He was barely audible, and his contained urgency was unmistakable. He glared in Barley's direction from under his grimy hat.

From the stage: 'Why, oh why, can't I?' The note hung in the air, a painfully clear treble. Now, the thundering of whistles, stomps and frantic clapping. I stared at the departing spangles. There was another rush to the bar.

'Drex! For fuck's sakes, man, Chris wants to leave!' Barley pulled my sleeve. I dragged my eyes away.

'Hey! Why don't we all go grab a bite?' Lion said cheerfully for the benefit of any listening bar-punters, and hissed in my ear. 'Chris says like now, man. Yee Chong's. Breaker's Yard.' Barley does subterfuge like panto.

I pulled myself together with an effort, back to the pressing business in hand. I downed the last of the Macallan, climbed down from my stool, felt the bulge of notes reassuring against my ribs, and nonchalantly we left.

'Who was that kid on the stage?' I asked Lion casually in the street.

'What kid? Look, the Whisper recognised one of the gorillas on the door. Ex-old Bill. And he says they've put CCTV in the bogs, anti-cottage campaign. Yee Chong's will be quieter.'

'Let's hope so. Let's just get there, shall we?' The street was fairly crowded. Revellers, tourists, the odd drunk, a youngish beggar with a dog on a rope and a notice telling passers by he was homeless in an educated hand. We dodged them at an unhurried pace. 'Tell me about that pink-haired chick on stage.'

'What chick?'

'The one who calls herself Mitzi.'

'*What?*'

'You're obviously a regular. So who is she?'

'She?' To my utter dismay, Barley whooped and nearly doubled up, causing people to turn round. 'Ow, shit, man! You're totally not *serious*? You don't mean... Oh, fuckin' wow!'

The Whisper looked away, dropped behind to stare into a window. Like me, he found advertisement scary.

'Shut the fuck up,' I told Lion roughly. Barley's insides were such a warring cocktail of chemicals that he was getting seriously unreliable, these sudden bursts of crazy emotion, all that. I should have dropped him right then.

'Sorry, man,' he said, his voice a stage whisper. He was wiping his eyes. 'I can't believe it! You fell for it! Oh shit!' He glanced round for the Whisper, probably wanted to share the hilarious joke. The Whisper was following, at a stroll, at a distance. I didn't blame him. 'Man, that chick! *Chick!* You totally shouldn't be allowed *out*. For one thing, she's far too young for you. For another, she totally ain't no chick! Oh fuck, man, that's priceless! Like *The Crying Game.*'

'I'd worked that out, you cretin,' I said viciously. And I had of course worked everything out. It had all slotted suddenly and perfectly into place somewhere between the foyer of La Pooche and the street. Now, we had turned into Breaker's Yard and reached the lanterned sanctuary of Yee Chong's. We entered the sickly-aromatic fug, ordered the vacant corner table near the back, near the exit to the bogs. The Whisper presently joined us, and we ordered a minimum taster menu we didn't feel like eating from a sweaty, jaded-looking waiter in a smeared tunic. Our business that evening was concluded successfully in the evilly-stained red-flocked men's room, somewhere between the greasy sesame prawns and the almost inedibly over-cooked Peking duck.

73

A pricking conscience? Possibly. A few days afterwards, I decided to do a little private detective work at that Pooche joint. It was a Monday, and I sidled up at about eight-thirty, before they were open. It was still light. There was a big slovenly guy on the door, out of shape, unshaven, rough-looking; smoking a fag, looking glum, looking thoroughly out of place even for 'La Pooche'. Not, I thought, the Whisper's ex-cop friend. He barred my way and grunted, 'Closed. Till ten,' and then spat messily onto the pavement. It was in his script to sound aggressive, but he eyed me in a way that suggested his heart wasn't in it: I surmised the Pooche wasn't paying its door staff very well.

'I just need a word with Laurie,' I said.

'Who?'

'Barman. Laurie, Johnnie. Can't remember. Anyway, I need a word.'

'Oh, you mean Wayne.'

'Yeah. That's him.'

'Fuck off, prick.' This geezer had manners as nice as his clothes. I showed him a tenner, and he cheered up a bit, his hand hesitating over it.

'Other night,' I said. 'Left my wallet behind. If Laurie, Johnnie, Wayne has been good enough to keep it for me, I might be feeling happier after that word.' His big, damaged, nail-bitten hand still hovered.

'You won't find Costa. He went.' He sounded as if he really didn't care.

'I'm not interested in Costa,' I said. 'Just want a word with Wayne. While you stay put, okay? This shouldn't take long.'

He couldn't quite make me out. 'Yeah...all right, I s'pose.' He took the note from my hand, peered at it through unpleasant bloodshot eyes as though to make sure it wasn't Zloti, trousered it. 'Go on in. And mind your head. It's all about to collapse,' he said with unexpected irony. 'You fucking queers – couldn't organize a tea-party in a cage full of fucking chimps.'

I went in.

There was a light above the bar, but that was all. In the gloom, the empty club looked desolate and smelled worse. Stained dark red carpet in the table area, with one of those metal rims where it met the dance-floor; dance floor pocked with splodges of gum and ancient fag burns; stationary glitter-ball hanging from the ceiling looking like a leftover from a bad Christmas party. The cartoon Pooche looked especially forlorn, like a kids' fairground ride in daylight, and I marvelled again at how you can get magic to happen at night with lights, music, gauze; make silk and diamonds. Try Las Vegas in mid-morning...

Squeaking sounds of glasses being rubbed behind the bar. I coughed. A black spikey hair-do, followed by a thin, white, spotty face appeared above its parapet. The face chewed gum with its mouth open.

'Wayne?'

'Who's askin'?'

'Your boss let me in. Guy on the door.'

'He shouldn't of let nobody in. And Gaz ain't my boss. Mr Costa ain't here. We're closed right now. What do you want?' The kid continued to chew, trying to do cool and failing.

'I'd like a nice glass of single malt. That Macallans will do...' I pointed to to a bottle on the shelf, and I showed him a tenner. 'One for you, if you'd like.'

'I don't.' The boy lifted his voice – he was different from the one the other night. 'Gaz? *Gaz?*' His voice rose into a wail. He was probably younger than eighteen, and he was frightened very badly for some reason. 'Gaz!'

But the man Gaz was doing a tenner's worth of guarding the door. 'Just pour me one, there's a dear good boy...' I fondled the tenner between my fingers. 'I'm not here about Mr Costa.' He poured the whiskey, giving me at least double with a shaky hand, spilling some, which he hastily wiped up with a grubby cloth. I drank, and he watched me. 'I'm here about Mitzi.'

'Mitzi?'

'That's what he calls himself. He sings, he dances. Last seen here about a week ago. I need to talk to him, on urgent business.'

'Oh shit,' said the boy, eyes rounding. 'I ain't done nothink! It was him! I don't know *nothink.*' He began to back away, and I grasped his wrist. 'H – have you come from Mr Costa?'

'No, as it happens. If I had, you'd have just sold your little friend out, wouldn't you? Where is he, Wayne? Where's Mitzi? Where's *Marty?*'

'I'm not Wayne! I'm Paulie. And Marty ain't a friend, he's – Ow! Mitzi's gone! He ain't here!'

'Did he go with Costa?' I kept the boy's pathetic bony wrist tight in my fingers. 'Paulie? Did – Marty – go – with – Mister – Costa ?'

'Ow! No! Honest.'

'Not in an office upstairs, maybe?'

'Ow! No, swear to God. Lemme go! *Gaz!*' Tears had sprung to his eyes. He looked about to shit his pants.

I let go. 'I'm not going to hurt you, sweetie. I just want to talk to Marty. I've got a message for him. It's important. From his mother.'

'I don't – I don't know where he's gone! They ain't together, I swear. He'd be *dead.*' He looked as if he thought he might be shot.

He'd left the Macallans bottle on the counter. 'Look,' I said, helping myself, prodding my glass towards him. 'Have a sip. You look like you could do with it.' Paulie hesitated, then took a sip as bidden, blenched. 'That's better. Tell me about Marty.'

'Oh shit! You're the Bill ain't yer?'

'No. A friend. Of Marty's mother. Call me Mr Todd. And get me a clean glass. Good boy. You can keep this one. Now, tell me. Tell me about him, about Marty...' I was still fingering the tenner, but Paulie seemed too preoccupied to notice. He gulped another slug of the whiskey, and a flash of colour flared in his mottled weaselly cheeks. 'Tell me, Paulie. I really am trying to help,' I said.

'But I *can't,*' wailed Paulie, anguished. 'I don't know nothink. Marty's gone, like I said. I don't know where. Swear to God. Hope to die. But he'd better be hidden

[282]

good, because he's *evil*, you know? And he's like got this thing about Marty.'

I wanted to sort his pronouns out, but I had pretty much got the picture already. 'We're talking about this Mr Costa, right? The one who owns this joint.'

'Right. Except he don't own it. Least not altogether. He like runs it, the manager like, but there's three of them, right? A consortimum, or somethink...except now they're after him.' Paulie leaned close over the bar breathing a gale of peppermint. 'There's another gaff somewhere – smart, not like this shit-hole. But I don't know *nothink*, right?'

'Okay, Paulie. We all have our little secrets. You know the names of the others, do you? The ones who're after the evil Mr Costa?'

'No!'

'You must do, Paulie. You work for them. They're your bosses.'

'I don't too! I ain't never seen them hardly. I just listen to what I don't want to hear, swear to God, least when it's in English. But Speros – Mister Costa – he was rippin' the others off, that's what I reckon, and they was after him and – well we ain't seen him for three days. It's weird. I just wish he'd come back. I thought maybe he'd sent you. We ain't been paid, see?'

I phrased the next question carefully. 'Why was Mr Costa so pissed off with Marty?'

He leaned closer. He trusted me now. Almost. 'Mr Costa, right? He's got another sort of business – know what I mean? And Marty, see, Marty was doing freelance. Mr Costa don't like freelance, he don't. Gets slappy. And Marty's – well, Marty's a favourite, if you get me.'

I got him. I could imagine all too well. 'So, if you were Marty, where would you go?'

'Me?'

'Yeah. If you were Marty. Where'd you go? I am trying to find him, Paulie. I want to help him before Mr Costa finds him.'

'I'd *hide*, Mister Todd. That's what I'd do. Before I got half a face.' The weak blue eyes watered again suddenly.

'What about you?' I asked. 'Why are you still here?'

'I ain't got nowhere to go, have I? And Speros – Mr Costa – he'll be back, an' he'll look after me. S'pose. *I* ain't done no freelance nor nothink.' He trailed off miserably, snuffling. I suddenly felt very weary.

'I bet you this tenner he won't, Paulie. I bet you he's gone back to Cyprus or Crete where they can't get him. Would you care to bet where Marty's gone? Did he ever confide in you in the secrecy of the seraglio?' I put the tenner on the counter between us.

'The *what*?'

'Skip it. Who's Marty's new minder, Paulie? Can you guess?'

'What minder? How d'you know? I mean, Marty just went, didn' he...' He wiped his nose on his sleeve and then looked as if he regretted it, regretted the whole interview. Then his face resumed its rodent aspect. 'I *might*,' he said, eyeing the tenner. I plucked out another.

'I've not got much time to waste, Paulie. And I'm only betting on certs. *Who?*' And I grabbed his wrist again before he could touch the notes, to show I meant business.

'Has Speros – Mr Costa – has he really gone?' I felt him tremble under my hand.

'I'm betting as much, aren't I? Now, spill.'

Paulie's voice slid into an adenoidal whisper, and his eye was as much on the door as the money. I held onto the wrist. 'Well…there's this club in South Ken. A sort of private drinking club, members only, bit of a restaurant. Cabaret, like here. Smaller. And other stuff in the basement. Women. But it's smart, toff clients, all that, and Marty – you know, the Mitzi thing – well, he's got talent Marty has. Class in his way. He's a real ladyboy, and sings like an angel. That's what Mr Polluty-Cough called him. The Angel. He tried to poach him. Get him to work at his place, like. But Mr Costa, he didn't like it. There was a bit of a fight. But then there was the other stuff with Speros and the other two. They're all in it.'

'Okay. What did you say his name was? At this South Ken club?'

'Ow!' I relaxed my grip a bit. 'Polluty-Cough. That's what it sounded like. Me and Laurie, we laughed, coz the guy was always coughing, you know, over one of them big fat cigars. Ow! I dunno nothink more, honest! Marty went. Mr Costa went. There ain't nothink more. Cross my heart. Hope to die.'

'You probably will if you stay here much longer,' I said, releasing him. 'Here,' I peeled off another tenner. 'Why don't you take that and get back to your gran in Catford before you lose even half of your unappetising little face?'

'How d'you know?' Paulie's sloppy little mouth had dropped, showing the wad of gum.

'Call it intuition, kid,' I said. On my way out, I gave the morose Gaz another tenner, and he looked incredulous too.

74

I almost never hang about on corners, almost never foot-pad anywhere. I don't sit in cold cars in streets with a flask and the radio and a driver for company. Not these days, and almost never on business. But this wasn't business; you could have called it a sort of labour of love, or at least of obsession. You could have also called it something I wasn't prepared to trust to anyone else. Except that the cretinous Barley was there, behind the wheel, and he was getting agitated, moaning on about his failed career. Barley never stops reminiscing about his glory days. Now, he's just this washed-up dur-brain with an expensive habit and a constant need for reassurance. And I'll keep reassuring him for as long as it suits me, for as long as it takes.

We had parked the red Fiesta round the corner in Somerville Gardens. Barley's brief was to look out for the Bill. I had my eye through my lens trained on the white Georgian brass-knockered door, where the glass fan-light above it glowed a subtle orange. There was nothing to distinguish this particular door from the many others like it in the row, except for its visitors. It was three in the morning, and we had been there for over three hours. The atmosphere outside the car was getting damp, misty; inside it was filling with smoke, the reek of a disgusting pizza slice Barley had insisting on eating, and Barley's intermittent whining. The door had been lively between midnight and two – smart-looking punters in ones and twos, mounting the steps, pressing the intercom, speaking (presumably there's a password, and presumably it changes – things haven't altered all that much since Groucho Marx said 'swordfish'). Punters being admitted into a softly-glowing interior by a butler-looking person, whose black tie and button-cuffed dinner-jacket I caught often enough in my lens, but mysteriously never his face. Now, the process was beginning to happen in reverse: the door would open, someone would leave, sometimes nodding goodnight to the Jeeves who held the door, sometimes not; pulling a scarf up round his face, which the night air warranted, but it was my bet that it could be in the sultry mid-twenties in August and the scarf would still go up over the chin. This is Furtive Land, my friend, and you never know – do you? – who might be watching.

The door began to liven up even more. Earlier, I had counted ten punters in. I now counted eight leaving, in the space of thirty minutes. Number nine now: in his fifties, swift, but walking not running, heading off briskly into the night, back to his home comforts. Number ten looked older and a bit the worse for wear; lurched a little on the whitened steps, grabbed the railing, braced himself as the night air hit him, pointed himself in the right direction on the pavement and assumed a semblance of dignity with his overcoat clutched to his neck, his shoes going scup, scup, growing fainter. Now, we had to wait, and we waited.

'They've all gone,' Barley complained. 'You've taken enough pictures. Can't we go? It's nearly four ay-em, and I'm freezing my nuts off.'

'Oh shut up, Barley. Watch the lights. Just shut your trap and wait.'

We sat in silence for a few moments, Barley's head swivelling between the lights on the corner and the door.

'But why are we –?'

'Shhh! Okay. I'm getting out. Drive round the block once. Take your time, but don't go too slow, don't attract attention. Meet me here, by the lights. Five minutes.' I got out, sauntered to the corner, hidden by the Gardens' bushes. Gradually emerging in twos and threes came the 'staff'. I saw the one I wanted almost immediately, for it had pink hair and was dressed in a leather overcoat, the sort that Italian male models wear. It was chattering to a colleague, also wearing a leather overcoat. I emerged from the bush, stepped across the street. The pink-haired kid was walking on the outside. I followed them at a quiet distance as they chattered their way up to the lights. The other one said goodnight, Mitzi, babe, and crossed, leaving Pink Hair on the pavement, hesitating, casting about the way people do when they think they might be followed; and before he could head back towards the tube I grabbed his elbow, fairly gently. 'Hello, Marty,' I said.

We lie in bed as the dawn comes up, or at least he does. I'm by his side, still dressed, staring first at the ceiling, and then at him. Marty's tears have subsided, a bit, the over-theatrical little wretch, and he's sleeping, or doing something that passes for sleep. There isn't much sleep where Marty's been. Not much where I have for that matter. I watch his fine-boned, freckled, tear-blotched face in its repose. It will mend remarkable quickly; at his age faces do. His mouth is slightly open, but not drooling, like an older mouth might, like mine almost certainly does. And now he comes suddenly awake, his eyes – very blue, oh God, how blue – gazing at me.

'Where am I?' he asks, snuggling like a child, because this is his default mode until the nightmares surface.

'You're in the East End,' I say. 'With me.'

A puzzled little frown creases his smooth white forehead. The roots of his reddish blond hair are visible beneath the electric pink. Pink, orange, a hint of violet. In the room, a faint yellow light through the wheat-coloured blind, dark blue shadows in the bedroom. Almost a rainbow.

'Who are you?'

'You can call me Todd.'

'Hello, Todd. I'm Mitzi.' He's bright as a little button now. 'It's not me real name, but it's what I like to be called.' His camp little Yorkshire voice is meant to be endearing. He cannot possibly know how much it stirs me.

'That's all right, Mitzi. Todd isn't my real name either. I like it, because spell it a bit different and it means 'death'. At least it does in German.'

'Coo. Are you German?'

'Not the smallest bit, as far as I know.'

'Death – are you going to kill me?'

'Not yet,' I smile, stroke his head, and he sighs. He trusts me. One can tell.

Earlier he would have tried to flee. Now he doesn't seem to want to, but a cloud comes over the rainbow. 'Can I really stay here?' he asks.

Earlier, I had assured him that he could. Earlier, he had been like a scared little animal. He thought I was one of Costa's heavies, come to drag him back. He could have been forgiven for thinking this – I had had to practically jump him into the red Fiesta, cover his mouth, hold him down in the back. He took a bit of convincing. Now his hysterics have subsided and he has calmed down, he's back in the only role he knows, with a bit of an adventure thrown in.

'That depends. Yes, if you're not too much of a hostage to fortune.'

'A what?'

'Skip it. I need to know things, Mitzi. If I'm going to help you. Like why are you hiding? Tell me about Mr Paluticowski.'

'Depends...' He flutters his lashes a bit. 'How much do you know?'

'Don't fence, sweetie. He's been your – sponsor, let's say, hasn't he? Since you left the employ of Costa at that disgusting Poochette joint.'

'Yeah... oh, bloody eck, *he's* going to kill me. I just know, I just know...' Mitzi-Marty, whoever he really is, has got the shakes pretty badly. I diagnose a serious habit, but there's a serious, animal fear there too. I can smell it on him. I keep good first-aid remedies for both, but at this moment I want to get some sense out of him.

'Costa?'

He nods and gulps.

'I think you'll find Costa has got other things on his mind, Mitzi. There are people who'd like to put him out of action. I think you'll find he's done a bunk with most of the Poochette takings. That's my guess.'

'You mean Costa's really *gone*? Yer sure?'

'I would think so. If he's any sense, Costa will have gone far away. Mr Paluticowski doesn't forgive and forget, I gather...' Marty shivers. 'But I'd like to know more. And about Mr Paluticowski's clients.'

'Oh eck! But now Polluty-Cough'll kill me too.' More tears. Fear is winning. I coax him to talk, and incoherently he tells me a squalid tale: a greedy brutal Greek who pimped a ring of sad little catamites he literally whipped into submission and kept half-starved, and of his own attempts to escape. 'I thought I could get away-like. I tried to work on me own, and Costa had me beaten up. But he still wanted me at the Pooche, so they didn't do it so bad I couldn't dance. It was – it was –'

'Shhh, shh. Sta' calmo, figliolino, mio. Then? Tell me.' I wonder if he had been beaten the night I saw him on stage. Somewhere over the rainbow.

'Then Laszlo – Mr Polluty-Cough – he sort of fought Costa for *me*, like.' His pretty lashes flutter. 'Wanted me for the club. And Costa, he went ballistic, but there was this other trouble – him and this other guy who ran the Pooche. They fell out. Big time. I don't know what that was about, really. Money, pr'aps. They argued in foreign-like. But Laszlo wanted me – you know, to sing and all that – and there was some deal, and one night, Laszlo just said, Mitzi, angel, you're coming with me. I thought – I thought I'd been rescued like! Lovely club, big rooms, clients who gave you tips n' stuff. And food, after hours when the buffet closed, and all I had to do was dance and sing cos the punters mostly just wanted Millie, or Mandy or one of the girls.' Then Marty begins to weep again, softly, a small rain of tears down his little face. He's not twelve or anything like, but he is very young.

'The frying pan into the frying pan, if you ask me, Marty. Sorry, Mitzi. Sounds as if this Polluty-Cough as you call him was almost worse.' It does, too.

'He was kind. At first. You know, presents n' stuff. Lovely clothes. And plenty of gear. And gentle, at first.' Marty hiccups on a sob. 'But he had this thing, y'know? He'd get whipped stupid by Millie – she was his favourite, or Mandy if Millie was busy – and then take it out on me later, all fired up, like. He called it pay-back time. He was enormous – he used to make me bleed, everythink! I can't hardly dance no more, honest.'

'*Poverino*... Poor baby...' I get off the bed and go to the fridge. Return with first-aid. He is examining his face in a hand mirror.

'Drink this.'

'What is it?'

'They call it 'bloody mary' in America. It's tomato juice, nourishing. Worcester sauce, celery salt, lemon juice. And vodka. Just enough to drive the demons away.'

'Ugh – bitter...' He sips some more. 'It's quite nice, really...' I don't know if he means it, but he finishes it up.

'Now this, for those shakes...' I take the mirror and divide a generous line between us, give him my silver snorter, watch him hoover it up into his delicate little nostril, take it and snort myself without wiping it.

'Bloody Norah,' says Marty after a round-eyed interval.

'Better?'

'Yes, Mr Todd.'

'You can call me Drex.'

'Wow – that's dead cool, that is! Drex! Sounds like really cool chemistry.'

He slides his thin, milky white arms round my neck and kisses me. This is Marty's notion of gratitude. I am suddenly taken aback, with this strange little rainbow-haired boy, shocked into a tenderness I have not known since I loved Marie, so very long ago.

Later, he asks, 'Can I really stop here for a bit? Be safe?' Marty has a tart's practicality.

'Yes. I promise you no-one will ever hurt you again, sweetie. But Mitzi will have to go into hiding. All that punk pink will have to go. A bleach. We'll make you blond as a little angel.'

'You can call me Angel if you want.'

[288]

75: Last Year – The Run-up to Christmas

Celebrity Spotters: Is the Fairbrother family re-united? This seasonal visit to Hamley's certainly suggests that Charlie (11), Emily (9) and Jemima (6) might have both Mum and Dad under the tree this year despite constant rumours of impending divorce, but Mandrake hears that Christmas lunch will be a barbecue on the beach on Grand Bahama, where Lady Fairbrother's hideaway home, a gift from former beau, the late fashion-house tycoon Giorgio Ginelli, awaits...

It was their pre-Christmas ritual. Jerry treated Shelley Tasker to an excellent lunch at the Connaught, which neither of them much enjoyed. Shelley's appetite was bird-like, existing as she did on snatched mouthfuls, and these days a great deal of red wine, and she was frustrated by not being allowed to smoke between courses. Jerry enjoyed his food as a rule, and sighed inwardly as Shelley pushed away a plate of half-eaten sole fillet and did the same with the roast goose, while he himself tucked in hungrily despite his companion's reluctance. This was partly business. Determined not to retire, Shelley had been concentrating most of her energies on himself, of late becoming querulous and exhausting, seeming to regard him as her own personal property. She was currently furious with him for dropping *Sort It!*.

'I've no choice, Shelley. I'm doing way too much as it is. My priority has got to be this negotiation with Louise. One of her chief weapons has been the suggestion that I'm simply not around enough to be a proper parent. Everything's pretty, well, delicate. Surely you can understand that?'

'I understand she's got you by the short hairs, kid. I hope she's worth all this sacrifice. Do I take it she's won you over?'

'Shelley! Shelley, I think you don't quite *get* it. Something's got to go, and it's not going to be my kids, right?'

He felt himself about to lose his temper. An embarrassing memory surfaced unbidden – Louise had padded into his room and slid into his solitary bed one recent early morning, and in his semi-sleep, not only had he begun to make love to her, but had accidentally, from the depths of a dream, called her 'Jenny'. Louise, climbing on top of him, had said in a sort of hissing purr, 'No, not Jenny, not Jenny...I am Louise, I am Louise, Louise, *Louise!*' climaxing to the triumphant sounding of her own name. Treacherous body, in its wilful physical loneliness. He had climaxed too, flooding into her, almost sobbing. Treacherous body and treacherous subconscious! Thoughts of Jenny had haunted him lately more and more.

'Jerry, kiddo, keep your hair on. I understand, I do truly. It's just such a bummove, career-wise. You know you'll be giving everyone the impression you're over the hill.'

'Well, perhaps they're not wrong. I do need to slow up a bit. Besides, I'd have thought even you might admit that career-wise, I hold quite a lot of bargaining counters these days. I don't have to do any work I don't want to. I still have the *Quiz*. I know what I'm doing, Shelley.'

'Well, I hope so, kiddo. You know Jilly Tantram is after *Sort It!?* Haven't you heard? She's aiming to become a face on TV as well as a voice on radio. That face-lift story would have been hilarious if it hadn't been obviously true. That woman's a bitch and a half.'

Jerry cared nothing for Ms Tantram's cosmetic surgery. 'Jilly? Well, good luck to her, I say. She'll have fun and games with Lynne Berry. Blimey! What a thought! I shouldn't mind being a fly on the wall in that office if she gets it. Poor Lynne!'

'Lynne Berry can look after herself. I'm worried about you. Brian Burton's manoeuvring himself into position for the *Quiz*. Did you know *that?*'

'Burton? You're serious?'

'Yes, kiddo. Wise *up!* Everybody's hovering like vultures, waiting for you to come down. It's a cruel world as we know. Burton's a foul-mouthed oik, but he's popular in some circles. He'd get it, too. God, it makes my blood boil to think about it!'

'Well he can wait for the *Quiz*. I'm not finished there.'

'Nobody's indispensable, Jerry, not even you.' Her carmine mouth was a hard thin line. He knew her in this mood.

'What about a spot of Christmas pud, Shelley? Brandy butter?'

'Brr, no thanks all the same. Haven't room. Shouldn't mind a brandy without the butter.'

They ordered brandies and coffee, and Shelley bit into the chocolate mints with gusto, and he felt almost sentimental. 'You don't change, Shelley.'

'No?'

'No. Thank God. Truce?'

'Truce.'

'Merry Christmas, Shelley.'

'Merry Christmas, Jerry. Look, kiddo, I know this is appallingly rude, but if I can't have a cig I'm going to go spare.'

'I can summon the car,' he said. 'I'll take you home.'

'I'd sooner walk for a bit, look at the shops. You don't have to if you're worried about the screaming hordes.'

'I'll brave them,' he said in the foyer, wrapping the lower part of his face in a scarf.

'You look like a celebrity with a bad toothache,' she said with a flash of her old humour.

But as they wandered towards New Bond Street and Shelley smoked, she struck him as more than usually agitated, tottering a little on her high-heeled red boots and clutching at the bright cashmere scarf at her neck. In the stark wintry light, her face despite the farinaceous make-up had a pallor that rather alarmed him and he even wondered if she were ill.

'I do so hate bare plane trees,' she remarked. 'Depressing.'

'Hmmm.' He was thinking of palm trees, the villetta in Grand Bahama, to where he was due to fly as soon the Christmas Specials had been recorded, *en famille* with Louise and where her parents would join them from Long Island, New York. He suppressed a shudder. At that moment, a taxi drew up by the kerb and a thin middle-aged man dressed in a black overcoat alighted in front of them, glanced at them briefly and made to cross the street. 'Oh my God!' Shelley gasped, and clutched Jerry's arm. Her face had blanched, and she staggered into him, suddenly a dead weight at his side.

'Shelley? Shelley! Oh, Jesus Christ!' Along the street there was a cafè with pavement tables which were deserted, apart from a pair of young girls wearing padded jackets and furry boots, drinking milkshakes and smoking, examining purchases, absorbed in conversation.

'That man... the one who got out of the taxi... you must have seen him! Oh, shit! I need my inhaler...' Shelley was beginning to struggle for breath.

'Shelley! Oh God. Look, sit down. Here!' He guided her onto a metal chair and stood, feeling helpless and suddenly exposed. The girls at the next table were whispering and staring. He turned his back, but it was too late. They had recognized him. 'Shelley?'

Shelley Tasker was taking long deep breaths from an asthma inhaler, and colour began to reappear in her cheeks. 'I'm fine, I'm fine – sorry, kiddo.'

'Can I get you anything? Do you need some water?' He was considering the practicalities of going into the bar and ordering something by himself.

One of the girls had got up and was sidling over. '*Sarah!*' cried the friend, giggling. 'You can't just – !' He felt a soft tap on his sleeve.

'Excuse me, Mr Fairbrother,' said the girl. She was no more than eighteen, probably still a student, and she gave him a toothy grin from under a perky pink velour hat. 'I'm sorry – I mean Sir Jerry!' She giggled awkwardly, glancing at Shelley, perhaps to see if she was famous too. 'I knew it was you! I'm like it can't be, not in the street, but I'm like wow! I mean, could I have your autograph? Like for my mum? She's one of your biggest fans.' The other girl had joined her.

'Look,' he said, with one of his best smiles. 'I'll give you ten autographs if you do me two enormous favours, okay? My friend isn't feeling very well. Take this inside and get her a brandy – no, make it two brandies. Cognac if they've got it. Martell or something. And the other favour is not to say a word about this until I've popped her into a taxi. Okay?'

'Okay! It's a deal, Sir Jerry! This is just amazing! Wow! C'mon, Tanya!'

Jerry readjusted the disguising scarf. 'Shelley, darling, what on earth was all that about?'

'Asthma... I'm okay. I'm sorry, kiddo. Bit of a shock. Better now. Whew!'

The girls brought out the brandies and the small change from Jerry's ten-pound note. 'You can keep that,' he said. 'I'm extremely grateful, Sarah...and Tanya...there. My very grateful thanks.'

'I'll never spend this,' said the girl Sarah, stowing a pound coin and a twenty-pence piece into the pocket of her jeans. 'I'll give it to my mum in her Christmas stocking. She'll be like over the moon! Her name's Sheila. Sheila Lewis. Oh, wow!'

'Sheila. Here we are...' He signed a notebook, a diary, a packet of Marlboro Lights, the inside page of a new pink address-book, the gift tag round the neck of a small furry teddy-bear, and two menu-cards taken from the table, gazing up at them with smiling eyes. 'If you write to me at the BBC, Sarah, I'll send Sheila some complimentary tickets for the *Big Quiz*. Enough for all of you. Schtum for now, and tomorrow, you can Facebook it all you like. How's that?'

'Oh, wow! That's fantastic! Wow – oh, thanks a *million!*'

'Merry Christmas!'

'Spread a little happiness,' said Shelley, lighting up a cigarette when the girls had clattered happily up the street.

'Shelley...'

'Now don't boss me, Jerry, for God's sakes. I'm better. Truly. Cheers, kiddo. Don't know what came over me. Nice kids. Now, let's hope the press doesn't arrive in about fifteen seconds.'

'They seemed genuine.' But he spoke into his mobile. 'Craig? The car, please, soon as poss...yeah, you've got me. Just off Bruton Street. Crouch End first...' He began to relax a little. 'Shelley, what was all that about? Can you tell me?'

'Not without sounding like a complete loony, I can't. I'm – well, I think I'm either being stalked or haunted. It was him, I'll swear it was *him*.' She gulped brandy.

'Who, Shelley? Who?'

In the back of the big Mercedes as it purred towards her home in Crouch End, she told him, and he took her thin gloved hand which still shook slightly, and said, 'You need a good holiday, Shelley.'

76

Veronica Dearborn climbed onto a 74 bus in Oxford Street clutching several bags, feeling tired but triumphant. She had submitted her first draft of the *Life* and had lunched with her agent, who had made very encouraging noises, and promised a full discussion with the publishers early in the New Year.

Now, free for a blessed couple of weeks, she had indulged herself with some Christmas shopping. She had found exactly what she wanted: for herself, a frock in a heavy woollen-silk fabric, cut on an almost medieval pattern in a subtle shade of dark orange that had caught the lights in Nicole Fahri's changing rooms like an oriflamme; and for him, the softest possible cashmere sweater, of a colour that was not quite petrol, not quite charcoal. I'll wean him off black very gradually, she thought, and smiled privately. How very, very nice, she reflected, to be able to actually enjoy Christmas for once. That morning, she had printed off her tickets to Italy: *la Casa dal Ruscello* – the house by the brook. It was part holiday, part investigation: she could sell the property – there had been a particularly handsome offer – or she could continue to run it, as Leo had, as a letting. Or – and this was the thought tugging in her mind – she might even decide to live in it. Or part of it. For part of the time. So much (and this thought was far more troublesome, in its way) depended upon Andrew Todd. She groped inside one of the bags as the bus stop-started along festively-lit Oxford Street, felt the sensuous fabric of the sweater under her fingers. The colour was wonderful, just right; the same shade, almost, as Greymalkin's fur. Poor old Grimble, who had protested loudly at having to go into a cattery! But cats are forgiving, and he might even have to get used to being an Italian cat.

She did a rough calculation of the hour. He would probably be sleeping now. New York on business, always the mystery-man. 'C U 24/12 Vx...', she texted into her cellphone. Maybe she would try to speak to him before she got her early flight to Pisa the next day. Extravagant, but so what? She would prepare everything, get everything warm before he came. She imagined them both tucked into the Tuscan hills, a roaring log fire, chestnuts. She would put up some greenery, roast a couple of guinea-fowl on Christmas Day, find something delicious in Leo's cellar. Her cellar, now, but she still thought of it as Leo's. Dear Leo! She could never think of him without a certain poignant sadness – she missed him – nor without a sense of immense gratitude. He had left her everything, left her free, and she honoured his gift with an almost humbling sense of responsibility. It was far more than she had ever deserved. She might even light a special candle for him, and for Lottie too, in the little fourteenth-entury church in the village. When the bus jolted her out of her reverie, she realised she must hurry if she was to pack and organize herself.

'Special delivery,' says the man in black to the woman cleaning the staircase. 'Number thirty-eight C. A Ms S. Tasker.' He is carrying a big box plastered with labels, and seems to be staggering under its weight.

'Ain't nobody there, mate. She don't normally get in till ten.'

'Well can I leave it somewhere, love? It's killing me.'

'You can't leave it here on the stairway – health and safety. Take it away.'

'But she's expecting it. Important. Come on, love. Let me leave it outside the door, at least. Or as you're here, why can't you let me in with your key and I can put it inside her office so nobody trips over it?'

'Can't do that. Rules. Lose my job. You could wait half an hour and come back.'

The man lets the box rest on the third step with a grunt, rubbing his lower back. He removes his dark glasses, wipes his forehead on his sleeve and gives her a very special smile. 'Look, love. I've got about three seconds more street parking before the wardens come and arrest my van. Have a heart!'

The woman – she is not very young, a little overweight, fed up, a little suscep- tible – thaws. During a normal day – she works as a contract cleaner for a small local firm that does offices and pays the going minimum – a smile, especially from a good-looking stranger, is a rarity to be savoured. 'Oh, go on then. I'll let you in just this once. Not supposed to, but it can't really hurt. S'nearly Christmas, innit?' She removes an earpiece and returns the smile like a conspirator.

'Thanks, darlin'! You're a doll.' She runs ahead of him up the steep staircase and unlocks the door to Shelley Tasker's office on the first floor. He humps the box slowly behind her, puffing, saying, 'Books, I reckon. Blimey! Weighs a ton, this…' She sees that he is slightly lame, with a built-up boot, and she thaws some more.

'There. It's open. Just stick it on the floor, I would. It's a right tip in there. Take yer time. I'll lock up after. I'm almost done here.' She squeezes past him on the stairs, giving him a close-up view of the gold pendants snuggling between her ample breasts. 'Ooh!' she giggles like a teenager. 'Passing on the stairs is sup- posed to be bad luck, innit? I gotter get on. See yer downstairs, mate!' She runs on down, the soles of her trainers squeaking as she descends to her broom and bucket, and he hears her sing tunelessly as she clatters about below him, hears her open a door, presumably to a broom-cupboard, the singing getting fainter. Swiftly, he picks up the box – it is as light as air, being entirely empty – runs silently up the rest of the stairs and enters Shelley Tasker's office. He places the box on the floor in prominent view of the door, which he leaves fractionally ajar. Then after a glance round the office – more a large cubby-hole with a grimy street window, and indeed a 'tip' as the woman has said, with mountains of paper and box-files stacked haphazard everywhere, several over-flowing waste-paper bas- kets and a pungent odour of stale cigarette smoke – he makes for an inner door, behind which he knows there is a small annexe kitchen with a kettle and coffee things. He opens it, goes inside, leaves this door open a tiny crack, and waits…

Presently comes the audible squeak of the cleaning-woman's trainers on the bare tiled stairs. Sound of the office door opening. 'You finished, mate?' Pause. 'Mate? You still here? Hmph!' Through the slit, he can see her deduce the obvious – he has dumped the box and hurried back to his van. Sees the shrug that might be mild disappointment. Sees her take a last glance round the room, hears the definitive click of the office-door's yale, more faint squeaks on the stairs. He emerges and opens the office door again, very softly, listening, identifying sounds. Some door below – the broom-cupboard? – shutting to, then squeaking feet on the entrance hall tiles and the unmistakable clang of the street door. The woman has left. He checks the time. Nine-fifty. Now he picks up the box, takes it into the kitchenette and dismantles it with the aid of a penknife, folding it flat, as small as it will go. The kitchen has a long narrow window, with a view of a dingy yard that contains wheelie bins and several heaps of squashed cardboard boxes stacked by them. One more will make no difference at all. He shoves the flattened cardboard through the window, and watches it flop untidily down, sees it land. Goes back to the office-door.

Five past ten. A faint rattle, someone entering the main door. He stiffens, listening intently. Clack of high heels in the entrance hall and on the stairs, getting louder, closer. Noisy, asthmatic breathing and a thick, glutinous cough. He closes the door silently. Jangling metal, someone taking out a bunch of keys. He darts back to his hiding place and through the slit watches her enter: Shelley Tasker, saying 'ouf', and looking almost unchanged since he saw her last – silver hair in a neat bob under a black beret, shiny black mac, red Ginelli scarf, narrow black trousers, red ankle boots with high heels, a gash of scarlet lipstick, and of course, the trade-mark outsize specs.

She removes the mac and slings it over the back of her chair. He lets her rummage in her red patent bag for cigarettes, lighter and her laptop, hears her mutter under her breath. Sees her pick up the desk telephone, sees her change her mind – a woman, he discerns accurately, who badly wants a cup of coffee before she begins her busy day. Now she stands up, lights a cigarette, her back towards him, glancing out of the street window. He opens the door silently, waits for a fraction, flattening his breathing to almost nothing, enjoying this – that he is so close, and that she is so completely unaware. Ballistics experts probably feel something similar just before the controlled explosion.

'Ciao, Shelley.'

She screams involuntarily, her hand on her chest. She wheels round, her clownish face a mask of shock, and she bends over as if winded. But Shelley Tasker lacks neither guts nor nerve, and now shock gives way to fury. 'Just who the *fuck*?' He emerges from his hiding-place, stands in front of her, silently. For a second her eyes goggle. She takes in the dark glasses, the built-up boot, and blanches. 'Oh my God...oh!' The cigarette falls from her fingers into an overflowing bin. She backs away from him, half falls into her chair, her breath coming in jerky wheezing gasps. She scrabbles ineffectually for the inhaler in her bag.

The man in black leaves, swiftly, silently. Behind him, the sounds of choking, and the unmistakable reek of paper beginning to burn.

[295]

78: La Casa del Ruscello, Christmastide

'Arr. Casa Ruscello! See U soon..vxxx.'

'A – where are you? Pls ring/txt. Vx'

Voice message: 'Andrew – this is Veronica. I waited and waited at the airport this morning. What's gone wrong? Are you okay? Please let me know…'

A tap at the door of the sitting-room. The wood-burning stove blazed invitingly in the darkening afternoon. Veronica had draped holly and ivy over the chimney-piece. A small cypress in a terracotta pot did service for a Christmas tree, and could live outside afterwards. On the top, she had tied a small plaster angel she had found in a kitchen drawer – she liked to think it had been Lottie's – and round the base of the pot she had placed big bowls of walnuts, pistachios and tangerines, and a wrapped present, his sweater. She was sitting anxiously in an armchair with her mobile phone on her lap and a glass of wine by her side. There was a polite tap on the door. '*Si? Prego!*'

Marisa Bindi entered. '*Permesso, Signora Veronica! Va tutto bene? Sei abbastanza calda? Le camere sono tutte preparate. Il tuo ospite non è ancora arrivato, no?*'

'No, Marisa…*forse il vole è stato ritardato. Grazie mille…*' Indeed, it was only the thought of a delayed flight and the inevitable blanked mobile that was preventing her from panic. Veronica forced a smile at the bustling, sprightly little woman who wore a woolly hat and thick quilted coat, obviously about to leave. She held a letter in her gloved hand.

'*Allora…Ho finito qui per ora. Vado via. Penso che siamo per la neve! C'è un messaggio per te…è venuto stamani, cara, mentre tu eri fuori…*' Snow. A letter that morning while she was at the market.

'Oh! *Grazie, Marisa, grazie tante. Buon Natale. Prego salutami la famiglia…*' She got up and gave the woman a hug, taking the post.

'*Senz'altro, Signora Veronica! Buon Natale! Ci vediamo il giorno dopo Santo Stefano!*'

She heard Marisa's car drive away. She looked at the letter in her hand, recognized the writing on the envelope. Saw it had been posted in London. Opened it. Read it once in hurried disbelief; then she read it again, through a blur of tears.

The day after Boxing Day. Jerry sat on the veranda with his in-laws, in more or less companionable silence, sipping orange juice and coffee, staring out over the ocean. John Van Deer was tackling a holiday edition of the *Herald Tribune* crossword. Sonia Van Deer was writing postcards, thumbing through an old-fashioned address-book. Simeon, the house-boy, arrived with a tray of hot croissants and marmalade, and they buttered and spread, each with his or her own thoughts. Jerry watched as Charlie climbed out of a fishing boat and ran up the beach towards them, brown, happy, waving a small fish.

'Cute kid, that,' said John Van Deer, looking up. 'Nice youngster.'

'I like him,' Jerry said, remembering too late that irony was not something the Van Deers 'did'.

'*Like* him? I just love him to bits,' cried his mother-in-law. 'Why, he's like one of my own. Now, where have those girls got to?'

'Preparing themselves for the big entrance, maybe,' said John Van Deer. 'You any good at these things, Jerry? Eleven letters, two words beginning with "C" Eliminates undesirable parts.'

'Er, cuts out? Chucks out? No that's too few. Sorry, John. I can't do sudokus either.'

'Dad!' shouted Charlie, now in earshot. 'I've caught a merlin, and Santo says he's gonna take me night fishing, for squid, if that's okay.' The boy, out of breath, arrived smelling salty at the table, eyed the croissants hungrily. 'You can come too. Santo said.'

'Take that – that thing away, Charlie, sweetheart! Ugh!'

'Sorry Gran'ma. It's only a fish. Santo and me, we're gonna gut him and then we'll put him on the grill!'

'You go put that thing in the cooler in a cooler-box, and then when you've washed up and had your breakfast, we'll think about lunch, okay, Charlie honey?'

'Dad? He's fairly big, isn't he? Santo catches monsters!'

'He's great, darling. Of course we'll have him for lunch. We might have to put him in with some others, because there's quite a lot of us. Now do as Gran'ma says. Clean up, and come and have some breakfast.'

'Okay, Dad. But you gotta come fishing.' Charlie ran off into the house, clutching his prize.

'You're a lucky man, Jerry. Your son obeys you. Our daughter never did. Got it! Cleans house.'

'John! Now, honey, that's not fair. Louise was just a bit wayward. Girls are, isn't that so, Jerry? My, my – what's all this ruckus?'

'I absolutely *vetoed* news, and that's how it's going to stay, Dorota!' cried Louise's voice shrilly from inside.

'But Madam, this is very serious news. Mister Jerry, he needs to know.'

'And I say he does *not*! He's on vacation – no news, Dorota! He's not even brought his blackberry. How many *more* times do I have to –'

'What's up, Dorota? Something wrong?'

Dorota came out onto the veranda looking determined; Louise followed her, a sarong wrapped round her bikini-clad body and looking furious. Emily and Jemima in flip-flops and beach dresses followed their mother, agog.

'Jerry – this – this – *girl* refuses to obey me! If she has to text home that's her own business, but she's got no business taking messages for you. You promised! He *promised!*' she said to her parents. 'It's just not fair!'

'Louie, honey, I guess if it's truly important, then.'

'Nothing's that important, Momma! We're supposed to be having a *holiday!*'

'What is it, Dorota? It's all right, Louise darling. This is obviously serious.'

'It sure is serious when staff don't obey their employers. She's the nanny help, for Chrissakes, not your secretary. As far as I'm concerned, Dorota, you book yourself on the next flight out of here. You two – eat some breakfast with Gran'ma and Pops. I'm going back to the pool!' She gave a furious sigh and stalked off.

'Dorota?'

'I'm very sorry, Mr Jerry. I just got this.' Dorota handed him her cell phone. He read the message on it.

'Oh my God! Oh God, Dorota. When did this come?' His in-laws were staring at him; Jemima dropped a knife and her older sister nudged her.

'Just now, a few moments before. I did wrong, Mr Jerry?'

'No, no of course not. Oh my God!'

80

Shelley Tasker Death: Inquest Rules Accident. After hearing evidence from expert witnesses, Coroner Dr Eric Simpson gave his opinion that the fire in which Ms Tasker died from smoke inhalation started accidentally, probably as a result of a lit cigarette falling into a waste-paper basket. He said, 'It would appear that this unfortunate lady suffered an asthma attack, tried and failed to find her inhaler, and dropped her cigarette as she struggled for breath. She probably fell unconscious and it is unlikely that she suffered. Her office contained a great deal of paper which in these very tragic circumstances proved a death-trap...' He delivered a verdict of death by misadventure, and went on to order a separate inquiry into the adequacy of smoking bans, warning that smoking, even in private rented offices, must be strictly forbidden at all times. He also commented on the prompt action of the emergency services that had prevented the Grade II listed building in Montague Street, Bloomsbury, from suffering serious damage. The fire was largely confined to Ms Tasker's office, although it is understood that there was some damage to a corridor.

Shelley Tasker, 67, a colourful figure in the media world with her trade-mark designer spectacles and inevitable cigarette, was most well known as the agent and personal friend of Sir Jerry Fairbrother, who has cut short his Christmas holiday with his family in the Bahamas to attend the funeral, to be held at Golders Green next week. A source close to Sir Jerry said, 'He is devastated. It's a tragedy. She was one of his oldest friends, and it was she who helped launch his career. He is very, very upset...' Sir Jerry was himself unavailable for comment, but is understood to have requested that his privacy be respected at this very sad time. See related articles: Shelley Tasker obituary; Smoking bans still too lax? asks Robert Macfee.

The funeral had been strange – a circus, naturally, but also something of a shock: just when he had been imagining that he would be cast in the role of Shelley's chief mourner, amid all the other celebrities, actors and television writers, suddenly the crematorium was filled with Shelley's relatives from far and wide – a nephew, a couple of nieces, their families, and a younger sister from Australia who, being plump and homely, was about as different from Shelley as one could possibly imagine. He had rather warmed to them all. They had treated him much more as a grieving friend than a celebrity, and he had joined the sister and her husband at a private drinks do afterwards. 'I'll just feel lost without Shelley,' he said, and it was all he could do to prevent himself from weeping.

There had been a flood of correspondence – some of it perfunctory, most of it well-meant. A hand-written letter from Spain: Gwil Jones, currently wrapping up his lush new film of *Twelfth Night*, offering condolences and suggesting a meeting when he returned. An email from Ben Young. How much he missed Ben! Another from Suzy Merritt – the tone a little distant, perhaps, but the commiseration genuine. He hesitated as he worded a careful reply, wondered about ringing her. Shook himself.

Soon, his family would be home from their holiday. He was in no doubt at all that this trial reconciliation with Louise had been a failure. Her petulant fury had blazed when he had insisted on his immediate return to London, and she had barely spoken to him afterwards. Now, a telling silence. Talk about starting from square one.

All he could do, as he saw it, was to open up the Wimbledon house and make everything as welcoming as he could, and hope. Miserably, he took the car and went to the *Big Quiz* offices where he was greeted with warmth and more commiseration. A young man in the studio offices handed him some private mail. 'Sir Jerry!!! Private, personel & confidental!' said one, carelessly spelt, in vivid pink felt pen. It was a request from 'Sarah' for tickets, as he had promised. He remembered, sadly, his last meeting with Shelley. He instructed his secretarial staff to send ten comps, and then, impulsively, made it fifteen.

Now, alone in the Barbican flat, he fretted, exchanging text messages with Charlie. The boy had wanted to come back to London with him, and it was only the promise that Dorota would be allowed to stay on in Grand Bahama for the remainder of the holiday, much to Louise's chagrin, that had persuaded him. 'After this, I go back in Poland,' Dorota had said to him. 'Of course, Dorota. Just please do this last thing for us. Please, Dorota. For Charlie, mainly. Bring the children back to Wimbledon in ten days or so, see us a bit settled, if you could – well – find it in your heart?' and Dorota, whose heart could be generous and was not solely motivated by the very considerable financial recompense that Jerry was offering, had agreed. Jerry had no illusions that Louise was making her life hell. 'Nxt wk, kid!' he texted. 'Catch bg fsh! Hng on in thr! Dadx.' He was still horribly uncertain about what Louise would do next, and fretted that the children were thousands of miles away… He wished, passionately, there was someone in whom to confide his doubts, but now there was no one.

He went back to Wimbledon and prepared for his returning family, and it was there, on his desk in the den, that he found another item of post: 'jerry fairbrother, private & confidential', perfectly spelt this time in the familiar lower-case felt-tip print. He threw it across the room without opening it and left it where it fell.

'How's Mitzi these days, Angel? Too fat for the tu-tu?'
'Why d'you want to know?
'Wondered if she'd like a little outing. Call it a professional engagement.'

'Hi, Barley? I've got a Christmas present for you. Well, New Year present. Yeah, that's right. All you have to do is arrange overnight accommodation and a little party, nothing elaborate. No, just small party-bags. Like I said, nothing elaborate. I'll be bringing a fugitive. Here's what I want you to do.'

Jerry ran. A cloudy morning ominous with unspilt snow in mid-January, early enough to be almost dark still. Jerry jogged on at a steady pace in the chilly gloom through the bare trees, his trainers scrunching on the recently gritted path, trying to force his mind away from his troubles, force himself to concentrate on his breathing, his pacing, the well-maintained track, the familiar landmarks of trees and bushes and discreet rustic litter bins.

His familiar bench. The elderly early-riser with his labrador, whom he hailed as usual with a wave. An early plane disappearing into the blustering greenish clouds. Thoughts of planes descending. He paused and tried to breathe slowly, put his head between his knees, willing himself to think of nothing, make his mind blank. A sudden slight pressure on the wooden slats made him start up.

A thinnish man in shades, dressed in a black leather jacket, a thick grey muffler and black jeans. A man struggling to light a cigarette in the sharp breeze, his face shaded by his hand. Jerry turned his back, feeling resentful that 'his' bench should have become occupied, and the more or less automatic resistance of the celebrity to the sudden close presence of strangers, of being recognized unprepared. But now came a terrible thrill of panic. Lunatic to have come here, alone and unprotected! His calf muscles flexed, poised for immediate flight.

'Jerry?'

'No, wrong man, sorry!' He was on his feet.

'Sure about that, Jer?'

He started, turned.

'Good God! *Christ!*' He was unmistakable. Age had etched deep lupine grooves between the nose and mouth. It had greyed and thinned his curly hair, exposing the temples. But his eyes, when he removed the inevitable shades, were just the same: opaque, inky, ironically amused. 'Drex? Jesus, I thought – I mean I thought…' Jerry felt the blood drain from his head. He sat down suddenly.

'You thought I was dead.'

'Yeah, shit!' Jerry squeezed the top of his nose between thumb and forefinger, shaking his head. 'It really is you?' he said, stupidly.

'The very same. Look, why don't you stop acting as if you've seen a ghost, and we go and have a quiet pint? The Hand in Hand opens for breakfast. That's your local, isn't it? Quiet, no cameras.'

Too stunned to protest, Jerry allowed himself to be led.

Decent filter coffee. Bacon and egg sandwiches. A discreet youngish landlord surprised by the earliness of the hour but who, as ever, greeted his famous local patron simply as a 'regular', and if he recognized the man in black, he only smiled vaguely.

'Nope. Alive and kicking. Reports of my death greatly exaggerated, as you see.'

'Christ! But this is a shock, Drex. I mean I keep thinking I'm dreaming. *Shit…*'

'No you're not. It's true I did go underground for a bit.'

'Christ,' said Jerry again. 'Where in hell have you been? What have you been doing? And – um – well, what are you doing *here*?'

'I came to see you, Jer. Eat, go on. You look as if you could do with it. I'll eat too. Prove I'm not a phantom. *Salute, e buon appetito!*'

'Yeah, sure, *salute!*' Jerry was hardly taking anything in. 'I mean hell, Drex, I was fucking convinced you were dead. Someone wrote. I don't remember all the details. Overdose, or something. It was Shelley Tasker who got the letter. From a hotel, Venice, or somewhere.'

'Ah. Dead men can't pay bills, can they? I needed to – well, disappear. For a bit. Then, well, you know, I slid off, got involved in things. It's nice in California. Apart from the sun...' The contrast between Drex's pallid complexion and Jerry's tanned one was marked.

'Still the same Drex. But you disappeared pretty thoroughly. I even got something from someone – Roland? Robbins? A friend of yours, some sort of brass hat, sent me a photo. It was ages ago. Eons. Before I married Jenny, everything... fucking hell!'

'Rumours get blown up. Let sleeping dogs lie, I say.'

'Did you know Shelley died just before Christmas? That wasn't a rumour.'

'Yeah. Read about it. Must have been a shock. Sorry, Jer. She was never one of my favourite people.'

'No.' He recalled Shelley's absurd-sounding story. 'Before she – before Christmas, she thought she might have seen *you*.'

'Only in her dreams. I only got in from California a couple of days ago. I've not been anywhere near this smelly little island for years.'

'California... Jesus Christ, I want to pinch you, or something. This is surreal.'

'*Noli me tangere*, my friend. I'm real enough. Fancy a pint of Guinness?'

'Yeah, okay. Bit early, but, well, hell, why not?' Drex went to the bar, and Jerry stared at the utterly familiar narrow, slightly scruffy black-clad shoulders, the thinnish frame, the uneven feet... When Drex came back with frothing tankards Jerry forced his voice to sound normal.

'So, Drex. Tell me what you've been doing. In California.'

'Living on my wits, Jer. As ever. Bit of reviewing, all that. TV. Bands, too. A bit of creative stuff as the mood takes me. I wrote a bad book that was turned into an execrably awful TV film script a few years ago, much to my shame, but I used an alias. It pays a bit in royalties. Nothing big, but it had a cult following for a while over there. Don't worry, Jer. This isn't a touch.'

'I didn't think it was – I mean...' Jerry looked embarrassed.

'You must get them all the time. Nope. I'm not exactly rich, but I eat, I amuse myself. Fly.'

'I still don't understand – er, why you flew here.'

'Simple. It's work, right? There's a big market these days for ancient British crap. The Yanks love it. You might even like it yourself.'

'Okay. Go on. Talk to me.' Jerry drank his pint. He was still reeling.

'You're not going to credit this. It's our old friends *Plug & Socket*, believe it or not.'

'*Plug & Socket*? Shit! You're joking!'

'Nope. Straight up. There's this American TV channel dedicated to antique British alternative humour. Python, all that shit. They want to do a re-run of Puke & Soddit. They'll be getting in touch regarding rights and royalties. But there's something else. They'd like a new series. I couldn't agree without your say-so, so I'm here in person. Simple as that. I thought it was better than trying to write. After all this time you might have thought it was just a hoax. Well, wouldn't you?'

[302]

'I suppose so. It's – it's good to see you, Drex.' He meant it. There was something comforting in Drex's presence. It was as if he had prayed for a friend, and now here he was.

'Me too. You've always been – well, close to my heart, Jer.' Drex took a swig of his pint. So did Jerry. Drex watched him: a big, tanned, friendly-looking man in jogging gear, the star off-duty. Right now, the star was looking distinctly dimmed. 'Okay. *Plug & Socket*. It's going to be an update – but rather than their idea of a similar young pair in a modern setting, I want to do something with the original pair – older, still down and out, reminiscing rather than fantasizing and bewildered by all the hi-tec developments which have just gone over their heads. Think it'll work?'

'This is crazy! Mad!' But for the first time, Jerry grinned. 'Probably! Yeah, it's great! I mean, why not?'

'So you'll do it? Help me write it? I've drafted a treatment for a pilot, but it's gappy. There needs to be quite a bit of work on the dialogue. We'll go fifty-fifty, but you don't have to appear on the creds, not if you don't want to. Let's fix a date soon to do some work on it. If you want to, that is. I know you're a busy man, Jer.'

'I – I'm at a loose end for a few days, matter of fact. I've been in the Caribbean. I only came back for – for Shelley's funeral.'

'Well that's great news, colleague. I mean about you having some time, not Shelley. Trouble and strife still away, is she?'

'Yes. My wife – um – we – we're supposed to be in the middle of a reconciliation. You must have read about most of it. It's all been fairly public. It's still all touch and go. I'm just waiting for Charlie and the girls to come back from the Bahamas. My children…' He realised that all of his current life – his marriages, his children – these were unknown to Drex. There was so much he suddenly wanted to tell him.

'From all I read, the fair Lady Louise is a bit of a ball-breaker.'

'Whoa! You're speaking of the woman I don't quite love. Look, I – I'm going to tell you something, Drex. As a friend. An old, old friend.' The telling took another pint of Guinness, and Drex listened in silent attention.

'Mmm. Sounds disturbing.'

'You can say that again.'

'But it doesn't sound like her. Forgive me, Jer, but she frankly doesn't sound bright enough for this. I mean, she sounds ambitious enough for anything, but this has taken planning. A fine Italian hand, as the man said.'

'She might be – that is, I thought she might have been working with someone. There was this lawyer guy I suspected for a bit. Drew blank.'

'Uh-hu. Why?'

'Well, there were things – things he couldn't possibly have known. Louise too. That's what's so weird. Some of this stuff just seems to come out of the ether.'

'Have you kept them? These anonymous communications?'

'Some. Something arrived just yesterday – or at least that's when I found it. I didn't open it.'

'It might help to see.'

Jerry was hesitating. Now he made up his mind. 'Look, if you're not in a hurry, come back to the house. It's only over the Common. I'll show you.'

It was almost like confiding in the dead. If Drex's breath had not puffed in clouds of vapour on the chill air like his own, Jerry could almost have believed the man at his side was truly a phantasm. He punched in his number at the electronic gate and the pedestrian entrance swung open. 'No-one here for the rest of the day,' he explained. 'Everyone still on their Christmas hols. Almost feel like an intruder in my own house. How silly is that?' He punched in more numbers at the front door. 'Come on in.'

'Shee-it!' I gaze round the enormous sitting room, suitably impressed. Vaguely north African, the upper end of the market. Low carved tables, some large and intricate Tunisian woven rugs over a polished wooden floor, and another, antique by the look of it, on a wall. Vast squashy sofas, discreet lamps with vellum shades; a carved wooden head, museum piece, primitive, rather sinister; a large wood-burning stove. Very expensive abstracts on the walls. A signed Escher print, the one of the stairs that lead nowhere – a familiar stamp. 'Elegant, and yet almost user-friendly,' I murmur.

'You should see the bathrooms.' Jerry gives a chuckle.

'It reeks of understated success, if I may say so, Jerry. Bravo!'

'Not me. Louise. She's the interior designer.'

'When she isn't breaking balls.'

'Quite…' He seems more confident on his own ground. 'Come into the den. More civilized, by which I mean more of a tip, but it's mine.' The den is cosy, cluttered. A room where a man lives and works. A comfortable chair at a large old-fashioned lawyer's desk with serious hi-tec on it. An untidy sofa for reclining on. Books. DVDs. A large but not over-imposing plasma screen. The sort of room one could envy for its sheer prosperous practical comfort. Photographs of children. A studio portrait of Louise. Another woman, sweet-looking rather than beautiful, smiling, sitting on a rock with windblown dark hair, holding a little child… 'That's Jenny, my first wife. Charlie's mother. She died more than ten years ago. Car crash. I still miss her. Now then, more beer? Whiskey? Or wine. I've some very decent Bergerac if you prefer.'

'Pretty lady. I'm sorry, Jer. What's the whiskey?'

'Lagavulin, Islay single malt. Some people think it's too peaty, but I rather like it.'

'Sounds good to me.'

'I'll join you. Smoke if you want to, Drex. I packed it in years ago. Here, have an ashtray…' Jerry opens a bottle at a corner table. Pours and hands me a glass.

'Salute!'

'Cheers! Bloody hell, Drex. I mean, blimey!' He still looks light-headed.

'This is very fine indeed…' I snuff the fragrant glass. 'You were going to show me something, Jer.'

'Yeah, okay. Yes, I was.' I've already spotted the jiffy-bag lying on the floor by the book-case, and he picks it up and hands it to me. 'This was waiting for me when I got back here yesterday. Don't know when it came. Mrs Wylie must have put it on the desk. The envelope, the writing – it's just like all the rest, but this actually came in the conventional post. Stamps. I just hurled it at the wall when I found it. I was a bit, you know...' He looks awkward, uncertain.

'Well? Going to open it? I take it you wanted a witness.' I pass it back. 'It doesn't feel like a bomb.'

Jerry hesitates. 'One never knows – quite – what to expect...' I realise how much he must be trusting me. The thing could be anything, all sorts of unpleasant secrets about to jump out at him. He prises open the staples, extracts the contents. A disc. He feels inside the envelope. 'Oh. Just by itself. Often there's a note...' He takes a good slug of Lagavulin.

'Go on then,' I urge him. 'You've got to do it, Jer.'

He puts it into the machine and waits. I can hear his breathing. We both wait. A longish pause.

Then: 'I suppose you mean I might have him killed. Rubbed out. Of course I've thought about it, believe me.' Crackly pause. 'You're not shocked? Of course I've thought about it. But I thought it was a bit drastic. Anyway, I don't know any of the right people. You can't just look hit men up in the Yellow Pages. Can you?' Another pause. 'Do you? Know people, I mean?' Pause. 'How much? Theoretically?' Pause.'Perhaps it's too much of a risk. I mean I – one – would be in their power for one thing. And it is a bit well, extreme. Silly, maybe. No. It's absurd, isn't it?' A little laugh, very familiar. 'No – yes!.Okay. Do it, then. Inquire...' Louise's voice is eerily loud and clear through the speakers. Then the disc whirrs into silence.

Jerry's head is in his hands. 'Oh Christ,' he murmurs.

'Jesus, that's a bit definitive. Do you know who it is?'

'Yes! God help me, that's *her*! Louise! That's my wife – oh *Jesus*...' Jerry looks as if he's about to vomit.

'Sure? No mistake?' Jerry shakes his head like a man with a wasp.

'You don't know who she could have been talking to? The other half of that dialogue's been edited.'

'I realise that! No! Oh *shit!*'

'Well, you can be sure of one thing, my friend... Here, look, have another whiskey. May I?'

'Sure, of course...' I take Jerry's glass and refill it. He mumbles, almost to himself. 'I went out running this morning! Alone.' He stares at some unseen demon in the middle distance. 'Louise. All along. She's been planning to – to have me *killed.*'

'Seems likely. Here, Jer. Drink...' I've poured a small drop for myself, but I want to keep a level head. 'Let's be logical. One, whoever she was talking to is in a position to know some fairly shady people. Obviously. And two, whoever sent you this is on your side, I'd think.'

'What? How do you mean?'

'I mean this is a warning. Otherwise why send it? Either that, or they're out to get her. Maybe both. Listen, Jer – you need protection, and fast.'

'I'll call Craig. He's my driver. He's in charge of the security. He's in Maidenhead with his family, but he's on call, and –'

'And you trust him?'

'Yes. Shit, I suppose so. Oh *God!*' Jerry's eyes widen, horrified.

'Jerry, man. This is serious. You're not going to like this, but I think we'd better call in the Bill. You need real protection. This disc's evidence. You've got to get that bitch, Jer.'

'Shit, Drex. I can't! Louise has got the *kids*. They're thousands of miles away. And if she's got someone onto me, they'll be *here*, lurking round this house. Or the Barbican flat. Or the studios, checking me out. But *who* would send me this, blow the – the *plan?*'

'Someone with a conscience? They don't want to open up and announce themselves, obviously, if they're professionals, but they don't want you gunned down in the road either. That's how I'd read it.'

'Oh Christ...' He puts his head in his hands again.

'Okay. Look, we need to think. To get this straight. You need a safe-house for a start. We'd better act quickly. Look, I reckon this is what we have to do...' I tell him my plan, and he listens, drinks and stops shaking. A bit. He takes a bit of persuading, but the way I put it, he knows he doesn't have much choice.

'You're sure? I mean – well – I'm too well known, everywhere.'

'Which is why you have to hide, Jer. My mate, this geezer I'm staying with, he was famous too. For a bit. Knows the downsides. He's got the ideal gaff – three storeys up and almost as much security tec as you. He's a bit down on his luck, but we can trust him, Jer. All he'll want is a spot on some pop-talent thing, judging. He's discreet. It'll buy us a bit of time while we think. We just have to get you off your usual beats for a bit, okay?'

'Oh God. Okay.'

He goes to change out of his jogging gear and pick up some essentials. 'Best not bring that,' I say, seeing him stowing his blackberry into the pocket of his overcoat. 'Traceable.'

'Oh! Oh God!' He hides it in a drawer in his desk. 'I suppose we can't be too careful. Hell!'

I pad a number into my own mobile. 'Lionheart?' This is our code. Very soon, the car – a nondescript Renault Clio with the plate muddied the way I like them – arrives.

81

Scene: large open-plan sitting room in Lion Barley's third storey riverside apartment, doubling as a local authority hovel. Props: a large and dilapidated leather sofa that had cost a bomb once, doubling as a much shabbier second-hand affair with bad springing – you have to use your imagination, but you're actors – a half bottle of Bell's and a ten pound note, placed on a coffee table between...

...'Plug', a smallish man with an unattractive paunch and thinning longish blond elf-locks dressed in leather trousers and a white Armani shirt, played by Lion Barley, a washed-up pop-star whose ambitions have very recently undergone galvanic optimism, and 'Socket', a well-set-up fit-looking middle-aged man in jeans and trainers, played by Jerry Fairbrother, a pleasantly overweight television celebrity with a great deal on his mind.

Behind the sofa is a well-stocked drinks-table with glasses and an ice-bucket, and a door – 'off-stage' for now – that leads to the rest of the apartment.

Both actors hold scripts. Straddled on a cube-shaped leather pouffe opposite the sofa, also holding a script, sits the Director, a thin man in black, a man of parts.

This scratch cast has been introduced over good deli prawn sandwiches washed down with the fizzy white wine that Mr Barley keeps on ice in his fridge. It has also partaken of a generous line of very decent Uncle C (JF: 'I don't these days, but...' DB: 'Oh, come on, Jer! As you veto calling in the Old Bill you might as well have a bit of a party while you're in hiding...') and the anxious mood has lifted a little. By common consent, after Jerry has inspected the guest room ('Look, Jer – handy fire-escape through these French windows, just in case.') and expressed his gratitude to his saviours ('I'm incredibly indebted to you both. God, I don't know what to say.') and all three have satisfied themselves that there are no lurking parked vans, nobody patrolling the footpath below where in the darkening afternoon fake gas-lamps light the little thoroughfare with a reassuring glow, Jerry's problem has been temporarily shelved. ('You're among friends now, Sir Jerry! You just make yourself at home.' 'Just Jerry, please, Lion. I'm amazingly grateful, truly. I'll help you all I can.')

An informal read-through of the new *Plug & Socket* draft, by way of a diversion, has been Drex's suggestion. Lion Barley has acquiesced eagerly, doubtless keen to show off his versatility to this luminary suddenly in their midst; Jerry has merely acquiesced, but his fears have subsided and he feels brighter, almost recklessly so in this warm and bonhomous atmosphere. He still feels, in a curious way, as if he is in some sort of dream, as if none of this – the whole day, so far – is quite real.

The Director speaks: 'Gentlemen! Okay. Outline plot for a pilot. *Plug & Socket*. Exactly the same scenario – hopeless down and outs sharing nasty accommodation, but now they're older it's not so much dreaming as reminiscing, right? All those lost opportunities and now some old-man jokes about bladder trouble, impotence and indigestion. There's still the old rivalry, still the old dependency.

Now, they're each trying to do the other out of pathetically small gains. The Socket character – you as was, Jerry, but some ageing Yank actor will get to play it if I can't find a Brit – he is determined to steal what he thinks is a serious win from Plug, who hangs out at the local betting shop with his dole money. Plug's dog has come up. Keeps mum about how much. Socket's stolen this bottle of whiskey from the offie and offers it to Plug, ostensibly to celebrate, but he's drugged it with crunched up tranquilizers, so he can steal the winnings. Plug twigs that Socket's trying to get him drunk – lot of business with the loot shoved first into his jacket and then when it gets too hot and he takes his jacket off, into a back-pocket, or maybe down Plug's foul underpants – but he can't resist the odd wee sip. Hide that tenner somewhere, Lion. Your shirt pocket will do for now – it's only a read. Now then! Socket only pretends to get legless, but Plug really drinks – lot of dialogue here, with Plug teasing that he's carrying a wad, but of course he knows something Socket doesn't, and...'

LB: 'What does he know?'

DB: 'The amount of the winnings, cretin. Concentrate!'

LB: (Giggles) 'Sorry. Was he always this fierce, Jerry?'

JF: 'Yep. Pretty much.'

DB: 'Okay. Plug's already drunk most of his winnings in the pub. All that's left is a tenner which he's hidden with a lot of mystery-business the audience can see. Now he gets plastered on the whiskey and anxiolytics and falls asleep, and once he is snoring, Socket raids Plug's pocket and discovers the loot in question is a measly ten quid – less in value than the stolen scotch. – so he swears, and glugs the rest of the drugged whiskey himself, mumbling that innocent sleep knits up the ravelled sleeve of care or somesuch squit and falls into a heap at Socket's side, at which point the credits will roll, okay?'

LB: 'Sounds like a lot of bollocks to me. I mean sort of totally insane.'

JF: (Seriously) 'It's the dog's bollocks, Lion. Shall we start?'

LB: (Slaps thigh) 'Dog's bollocks! Oh shit, this'll slay me!'

DB: 'Shut up, Barley, wipe your nose and stop being a twat. There's a lot needs filling in, Jer – you can both ad lib all you like, okay? Okay. We have to imagine a bit of business when Plug first comes in from the betting shop – perhaps Socket accuses him of losing his week's dole again and refuses to help him. Okay? Cue!'

Barley-Plug: 'She was called "Princess Tazer" and she went like the clappers.'

Jerry-Socket: 'Tazer, eh? Funny name for a princess. Funny name for a woman.'

Plug: 'Bit of a dog, actually. Well, a bitch, I suppose.'

Socket: 'Bad luck. Desperate times then, mate. Where'd you meet her?'

Plug: 'Ladbrokes.'

Socket: 'Oh well, all sorts of low-life hang out in Ladbrokes. Er... went like the clappers, you say.'

Plug: 'S'right. Little darling! Came in ten to one.'

Socket: 'Ten to one? Hang on! Are you telling me you had a win?'

Plug: 'Might have.'

Socket: 'How much?'

Plug (primly): 'That's my business.'

Socket (wheedling): 'Go on. You can tell your old mate. How much?'

Plug: 'Enough…' (Looks sly): 'Perhaps more than enough.'

Socket: 'More than enough to pay your debts? You owe me, remember?'

Plug (ignoring him): 'I'm off to Town later. Pint in the Two Grafters, a club maybe, pick up a bit of young frilly, bit of dinner perhaps, well, a curry take-out, and then tonight's the night, her place if she's got any sense…' (Pause): 'Eh? What do you mean, I owe you?'

Socket (with notebook): 'Let's see. I've done the gas bill five times…and bailed you out the last time you spent your benefit and couldn't afford the bus. And a tenner for the last time I let you share my take-out vindaloo. That's, let's see…' (adds up very quickly) 'four hundred and fifty-seven pounds and eighty-one pee.'(Cue laughter.)

Plug: 'Get stuffed! What about all the times I've paid for you in the pub?' (He sings softly): 'I'm in the money. And I don't owe you for that last vindaloo. I was on the bog for half the night. Lost the lot.'

Socket: 'Caveat emptor.'

Plug: 'What?'

Socket: 'It means 'tough shit' in Latin. Where is it then?'

Plug: 'Down the bog, like I said.'

Socket: 'Don't start getting clever with me, Plug. Where's the loot, the dosh, the folding?'

Plug: 'Wouldn't you like to know.'

Socket: 'Your pocket! What have you got in your pocket?'

Plug: 'A man's pocket, Socket, is his own private domain.' (slyly): 'Suppose it's too big for a pocket?'

Socket: 'Too big for a… the kitchen! You've hidden it in the biscuit barrel!' (Leaps up from sofa.)

JF: 'Okay – I've leapt up from the sofa…'

DB: 'Right-ho. Now a lot of racket while Socket turns out cupboards, clattering pans, breaking china…we can imagine that bit, but it's supposed to take a few minutes, cue audience laughter as the thing becomes excessive. Meanwhile, Plug looks smug. Look smug, Lion. Shouldn't be too hard. You can sing again if you want. You register you're too hot and you take off your coat and hide the money in your jeans. Pretend that bit. Your cue, Jer. Socket's punchline.'

JF: 'Okay. Returned from making noise in kitchen.'

Socket, (returning from kitchen): 'Nope. It's not in the biscuit barrel.' (Cue more laughter. Hunts round the room for possible hiding places.) Eventually: 'Right, cretin! Where've you put it? What's that bulge down your trousers?'

Plug: 'A man's trouser-bulge is his own private business.'

Socket: 'And you haven't had one of those since the prostate job.' (Grabs Plug's throat.) 'You owe me, you bastard!'

DB: 'Go on, Jer. Grab his throat! Pretend to throttle him… that's it! Nice one. No, Barley, stop giggling like a frigging schoolgirl – this is slapstick, but it's serious. Now a thump on the ceiling from the neighbour upstairs – we have to imagine that too. Oh Christ, shut up, Barley! Let's take five.'

[309]

JF: 'Sorry, Drex. I seem to have got the giggles too.'

LB: 'Fancy another line, anyone?'

DB: 'Yeah, why not? Is it okay so far, Jer?'

JF: (snorting) 'Yeah. But you should stick in a bit about a man's private lunch-time, you know, when Plug first comes in, maybe?'

DB, making note: 'Yeah. Okay. Good. Keep that as a running joke.'

Director and cast break for refreshment. Lion Barley rolls and lights a small spliff. 'I just totally love this,' he says, taking a deep drag. 'You know, I was about thirteen when *Plug & Socket* first hit the screens. My dad, he used to say it was crap, gave kids ideas, made delinquency glamorous.'

'Barley's father was evidently a bit of a social realist. I can't actually imagine a better accolade, can you, Jer?'

'Nope. So now it can give elderly delinquents ideas.' The notion suddenly strikes him as hilarious. 'Hey, your dad still with us, Lion? Still alive?'

'Sure is. He's a retired traffic warden. Mum was a school cleaner. Melksham, Wiltshire. I bought them a villa in Spain.' Lion snorts with laughter. 'A traffic warden! My old dad! He still misses writing the tickets out.'

'My dad, God rest him, was a country solicitor, and a coroner to boot. All those upholders of law and order, and just look at us! Say,' he says through parox-ysms of mirth, 'Any more of that nice fizz going?'

'Sure, man,' says Barley, dabbing his nose. 'You're more than welcome. More for you, Drex?'

'Please, Lionheart.'

Lion opens a fresh bottle. 'Hey, this is great! Sorry you've got issues, Jerry man, but it's great you're here... have a toke on this?'

'Thanks, Lion. Cheers. Oh God, this is so weird – surreal – what happens next?' He wipes streaming eyes and inhales. 'Jesus, this packs a punch...woosh! Go on, Drex. What happens? To our heroes?' He takes a deep slug of wine.

'Next? Well, Socket comes back in with the whiskey bottle. There's been a bit of business in the kitchen with Socket grinding up some sleeping stuff and shaking it into the whiskey. Yes, Barley? It doesn't *matter* what it is. Mogadon, or something. Herbal valerian, for Christ's sakes. And probably from out of a bottle marked 'Happy Dreams' or 'Silent Night'. Think cartoons. It doesn't matter as long as the audience gets the point. Anyway, all the while there's a parallel fantasy-bit with Plug imagining himself on the tiles in the money. One of his old reveries – perhaps cue a guest babe, Britney Spears, Silvie Snape? This harks back to the *Plug & Socket* series that never got made. Series number three, remember, Jer?'

'Yeah. Pity. But it will now, eh? Like old times, Drex, maybe?'

'Yeah! Wow! Like that pair of medics on *Earthwatch*, remember? You both did that too, didn't you?'

'Not me on that occasion, Barley. Officially that is. I was a bit tied up at the time, entertaining Her Majesty who wasn't in a joking mood. Eh, Jer? Still got half a mind to do you for plagiarism, my friend.' Drex winks, and Jerry looks a little uncomfortable and coughs.

[310]

'I owe you there, Drex. It just sort of came up, all Webster's idea, really. These things sort of happen. Perhaps we might talk about it privately sometime.' He glances over at Lion.

'Well, it was dead good, that. Brilliant! Totally loved it,' says Lion Barley bathetically into a tense little silence.

'Thanks. History...' Jerry glances at Drex, whose nose is in the script.

'Yeah. History,' he murmurs. 'Funny thing, history. They say it repeats itself. But then they say pigs don't have wings and daleks can't climb stairs. I just say sleeping dogs wake up, eh? Oh, do shut up, Barley. It wasn't that funny. Okay. Back to dogs. Greyhounds, in this case. Ready? Skip to where Socket produces the whiskey. Page four. Places, Barley, please. Plug on the sofa, Socket entering with a bottle. You've come in with the bottle, Jer.'

'Er. Okay. Got it.'

Socket: (sing-song) 'Plug! Plu-ug! Here. I got you a little present! One I pinched earlier! Let's celebrate your big win, shall we?'

Plug: 'Wow, man! That's very kind of you. Real Haig.'

(LB: 'It's Bell's, Drex – can I say Bell's?' DB: 'Say anything you *like*, Barley – Christ! Just don't laugh till you're supposed to!')

Socket, (unscrewing the cap and pretending to drink deeply): 'Me first. Cheers, man!'

Plug, (shouts): 'Here! My turn.' (Grabs bottle, unscrews top and takes big slug.) 'Wow! Hmmm.'

(LB, spitting messily: 'Fuck, man! It's just *tea!*' DB: 'It's a stage-prop, Barley, you cretin. You just *pretend* to drink, you twat – you're supposed to be an *actor.*' LB, giggling: 'Sorry man. Fucking hell! So I'm really drinking, but he isn't. I'm confused, man.')

DB: 'Jesus wept! Tell him, Jer.'

JF: 'Okay. Look Lion, It's Plug who's really drinking – your character, Lion, not you yourself. You have to make it look realistic. On set, you'd have to drink cold tea. Socket's pretending and he needs to make it realistic to Plug, but obvious to the audience that he's only pretending. But as actors we're both miming. That right, Drex?'

DB: 'Exactly. Spoken like a true pro. Jesus Christ! You're a liability, you are, Lion. He can sing, Jerry, which is the best that can be said of him. Ready? Jer, your cue.'

'Okay.' Jerry takes another thirsty draught of the fizzy wine.

Socket: 'Drink up, Plug... not every day your dog wakes up...er, comes home.' ('Sorry.')

Plug: 'Too right.' (drinks some more from bottle): 'It tastes a bit funny. Is there something in this?'

Socket: 'Only the usual amount of E-numbers. And no water this time.'

Plug: 'That'll be it then.' (Drinks more): 'You're drinking it too? I don't trust you!'

Socket: 'I'm jusht about leglesh, man. A little goes a long way.' (Acts drunk, grabs the bottle again and pretends to drink.)

[311]

DB: 'Okay. Jer, pretend to get drunk.'

JF: 'Not much pretence needed. Christ!'

DB: 'Okay. Socket watches Plug closely for a moment or two. Plug's eyes go droopy. Plug snores. Snore, Lion. Socket watches him. Then Socket begins very gently to feel inside Plug's trouser pocket.'

Plug (sleepily): 'Tazer... Princess... baby... touch me there, yeah!'

Socket (groping in Plug's pocket): 'Shh, shh! This won't take a moment.'

(DB: 'Stop giggling, Barley!' LB: 'Can't help it – I'm being groped by Sir Jerry Sort It!' JF: 'Christ, Drex, I *can't*...' DB: 'All right, take another five. Relax. More fizz and whizz, Jer?' JF: 'No more whizz, just fizz thanks... whew!' LB: 'Sorry, Jerry. It was just –' DB: 'This is getting too silly.')

Lion helps himself to a generous line of cocaine, then refills Jerry's glass. 'Not too much, Lion. I'm beginning to feel a bit light-headed. This stuff's not bad. What is it?'

'Prosecco, best Waitrose. Italian.'

'Nice. Nice and lightsome. Cheers! Whew, I'll sit down again, if I may...'

'Cheers. This must be totally like old times for you two,' Lion Barley says.

'Yeah. All we need's Gwil. You ever hear from old Jonesy, Jer?'

'Jonesy...Jonesy-Jones. Not much. He wrote after Telley Shasker died...Shelley...she died, y'know.'

'I know, Jer...poor old Shelley, eh?'

'Burned up. In Barbados... Gwil. He's in Barbados. No, Barcelona... With *Twelfth Night*... the movie. Poor old Gwil Shakespeare with the Twelfth Movie. I stayed in Barcelona with little Suzy... wake up, little Suzy... Everly Brushes... Remember that LifeBoyz band? Gave them top marks.'

'That was *me*.'

'I know... you were jus' great... great.'

'Lionheart – ?'

'Yeah? Oh. Yeah – excuse a sec. Nature...' Lion Barley leaves the room.

Drex says, 'Well, Jer, my friend, we can't have Jonesy. But we can have the neighbour, Gracie, from the first series. Remember her, Jer?'

'Remember who?'

'Gracie. Marie.'

'Gracie, just fancy! Takes you back. We both fancied her, didn't we? Little Marie Oldroyd. Haven't thought about her in aeons. She died too, d'you know, Drex? Everybody's *dead*, Drex... dead as dirt, dearth. 'Cept you. It's crazy. You're not dead after all.'

'No. I'm a waking dog.'

'You know, you *look* a bit like a dog. A wolf, anyway. Sorry. Rude. Fucking hell, Drex, I'm plonked! I can hardly move my feet... everything's gone a bit... fuzzy.'

'No matter, Jer. You just stay nice and comfy.'

Theatrical ratatat-tat on the sitting-room door. Behind the sofa, the disembodied voice of the upstairs neighbour, Gracie: 'Cooo-eee! Can I come in? You was making that much of a row.'

JF: 'Eh? Bloody hell! Is there someone else here?'

DB: 'Only Mitzi – she's cool. An extra. You're too soon for your cue, Mitzi-poppet...'

Mitzi: 'I want to come in anyway.'

JF: 'Her *voice!* Who?'

DB: 'Okay, Mitz – you're on.'

Enter 'Gracie', a small girl of about twenty-two, dressed for Town. She wears a black beret over short peroxide hair and sparkly earrings, and a short trenchcoat mac over a black leather mini-skirt and high-heeled black patent boots. Her fingernails are painted silver. Gracie is played by Angel, aka Marty, aka 'Mitzi', a versatile performer. (DB: 'Say your lines, Mitz. I'll be Plug. I'm supposed to be comatose.' Drex-Plug sits on the sofa beside Jerry-Socket, and snores dramatically.)

Mitzi: 'Coo-er.' (Clears throat. Reads from script, a bit woodenly from behind sofa.) Mitzi-Gracie: 'You two are making far too much racket. My mam wants a bit of peace and quiet. She's trying to rest upstairs. Ay-oop! Is Plug all right?'

(DB: 'Go on Jer, your line. You're supposed to be raiding my pockets.' JF: 'Shit, er... I can hardly see.' Reads, screwing his eyes onto the dancing print.)

Socket: 'He's fine, just rat-arshed. He's been shelebrating a big win. He's...'

Mitzi teeters round to where Jerry can see her. 'Oooh! Hello, Sir Jerry-love! This is a proper thrill. Oops, sorry, Drex. That was out of role like. Can I say me lines, Drex?'

JF: 'Jesusharrychrist! Fucking *hell!* How? You're...' He blinks as if his eyes are failing, struggles to sit straighter on the sofa. 'Marie? God, Drex – who?'

DB: 'Jer, meet Mitzi. She's a friend of mine. Mitzi, this is Sir Jerry Fairbrother, a very important person whom I once called colleague.'

JF: 'But she's... she's...' His eyes bulge in disbelief.

DB: 'Good, isn't she?'

Sudden noise off-stage. Fearful knocking on the downstairs door, and some shouting outside. Lion's voice, yelling, 'No you fucking can't! Wait down there!' and the sound of urgent feet on the stairs. LB, rushing in suddenly, red in the face and out of breath. 'Drex! Shit, man – quick! There's some guys downstairs – almost forced their way in! You've got to hide, Jerry man! Quick – into the back bedroom!'

Fear pierces Jerry Fairbrother like an electric charge and he struggles to his feet, which suddenly won't obey him. He tries to straighten up and staggers, stumbles over a pouffe, clutches the sofa, weaves his way through to the passage, to the bedroom. The others are behind him, as is a great deal of commotion.

'Hang on, Jer! It's okay!'

'No, no!' Panicked, he casts wildly about for somewhere to hide in the darkness of the bedroom, while the phantasms of nightmare approach. Under the bed is too narrow. 'Quick!' cries someone. 'The closet!' Someone holds the door open, but the darkness is too much. He can't breathe. The others, the ghosts... Drex, Marie... in the dark they will get in beside him. He blunders out. The French window, the fire-escape... he must have air... The shouting gets louder. Out on the platform of the fire-escape steps, the world swirls. Cold air, freezing air. He looks down on a dimly-lit courtyard which whirls and seems to come up

[313]

towards him. He clings heavily to the rail. More noise. His feet tangle together in his erratic flight, but he stumbles on, downwards

LB: 'Oh shit, man…shitting Christ!'

Drex firmly closes the French window.

Angel: 'Will he be okay-like? He seemed that scared.'

DB: 'Don't know, don't care. Barley – get away from there. Come on, both of you. Back into the sitting room.'

LB: 'But that crash! He might have had a bad fall, man. Shit! This is a bit of a downer…' Glances at the bed where a padded jacket and an overnight bag sit on the duvet. 'He's left his stuff.'

'Leave it, Barley.'

'But –'

'Shut your trap, Barley. He's gone. I expect he's in a taxi home to sleep it off. Come on. He's gone.'

'But he left his *stuff*, and we totally never got to talk about me and the judging panel. Shit, man!'

'Have a line, Barley. Shut up.'

'You said it was all a joke, man! Get him out of it and pretend there's someone after him, just a joke, you said! I did what you *told* me! Now somebody'll find him, and he'll tell, and then the Met'll be here and – ' Lion Barley suddenly bursts into tears.

'Listen, you puling little cry-baby – just shut *up*, okay? Barley! Barley, Lionheart, *calmati,* this is no time for hysterics. Have this, come on. Wipe the nose. Big breaths. Better? Now snort. That's better. Sit here. That's it.'

'Here! Lemme have some of that, will you?' Angel grabs the mirror and the little plastic bag. 'Bloody Norah! He looked like summat'd hit him when he saw me. I started that – he was peaceful-like before. It was me, *me* – weren't it?'

'No, Angel! Not that! *No!*' Drex swipes the mirror out of Angel's hand. The plastic bag falls to the floor, spilling some of its contents.

'Ow! What'd you do that for?'

'There's lots more at home, Angel. Leave it! Come on, we're leaving. Now!' Grabs Angel's wrist.

'Is – is he okay?' Angel is staring round-eyed at Lion Barley, who appears to have slumped on the sofa. 'He's gone a funny colour, Drex. He looks reely peculiar. His eyes have gone into the back of his head. Oh God, I'm *scared.*'

'Angel! Come on. *Now!*'

In the chilly gloom by the river, the rising mist reminiscent of some Dickensian television drama, their breaths making thick vapour clouds as they walk without speaking, two people, a lupine-looking man dressed in a black overcoat and a muffler who walks with a slight limp and wearing sunglasses (eye complaint?) in spite of the deepening dark of the evening, and a vibrant-looking, much made-up young woman in a beret who clings to his arm shivering, walk steadily towards the Tower Bridge, entwining arms like lovers, silent, oblivious. Somewhere, somewhere fairly close, a siren sounds.

Coda

'So, farewell to Sir Jerry Fairbrother...and that's all from me, Mike Bennett, on this sad day in Hatton, Cambridgeshire. Back to Suzy Merritt in the Round Britain studio...'

Old 'Gordon' signing out from Jerry's final show. Well, that about wraps it up, there in Cambridge. And here. My fuggy, cramped sitting-room with the large TV screen, the hissing gas fire, the dark blind drawn and Angel sitting uncomfortably close, legs tucked under his chin on a pouffe by the side of my chair, watching, waiting, twitching...

'So that's it, then,' Angel says.

'Yep. Just about.'

Not everything is entirely finished, and I daresay there'll be a few more little surprises to tantalise the public. I'd give a lot to see Louise's face when they call. By today, there'll be a CD in Wragg's in-tray at the Kinseyder offices. A similar one will have reached the offices of Superintendent Callum Berrisford at the Yard. It's the same one Jerry received, and Louise – with one difference: I've edited in the other voice, Louise's interlocutor in that singularly incriminating little exchange. Call it a last squeak from a dying ego. The Met won't have a clue, but Wragg will. I wonder what they will make of it. I swig my scotch from the bottle.

'Thank you, Mike.' It's fairly obvious that little Suzy has been having a little weep, but she's too professional to let it show much, and someone from make-up will have dabbed her face a bit. Now she says, matter-of-factly: *'And now, more news of the investigation into the mysterious death of the former Boy-R-Us star, Lion Barley, found dead three weeks ago in the Southwark Thameside apartment where it is has been established that Sir Jerry spent his last evening before he was found dead behind the building in...'*

'Drex?'

'Yes, Angel?'

'What are you going to do?' His voice is barely a whisper.

'Do?'

'Yeah.'

'Hang on. I want to see this.'

'...Earlier, Superintendent Callum Berrisford who is in charge of the investigation spoke at a press conference...' Over to a solid-looking senior cop in uniform with a lot of pips and flash cameras going off in his eyes. *'We can announce that post-mortem results show that Mr Barley died from an overdose of extra-pure cocaine. No, we do not rule out foul play. Yes, there is very clear evidence that there were others present. I'm sorry I cannot comment further at this time.'* Shouts from assembled journos. 'Was Jerry Fairbrother murdered, sir?' 'Did Lion Barley kill Jerry, Superintendent?' 'Have you found the others?' *'I'm sorry, I can make no further comment at this time. Investigation is proceeding and we will let you know.'*

Back to anchor. *'And now, more news from Afghanistan, where another British soldier, Corporal Jason Cox...'*

'Drex?'

'Yeah.' I'm feeling a bit woozy now. Dreamy. Little flickers of memory. A vain, silly kid called Lionel in jail with ambitions who turned into major liability.

'Drex? I keep remembering Lion. I'm scared, Drex.' Lion wasn't nearly scared enough. Something in his survival antennae got blunted. His face, going blue, and his eyes turned into his head, his nose bleeding. It would have happened sooner or later with or without me. Well, wouldn't it?

'What – what's going to happen?' I am supposed to have the answers to these things.

'You've had all the time in the world to vanish, Angel. I gave you the choice.' Choice! For some, it's just reason-spiting sentiment. Veronica chose to see me as a leprechaun, something mysterious, magical. Her arms, big-boned and warm, wrapped round her dreams... Veronica, stroking my face in the dark, back in London now, doubtless, on the other side of Town, back in her snug little basement in Fulham where I grew up, where I learned to hate, and learned, briefly, the other thing. Or something. Veronica, imagining a life that might have been, loving a fiction. As it is, I've saved her a whole heap of heartache. She won't realise this now, but she's a survivor. Writers are. Nothing gets wasted. She'll heal in time, or she'll write about it.

'You – you – killed him. Lion. And Jerry Fairbrother. And that woman you got me watching, her that died in the fire.'

'So?'

'So why? I thought he was a lovely feller, that Jerry. He panicked when he saw me – it was something about *me!* I can't forget his face...' Lovely Jerry, the lovely feller...and yes, I killed him, I suppose. Or least he saw me as Death, Death and the Angel, and he ran, and he fell and he died. Jerry and me, the writing combo that almost captured the imagination of a decade. Pity about old Jerry. Hubris, you see. He brought it all on himself. But I almost loved him.

'I'm really scared, Drex!' Angel's teeth chatter. We've been holed up here ever since that night, edging round each other, watching the news. Every day he's been urging for us to leave. Every day, I've refused to budge. So has he, staying put by my side.

'So why stay, Angel? You could have scarpered. You could have turned me in, had a drama, been a little heroine. Huh?'

'I – I'd never do that. I didn't – don't want to leave you.' He sobs a bit. Little Angel. I stopped him. His little nose about to snuff up all that lethal purity. I might have let him, but I didn't. Don't ask me why. 'I – I love you.'

'For fuck's sakes don't snivel so close to me, Angel.'

He furiously wipes his face. 'Why don't you run, Drex? Get out of here? Before...' Shame I shan't see Lulu's come-uppance. Lulu, beautiful, lame-brained, ambitious, soulless Lulu. Maybe we deserved each other after all. 'Drex. Come on, now, you soft pillock! Beautiful! *Please*, let's get out, let's go.'

'Too late, Angel. I've set things in motion. They'll be here within – well, given the Mr Plod mentality, I'd give them another eight hours or so.' I've not made it exactly easy for them. They might not come at all. Good stuff, this. Soft. Gentle. A soft black blanket.

'Come *on!*' He's grabbing at my sleeve, trying to pull me up out of the chair.

'Angel! For fuck's sake, lay off. Eight hours is enough for you to get away. You don't want to get pulled in. They'll mangle you and you'll go down.'

'But I've nowhere to go.' He's on the verge of sobbing again.

'Neither have I, Angel. I'm staying. Get Mitzi…hide where she'd go. Go somewhere over the rainbow…' Mitzi, Marty, Marie.

'Come on, Drex, love! Don't drink any more of that stuff, your eyes are going all funny. You can do it – you can do anything.'

'Anything' is an exaggeration, but I can do this. Before the blanket falls. I look at him seriously. 'Angel.'

'Drex?'

'Angel, Mitzi, Marty, Marty Oldroyd.'

'Marty *Oldroyd*? My name's Baxter!'

'Marty, Baxter was the name of your grandparents. I think you'll find your grandmother's maiden name was Oldroyd. It was also your mother's stage-name. She thought it sounded more authentic. That actress girl in *Plug & Socket*. And *The Husband of the Bride*. She was your mother, Marty. And if she ever named anyone on your birth-certificate as your father, it would have been Fairbrother. Get it?'

He's staring at me with round, blue, unbelieving eyes.. 'Oh! Oh, bleedin' *Norah!* You don't mean?'

'Yes, Angel. In all likelihood, old Jerry was your dad. He thought Mitzi was Marie. I intended that he should. That's why he jumped. He'd seen enough ghosts for one day. Get it?'

'This isn't *real!*' He makes a noise like a terrified rabbit. His eyes get rounder and more frantic.

'It's as real as it's going to get, Angel. Now get out, for Christ's sake. Listen. You've got an aunt Janice in Filey. Her married surname's Ladkin. It's not that common. You'll find her, and she'll explain everything. She's a decent woman. She might help you. She was your mother's sister, Marie's sister.'

'Oh God! Did – did you kill her too? Marie?'

'Yep.' Some good I mean to do, as the man said. 'I killed her. I strangled her in her hospital bed as she lay helpless.' I smile very nastily, and he backs away. As I mean he should.

'No! Oh, Norah, *no!*'

'Fraid so, sweetie.'

'You're… you're mad, Drex.'

'Mad north-north west. It's your turn next, Angel-mine. You know far too m-much, sweetie.'

I'm struggling a bit. Words difficult. Black blanket…

'Would you like a little of this nice medicine, Angel?' I push the bottle towards him. 'Go on! Why not, sw-sweetie? Couple of s-slurps… ob-b-blivion…'

[317]

If he takes it, what can I do? The life-instinct is strong, however.

'No! *No*…Oh shit…No!' He's on his feet, backing away from me. I'm aware of noises… the TV blathering quietly… Angel putting stuff into a bag… not long now…

His head round the door. One last look. Now his feet on the stairs… light as a ballerino… light as air… Angel fleeing, flying. Little Angel who said he loved me. The outer door clanging. Black blanket… I smile, very softly, as it envelopes me…

~